DEDICATION

I'd like to dedicate this story to my mother. Thanks for all your assistance in bringing me up to be "an achiever in life," which I've really become, and thank you for your assistance in making this book a reality! Love ya, Ma.

SPECIAL ACKNOWLEDGEMENTS

I'd like to specially acknowledge my team of artists and graphic designers—all you guys did "a tremendous job" in making the swords/book-cover design: "*BLING-BLING-BLING*!!!"

Brenton P. Wilson
"Joliet James"
Philipp Leibelt

"That's what being young is all about ...
You have the courage and the daring
to think that you can make a difference."

- Ruby Dee

The Swords of the Sultan

CHAPTER I

In a remote galaxy on the opposite side of the universe....

There once existed a world just like ours, except for these four major differences.

The first difference was that two moons safely orbited her skies, moving in nearly opposite directions. While the nearest moon looked identical to ours, except for the meteor markings, the farthest moon—twice as far away—appeared to be half the size and even had a slight red glow, due to the trapped surface gases.

Second, the land and water masses on this planet possessed their own unique shapes and sizes.

Third, a little over ten million human inhabitants existed here—all living in an age far more primitive, barbaric and ruthless.

Lastly, located upon the western borders of the single largest continent, the central latitude of which rested a hundred miles north of the equator, there dwelt a great and powerful city named Pavelus.

Now the first-of-many striking features about this particular city was that although the sun rose from the eastern horizon between five and six o'clock every morning, it still took nearly two additional hours before the sun's rays could touch the dusty streets.

This manmade delay was caused by all of the lingering shadows cast from the six-hundred-foot tall by one-hundred-foot thick by seven-mile long walls of fortified stone, spanning around the eastern, northern and southern borders. There was only one heavily guarded entrance in the very center of each quadrant.

Added to that formidable defense was the Sharia Desert—blistering hot, dry and windy desert terrains of all types that spanned for hundreds and hundreds of miles in just about every direction.

1

Just because there were no fortified walls or desert on the western banks of this capital city ruled by the Sharia Empire, do not think for one single second that this side was unprotected—actually, there were two equally powerful defenses.

The first defense was the seven-mile stretch of mountainous harbor, also manmade, consisting of hundreds of thousands of massive boulders all stacked upon each other at a distance of five thousand yards from the beach—the seagull-infested peaks rose about five hundred feet above the seawater.

There was only one entrance in the enclosed harbor's middle, just big enough to allow two large ships to sail in opposite directions. Comfortably built inside this harbor were five thousand docks of various sizes, all made from waterproofed steel.

Parked inside was the second defense, the Sultan's five-star naval fleet that consisted of two thousand ancient battleships ranging from sleuths, to transport ships, frigates and galleons. More than half of this fleet consisted of a brand-new type of patrolling sleuth proudly heralded by the citizens of Pavelus as "The Swordfish!"

This very sleek sailing and/or rowing ship possessed an armed crew of thirty sailors and one captain, and resembled an actual swordfish because of the abnormally long and pointy bottlenose located in the bow—made of the same steel as the docks, yet always kept polished until gleaming like platinum. Bolted side-by-side onto the entire ship's most outer railing (starboard and port) was a large number of rectangular steel shields—equally shiny.

Swordfishes had not been designed and built by some of the greatest shipbuilders in the world for looks, but for purpose: ram through small-to-midsized enemy ships at top speed and survive the impact. There were always a dozen swordfishes on patrol—both inside and outside the harbor.

And there were two crucial reasons that this harbor was so safeguarded—one, protect the city from the sea's furies; two, protect the scores of merchant ships that continuously departed and arrived every day, importing and exporting exotic goods like spices, animals, silks, and oftentimes, slaves.

After all, the key to Pavelus's incredible success and wealth—trade—was its centralized location to more than a dozen major cities and seaports around the Sea of Albusina—the largest sea on the planet.

Approximately eighty thousand citizens and forty thousand soldiers—both army and navy—populated this thriving metropolis, ranging from the "desperately poor" to the "opulently rich."

Yet very few ever dared to oppose the "tyrannical will" of the Sultan—he and his ancestral family had ruled this capital city with an "iron fist," as well the entire empire that included another thriving city and thousands of miles in between ... for a little more than five centuries.

Not surprisingly, most of the population greatly feared that the Sultan had spies everywhere, which he did. Those even caught hinting of rebellion were typically found impaled, as both a promise and warning to others, just outside the eighty-foot high defensive walls of fortified stone that surrounded the palace (literally made of gold), located at the south-central part of the city.

The final necessary-to-mention piece of trivia about Pavelus was that it had been broken up into seven sections, bearing forty-foot stonewalls that prevented the lower castes from entering the higher castes' sections; for stationed twenty-four hours a day at each checkpoint, there were guards who checked everybody's citizenry identification and status paperwork.

Three hours after sunrise one such morning, just near the northeastern border within the "lower middle class" section, the sun's rays finally entered the alleyway in between two abandoned factories.

Minutes later, that light peeked through the hole of an old, wooden floorboard balcony.

That ray of light, soon after, skimmed across the dark-brown face of a thin and dirty boy, who slept underneath a blanket of the same quality. Even though there was no facial hair to speak of, the color of his unkempt hair on his head was black. This twelve-year-old boy went by the name of Baltor.

Due to the very annoying sunlight that penetrated through his shut eyelids, he turned over, yawned, and tried to fall back to sleep. Only a moment or two later, however, he heard and felt his stomach grumbling in angry tones!

Realizing that it was time to eat, the boy got up, but felt that all of his muscles and joints were very sore and stiff from sleeping on the cold, hard ground.

Originally, and for most of his life, he had lived the middle-class lifestyle with both parents and without any brothers or sisters. His father had been a modest blacksmith who preferred to repair weapons of steel but mainly replaced horseshoes for a living.

His mother tended to their only child until he had turned eight, when his father began to apprentice him in the craft of blacksmithing for the next several years to come....

Unfortunately, Baltor's memories were still haunted by that horrific night, only fifty-five nights ago, one week after his twelfth birthday. He and his family had long been asleep when the robber had broke his or her way in, in the middle of the night.

He had only awoken out his own deep sleep upon hearing his father yell angrily from downstairs, "I thought I heard some funny noises going on in my shop! Don't make me use my mace on you, but slowly lay down that sword and surrender! You...I know who—"

What interrupted his father's words was his "death scream," which in turn caused his mother to begin screaming! Apparently, she had followed behind her husband, witnessing *the murder*!

Frightened out of his wits, Baltor could only lie frozen in his bed and sob. Only two seconds after, his mother's screaming abruptly stopped, and he knew that his mother was also dead!

At that moment, he somehow managed to get his wits together, slip on his clothes and shoes, crawl out his second-story window, slide down the gutter, and take off into the night—he escaped seconds before the unknown murderer had kicked his door open....

However, with nowhere to go, and no one to care for him, this hole is where he ended up—traumatized, homeless, destitute and orphaned. Ironically, he had no choice than to turn to thievery—stealing bread, meat or fruit from vendors, in order to survive.

Of course Baltor had only recently become aware that one of the strictly enforced laws of Pavelus, due to all of the trading and commerce, was that thieves minimally had a hand cut off, though the typical penalty was death. Only three weeks earlier, he witnessed a six-year-old orphaned girl who had her hand chopped off by one of the Sultan's guards—she had only stolen an orange.

He had also been quite aware that she had belonged to the local street gang—fourteen other orphans of both genders, ranging from the ages of four to nineteen. Not only did they steal food and other goods from vendors, yet carried weapons and even mugged people.

Thus, Baltor made sure to stay out of sight whenever this gang was nearby, including this day—his fifty-sixth as an orphan.

After tucking the blanket away into a little nook and making sure the coast was clear in the alleyway, he exited the hole, and of course, stretched his thin arms and legs out to get nimble and loose.

Once so, he proceeded his way to the bazaar located on the main strip. His stomach grumbled angrily yet again, as it demanded food!

Upon reaching the bazaar, nearly ten minutes later, he happily observed that a few of the merchants hadn't yet finished setting out all their wares. Nor were there any gang members or guards patrolling about—yet. The one thing he wasn't happy about was that this place was already getting pretty packed full of shoppers.

Right away he began walking close by the tented stalls, while always keeping his head locked straight ahead. His eyes carefully scanned all around for the right moment when a vendor had his or her head turned away—most were looking right back. Located between each stall, he also happened to see and/or hear an entertainer, or two, or three, ranging from jugglers of sharp weapons, to singers, to musicians playing all types of musical instruments. Why, several musicians were blowing exotic tunes from their horns in front of swaying king cobras.

"The moment" came, and as quick as a cobra strikes, Baltor's hand had already tucked a half-pound cooked sausage link into his shirt. As he casually walked away from the stall, he prayed that no one had witnessed his act—his heart continued to beat rapidly.

Luck wasn't with the boy this time—perhaps thirty seconds after the theft, he first felt a hand clamp hard onto his shoulder from behind, and then he heard a woman who had a strong foreign accent exclaim, "Hey there, boy!"

Without looking, he easily slipped out of her grip, and took off like a bat out of hell.

After reaching the next intersection only ten seconds later, he turned right off the main strip, ran to the next intersection of this semi-busy street, turned left into a small alleyway filled with tons of clothes hanging on dozens of clotheslines, and then made another right onto the very next street without looking both ways.

Baltor almost became roadkill, but in the nick of time, he jumped back from the first pair of galloping horses carrying soldiers! These men wore polished swords, helmets and armor, and also black capes bearing the gold emblem of crossed sabers—the symbol of the Sultan.

While the stampede continued to pass, Baltor tried his best to look calm and casual as he hurried on over to the sidewalk. However, due to the earlier running, his breath had turned ragged while sweat poured down his head, face and body. Even worse, thanks to the dust that the horses had just kicked up, coupled with all the accumulated sweat, caused it all to cling to him like mud.

Once the last pair of soldiers had passed, sixty of them in total, he coughed out quite a bit of the dust that had gotten into his lungs before turning around and walking.

As he breathed a small sigh of relief, he wiped the sweat off his forehead with the back of his hand—this action definitely caused a mud-like substance to smear on both areas, though he didn't care.

After scanning his horizons one final time and observing that the coast was clear, he pulled out a chunk of the sausage and began to munch. Already had he begun to look for an animal trough to quench his ever-growing thirst.

Just after he had swallowed the first bite of meat, he heard that same woman melodiously ask from behind him, "Where are you running off to so fast?"

Frightened out of his wits, he nearly jumped five feet into the air. The moment he landed back on the ground, he had already performed a complete one-hundred-eighty-degree turn, and he could now see, for the first time, the young woman with the accent.

Holy moley! You are the prettiest thing I've ever seen....

True, her complexion was nearly white as a ghost, but she had a beautiful face, sea-blue eyes and golden-blond hair that gently cascaded all the way down to her waist. As for her stylish attire, she wore a pair of shiny-blue, knee-high boots that had a strip of white fur sewn around the top, which met up with a snug pair of white, silky breeches. Despite the black-and- blue- striped cape of silk that gracefully draped over her shoulders, clasped together by a jeweled broach, the v-necked/silvery tunic she wore underneath revealed a small portion of her full cleavage.

Everything about this gal, perhaps only a foot taller and only a handful of years older than the boy, was wonderfully exotic and beautiful, and couple that with the fact that he was still startled from her most-unexpected appearance for the second time, all he could do was to continue to stare in awe.

After an unknown amount of time had passed, as the two unwaveringly stared each other in the eyes, she was the first one to ask, "Well? Aren't you going to answer my question?"

"What question?"

"Where are you running off to so fast?"

"Ummm—" he lied, "you have me mistaken for someone else."

She unexpectedly began to laugh for a few seconds, before abruptly stopping and sighing, "Nope, no mistake."

"Listen, lady," he said. "I really do think that you have me mistaken for someone else, so if there's anything else—"

With a wag of her index finger, once to the right and once to the left, the gal interrupted, "Fine. Maybe I'm mistaken—maybe I'm not. Open up your shirt and prove that you don't have a link of sausage in there. If I'm mistaken, then I will apologize and go. Deal?"

His gaze darted around as he lied, "Trust me—I don't have—"

As if reading his very thoughts, she interrupted, "Don't even think about running again, boy, for if you do, not only will I catch you yet again, I'll turn you into the guards myself."

"Well, fine," he sighed in resignation. "I'll show you what I have in my shirt."

Slowly he began to reveal the remaining link of sausage tucked inside. Halfway through, she immediately gestured with her index finger to tuck it back, while saying softly, "There you go, all you had to do was tell me the truth."

After considering her statement for only a single second, Baltor easily explained the full truth: "I am an orphan. I am homeless. I do what I have to do to stay alive—there's your truth! So if you're not going to turn me in, then what is it you want?"

The gal laughed merrily yet again! Perhaps because of her laughter, for the very first time in the boy's life, not only did something strange, unexplainable and pleasant stir within the pits of his stomach, his heart began to race and his mind began to swoon.

As the wind suddenly threw her cape up into the air, which wind also caused a lengthy portion of her golden hair to blow over her eyes, she cast a friendly smile before introducing herself, "My name is Lady Lydia. You seem to have some remarkably quick talents, young man. Oh, and by the way, what's your name?"

"I am Baltor," he tried to say but found his voice getting raspy from being very thirsty, especially because he had eaten that salty meat and was now standing there in the middle of the street with the very hot sun beating down.

As if reading the boy's mind again, Lydia's eyes spotted a nondescript building made of sandstone just down the street, which had a wooden sign hanging above a door that read *Myrkshia's Family Restaurant and Tavern*. She suggested aloud, "Would you like to get something to eat and drink, Baltor?"

The boy simply nodded his head.

"Good!" Lydia chimed, just before she unexpectedly spun her body the opposite way in one surprisingly swift movement. This action caused both her hair and cape to fly chaotically about for a few additional seconds.

Once both objects had resettled, she cocked just her head around, smiled and said, "Follow me, Baltor."

Without waiting for an answer, she looked forward and began walking toward the restaurant. He followed.

In about a minute or so, the two entered the restaurant. While walking behind her, the boy observed that this cozy-looking establishment was packed full of noisy patrons, and that there was only one empty booth left that sat in the left-hand corner.

He continued to follow her toward that booth.

Only a couple of seconds later, however, a bald man—who was standing behind the bar, wearing a clean apron, and washing glasses—looked up, observed the boy, and yelled over the din of the patrons, "Hey there, you filthy rat! You need to leave now!"

Everyone in the place instantly quieted as he or she turned to look with disgust or shock at the "filthy rat."

Lydia stopped in her tracks, looked over at the bartender, and flipped back her cape with her right hand, revealing a plum-sized leather bag hanging from a string on the back of her belt.

As she began to shake the bag around with the same hand, jingling a whole lot of coins, she replied just as casually, "The boy's with me."

The man's eyes bulged at the sight of the bag of coins, just before he sighed. "Fine, fine."

The chatter in the room picked back up even before the two had taken the booth.

Not even two seconds later, a serving girl approached. With both a chipper tone and a friendly smile, she asked, "Top of the morning to the both of you—so, what'll it be?"

After Lydia had turned to look at the waitress, she politely said with a smile, "Two glasses of cold water, and two orders of a breakfast type of food that won't take long to serve, please."

"No problem," the girl said. She immediately left to place their order with the cooks, retrieve their drinks, and then hand a bill over to an elderly couple that had just completed their meals.

Nearly ten seconds after the waitress was gone, Lydia slid forward in her seat, and then she half-whispered, "I noticed that you displayed not only unusual skills, but you're also unusually quick. And despite all that muddy dirt currently hiding you away, I can tell that you'll one day become quite an attractive young man."

Baltor didn't know what to say, so he just simply shrugged.

She asked, "What do you think about the idea of getting some help by enhancing those skills?"

Instead of answering her question, he asked his own, "Why in the hell would you want to help me?"

Just then, the serving girl returned with two empty mugs and a pitcher that contained both chilled water and ice cubes. After setting everything down on the table, she left to take the order of three new customers—two ladies and a small boy—who had all taken seats at the far end of the restaurant.

Instead of answering Baltor's question, Lydia picked up the pitcher, filled both glasses, set the pitcher back down, picked up her glass, and took a small drink. Without hesitation, he took his glass and drank.

He was quite delighted that this icy water was quite delicious, refreshing and clean—not like the warm and dirty water from animal troughs he drank ninety-nine percent of the time. That water was extremely yucky in his opinion.

After taking two more small sips, she said in just above a whisper, "I want to help you for two reasons. First, I have a soft heart for those in need. Second, you have the rough skills that once developed and refined, could make you a master thief like me." Upon conclusion, she allowed a slightly mischievous smile to cross her face.

Rather loudly, he blurted out, "You're a—" Catching himself before he could utter the final word to his question, which "word" would certainly get them both into a heap of trouble, he mouthed out the word, "—thief?"

Lydia, who had already been observing the waitress's approach peripherally, remained completely silent until after the waitress had deposited the food and left. With a lingering smile still on her face, she finally asked, "Surprised?"

"Wow—not in a million years would I ever have guessed that," the hungry boy whispered, picking up his spoon. Without looking down, he scooped a portion of the porridge and took a bite— quite tasty, as he happily discovered.

"That," she added, "is exactly what makes me a master."

He glanced down at his food and began eating. The more he ate, the more he realized how hungry he was!

Lydia didn't eat a bite but silently stared at Baltor. Whenever he looked up at her, she threw sweet smiles.

Even though the boy's mouth was continuously refilling with food, his mind was completely in awe—he couldn't believe that this really, really, really beautiful woman was actually a master thief! However, he could believe that she was looking out for him, and the more he thought about his future, or the lack thereof, the more he wanted to agree to her proposal.

The second that he had finished his bowl of food, she asked, "Would you like this bowl, as well?"

He gave her a sweet smile, answering, "Please."

She slid it across the table. He picked it up right away and began to slurp down all of the contents. At the end of breakfast, which had a grand timeframe of a minute and twenty-five seconds, he agreed, "Okay. I'll do it."

After nodding her head one single time, Lydia replied with an elated smile, "Perfect. Then we'll begin your special training in one hour—after of course, we get to our next destination, which, by the way, is *top secret* to your little ears at this time. So please don't ask me where we're going. In fact, just keep your mouth shut the whole time and let me do the talking if the need should arise. Your food should have had enough time to digest by the time we arrive."

As the waitress was just about to pass by, Lydia looked on over and asked, "Waitress… check, please?"

CHAPTER II

After paying the bill with a decent tip and exiting the restaurant, Lydia led Baltor through three different sections of the city, displaying her ID to the guards posted at the checkpoints.

He really found it strange that the guards treated her with such a high amount of respect, especially after the way he'd seen the guards treat others, especially himself! Yet, at every gate, they would all bow low and call out, "You may pass, my lady."

The boy didn't find it strange that they were already looking at him both suspiciously and disdainfully; that is, until Lady Lydia nonchalantly explained that she had just bought him at the slave market and that he would be getting his ID that very afternoon—slavery was both legal and very profitable in Pavelus.

They let him pass.

Approximately an hour later, now traveling through an upper-class neighborhood, the two made a right at a four-way cobblestone intersection and traveled down yet another road with concrete sidewalks on both sides. Most of the people around here traveled around in horse-drawn carriages, everybody and everything looking unique yet very, very expensive. Inevitably, Lydia and Baltor made their way onto the sidewalk on the far side.

Just beyond the sidewalk, there stood a thirty-foot wall made of polished granite, spanning as far as Baltor's eyes could see—painstakingly carved into it were the detailed images of heroes battling dragons, as well other beastly monsters. A massive black palace existed far in the distance on the other side of this wall.

On the other side of the road, there stood a simple black-gated fence, which revealed a very lush and colorful garden inside. This property ended about a thousand feet down, as there was a three-way intersection going to the right.

After walking nearly a half of a mile down this same road,

and passing three more three-way intersections on the right, he saw a pair of iron-plated gates separating the wall on the left, which wall continued on for at least another half-mile.

On each side of this closed gate stood an armed guard equipped with a sword notched on his belt. Their yellow uniforms were different from any of the uniforms that the Sultan's forces wore.

Upon Lydia's approach, the guards opened the gates in unison, and without as much as a word spoken to either she or the boy.

Baltor became utterly amazed as they passed through those gates and into a luscious tropical paradise. His mouth dropped open in astonishment, as he had never before seen a place like this!

After all, this huger-than-huge oasis possessed a small cobblestone path, wide enough for a carriage, that gently wound itself around all of the clustered groups of exotic flowers and palm trees, and led up to a wooden bridge that arched over a small stream.

The stream of water wound around back and forth, until depositing itself into a small lagoon nearby, also contained within the confines of this magnificent property. Small groups of people walked here and there, mindful only of their surroundings.

A smile finally crossed the boy's face as soon as he stood on top of the bridge, looked over its side, and discovered the schools of multi-colored fish that playfully swam below.

Lying just ahead at the far end of the path, just beyond the empty parking lot, his eyes had never stopped seeing that five-story palace, sculpted from black marble. Four enormous cylindrical pillars—white marble—held up the front balcony. Located on both sides of the building, there was an outdoor room.

Both rooms had been constructed from four narrow white pillars that rose from the white-and-black-checkered tile floors at each corner, and each pillar held up a corner of a white marble ceiling. No walls. Perhaps an eighth of this ceiling had been artistically chiseled out, allowing that same portion of sunlight to shed in hundreds of swirly patterns throughout the shaded area.

In the very center of both outdoor rooms was a large square pool that had thousands of reeds jutting out of the waters. Exotic and colorful birds chirped noisily away from inside wooden cages, which hung over each pool within a small marble gazebo. Baltor silently bet that there were colorful fish in those pools too...

All the while, Lydia casually led him down the path and toward the palace's main entrance—fifteen-foot tall mahogany doors with doorknobs made of polished gold. An armed guard stood on each side, and upon their approach, each opened his door.

Inside was an enormous chamber—bearing an octagonal shape and made entirely of white marble—that contained a set of mahogany doors at each of the three other main quadrants, as well two guards at each exit. Hanging on the walls in between each exit was a large and beautiful tapestry, each revealing a different scene of nature.

In the smack center of the room, eight black leather couches had been placed loosely together, also forming the shape of an octagon. Sitting or standing around these couches were twelve attractive and richly dressed young adults, seven males and five females. All were engaged in some type of social chitter-chatter.

As Lydia and Baltor passed by the group, most bowed their head in recognition and greeting toward Lydia. A few of them, however, stared at the boy with a snobby expression.

Upon the two nearing the entryway on the left side of the room, the pair of posted guards there simultaneously opened his door, yet again without a word spoken.

As Baltor entered the long hallway—mainly made of gray marble except for the black-and-gold carpeting—he saw that there were six doors to the left and six to the right. In addition, hanging in between each unguarded door was either a beautiful scenic painting or a mirror—at the far end of the hallway, which traversed for approximately a thousand feet or so, there existed another set of double doors and two more posted guards.

Halfway down this hallway, she cocked her head to look at Baltor, noted the bewildered expression on the boy's face, and hinted with a slightly mischievous smile, "There are many more surprises waiting to be discovered."

Only seconds before their arrival at this set of double doors, the two guards opened them—only a second after Lydia and Baltor had passed, the guards closed them.

It was then that she stopped in her tracks, turned around, and gestured with her arms for the boy to take a good look around.

Of course, he couldn't help but gape in shock and awe at the fifty-foot tall brass statue of a beautiful woman who stood upright in the very middle of this enormous and aesthetically pleasing chamber, filled with artworks of all types just about everywhere.

Upon closer examination of the statue itself, he not only observed that she was barely clothed, yet stood on a blue marble pedestal that rose three feet over the top of a blue marble pool. A very large, square pool filled with water on the inside, and tons of imbedded "sparkling jewels" on the outside.

Only a few seconds later, he observed that this statue's right hand held a marble seashell that continuously, and mysteriously, poured water into that pool. His immediate opinion was that this artistic masterpiece's value had to be "p r i c e l e s s !"

Soon after, he began to look at all the other very beautiful, yet much smaller statues or sculptures—made of all types of expensive metals or woods and bearing a wide variety of poses. Some statues were resting upon black or white marble pedestals.

A minute or two afterward, he began to look at the hundreds of beautiful scenic paintings of all shapes and sizes hanging on the black marble walls—there were no exits out of this room anywhere he looked, nor were there any other living occupants besides he and Lydia.

Perhaps as long as five minutes after arrival, the boy double-checked to make sure no one else was around. There still wasn't, and so he whispered, "With all of this wealth you already possess, why do you need to be a thief?"

Lydia smiled and answered in a normal tone of voice, "Everything will be explained when the time is right, and you are ready to understand."

She walked up to the front of the fountain and reached out her hand. Grabbing a hold of an emerald that jutted out, she twisted it.

A black marble tile on the floor slowly tilted upward, revealing a hole underneath. Just below the hole, there was a ladder that led down into the darkness.

As she began to descend, her left eye winked before she hinted, "Follow me… if you want to learn more."

Only a few seconds later, he was already climbing down the ladder. Upon reaching the floor of this underground tunnel, he observed that there was only one burning torch nearby, providing a bit of additional light. It was hanging in a post fastened to the wall.

As he glanced back up to the top of the thirty-foot ladder, the light from the entrance slowly disappeared as the lid shut. Now this torch was the sole source of light, providing just enough to see.

After waving for the boy to follow, she walked down a very long and zigzagging tunnel, where m o r e f l a m i n g torches s a t in posts at every corner in this quarter-mile-long passage. From somewhere ahead, they could hear a multitude of e c h o i n g noises, ranging from the clanging of metals and other objects, to people yelling.

This tunnel inevitably opened u p into a gargantuan underground cavern that contained tens of thousands of stalagmites and stalactites spread all about in variously sized and shaped clusters, as well nearly a dozen other tunnels that Baltor could see, thanks to all the lit torches posted on all three levels.

Also spread all about this rather noisy cavern were dozens of people engaged in hardcore-training—most looked to be teenagers or older. A few raced through obstacle courses, while some taught others how to fight or wrestle. The remainder of the people sparred violently and ferociously with other opponents, some using weapons of wood, or steel!

As for Lydia, she stood quietly by and allowed the boy his time to explore his new surroundings.

Finally, he walked right up next to Lydia and whispered so no one else could hear, "Would you now please answer my question?"

"We are thieves," she began, "but not the conventional type. For all around this world are priceless treasures and artifacts waiting for the properly trained thief to discover and steal. Most are not only heavily guarded, but also booby-trapped!"

After taking a deep breath through her nose, she added, "We never steal from the poor, and quite often, we give them a portion of our wealth. Still, good and honest thieves are hard to come by, especially these days. Therefore, we have certain secret oaths that a prospect must swear to before that person can join our very special thieves' guild—what we simply call 'The Guild.'"

Once she had given the boy about five seconds to digest this information, she continued, "Before I go on any further, I should inform you that if this place was to be discovered, the Sultan would not only plunder our rich treasures, but have us all executed."

"So why are you showing all of this to me?" he asked. Without waiting for the answer, he asked another question, "How do you know that I will not spill my guts out to the Sultan once I'm gone?"

She laughed for a few moments, but did not answer his questions—his facial expression instantly turned suspicious.

Once she had stopped laughing a few moments later, she answered quite seriously, "Well, Baltor, I'm showing all of this to you because I'm about to give you the opportunity you never had. However, should you try to leave now; you'll have your guts spilled out before you even make it to the ladder, as this place must remain *top secret.*" She whispered those last two words.

The boy gulped.

She laughed yet again for two seconds, before she sighed. "Relax—if I didn't think I could trust you, I wouldn't have brought you here."

"I see," he answered. "I won't tell anyone."

"Great!" she said with an elated smile. She then said, "I have a couple questions for you, Baltor. First question—would you like to become powerful, get rich and become a master thief? Second—are you ready to begin your training?"

Without hesitation, the boy answered, "Yes to both questions. Are you going to train me?"

She shook her head one time, before answering, "No, not right now... perhaps later. I only train those who have completed all their student training, completed their quest, achieved the official rank of Thief, spent at least five years of loyal service with us, spent an additional six years successfully training students as a Drill Instructor, spent five more years successfully training Drill Instructors, and passed all the pretests to be trained as an Officer of the Guild. Even though there are many h i g h e r grades before one can become a ruling member of the High Council like me, it is obviously possible, even at my young age. Finally, the last thing I do, though in very rare circumstances like yours, I recruit."

He asked, "What do 'circumstances' and 'recruit' mean?"

She answered, "A more common word for circumstances is 'situations.' And recruit means 'find new talents like you.'"

"Oh," he said. Once again very curious about all that there was to see in this room, he began to look around.

She had already begun to scan throughout the room herself. About thirty seconds later, after having found who she was looking for, she called out loudly, "Drill Instructor Humonus!"

Having heard his name, a man who had been watching two women viciously fight with quarterstaffs, turned around and began to approach at a quick and steady gait. Even from this distance of two hundred feet away, Baltor saw that he had muscles.

His simple attire consisted of a short-sleeved green tunic, black breeches and boots, and his rugged-good looks consisted of shoulder-length brown hair that was slightly wavy, a five o'clock shadow and brown eyes. As he drew closer, Baltor observed a thin scar that ran up and down the left cheek on his mocha-colored face.

After arriving and bowing to the lady, the six-foot-tall man asked, "Yes, my Mistress, how may I be of service?"

"Good Sir, are you currently training any students?"

Humonus answered, "To answer your question, nope. My last student Shami passed his final exam yesterday, though not without a scratch. Were you not able to attend, Mistress Lydia?"

"No, I just arrived back in Pavelus this morning from a month's long vacation—what do you mean not without a scratch?"

After sucking a deep breath through his mouth, Humonus explained, "Well... On the seventh and final obstacle course, Shami paused a nanosecond too long and one of our archers smacked an arrow into his right buttock! *Ouch!!*"

Both he and Lydia began to chuckle with quite a bit of amusement at that, which drew the boy's attention back to them.

Once the man's laughter had dissipated, but a few seconds later, he added with a whole lot of pride, "But seriously. I am so very proud of Shami, especially the way that he determinedly maneuvered himself through that final obstacle, to the finish line, and won!"

Humonus couldn't help but chuckle again, before he concluded, "Still, it'll probably be a month or two before he is able to sit down... and his new teachers will allow him to 'sit in' on their classes! Get the pun?" No longer able to contain himself, he laughed very hard while slapping himself on the knee.

Lydia laughed along for a few more moments, too. Even though Baltor had been listening, he hadn't been amused, nor did he join in the laughter.

As soon as she glanced back at the boy and his serious look, she stopped laughing. "Well, I'll be sure to congratulate Shami later on today. Now, I have a couple of related questions for you. Are you going to take a vacation or something, or are you all ready to take on another student?" With a point of her thumb, she introduced, "This is Baltor."

Humonus looked over to the boy for the very first time, and after only a few seconds of baleful study, he replied with a sneer, "This boy doesn't look like a thief. In fact, he looks like a coward that would turn yellow and run at the first sign of danger!"

Baltor, who was quite aware that *he* was the boy Humonus was talking about, defended aloud, "That's not true! You have no idea who I am or what I'm capab—"

"Well," Humonus interrupted, "that remains to be seen, or better yet—not seen! Follow me, boy." Right away, he turned around and proceeded toward one of the tunnels located at the far-left side of the cavern.

Baltor followed Humonus into a straight and narrow tunnel— every seventy feet was a blazing torch fastened to the wall.

Twice, Humonus came across forking tunnels and both times, he took the left tunnel, until finally, halfway through this third tunnel, again on the left side, there was a lit alcove.

17

Sitting on the floor inside was a beautiful wooden desk, and resting upon that, two small oil lamps burned. Behind the desk sat a matching wood chair with a plush black pillow on the seat.

Humonus walked around the desk, took a seat, pulled open a drawer, took out a sheet of paper, closed the drawer, set the paper on the desk, looked the boy directly in the eyes, and asked, "Do you know how to read and write?"

Baltor answered, "No."

"Well," Humonus replied, "you'll learn soon enough. In the meantime, what I'm about to do is to read this contract for you. When I tell you to repeat something after me, you will be swearing to it. When I've gotten through the entire contract, you can just put an X at the bottom, signifying your name. Any questions for me, boy?"

"No."

"Good, now raise your right hand and repeat after me," Humonus ordered. He next picked up the contract and read aloud, "I, state your name..."

"I, Baltor," he began, raising his right hand.

"Do solemnly swear..."

Baltor repeated.

"Never to reveal the secret location of this thieves' guild..."

Baltor repeated.

"Nor to reveal the secrets of this thieves' guild that are about to be taught to me..."

Baltor repeated.

"Nor will I reveal any of the members of this thieves' guild under any circumstances—ever!"

Baltor repeated.

"And if I even begin to think of betraying this solemn oath, I swear that I will first acquire a dagger, cut my own eyes out, then my tongue, then each of my fingers and thumbs, and finally, plunge that dagger into my heart with my feet." Humonus finished reading.

The boy got about a quarter of the way through before he forgot the rest, and so his eyes began to squint, which was his "thinking look." Humonus was on the ball, and assisted him where he had left off.

Once done, he turned the piece of paper around, handed a feather pen to the boy, and said, "Now, sign here."

He signed with an X.

"Good—I am now officially your drill instructor." Humonus extended his hand, which the boy immediately shook.

Before the drill instructor let go, he promised, "One more thing—if you do happen to violate your oath, it would be better for you to do all that you have sworn to, than for us to take the matter into our own hands. Now you begin basic training... follow me."

CHAPTER III

Humonus left the alcove and led the way back down the tunnels, while the boy followed.

During this trip, the drill instructor began to teach, "Our Guild has been in existence for a little less than five centuries—not too long after this city had been conquered by the empire. Yeah, it's true that we have had members caught, tortured, tried, hanged or worse—but none has ever stupidly revealed the location of our headquarters or our members, yet why should they want to? After all, they remember that we have always taken great care of them, and it was solely by their own stupidity and/or clumsiness that they got caught. But now, onto more pressing matters."

At that moment, the two had entered back into the main cavern—he continued, "One of the first things that we shall do for you is to build up your strength, dexterity and endurance through intense physical exercises and challenges. Later, once you pass the basic tests, you will then learn how to use a broad selection of weapons, and of course be tested.

"Once you pass all of these physical tests, you will learn how to read and write, even foreign languages, and you will also learn etiquette, manners and customs..."

After a five second pause without interruption, the drill instructor concluded his spiel, "In time, should you pass all of the tests, you will know how to bust into any lock or door, how to talk or fight your way out of any situation, and ultimately, you will know how to blend in anywhere... as a master thief! Do you understand?"

With quite a bit of enthusiasm, the boy answered, "Yes!"

With just as much anger, the drill instructor snapped, "Oh—from here on out, worm, you will only address me as 'sir.' Do you understand?"

No longer sounding excited at all, especially because of the insult, the boy replied, "Yes, sir."

The expression on Humonus's face contorted even more furiously as he screamed out, "I can't hear you—worm!"

"Yes—sir!"

Still bearing an angry expression with arms defensively crossed, Humonus stated in a gruff tone of voice, "Good... Now, drop and give me twenty."

The boy looked very confused as he asked, "Twenty what, sir?"

The drill instructor growled, "Twenty pushups, you knucklehead!"

"Sir, what are pushups?"

After giving a very disgruntled sigh, he explained how to do a proper pushup—upon having done ten, he stood back up and yelled, "Now drop and give me twenty pushups!"

The boy dropped to the ground into the pushup position— he pushed out one, two, three, three-and-a-half pushups, before his arms and chest buckled, and he collapsed onto the ground.

"Are you freaking kidding me? That's all you got—three miserable-looking pushups?" the drill instructor asked, just before he knelt down next to the boy's head. Only a second later, he barked, "You'd better give me more than just three, maggot!"

With all of his might, the boy tried again but failed to get even one pushup.

After looking up, he whined, "Sir—I can't!"

"I somehow knew that you were going to be a lot of work," Humonus sneered with a whole lot of derision. "Give me twenty sit-ups!"

"Sir, what is a sit-up?"

The drill instructor howled out with such severe agitation as if he had totally lost his marbles, but instead of saying another word or making another sound, he laid his back down upon the ground. He then laced his hands and fingers behind his head, crossed his legs as he lifted them into the air, and bent his knees to a forty-five degree angle. Repeatedly, he began to pull his hands and head into his knees.

After he had performed ten sit-ups, he stood back up onto his feet and said, "Make sure that you pull with your stomach muscles, not your hands—now, give me twenty sit-ups."

The boy flipped over onto his back, lifted up his legs and knees, put his hands behind his head, and squeezed his abdominal muscles by pulling his elbows to his knees. One, two, three, four... five...

Even though five-and-a-half sit-ups were all he could do, Baltor still felt his stomach muscles burning ever so badly!

He looked up at his drill instructor, of who he saw was simply shaking his head in baleful disdain.

Instead of yelling, however, Humonus clipped, "Give me more pushups."

Many long hours seemed to pass, though it was impossible to tell exactly how many, especially underground, before the utterly exhausted boy was finally granted a break.

Right after the drill instructor ordered, "Rest ten minutes," he disappeared into one of the pitch-black tunnels.

As Baltor sat down on the cold, hard ground, and tried to relax, exhaustion and fatigue hit him all that much harder, and he began to crave sleep.

Only a few seconds seemed to pass, however, before the drill instructor was already back, screaming at his student to do more pushups, sit-ups and running.

Soon after that, he began to teach the boy how to do more types of exercises like jumping jacks and pull-ups, and then many more long hours seemed to pass as the boy performed them, along with still more pushups, sit-ups and running.

Finally, the time came when "the very, very cruel drill instructor," in Baltor's unexpressed opinion, said, "I'll now take you to your bedchambers, so you can rest."

Through his exhaustion and sweat-caked body, the boy could only pant, "Yes.... sir...."

The drill instructor led his student into a pitch-black tunnel located at the far right side of the cavern.

The student was able to follow in the darkness solely by listening to his drill instructor's voice. "A thief must rely on his other senses besides sight. Therefore, we have left many of our tunnels without any lights, so that our students can learn how to maneuver around in the darkness. Soon enough, you will have to learn and master this skill. Of course you will be tested in this area."

The very second Humonus finished saying all this information; Baltor saw a lit cavern up ahead on the right-hand side.

Nearly twenty seconds later, they entered into the cavern. There, the boy observed about two-dozen bunk beds, and that every bunk but one was occupied with sleeping people. Lying against the wall on the right stood a huge metal table filled with fruit, vegetables, small loaves of wheat bread, wood pitchers filled with water, and empty, wooden mugs.

"This is where you'll be sleeping," Humonus informed him while pointing to that empty bunk, "Better take advantage of it while you can."

"Yes, sir!"

Without another word, the drill instructor turned around and departed the room.

Even though Baltor was hungry, he was too exhausted to care. Immediately he plopped into bed and fell asleep.

Only minutes seemed to pass before the boy heard a screaming voice that brought him back to consciousness. As he slowly opened his eyes, he turned his head toward the screaming. Drill Instructor Humonus.

"I said get the hell up, for the dozenth time!" the drill instructor screamed, looking very ticked off. "From now on, when I tell you to do something, do it the first time! Do you understand, maggot?"

Hurriedly sliding out of bed, the boy cried, "Yes, sir!"

"You have five minutes to eat, and three of those are up," the drill instructor continued to yell.

While yawning, the boy ran over to the table of food, plucked off a loaf of bread, and stuffed a piece of it into his mouth. As he chewed on the hard bread, he quickly poured a glass of water from the pitcher.

From his peripheral vision, he noticed that his instructor was standing right behind him and silently waiting—he also saw that the rest of the room was void of occupants. Baltor took a swallow of water, stuffed another piece of bread into his mouth, chewed on that for a few seconds, and took another swallow of water.

It didn't even feel as if he had even two minutes to eat, for upon swallowing his sixth chunk of bread and fifth gulp of water, Humonus barked out, "Time's up—let's go! Lead the way back to the training area!"

The boy first cried out, "Yes, sir," before he ran into the pitch-black tunnel.

Making his way back to the training area turned to be an unbelievably frustrating task indeed, for many times over, he crashed into a tunnel wall, crashed into his drill instructor, or simply became lost.

For the most part, Humonus remained silent during this rather long trip, except for the times that Baltor screwed up. When that was the case, he was on the boy like flies on feces—screaming away in the pitch-black, tunnels that reverberated with even more yelling, which was a very disorientating thing for poor Baltor.

It seemed as if an eternity had passed before the student finally saw the torch light ahead. Unfortunately, as he came to discover, the light came from the bunkhouse.

Once they finally had gotten to the training area, perhaps hours later, Humonus pointed, while howling, "Now I want you to follow the trail marker and run through this obstacle course as fast as you possibly can! Move it—move it—move it!"

After observing a chiseled line in the ground with an arrow pointing in the direction he needed to run, the boy ran at top speed.

The first obstacle that he came across was a knotted rope that reached all the way up to the ceiling; not surprisingly, his muscles were so fatigued from the day before that he could only climb up halfway, about twenty five feet, and that was it—despite the outraged protests, and curses, from his drill instructor.

Eventually, Humonus yelled up, "Get the hell down and move on—you sluggish puke!"

As the boy climbed back down, luck was with him that he didn't fall because of his already fatigued and sore muscles. Once he hit the ground, which felt like hitting a ton of bricks, he then ran down the chiseled line and up to the next obstacle—a rope that gradually angled its way up to a platform some forty feet high!

"How do I—" the boy tried to ask, only to be interrupted.

"Turn yourself around, slide your legs over the rope, and pull yourself with your arms and legs up to the top—do it!" the drill instructor screamed.

Doing as instructed, it took the boy about ten minutes before he finally reached the top. He was completely out of breath, his heart raced frantically, and sweat soaked his body.

The drill instructor shouted from the ground, "Climb down the ladder and move on to the next obstacle—you're not done!"

As Baltor ran to the next obstacle, he saw that he had to leap across a circular pit that spanned about ten feet in diameter, which had a rope that hung in the middle and was attached to the ceiling—once there, he leapt and successfully grabbed the rope.

The momentum allowed him to swing to the far end, and once on the other side, he dropped to the ground. Turning back around in shock, he confirmed that this pit was bottomless!

"Well, what are you waiting for? Homlick Day?" Humonus snarled.

Baltor continued to run down the chiseled line. Ahead, he saw six bags of varying sizes that hung from metal railings, which automatically swung back and forth, but at different rotating speeds.

24

Upon getting closer, he observed that the bags were connected to a bunch of interconnected mechanical gears that somehow maintained a continuous motion.

He was able to slip pass the first two bags, but the third one smacked into him unexpectedly hard—the impact caused him to crash into the ground, painfully, and see shooting stars!

The drill instructor was all over the boy, as he ranted and raved and spitted, "How in the hell are you supposed to be a thief if you can't even make it through my obstacle course? Well?"

As more stars appeared in the boy's field of vision, as well gobs of spit flying on his face, he tried to answer, "Well, sir... I'm—I'm trying... the best that I can."

"You need a hell of a lot more work!" Humonus retorted. With a point of his index finger, he ordered, "Get some water from the lunch table over there... and eat some fruit. You'll get a fifteen-minute break before we begin the next training exercise."

Just after the drill instructor had turned and begun to walk away, he stopped—without looking back, he said without an ounce of compassion, "Oh, if you want to quit because you can't handle my training anymore—you might as well fall into that pit you just swung across."

The boy said not a word—instead, he stumbled himself over to the table, picked up the pitcher and drank. His poor body ached beyond comprehension and his mind was completely exhausted—yet the day had only just started.

If it's even day.... he silently mused to himself while taking another drink.

He began to get very exasperated as he thought aloud, "What in the hell have I gotten myself into? At least before, I was free. Definitely not wealthy, certainly homeless, but still, at least I was free! Maybe I should just jump into the pit and end my agony."

Yet, another voice inside the boy's head countered, sounding suspiciously like his mother, *No, Baltor! You will not give up! Look at everything else you've survived! And now—now you've been given the chance to succeed, my baby boy!*

Those new and encouraging thoughts seemed to stimulate Baltor, and at least for the moment, he no longer felt any pain or frustration whatsoever.

Reality, however, abruptly pulled him from his thoughts as an all-too-familiar voice screamed out, "Your break's up. You were too slow and too weak during your last exercise! Let's see you try again!"

With a zeal that the boy had never known before, he roared out, "Yes, sir!"

He bolted down the chiseled line, leapt high for the rope ladder, caught it at eight feet in the air, climbed his way all the way to the top, and then made his way back down.

Refusing any negative thoughts that might break "his concentration," he pushed himself through the next two obstacles, meeting them both with success. Finally, he knew that his next obstacle was the swinging bags.

As he began to draw near, he mentally noted the time it took for the first bag to cross from one side to the other—approximately six seconds. By the time he approached the obstacle, he had also noted that the second bag was a bit smaller yet only took three seconds each way.

The boy stopped right before the first bag, waited for it to pass, and then entered its path. The second bag crossed and he rushed six steps forward, in between the second and the third bag.

The third bag was even bigger than the first bag but only took seconds to cross—it was on its way back—and as he waited for it to pass, he observed that the fourth bag was a lot smaller and faster than all of the other bags, taking only a second for each direction. He couldn't make out how big or how fast the fifth bag was going.

Once the third bag had crossed yet again, the boy instantly leapt toward the ground, tucked into a tight somersault, and rolled right underneath the third and fourth bags—his right shoulder began to ache.

Without pause, he stood himself straight up, so that the fifth bag wouldn't clobber him. This bag was very big and slow, with an estimated time of nine seconds to swing each direction.

However, the boy also observed that the sixth bag was the same size and speed as the fourth bag, but with one noticeable difference. The frame that held the final bag was built much lower to the ground, so rolling underneath it would be impossible.

Once the fifth bag was clear, the boy leapt, but this time straight up! He successfully grabbed the frame above him. He pulled the rest of his body up and over, and then he safely dropped to the ground on the other side. It was then that he observed that the chiseled line/path continued onward.

"Well?" Humonus shrieked, "Keep going!"

Baltor pushed onward with all he had. He soon observed that the chiseled line appeared to lead him up to a sheer cliff face. Even as he drew closer and closer, he observed that there was no ladder for him to climb and very few decent hand- or footholds. Yet looking up, about forty feet up, he confirmed that there was a mouth of a tunnel way up there.

About four feet from the ground, he spotted a rock that slightly jutted out from the cliff face—he clasped it with his left hand and then leaned himself into the wall.

He soon scanned a tiny crack in the wall about two feet above that—he reached for it with his right hand, while trying to pull his body up. Again, he was successful with his attempt.

The boy next lifted up his left leg, and then placed it onto the next rock, while pivoting his entire body again so that the whole of his body weight rested on his left side, and then he looked for the next handhold.

There was another crack, but it was a good three feet up and about four feet to the right. With all of the elasticity he could muster, he reached for it.

This time, unfortunately, he missed the handhold and fell to the ground—his knee smashed into the pebbled earth first, which sent shooting pains up his knee and throughout the rest of his body!

Despite the pounding pain in his kneecap, he heard his drill instructor once again screaming right in his ear, "Come on, you weakling! Get the hell up there!"

With tears now steadily flowing down his cheeks, both from the pain and the frustration, the boy turned his head to face his drill instructor. "I can't! What you ask is impossible!"

Humonus began to laugh like a crazed maniac.

"Damn you to hell!" the boy screamed as he tried to wipe the muddy tears away.

With lightning speed that defied the laws of physics, the drill instructor had already pinched his dagger into the boy's neck, slightly drawing blood. He hissed, "The next time you curse me like that, boy, I will kill you...."

Frightened out of his wits, Baltor could say or do nothing.

After a few moments, the drill instructor finally put his knife away behind his back, before saying nonchalantly, "This time, however, I will show you how to make the impossible—possible."

With that, Humonus took a few steps back, leapt over the boy, and then climbed the wall with ease, almost as if he were walking on the ground. It had taken him ten seconds to accomplish this astounding feat, while the student watched in total amazement.

From up above, the drill instructor ordered, "Now climb on up here, boy."

Trying to follow suit, the boy was able to scale the wall successfully, though it took him more than four minutes.

Once he stood on solid ground inside the tunnel, the drill instructor simply shook his head balefully, as he informed, "You need much, much, much more work—now continue on."

The boy answered, "Yes, sir!" He then bolted ahead. Not only did he find that this very windy tunnel twisted right and left, yet up and down.

A minute later, he finally made it to the end, just before scanning his horizons. He saw the rope with the knots in it that he had first climbed, but it was more than twenty feet away!

From behind him, he heard his drill instructor order, "Back off a bit, run, and then jump for it!"

Baltor sucked in a deep breath in order to regain a control over his fears—the fear of heights and the fear of plummeting to his death. Even though it didn't work, he still backed off as ordered, ran forward at top speed, and then jumped at the last second.

Whether it was luck or skill, the boy did not know or care, but he was quite relieved when he saw himself flying straight toward the rope ... and even more relieved when his hands gripped the rope securely!

From all of his momentum, the rope swung about seven feet out, but he had already wrapped his legs around it.

Seconds later, once the rope had finally settled, the boy climbed his way down knot-by-knot and waited. He was out of breath, soaked with sweat, and worst of all, he was exhausted beyond comprehension.

As for his drill instructor, he climbed down the rope with ease.

Baltor saw that this man hadn't even broken a sweat—not even on his forehead!

As Humonus began to shake his head balefully, his words confirmed, "You need a hell of a lot more work. It took you more than fifteen minutes to complete this course. Next time, I want you to accomplish it in under five minutes."

Still out of breath, the boy replied, "Yes... sir..."

"Take a half an hour lunch, and then we shall commence to doing some more physical exercises for the rest of the afternoon," the drill instructor concluded, just before walking away.

"Yes, sir!" Baltor slowly and painfully made his way over to the lunch table, and began to munch on a loaf of wheat bread.

"So," Lydia most unexpectedly asked from behind him, "how are you enjoying it here?"

Too exhausted to jump and do another one-eighty even though he was still startled, he turned around, and answered with a small portion of food still inside his mouth, "It's tough and I don't think I'm doing so well, if you want to know the truth."

She laughed melodiously for a second, before answering, "That's all I've ever asked of you, Baltor. As for you not doing so well — nobody does well in the beginning. Remember this... Soon enough, any and all challenges will eventually be overcome. And also remember this—success is a road that you must pave."

The boy pondered her information for a moment. "Did you have to go through all of this yourself?"

"Yes, I did. As if you can't tell already, I'm not exactly from around here," Lydia added. "At the tender age of twelve, I was kidnapped from my parents and home in a land far away from here and sold as a slave. After nearly a year of me riding in one of their cages going from town to town, I was bought. Unfortunately, the one who bought me would beat me senseless whenever I didn't do as he commanded."

"You were a slave?" Baltor asked in disbelief. "Then who was your master?"

Lydia replied, "I was one of the Sultan's harem girls."

The boy looked at her in both shock and wonder! "How did you escape? Doesn't he still look for you?"

"In answer to your first question, I escaped with the help of one of the Sultan's generals," she answered.

A wistful look suddenly appeared in her eyes, as she revealed, "He had, upon seeing me for the first time in the Sultan's private quarters, immediately fallen in love with me. I didn't find any of this out until several months later when he told me of his feelings and delivered a potion for me to drink. He then explained that its effects would only simulate death, but that I would return to normal within twenty-four hours. He promised me that he would take good care of me, if I wished."

She shrugged, before continuing, "Without any other choice, I agreed, and immediately drank the potion. After the Sultan believed that I was dead, and after the wagon cart had taken me outside of the city to the gravesite, the general waited there. He took my body and hid me away in his place of residence. For the next year, I lived with him, and truth be told, I fell in love with the man. Sadly, he died the following year in a battle with the Mauritians."

After releasing a sigh of sorrow, she concluded, "Once I had found out this information from another servant, I immediately left his place, took to the streets, and soon after—the Guild brought me in and gave me a new identity. To answer your second question, the Sultan doesn't know I'm still alive."

Baltor listened, enraptured to Lydia's tale. Once he was sure that she had finished, he asked, "How old are you, if you don't mind me asking?"

She laughed again before answering, "I'm twenty-five."

"Wow!" the boy sighed, as he felt his heart fluttering strangely, "I never would have guessed that—I thought you were like sixteen."

She laughed yet again, before she said, "Thank you."

Just then, the boy peripherally observed his drill instructor fast approaching. He said to Lydia, "Well, it looks as if I'm going to have to go do some more hardcore training, as my drill instructor likes to call it. It was definitely a pleasure to listen to what you had to say!"

With a smile, she nodded and added, "Don't give up hope and you will see your own 'moment of glory'—soon enough."

Though Humonus was now nearby, he still yelled at the top of his lungs, "Baltor! To me. Now!"

"Yes, sir!" the boy replied with confidence in his voice, as well a small smile. Immediately he ran over to his drill instructor.

Because Baltor could not see behind him, he missed the smile that lingered upon Lydia's face. Still, for the remainder of the day, he pushed himself way beyond what he could have ever conceived possible....

CHAPTER IV

After every long and grueling day that passed, Baltor found that he got fatigued less and less—even with only a minimal amount of sleep. As the days turned into weeks, which there were eight days every week, and the weeks into months, which there were four weeks a month and thirteen months a year, he learned quite a few new positive things.

For one, his timing and ability to maneuver through all six of the obstacle courses, each progressively harder, had drastically improved. Though the drill instructor rarely ever expressed any satisfaction, he did reveal his student's timeframes and physical training tests that were getting better every time.

For two, he had learned how to maneuver through darkness by relying on his sense of sound alone. It became easy as pie to find his way from the bunkhouse to their training area, which non-dangerous route actually had five different routes he could choose. The drill instructor had long ago warned to the boy that he was not allowed to explore any other pitch-black tunnels, as they were both dangerous and deadly. Baltor didn't.

And for three, he discovered that his muscles were not only becoming stronger, yet *bigger*!

He had also learned a couple of negative things. Despite the hundred or so nights that he had lived in the bunkhouse—he didn't know how many—he still hadn't made a single friend. He had tried twice, unsuccessfully.

Even worse—for some unknown reason, whenever he had tried to instigate a conversation with any of his classmates, they would all studiously ignore him, or if together, even bully him. Fortunate was the fact that for ninety-nine percent of the time, all of Baltor's fellow students were asleep or gone when his drill instructor woke him up in the morning and released him at night.

Of course, there were quite a few times that he had awoken prematurely, due to another drill instructor who was yelling at his or her own student. Baltor knew to keep quiet, as one other boy student had made the stupid mistake to yell back a month or so ago, although it wasn't the boy's instructor who had woken him.

In front of everyone at lunchtime that day, that boy had gotten his hands smacked hard with a switch twenty times, and not only by his own drill instructor, but also by the one he had yelled at. In the end, that boy's knuckles were busted open and bleeding and his eyes filled with pain-stricken tears!

The last, and the hardest, thing for Baltor to learn throughout these last few months was the fact that he hadn't seen Lydia even once, yet every day that passed he missed her that much more.

One day, or possibly night, the drill instructor arrived at his student's bunk. This time, unlike all of the other times before, he didn't yell and scream. Instead, he quietly tapped Baltor on the shoulder until awake and then he half-whispered, "I want you to report to my office in thirty minutes. We have some important matters to discuss. When we're done with our meeting, you can go back to sleep until morning."

"Yes, sir," the boy replied, just before rising to his feet and heading for the food table. Meanwhile, the drill instructor left the bunkhouse.

After Baltor had peeled and ate an orange, he next consumed a whole loaf of bread, amidst washing it down with a mug of water. Once done with breakfast, four minutes later, he made his way through the tunnels until he reached his drill instructor's office, which journey took about twenty-five minutes.

Once he stood before the desk, he quietly assumed the position of attention. The drill instructor had been sitting in his chair reading a notebook, but he didn't even look up once. He just continued to flip from page to page and read.

Eight to ten minutes passed before Humonus closed the notebook, looked up and said with a smile, "Baltor, you have passed through phase one of the training program. Congratulations!"

"Thank you, sir!" the boy barked.

"Now, phase two is to commence in the morning," the drill instructor revealed. "Within this phase, you will learn fighting skills that range from hand-to-hand techniques to a wide range of weapons training. Some students are slow learners and take many years before they even learn the rudimentary skills of fighting. Some students never make it through phase two at all."

Humonus paused for ten seconds to let these words sink in—Baltor simply waited in silence for his drill instructor to continue.

"Before you can be passed on to phase three, you will have to prove your fighting skills. Most likely, you will find a favorite type of weapon. But remember this—a thief may not have any weapon except his own hands, so he better damned be able to use them if he expects to get out alive!"

The drill instructor paused for an additional ten seconds to let this equally important info sink in, before he continued, "From here on out, though it is not mandated, it would benefit you to greatly enhance your physical and dexterity skills through the obstacle courses during those afternoons I give you such free time. For now, as it is three in the morning, you can go back to bed until five when we begin training! Dismissed."

"Yes, sir!" the boy exclaimed with a proud smile upon his face.

Even though he returned to his bedchambers, and lay back down to sleep, all attempts failed, as he had become overly excited about this "new phase."

Precisely at 5:00 a.m., the drill instructor arrived — upon seeing his student lying awake in his bunk while all the other students still slept, he ordered, but did not yell, "Follow me."

"Yes sir."

Humonus led his student to a massive rack that contained a wide arsenal of weapons—both training and real ones. This rack sat in front of the opening of another smaller cavern, which happened to be the supply room.

After gesturing toward the weapons, the drill instructor taught, "As I stated earlier, the first and greatest weapon that you will ever learn how to use is your own body. All of these other lesser weapons must only be an extension of you. Do you understand?"

"Yes, sir!"

"Good. Hit me."

After a few seconds has passed, the boy asked with a very unconvinced sound to his voice, "Sir, you want me to hit you?"

Laughing, the drill instructor answered, "Yes. Come on now, just hit me."

"Where would you like me to hit you, sir?"

The drill instructor's humored look instantly disappeared and severe irritation replaced it. "I don't care, for crying out loud—just hit me!"

With all of his might, the boy swung his right fist at Humonus's face.

A nanosecond before it would have contacted, the drill instructor twisted his body out of the way, and the fist only struck thin air.

"Again!"

This time, the boy swung with his left fist—again, Humonus had already twisted out of the way, and the fist connected only with air.

The drill instructor shrieked at the top of his lungs, "*Try harder!!*"

The student quickly tried to anticipate which direction his drill instructor would dodge, and when he made his best guess a few seconds later, he swung his right fist out with all of his might.

Not only was Humonus able to evade the punch, yet it also threw Baltor off balance. The drill instructor immediately grabbed the boy's still-extended fist and yanked while twisting. This simple motion caused the boy's back to slam hard into the ground.

For a minute or so, he saw only shooting stars. Even though he couldn't see, he could hear his drill instructor say, "In order to beat the enemy, you must first become that enemy!"

Once Baltor had begun to regain clarity of vision, he looked up at his drill instructor in disbelief.

"Stand up," the drill instructor immediately ordered. "Let me show you how to punch properly."

The boy stood as ordered but instantly became afraid—he flinched in terror when his drill instructor cocked back his fist.

Still holding his cocked fist back, Humonus nonchalantly stated, "Quit shaking like a little baby and take it like a man."

The boy tried to calm his fears, but to no avail.

Humonus shook his head balefully, just before he explained, "Listen… In any sort of combat situation whatsoever, not only must you be able to dish it out, but you must also be able to take it. As I told you once before—if you don't think that you can do it, you know where you can go."

Baltor sucked in a deep breath in order to regain his nerves—in that same second Humonus launched a full-forced punch into his student's chest! The boy's body flew backward about five feet and rolled several times over until finally stopping.

This time, however, the boy was unconscious and did not get up.

A minute or so later, he awoke to the painful sensations of someone slapping his face hard and repeatedly.

Once the drill instructor saw that his student had opened his eyes, he stopped slapping and yelled, "Sit up!"

With tears still flowing down his face, and still barely able to breathe, Baltor did as ordered, slowly sitting up.

While pointing his index finger up as a physical prompt, the drill instructor said at a normal volume, "As you just learned the hard way, one good hit is all it would take to completely disable any opponent—just one. Understand?"

"Yes, sir," the boy said, as he began to wipe the tears off.

"One hit," the drill instructor continued, "in the right spot, with the right amount of force, and with the whole of your body to back it up."

He paused for a few moments to let it sink in, and then he asked, "But what if your opponent is wearing body armor? Well, certainly then, a punch into his gut won't work. What if your opponent is wearing a helmet? Obviously, a punch to the head is just as futile."

After taking in a deep breath through just his nose, he concluded, "Therefore, the first lesson is this: Learn your opponent's strengths and weaknesses before you attack, yet always be ready with a good defense in case your opponent attacks first. Do you understand?"

"Yes, sir," Baltor replied eagerly.

"Not yet you don't, but you will," the drill instructor countered. "Stand up, and then I want you to strike me again."

The boy stood and quickly tried to judge his drill instructor's weaknesses. His first thought was that maybe he could get a good swing into the side of his gut, as it didn't look guarded, so he threw his punch.

With but a tiny flick of his hand, Humonus grabbed the punch and twisted yet another direction—this simple motion caused the boy to literally fly over his drill instructor and for his back to slam hard yet again into the ground. For the third time that day, he saw shooting stars...

He stumbled back onto his feet, but his balance was so completely off that he fell right back onto the ground.

The drill instructor knelt on one knee next to his student, pointed two fingers into the air, and said, "The second lesson is this: Always, always, always keep yourself in a defensive position, even if you don't look like you're in one."

Baltor gulped before speaking, "Yes, sir."

Humonus stood, extended his hand out to his student, pulled him back onto his feet, and then ordered, "I want you take a fifteen-minute break and then meet me back here."

The boy muttered, "Yes, sir."

He slowly stumbled his way over to the break table, and with trembling hands, he poured himself a glass of water. It was only when he had finished taking a long swallow that he realized just how badly his stomach, his back, his head—hell, his entire body ached!

This is even worse than the first phase! At least I didn't have him beating the crap out of me then.

Suddenly, from out of the corner of his eye, he observed a beautiful, middle-aged woman enter the cavern from the entryway tunnel. Her age was evident solely from the thick and wavy silver streak that lined her raven-colored hair and certainly not from her youthful face. She wore a silky blue dress that loosely contoured around her shapely body, and would have been touching the dirty floor, had she not been holding a good portion of it with her left fist.

Only a second later, a six or seven-year-old girl dressed in dirty rags follow right behind. Once the two stopped, nearly two minutes after their entrance, the girl began to look all around in utter amazement.

As Baltor took another long drink of water, he saw the woman face a different training area and heard her call out, "Drill Instructor Manichai, are you training any students?"

Two men, who were fiercely battling it out with real swords and who were not wearing any shirts, stopped their intense battle. The man on the left had jet-black hair pulled back into a tight ponytail, thick angular eyebrows, as well a long and tightly braided beard. The man on the right was clean-shaven and bald. Both were very muscular and sweaty.

It was the man with the beard who answered in a very deep tone of voice "No, my mistress, I am not... neither am I looking either. But I know Instructor Jeramone here is, my Mistress."

The woman next asked, "Instructor Jeramone, are you willing to train this girl, Vakshia?"

With a sneer, Jeramone replied, "Her? You've got to be kidding me! She's nothing but skin and bones. Throw her back on the streets and let the sun rot her out!" His crackly voice sounded as if he was still going through puberty.

Baltor stifled back a laugh.

The girl, now looking angry, boldly declared, "How about we let the sun rot you out, which task looks, and sounds, almost done?"

Her retaliatory reply startled and amused Baltor. Even Manichai and the mysterious mistress stopped short of laughing.

Jeramone, on the other hand looked peeved off, especially with that evil glare on his beet-red face and that sword in his hand that trembled angrily. He looked like he was about to yell something back or maybe even chuck the sword right into the girl's heart! Vakshia was starting to look scared too.

Only six seconds later, that murderous look on Jeramone disappeared instantly, and what replaced it was one of total serenity.

He took a deep breath, released it, and after taking another breath, he said with an impressed tone of voice, "Perhaps you do have potential to become a thief because you did not run off like a little coward. Follow me! See ya later, Mani. My Mistress."

"Later, Jer."

Thirty seconds later, Baltor watched as the two — Jeramone and the girl—disappeared down the tunnel that led to Humonus's office. Already had Manichai and the woman begun to converse in very hushed tones.

Just then, he heard his drill instructor call out from their weapons rack, "Baltor—time's up!"

The boy replied, "Yes, sir."

As he ran over, he observed that his drill instructor was waiting over there. This time, he donned leather armor, a helmet and a mischievous smile.

"Feeling better?" Humonus asked, still smiling all the while.

The boy replied, "Yes, sir!"

"Good." The drill instructor laughed. Suddenly, his face changed from humored to menacing just before he yelled, "Find my weakness and strike—be quick about it! And I mean now!"

Because the student observed that his drill instructor did not have armor protection in his swaying legs, he tried to kick at the kneecaps.

Not surprising, Humonus easily dodged, yelling, "Quicker!"

Instead of kicking again, Baltor surprisingly changed tactics, for he leapt hard and low at his instructor's legs.

Humonus was initially able to dodge the leap, but was not able to evade Baltor's grasping hands around both of his kneecaps. As his knees buckled underneath him, he found himself crashing hard into the ground, with his student right on top.

When the boy realized that his tactic had worked—that he had actually bested his drill instructor—he beamed a big smile and exhaled happily, "Yes, sir!"

Still lying on the ground, Humonus said with enthusiasm, "Good job! Now get the hell off me!" His second statement had sounded very angry.

Only a second later, Baltor stood on his feet.

After the drill instructor had risen back to his feet, he nodded his head once before saying, "You have just demonstrated the third lesson: If one tactic doesn't work, switch to another."

"Thank you, sir!" the boy said with a huge smile upon his face.

"Don't get cocky there," the drill instructor countered. "You have a ton more to learn."

After erasing his smile, the boy replied, "Yes, sir!"

Humonus walked over to the weapons rack and pulled off a sword made of wood. As he casually tossed it from hand to hand, he barked, "Now come at me again!"

The boy didn't lunge into him this time but waited for the right moment to strike.

This time, unlike the first time, the drill instructor didn't wait—he slowly advanced upon his student, while twirling his sword ever so rapidly around the front of his body with his right hand.

Even though the boy hurriedly backed away from his drill instructor, he never turned his back either.

With a loud roar, Humonus swung his sword down in an angled attack that surely would have struck Baltor—had the boy not leapt to his right and crashed to the ground, a split second earlier.

Before the boy could get back onto his feet, however, he already saw the sword plunging toward him again.

Instinctively, he fell backward, the sword just missing him by mere inches. Before he could even think of moving, the tip of the sword was caressing his throat.

"Game over," Humonus declared with a tight smile. He then walked over to the weapons rack and placed the sword in its rightful place.

In the meantime, the boy stood again and waited for his next order.

After the drill instructor had taken off his helmet and set it comfortably into the nook of his right elbow, he began to wipe the beads of sweat that had accumulated on his forehead with his left hand. Once done, he revealed, "You need a lot of work with your form, which leads me to your fourth lesson: Unite your body as a whole, and make it fluidic like water. Do you understand what I mean?"

"Not exactly, sir," the boy confessed.

"Let me explain what I mean before I show you," the drill instructor said. He first held up his left hand with his thumb sticking out, and then he taught, "Most people make the mistake of dividing their body up into each individual piece. For example, here is my thumb, here is my pinky, here is my arm, here is my leg, here is my chest, here is my head, etc., etc. Yet only the best of the best of warriors know that the secret to fighting is by uniting their bodies and making it one single piece of machinery ready for anything. Do you understand me so far?"

"Yes, sir, I think I do," Baltor said with a single nod of his head.

Humonus set the helmet onto the ground, before he continued to explain with the physical gestures, "Therefore, the best stance is to keep one foot forward, while your other foot remains at a ninety-degree angle from it at all times. Ensure your knees are slightly bent. And ensure you evenly distribute your body weight between your feet."

The drill instructor ordered, "Assume the stance."

The boy did as told but felt incredibly uncomfortable.

The drill instructor confirmed, "At first, you will feel awkward, as well will you be very clumsy during any and all of your movements because you are still divided, but the more you practice and make your body one piece of machinery, the easier and more comfortable it gets."

He added, "Now watch the complex movements I can make based off this simple, ninety-degree stance."

In one swift movement, Humonus leapt forward, simultaneously extending his hands out in front. Upon making impact with the ground, he tucked his body into a roll; and once out of the roll, he was standing back in the ninety-degree position.

As soon as he had extended his hands out to his right, the drill instructor leapt, again tucking his body into a roll. A second later, his feet were, once again, in the ninety-degree position.

He added, "When you get good, you can even roll backward. Watch closely."

Humonus demonstrated his words—he first fell straight back, slapped his hands hard into the ground, tilted his head to the side, rolled his body backward, and was immediately back on his feet in the ninety-degree position. He ordered, "Now you try rolling forward."

Baltor tried, but his shoulder crashed into the ground, which sent shooting spasms of pain all across that area.

"Try again," the drill instructor stated evenly.

The boy stood up and retried his failed feat. This time he was able to accomplish the roll, though it felt uncomfortable and extremely awkward.

"Ninety degrees," Humonus said. "Try again."

Baltor tried several times over, each time getting a bit better.

Finally, the time came when the drill instructor stated with a nod, "Not too bad. Now try rolling to the right."

The boy leapt to the right, and even though he was able to get back up on his feet, his foot positioning was wrong.

"Ninety degrees," Humonus clipped. "Try again."

Again, the boy's feet ended up in the wrong position.

The drill instructor shook his head and said, "Work on it, later. Now, I want you to roll backward."

Baltor attempted the feat but failed miserably. His back slammed into the ground before his arms could stop the fall. This was the fourth time he saw shooting stars that day, and he couldn't even get his body to roll back over itself, much less move!

The drill instructor shook his head. "Slap your hands hard into the ground—it hurts a lot less than your back. Also, tilt your head to the side. Try again!"

After the boy had slowly stood back up, he retried but failed still again.

"Work on that too," the drill instructor said, "but later, and in your own free time—I have more things to teach you right now."

"Yes, sir," Baltor replied, now completely sore yet again.

After Humonus had resumed the stance himself, he ordered, "Assume the stance."

The boy immediately did as told.

While extending his hands and arms out into ninety-degrees, the drill instructor taught, "Within this ninety-degree span is the strongest area for both your offense and your defense. But really, with the simple pivoting of your feet, you can already have another ninety degrees covered."

Once he had demonstrated, he then ordered, "Now you try."

The boy was actually able to repeat the act without trouble—his feet were the only body parts that didn't hurt.

"Good, good," the drill instructor congratulated with a small smile. His smile faded as he continued teaching in a very serious tone, "Now each and every attack or defense, whether a punch, kick, block, or roll that you perform—all movements must be contained within the perimeters of your stance.

"If any part of you should fall outside of those perimeters, your balance will be off, and your opponent will easily finish you off! Any questions?"

"Yes, sir, I have one."

"Yes?"

"How do I protect all the other ninety degrees?"

"Good question," Humonus answered. "There are two other ways to do this. One is through a defensive roll, which we have just gone over—the other is through an offensive strike. Let me show you both ways through a variety of techniques."

He then launched into a one-minute set that consisted of punches, kicks and rolls that utterly startled the student. His drill instructor had every area covered: His speed was breathtaking: His movements were precise: His power was evident!

Upon completion of his demonstration, he stopped, resumed a normal stance and faced his student. He hadn't even broken a sweat, nor was he out of breath, nor did he speak.

"Oh, my God," Baltor could only say about twenty seconds later.

The drill instructor sighed, "I am not God. I am a man. In time, should you make it through phase two, you will be able to accomplish all of this and much, much more. Any other questions?"

"One, sir," the boy asked, "how did you learn all of this?"

"To briefly answer your question—centuries ago, there was a traveler from a very faraway land who came to us and taught us these fighting skills. Only higher-grade thieves may learn the full history," Humonus answered. "For now, concern yourself with some lunch."

"Yes, sir!" Baltor snapped, just before he painfully and wearily made his way over to the lunch table, looking at the ground most of the time.

Upon nearing the lunch table, he observed that the new girl was over there, heartily munching away by herself. He reasoned that it was probably due to the fatigue and the suffering that he couldn't remember her name for the life of him.

After stopping in front of the table, he silently poured himself a glass of water, picked off a piece of bread, and began to chew. From his peripheral vision, he could see that the girl was now throwing sidelong glances over at him as well.

Once she had wiped her mouth with the dirty sleeve of her shirt, she said a bit shyly, "Hi."

Without having turned his head to look, and with his mouth still full of food, he simply replied, "Hello." He next picked up his mug and took a drink to wash down the remaining bread.

"What's your name?" she asked, turning to face him.

"I'm Baltor," he replied just before he took another swallow of water. He grabbed a banana, and as he turned toward her, he began to peel it open. He observed that despite her dirty face and snarled hair, she appeared to be cute, for a little girl, that is.

41

Just before he took a bite of the banana, he asked, "You?"

"My name's Vakshia." Right away, she asked with curiosity, "How long have you been here?"

"I don't really know to be honest with you. Months, I suppose," he said just before he began to chuckle. A couple of seconds later, he stopped laughing and asked, "You just got here today, right?"

"Yeah," Vakshia replied. "Is this place tough?"

He laughed for like six whole seconds. After taking another bite of his banana, he muttered, "That's an understatement."

"Really?" she asked with a nervous tension to her voice.

He swallowed his banana first before he answered. "Yes, it is—I can't lie to you. But you seem like a pretty tough girl, Vakshia!"

There was still tension in her voice as she sighed, "I don't know. The things that my drill instructor is telling me to do are impossible. He never seems to be happy even though I'm trying my hardest!"

"Well, what helped me to get through all of this were the encouraging words from a friend of mine. Now how did she put it?"

Baltor paused to recall—he first scrunched his eyes nearly shut, and when the recollection came a few moments later, he opened his eyes while reciting, "'As for you not doing so well—nobody does well in the beginning. Remember this. Soon enough, any and all challenges will eventually be overcome. And also remember this… success is a road that you must pave.'"

She silently pondered the words. The boy wolfed down the final bite of his banana.

Finally, she said, "I will have—"

From the first obstacle course, Jeramone interrupted their conservation, screaming, "Vakshia, to me!"

Baltor watched as she ran over.

Most unexpectedly, Humonus had somehow gotten behind his student, just before whispering in his left ear, "Baltor."

Startled and frightened, the boy jumped nearly a foot into the air. With his heart still racing, he turned around while holding a hand over his heart, and asked, "Yes, sir?"

Speaking at a normal tone, the drill instructor briefed, "For the rest of the day, I shall let you practice today's lessons on your own. Practice as long as you want, but remember this… the more you do, the better you'll get. Do make sure you eat dinner and get some sleep too."

The boy snapped, "Yes, sir!"

"Dismissed."

Once the drill instructor had departed the area via one of the unlit tunnels, the student decided to practice his rolls. Despite the pounding that he added to his already sore muscles, he did continue to practice for nearly an hour or so—until an interesting idea sprang to mind.

He thought aloud, "Maybe I could just integrate the training and combine it all with the obstacle courses?"

The boy jogged over to the first obstacle course, noting that Vakshia was standing next to the knotted rope and listening to her instructor screaming reprimands, insults and curses. Upon drawing closer, he observed that tears had been steadily pouring down from her eyes!

In between one of her drill instructor's yells, Baltor asked, "Sir—do you mind if I jump in and use this obstacle course?"

Jeramone glanced over and muttered, "I don't care. Say, why don't you do just that and show this freaking weakling how it's done?"

Baltor leapt onto the rope, and only about fifty seconds later, he had already climbed his way to the top and back down. Without looking back, he booked for the next obstacle, while overhearing her instructor yell, "You see? It is possible! Now you do it just like that! Get the hell up there!"

Long after the rest of the students had departed, Baltor continued his hardcore training.

When literal exhaustion was just about to take the boy over, he decided to call it a night, and so he headed for the bunkhouse. Upon entering, he observed that Vakshia and all the other students were zonked out. After eating dinner, he went to bed himself.

The following morning, Humonus woke his student just like the day before—without yelling. While the boy ate a quick breakfast, he observed and noted that he was the only student in the bunkhouse this morning and figured that everyone must already be training.

As the two silently made their way to the training area, the student wondered if he had now acquired his teacher's respect.

Upon reaching the weapons rack, Humonus began, "Today, we shall review yesterday's lessons and see how far, or how little, you've progressed. Assume the stance."

The boy instantly did.

The drill instructor, however, noticed some imperfections, for he kicked his student's rear foot lightly until it was right and then he stated, "I said ninety degrees. Now roll forward."

Baltor leapt forward, extended his hands, tucked his body in, did the roll, and was back up on his feet.

Humonus yelled, "I said, ninety degrees!"

The boy looked down at his feet, and as he saw that they weren't so, he shifted his feet until it was.

"Roll left," the drill instructor next ordered without emotion.

Baltor made his roll, but his feet must not have been right—Humonus ran up and screamed at the top of his lungs, "Ninety degrees! How many times must I tell you this?"

"I'm sorry, sir, but I'm really sore," the student explained in truth. "My body's not working like it should."

The drill instructor balefully shook his head, sucked in a deep breath, and then relaxed.

"Fine then," he ordered, "sit down on the ground."

The boy sat.

"Extend your legs straight out, stretch your arms out, and without bending your knees, reach for your toes with your hands," the drill instructor ordered.

Baltor found that his flexibility wasn't that good, and that he couldn't reach his toes without bending his knees.

Humonus sighed in frustration, before he replied, "Well, then. I see we've found another weak spot—flexibility. From now on, we will begin to work on that area through stretching exercises before you begin your morning training sessions with me. For now, follow me."

"Yes, sir," Baltor said as he painfully stood up, and followed. The drill instructor led the way as they entered one of the unlit tunnels on the right side of the cavern.

Not only was this twisty tunnel one that Baltor had never entered before, eleven more dark and unique tunnels did they pass, along with six deadly pitfalls. The longest tunnel was maybe a half-mile, while the shortest was forty feet. In the tenth tunnel, they had to crawl on their bellies to squeeze through.

Finally, after what seemed an eternity to Baltor, sunlight streamed down from what appeared to be a sewage grill in the middle of this particular tunnel. There was a twenty-foot ladder leaning against the wall, right under the grill itself.

The drill instructor climbed up the ladder, opened the grill, looked around quickly, and after a gesture with his hand to follow, he disappeared.

The boy followed. Upon reaching the top of the ladder, he discovered that his eyes weren't used to the sun whatsoever. He narrowed his eyes until they were tiny slits. Barely was he was able to make out that he was in someone's backyard, as there was a blurry mansion that was far too shiny for him to focus on. Looking the other way, there was a mostly red, yet blurry garden.

"Well, come on and be quick about it," Humonus ordered.

The boy climbed his way out before the drill instructor shut the grill.

"Follow me," Humonus said—he led his student to a nondescript fountain and ordered, "Hop in and wash yourself down real quick, yet real thoroughly from head to toe. No dirt or mud on you."

By the time Baltor had finished washing his body down, a full minute later, he found that his eyes had gotten semi-used to the sunlight—only five seconds later, the drill instructor ordered, "Follow me."

"Yes sir."

He next led his student down to a large, round and cemented stone underground pool, whose waters were both bubbling and steaming even in the hot air. "Take off your clothes first, other than your underwear, and then sit down in the pool."

After the boy had taken off all but his underwear, he slowly stepped his first foot into the pool, immediately becoming very surprised by the intense heat of the boiling water. Upon sitting down in the neck deep waters, slowly but surely, he found his very tense muscles begin to relax and his eyes wanting to close.

In fact, nearly ten seconds later, Baltor realized that the pool felt really, really good! After opening his eyes, he looked over and surprisingly saw that Humonus was already sitting next to him in the spa—his boots, socks, pants and shirt were neatly folded on the ground behind him.

"Sir, how is it that the water is so hot?"

"*Ahhhhh...* They call it a spa," Humonus answered. "An underground furnace heats it. As for the bubbles, they come from compressed and heated air that continuously circulates through tubes into the bottom of the pool. I only discovered this place last week but have been here four times so far. Wonderful!"

As the boy's eyes had readjusted to the sunlight, he spent this time taking "a good look" around. They were in the middle of a beautiful rose garden, concealed from the outside world by a fifty-foot-tall cemented wall that surrounded the entire perimeter. Including the three-story mansion that looked just like a greenhouse, except for the fact that all of these window panels were darkly tinted, reflecting back dozens of brilliant, bronze suns!

By the time he had completed his look around, he felt so completely relaxed that he actually began to find himself getting a bit sleepy. After a short yawn, he asked, "Where are we, sir?"

After glancing around to ensure that the coast was still clear, Humonus answered, "Let's just say that we're someplace we shouldn't be. If the owner and his large entourage of guards should happen to come back home and discover us here, they'll probably kill us!"

Confused, Baltor asked, "Why did you take the risk?"

"I see some serious potential in you, Baltor. You have raw talent that most thieves never acquire. It has only taken you months what others have taken years. I considered the risk well worth it."

"Thank you, sir!"

"Don't get used to this nice treatment," the drill instructor countered neutrally. "You have much more to learn—I have much more to teach. Let's go."

He got out of the pool and began dressing, to which his student followed suit.

Once dressed, Baltor felt incredibly refreshed and great—by the time they had made it back to the training area an hour later, he felt more than ready to take on anything that his drill instructor had to teach.

Not surprising, Humonus was back to his old self as he began, "I shall now teach you those ten stretching exercises I was talking about earlier. Of course I want you to perform them alongside me. Later down the road I'll teach you advanced stretching exercises that'll really help you in your fighting skills."

The student replied, "Yes, sir!"

One after the other, the drill instructor began to teach and demonstrate the ten exercises.

The student, once he figured out how to do the exercises, performed them. Only twice was correction needed.

Fifteen minutes later, once everything was thoroughly stretched, the drill instructor made his student repeatedly demonstrate his somersaulting abilities for the next several hours until lunchtime. For the most part, he performed them perfectly.

Only seconds after Baltor had begun to eat lunch, Humonus said, "I'm releasing you for the day. See you tomorrow morning."

"Yes sir."

Humonus exited the area, via one of the dark tunnels.

Once Baltor had finished eating, he spent the entire afternoon and well into the night training hardcore on his own, though the last of the students and drill instructors had departed the training grounds two hours earlier.

After eating dinner in the training area—three loaves of bread, two oranges and some water—he headed back to the bunkhouse, noting that all of the students were already sleeping.

Right away, he hopped into bed, sleeping like never before—blissfully away!

Upon awakening early the next morning, he discovered that the other students were *still* sleeping—he simultaneously discovered that he was feeling in *tip-top shape.*

He got up and silently ate his breakfast in the bunkhouse, only then deciding to meet his drill instructor at their training area. Not a student had woken up by the time he had left the bunkhouse.

Upon arrival at the training area, five minutes later, still another idea sprang into Baltor's mind, and so he began his stretching exercises all on his own, so that by the time his drill instructor did arrive, they could immediately begin to train.

About twenty minutes later, only seconds before Humonus was about to enter the tunnel that led to the bunkhouse, he heard his student ask from their training area, "Sir?"

Looking over and seeing his student rising to his feet, the drill instructor's mouth dropped open a bit in astonishment, though that look lasted for only a single moment in time.

"Are you ready to perform your stretching exercises, Baltor?"

The boy replied with pride, "I already did them, sir!"

"Really," the drill instructor said with an impressed tone. As he began to approach Baltor and the weapons rack, he said, "Impressive. Roll left."

The student easily somersaulted to the left—in the end his feet were at a perfect ninety-degree angle.

"Roll forward."

Again, Baltor easily did as told.

"Roll backward. Roll right. Roll left. Roll forward. Roll back. Roll forward twice in a row. Quite impressive."

"Thank you, sir!"

"You are ready to begin lesson five: The attack," the drill instructor stated with an even voice.

The student replied with a whole lot of enthusiasm, "Yes, sir!"

"I shall now teach you the various styles of punches that utilize the entirety of your body," Humonus said. "Once I feel that you are ready to go to the next step, we shall go onto kicks."

"Yes, sir!"

For the remainder of the training session, the drill instructor revealed the four different types of punches to his student, each punch that began and ended in the same basic feet stance—ninety-degree angles.

Those four punches that he taught—in turn—were a straight-forward, a twister, a roundhouse and an uppercut. Before proceeding from one type of punch to the next—not only did he demonstrate, yet he made his student repeat many, many, many times over.

It was while this practicing was going on that Humonus refused to show any more of his feelings—in truth, he was very much in awe, because the kid got it right after only a few tries.

The drill instructor next began to teach the basic blocks to hits and kicks, which blocks did not mean just using a hand yet the entire body, all the while reestablishing the feet back into the ninety-degree basic stance at the end of the blocking technique.

Once the boy appeared to have this all down, around one in the afternoon, the drill instructor dismissed his student for the rest of the day.

Trained hardcore, Baltor did. He first went through the second obstacle course, while occasionally stopping here and there to practice a roll, throw one of his new punches, or block.

Just as before, long after the other students had left the training area, he continued training well into the night.

The next morning, Humonus found Baltor once again at the weapons rack.

Without saying so much as a "good morning," he instead ordered, "Roll right. Block up. Roll backwards twice. Throw a roundhouse. Block right. Roll forward three times in a row. Throw an uppercut. No, no, you need to use your whole body, like this. Try again! Good! Now throw a twister. No—like this! Try it again. Much better! Roll left. Throw two straight punches in a row using both hands. Block down. Throw two twister punches back to back. Block right. Roll right. Throw two roundhouses back to back. Excellent! You are now ready to learn the kicks."

"Thank you, sir!"

The drill instructor taught, "In the same way as the punches, your kicks must be used by the whole body. If they are not, then they become pointless. As there are four basic punches, so are there four basic kicks."

One after the other, he taught those four kicks: a straight-up, a roundhouse, a ground sweep and a flying kick.

The kicks, however, proved to be a lot more difficult for Baltor to learn and master than the punches. Humonus had him repeatedly demonstrate the kicks for the entire day.

The following morning, he attempted to test his student in these areas—however, as he quickly discovered, his student hadn't yet achieved the needed leg flexibility.

"Hmmm," Humonus said while shaking his head for a moment. "It appears that you are ready to learn some extending leg stretching exercises. Let's start with the splits."

The boy tried, but could only get himself halfway down ... and that was it.

Therefore, the drill instructor assisted, pushing his student down another quarter of the way down, until Baltor yelped out in pain. For the remainder of this day, he assisted his student with performing twelve additional "painful" leg-stretching exercises.

That evening around dinnertime, instead of dismissing his student, the drill instructor again snuck the two of them to the spa. Fortune smiled yet again, as there was no one around.

After a week of intense leg stretching exercises every morning, and another two "secret" trips to the spa, at night and all by himself, Baltor could finally and comfortably sit in both the side and front splits.

To increase that flexibility even more, the drill instructor often assisted by picking up one of Baltor's legs and stretching it as far as it could go.

During the afternoons of this same week, the drill instructor either tested his student on his punches, blocks and rolls, or simply dismissed his student, allowing him to practice and train on his own.

Once the next week had begun, the drill instructor reacquainted his student with the four forms of kicking. This time, Baltor was able to do all of the kicks with total ease. Once accomplished to the drill instructor's level of satisfaction, he tested his student in the rolls, the punches, the blocks, and the kicks—always in variation.

Once Baltor had passed this final test with satisfactory results, only two days later, Humonus's only congratulatory reply was, "Tomorrow, we begin with weapons. Dismissed."

As the boy lay in bed on the verge of falling asleep, after training and dinner of course, it suddenly dawned on him that he hadn't seen Vakshia for some time. In the very next moment, he happened to look over at the lunch table and saw that there was only one other student currently awake and eating, Thesmul.

Thesmul was not only three years older than Baltor, which made him much bigger and stronger, yet this freckle-ridden, dark-redheaded teenager was the ringleader of the social clique; and the meanest bully.

Still, Baltor's curiosity was greater than his fears as he asked, "Hey, Thesmul. Have you seen Vakshia lately?"

Not only did Thesmul not answer the question, yet he began to laugh cockily as he left the bunkhouse.

Baltor wondered silently to himself, only moments before he drifted off to sleep, *I wonder if something happened to her? I'm going to have to find out tomorrow.*

The following morning, just after he had completed his stretching exercises, his drill instructor arrived. Without as much as a "good morning," he first pulled two wooden daggers from the weapons rack.

He instructed, "Every weapon must be nothing more than an extension of your own body, and every attack or defense begins and ends within the confines of your basic stance, regardless of the size of the weapon or weapons you may be carrying. For the purposes of learning, we shall start off with the smallest and lightest of weapons, and gradually work up to the longest and larg—"

Baltor interrupted, "Sir, before you continue on, I have a question that I'd like to ask, please."

"What would... you like... to know?" the drill instructor breathed out slowly, while clearly sounding irritated at this interruption.

"There... there was this other student and her name is Vakshia, sir," Baltor said, "I haven't seen her for some time. Do you know what happened to her?"

With a nonchalant shrug to his shoulders, Humonus replied, "Nobody knows what happened to her. She abruptly disappeared a few days ago and hasn't been seen since."

"Do you think she escaped?"

"That," Humonus answered, "is extremely doubtful. Never before, since the Guild's origins nearly five centuries ago, have any of our beginning students discovered the secret location of the underground latch that opens the tile in the fountain room. Yes, it is true that advanced students are granted this 'classified information,' as they are free to come and go as they please. In fact, they have their very own bunkhouse that I'm ninety-nine percent sure you're not aware of, which is about a mile away down that pitch-black tunnel

I'm pointing at. It's filled not only with natural pitfalls that can cripple or kill, but booby-trapped for extra security reasons."

After looking at the tunnel that Humonus was pointing out for only a second, Baltor looked back and shook his head. He didn't know there was another bunkhouse.

The drill instructor added only a moment later, "And, yes, it is also true that no advanced student has ever stupidly revealed the location to a beginning student. And not just because of the oath that they swore to upon first joining the Guild.

"Baltor, I have two questions for you. Even though it has been a little over seven months since you took the 'Oath of the Guild,' do you perchance still remember it, and if so, would you please recite it for me?"

After scrunching his eyes in contemplation, and getting the answer, the boy cleared his throat before he answered, "Yes sir, I do remember it, and, yes sir, I will recite it."

He recited: "'I, Baltor, do solemnly swear, never to reveal the secret location of this thieves' guild, nor to reveal any of the secrets of this thieves' guild that are about to be taught to me. Nor will I ever reveal any of the secret members of this thieves' guild under any circumstances—ever! And if I even begin to think of betraying this solemn oath, I swear that I will first acquire a dagger, cut my own eyes out, then my tongue, then each of my fingers and thumbs, and finally, plunge that dagger into my heart with my feet.'"

"Excellent, Baltor," the drill instructor commended not just with enthusiasm, yet also a few enthusiastic handclaps.

"Thank you, sir!" the boy said with a very proud smile. For some strange reason, he had never forgotten that oath since he had taken it, seven months ago. To him, it felt more like seven years!

Only a few seconds later, Humonus continued, "Now I shall commence with the second reason that Vakshia couldn't have escaped that route. If you recall, it involves the lethally trained guards that protect all the sets of double doors leading to the outside world. Even if she had received the secret info from an advanced student and tried to escape through the fountain room, the guards would have instantly killed her. They would have then reported the incident to their commanding officer, of who would have reported it to the High Council. After all, the guards know exactly who is allowed, and not allowed, to pass."

After pointing his left index finger up in the air, he revealed, "The only other way Vakshia could have escaped was through a vast underground maze of very deadly tunnels that easily triples the entire city above us. Furthermore, the Guild sealed off most of those tunnels intentionally, in order to make escape nearly impossible. No beginning student has ever successfully escaped 'the labyrinth' since the Guild was first established."

"For all these reasons," Humonus concluded sympathetically, "it is presumed that she died in a training accident, Baltor."

Baltor's eyes slightly bulged, and his mouth dropped open in a bit in disbelief. Finally, he muttered, "No."

"I'm sorry, Baltor," Humonus said. "Instructor Jeramone was even called forth yesterday before the High Council to report what he believed had happened to Vakshia. Last night at the bar, after we had drunk a few rounds, he told me all about it."

After taking a quick look around to make sure no one else was nearby, he continued, "With sadness in his eyes, he told me that she had just begun to train through the obstacle courses at night without his assistance, even though he secretly oversaw her just about every night in order to make sure she didn't get killed. With tears literally flowing out of the man's eyes, he informed me that the very night Vakshia disappeared he had been busy catching up on his own personal errands. Because she is now 'missing in action,' he feels so guilty and horrible. I believe that Jeramone was telling the truth, as I have worked alongside the man for many years—he genuinely cares about his students! Trust me that Instructor Jeramone has sought her out to the best of his ability, but no luck. Sorry, Baltor, these things happen."

Baltor found tears welling up in the corners of his eyes, while his face betrayed grief and disappointment.

Curious, Humonus's left eyebrow raised while his right lowered, just before he asked, "Did you know Vakshia personally?"

Sniffing back the mucous that had begun to accumulate in his nostrils while simultaneously fighting back the tears that wanted to pour from his eyes, the boy answered, "I only talked to her once."

Another look of curiosity crossed the drill instructor's face before he asked, "So why the tears?"

After a pause to formulate the right words, the boy finally answered, "I don't know, sir. Maybe because I believed, I wanted to believe that she could succeed."

The second he had finished broadcasting his answer, his peripheral vision picked up Thesmul, who was about sixty feet away from their current position. He was casually making his way over to the lunch table, which was forty feet behind Humonus— never did Baltor's head or eyes turn, but neither did Thesmul's.

Humonus replied thoughtfully, "Hmmm...."

Baltor suddenly became quite angry as he recalled the cocky laugh that this worm had given to him last night, though he kept his voice tightly under control as he asked, "Sir?"

"Yes?"

Only because he was sure that Thesmul was now out of listening range, he threw a cock of his head up and to the left, and then asked just above a whisper, "What do you know of him?"

Humonus asked just as quietly, "Who?"

Baltor threw another cock of his head over, yet only answered, "Him."

Though the drill instructor made it appear as if he was yawning and stretching, what he was really doing was covertly looking over in the direction that his student's head indicated.

After completing his stretches about ten seconds later, he stopped, turned back to face his student, and asked with a bit of surprise, "Thesmul?"

"Yes, sir," Baltor muttered, while unconsciously averting his eyes; he saw that Thesmul had already reached the lunch table, picked up a loaf of bread, and was about to take a bite into it.

Though the drill instructor didn't understand the curiosity that his student had for this other student, he quickly drew Baltor's mind back to reality by snapping his fingers once next to his ear, and saying, "Baltor."

A bit startled, the boy turned his head and eyes to look at his drill instructor, and then he asked in a loud tone of voice, "Yes, sir?"

As soon as Humonus saw that he and his student were looking each other eye to eye, he said in a caring tone of voice, "I know what it's like to lose someone that you care about—believe me. I also know that I may sound like a hard-ass, but that is because it is my job to toughen you up. I have lost a couple students in the past that I believed to have potential, but really, they had already given up long before they ever met me."

For the next ten seconds, the drill instructor silently observed not only the sadness, fear, and grief reflected in his student's eyes, yet the squinting eyebrows and eyes that indicated his student was contemplating his words.

Taking advantage of the silence that had lasted eleven seconds, Humonus continued, "Baltor, I have two questions for you to ponder, which is really one question, but answer neither of them now..."

After taking a deep breath in through his mouth, he asked, "Are you going to focus upon the people that are lost, and shall always remain that way no matter what you do or say...?

"Or are you going to focus upon the people that have hope and are looking for a new and better way no matter what?"

Baltor looked toward the ground in dismay, as he asked, "Sir, how am I supposed to know who has hope and who doesn't?"

"Your heart will tell you that," Humonus answered. With his index finger and thumb, he gently lifted the boy's chin until they were looking eye to eye yet again and added, "and also your mind."

"But, sir, you've already told me twice that I knew where I could go should I give up! How can you call that caring?" Baltor dared to ask.

Humonus stepped back a couple steps, extended his hands and arms out in front of him, and answered very, very seriously, "I've known all along that you wouldn't jump into the pit and kill yourself!"

"But what do your feelings tell you about Vakshia?" the boy asked with quite a bit of frustration. Without waiting for an answer, he added, "My heart told me that Vakshia would surely make it as a master thief, and now she's probably dead!"

"Ah," the drill instructor said with an affirming nod to his head, "that is why there must be the defenders, so long as there are the oppressors."

Lowering his voice until it was just a whisper, the boy asked, "So, do you think she was murdered?"

Upon hearing that unexpected question, Humonus sucked in a deep breath while simultaneously raising both eyebrows. Instead of answering the question on that particular breath, however, he exhaled, and t h e n breathed in deeply yet again.

He finally whispered, "It appears that you have a mystery that must be solved, but not now. In my professional opinion, you are not even close to being ready to begin this quest."

Baltor whispered, a bit louder and with angry tones, "Sir, the longer we wait, the harder it will be to find out the truth. Then if she was murdered, we will never find the killer—"

With a wag of his finger, Humonus interrupted in a commanding but not a loud tone of voice, "Silence—do not say another word until I give you permission, my student. That is an order."

Baltor turned silent, though he was clearly upset.

The drill instructor said evenly, "This may be your personal quest, but it is not mine. My quest, my mission, my job, which is how I get paid to live, is to train you—not to try and look for evidence to determine if another student's disappearance was murder, or most likely, suicide."

After giving the boy a lengthy pause to let the important info sink in, he continued, "After all, most of the underground pits around the obstacle courses, and throughout all the tunnels, are truly bottomless, and how easy it is to have an accidental suicide? On the other hand, maybe it was an intentional suicide. Who knows?

"No matter what, I cannot permit this, because the High Council has already concluded that there is *not* to be an investigation in the matter. And the High Council has the *final* say-so in all things related to the Guild."

He first put his right hand on Baltor's right shoulder, before he said softly, "Just so you know that I'm sympathetic to your cause, after you've completed your training with me, then go ahead and complete your quest, but I order you not to do it now—you're simply not ready."

The boy remained silent, even though he obviously had wished to speak the whole time.

The drill instructor began squeezing his student's shoulder for emphasis as he added, "I know that I've said a lot already, but I have one more thing to point out before we get back to training—okay? Nod your head in the affirmative if you've understood all I've said so far."

The boy nodded his head.

Humonus took his left hand off Baltor's shoulder but then extended that index finger in front of him while the remaining fingers clenched into a fist.

A moment later he added, "Good—let's hypothesize that you decide to disobey my order, become successful in finding Vakshia in the nearby future, discover that she was indeed murdered, track down the murderer, and try to face him, or her or them, on your own. Most likely, all I've taught you will go to waste, as you'll become the next missing victim. So do not disobey me, understand? Now you can speak."

The boy's eyes disappointingly looked to the ground, but he dutifully responded, "Yes, sir."

Using that extended index finger, Humonus again lifted up Baltor's chin until they were eye to eye for the third time, and then he gently concluded, "Listen—all things will reveal themselves, if Destiny, Fate and God decree it."

"Yes, sir," the boy said, while holding the gaze firmly with his drill instructor.

A couple seconds later, Humonus let go of Baltor's chin, just before taking two steps back, and then crossing his arms.

Upon observing that the student still looked calm and serene, nearly ten seconds later, the drill instructor ordered, "Go ahead and take your lunch break. Meet me back here in a half an hour." Without pause, he started walking with a very quick stride toward the tunnel that led into the fountain room.

Meanwhile, Baltor looked back over to the lunch table, noticing that Thesmul was nowhere around there, nor was he anywhere else in the cavern at all, as he soon became aware of.

He casually made his way over to the lunch table. Once there, he wolfed down a large lunch that consisted of four loaves of wheat bread and two delicious red oranges, and then proceeded to wash it down with a whole mug of water.

By the time that he had finished eating, fifteen minutes later, he took a seat against the wall in the training area and waited and relaxed. Fifteen minutes later, he observed Humonus come back from whence he left, and so Baltor stood to his feet.

Upon arrival, the drill instructor began, "Baltor, as I was trying to instruct right before lunch, every weapon must be nothing more than an extension of your own body, and every attack or defense begins and ends within the confines of your basic stance, regardless of the size of the weapon or weapons you may happen to be carrying."

He pulled the daggers out of his belt. As he held a dagger in each hand with the blade extended out, he said, "From the four stylized punches that I taught you earlier, you can incorporate weapons into your movements just as easily."

He then demonstrated all four of the punches while holding the daggers. Upon completion, he asked, "Do you see what I mean?"

Baltor's eyes squinted in contemplation for a moment, before his mouth answered, "Yes, sir."

The drill instructor swiftly flipped the daggers around until the handles were facing his pupil, and then he said, "Good—now you try them."

The boy, after taking the daggers, attempted the four different punches with a dagger in each hand.

"Not bad," Humonus informed with a single nod to his head, "but you will need to practice this much more often, especially if you are to become fluidic like water."

"Yes, sir!"

"Now to the defensive rolls while in possession of weapons—hand me back the daggers," the drill instructor ordered.

After Baltor had clumsily twisted the daggers around until the handles faced out, Humonus took them.

The drill instructor next taught, "A strong defense is just as important as a strong offense. You must be extremely careful while practicing your rolls not to let the weapon or weapons touch the ground, or you will lose one or both weapons, and possibly even seriously injure yourself in the process...

"Simply watch my movements and you will see what I mean about how to do things right."

He leapt forward and after ensuring that the daggers were parallel with the ground so that they did not contact, he rolled back onto his feet and assumed the ready stance. The daggers were still in his hand.

He next leapt to the right while extending his arms that way, paralleled the daggers with the ground and rolled back onto his feet. Just like before, the daggers were in his hands and he was in the ready position.

He fell backward while extending his arms out, but before his hands slapped the ground, he had already paralleled the daggers with the ground so they did not contact, and then he rolled himself back over onto his feet—in the ready position.

Baltor look on in amazement.

Humonus swiftly flipped the daggers around in his hands, and then handed Baltor the handles. He ordered, "Now you try."

"Roll forward."

Baltor leapt forward and extended his hands out. He tried to keep the daggers from contacting the ground, but failed. Though he rolled back onto his feet, he was now disarmed from both weapons.

"Try again."

"Yes, sir!"

Over the course of the next week during the mornings, the boy practiced these very movements under his drill instructor's tutelage, all the while holding onto weapons of all sorts. During the afternoons until late a night, he practiced on his own, all the while trying to unite these new movements with his other learned skills. And all the while, he slowly-but-surely got better and better.

Ever so secretly, in the wee morning hours when everyone else was asleep, Baltor had begun to investigate into the disappearance of Vakshia, whether dead or alive, despite the orders and warnings.

After sneaking into the supply room for the very first time, he had found a coiled one-hundred-foot rope in a large and very dusty sack, and just as useful, a large wood box containing two-dozen torches and some flint.

For no longer than two hours each time, he would check the chasms, pits, and deep gorges around the obstacle courses.

First, he would secure twenty feet of the rope to either a nearby rock or stalagmite, and slide down approximately eighty feet while safely holding the end of a lit torch in his teeth. Once he got to the end of the rope, he would drop the torch to see where, and if, it would land. For the most part, he found that the torch simply disappeared into the abyss, thus enshrouding him in utter darkness.

Luck still wasn't with him even after the first week of diligent searching, even though he had already covered the first three obstacle courses, with no success. During the second week of diligent searching and covering three more obstacles, he had found a grouping of human bones, but they looked like they had been there for decades, maybe even centuries. By the end of the second week, he slowly began to give up hope.

After all, there was only one more obstacle course—eight possible spots—that Vakshia could have fallen. Grimly, Baltor reasoned that she probably had not advanced to this stage in the short amount of time that she had been here. He thus decided to explore only one per night, so he wouldn't be as tired during the day.

During the morning times throughout the third week of Baltor's search, his drill instructor mostly watched and said very little as his student went through all the various combinations of the basic fighting styles while holding onto a wide variety of training weapons: offensive attacks, defensive blocks and rolls. After all, Baltor's movements were "flawless" just about every single time!

For this reason, he was always allowed to spend his afternoons, evenings and nights—training on his own. In addition, during those early morning hours, he continued to search the gorges and valleys in the sixth obstacle course for Vakshia, but only one per night as earlier decided.

Finally, on the first night of the fourth week of the boy's quest to find his one and only friend, there was one last deep valley that he knew about and could check. He had earlier promised himself that if he didn't find her here tonight, he would give up for now.

After securing nearly thirty feet of the rope around a solid tube of rock that spanned from floor to ceiling, he rappelled his way down the smooth slope of the valley. Just like every time before, once he reached the bottom of the rope, he then dropped the torch and watched it fall—this time, however, the torch slid down to the bottom of the valley approximately twenty feet, and what Baltor saw shocked him.

For lying on the ground near the torch's light, there was what appeared to be a body—crumpled and unmoving. Even though Baltor's eyes began to flood with tears of grief, something else inside of him raged as he strongly suspected that the body below was Vakshia!

As there was no way for him to drop the distance down to the ground, and then climb back up the smooth face of the valley to get back to the rope, he reluctantly climbed his way back up to the top.

He untied the rope, rolled it back up, looped it over his shoulder and eliminated all footprints as he made his way back to the supply room.

While lying in bed and trying to fall to sleep, he resolved to find out for sure the following night after training was over and everybody asleep. However, sleep did not come for a long while.

The following morning, about an hour after training had begun, Humonus only then began to tell that something was bothering his student by the slightly furled expression etched on the boy's forehead, the dark shadows under his eyes, and most importantly, he wasn't as eager-and-focused to learn as he normally was.

The drill instructor asked, "Baltor, are you okay?"

While unconsciously looking away to his right and down to the ground, the boy answered, "Yes, sir."

"Don't lie to me," the drill instructor countered, bearing a very suspicious look upon his face.

Baltor looked back up and over with an even expression and then confessed with a yawn, "Well, maybe I'm just a little tired, is all. I didn't sleep so good last night, sir."

Sounding convinced, the drill instructor said, "Oh—that hits us all every now and then, but what I'm going to need from you is for you to be fully awake and alert, especially before we recommence." With a shrug and a nod, he asked, "Would you like to take a fifteen-minute break, and perhaps get a drink of water?"

"Yes, sir," the boy answered. He then began to stretch, all the while taking his sweet time in getting to the lunch table.

Several minutes later, he arrived at the table and poured himself a full mug of water, drinking most of it down in one swoop. With the remaining bit of water still in the mug, he splashed it onto his hands and then onto his face.

He next grabbed an orange off the lunch table, peeled it, ate it, and then picked up and peeled a banana. While chewing on that, he turned around and saw that Humonus was nowhere in sight.

Just after Baltor had made his way back to the weapons rack, all the while looking around, he confirmed his drill instructor wasn't to be seen anywhere in the cavern. He sat down on the ground.

A minute later, he saw Humonus walking out of the supply room. Hobbling beside him, using a cane, was an old man who had a long, gray beard and wrinkly skin. His one-colored outfit consisted of a light-gray skullcap and flowing robes, along with a ton of colorful jewelry, ranging from jeweled rings to dozens of glittery necklaces. As the two men were speaking in hushed tones, the boy could not hear their words.

Due to Baltor's late-night excursions and his borrowing supplies from the supply room without asking, he instantly began to worry that they might have been talking about the missing torches.

He decided otherwise upon seeing the old man warmly pat Humonus on the shoulder, while saying with a slight shrill, "It was so good to see you again after all this time, my young friend..."

Humonus replied warmly, "And it was good to see you as well, Master Lupan... By the way, this is my new student, Baltor."

Lupan gave the up-down look at Baltor, and with quite a bit of enthusiasm, he shrilled, "You've got the best instructor out of the bunch... you know? After all, he got instructed by the best! You know by who, right? Me!"

With that, both he and Humonus began to chuckle with quite a bit of merriment: Not surprisingly, Lupan cackled like an old man.

Even though Baltor did not laugh, nor was he amused, there was instead a very impressed look on his face. After delivering a low bow, which is what caused them to stop chuckling, he looked directly into Lupan's eyes before saying, "Thank you for revealing that information, Master Lupan. It truly is an honor to meet the instructor of my instructor, sir!"

Lupan looked over to Humonus, and then he replied with a laugh, "*Ha!* This kid's going places."

Humonus responded at first nonchalantly, "Perhaps.... but he's still got a whole hell of a long way to go first, sir!" Amusement filled his voice as he made that second statement.

Both Lupan and Humonus began to laugh quite heartily from the inside joke. In the same moment, Baltor looked over at his drill instructor in surprise because this man rarely ever cracked a smile, but noticed that he was now looking at Lupan and still laughing.

Perhaps five seconds later, Lupan's gaze had just fallen back onto the boy, just before he stopped laughing and said, "Well, I must be off—errands to run. You gentlemen have a nice day." He then began to leave.

After bowing low, Humonus pivoted his whole body to face his student, and then he asked, "Are you fully awake now, Baltor?"

"Yes, sir!"

"Excellent," the drill instructor replied. "Now I want you to take those two long swords off the rack I'm pointing at, and then I want you to show me all rolls, blocks and strikes while holding on to them securely the whole time."

"Yes, sir!" After locating and picking up the steely swords, the boy demonstrated all that Humonus had requested, all the while holding onto the weapons securely. Baltor finally looked at his instructor, who was silently observing him.

A few moments later, the drill instructor said with a smile, "Well, Baltor, you just passed the last basic test to my level of satisfaction—congratulations! Put them swords away and come back."

"Thank you, sir... Done, sir."

That smile instantly erased as the drill instructor taught, "The time has come for me to begin to train you in the advanced stages of fighting; and from here on out things will get very complicated and technical. At first, just like with the basic stages, we will practice solely with hand-to-hand. Later, we will incorporate weapons into the mix! Are you not only ready and awake, yet enthusiastic?"

Sounding very enthusiastic, the boy snapped out, "Yes, sir!"

"Ok—the way to best your opponent is by causing him to become unbalanced from his attack, and then to use that very attack to your advantage. Throw a slow punch at me, and I'll show you what I mean."

As Baltor threw a slow punch with his right hand, Humonus slowly twisted his own body ninety degrees until he was on his own right side, and then he grabbed the wrist of Baltor's fully extended fist with both of his own hands.

The drill instructor ordered, "Stop."

Baltor did.

"Observe as I ever-so-lightly yank your body the direction you were throwing your punch until the moment your feet become unbalanced. Watch as I twist your wrist wide around in front of me. Now, because you threw a punch with your right fist, I shall twist to my right. In seconds, you will find your body forced to the ground and you will be completely defenseless. Ready?"

"Yes, sir."

A second later, the student found his body slowly forced to the ground; and a second after that, his face burrowed harder and harder into the hard cavern floor, which quickly became an uncomfortable experience for Baltor.

Not only did the drill instructor still have a firm grip on Baltor's majorly twisted-up wrist, yet he still stood on his feet right over his student, though the student was not aware of this trivial fact.

Baltor heard Humonus say, "For the purposes of learning and understanding, you will feel only a tiny sliver of the pain that's involved as I twist your wrist only a fraction of an inch more... Imagine how much worse it would hurt if I twisted but a fraction farther?"

Without waiting for an answer, the drill instructor twisted his student's wrist that fraction. Because of the agonizingly sharp pains that erupted throughout the boy's left arm and shoulder, he yelped aloud!

Though the drill instructor did not release his grip, he did loosen three fractions. The first fraction caused the agonizing pain to not be so agonizing. The second fraction still kept him immobile but in a painless state. The third fraction even allowed his student a bit of mobility, which allowed him to turn his head around until he was looking up at his drill instructor.

Once Humonus saw that his student was looking at him, he continued with his lesson, "As you can now see, with my other free hand, I can punch you in the head as many times as I want, or kick you in the gut just as many times. Or, as you just experienced, simply keep on twisting."

After the drill instructor released the hold, he added, "One more thing about this defensive technique—it is effective against both punches, and even hands bearing weapons. So long as you grab and yank the wrist before the moment of your opponent's strike!"

As Baltor stood back onto his feet, he replied while moving around his stiff arm, "Yes, sir!"

The drill instructor continued, "Now I'm going to throw a slow punch at you, and I want you to try the move on me." Slowly but surely, Humonus threw a punch with his left hand.

Baltor twisted his body the ninety degrees, until he was on Humonus's left side. Even though he had grabbed his drill instructor's extended wrist with both hands, as well twisted that wrist widely around in front of him with both hands, his drill instructor strangely did not end up on the ground.

Moreover, not only was Humonus able to break free of the grip, he then launched an upward kick that stopped an inch of hitting Baltor's gut. A second later, he set his foot back onto the ground.

"What am I doing wrong, sir?"

"The first thing you do," the drill instructor answered, "after you securely grab my wrist, is to lightly yank it, which will cause me to become unbalanced—after all, when your opponent is unbalanced, you can do anything."

After taking a deep breath through his nose, he then ordered, "Let's try that again." Right away, he slowly launched his punch, this time with his right hand.

Meanwhile, the student twisted his body ninety degrees to his instructor's right side, caught the wrist with both of his hands, and then lightly yanked upon his drill instructor's still-extending fist.

The student then twisted that wrist to the right with both of his hands, until his drill instructor's face had buried itself into the floor, and the student was standing on top and in control.

Lying on the ground face down, the drill instructor commanded, "Stop!"

Baltor did.

Humonus ordered, "When I tell you to go ahead, in just a few seconds, slowly twist just a bit more, but only a fraction. As soon as I tap the ground repeatedly with my free hand, then that means that you are to loosen your grip, but do not let go, okay?"

"Yes, sir!"

Baltor must have accidentally twisted a fraction or two too much, for Humonus howled out in pain while slapping his hand repeatedly into the ground very hard and snapping, "*Owww*, damn it—let go!"

The boy immediately let go. "Sorry, sir!"

Humonus stood back up to his feet, and as he began to rub his sore shoulder, he said with exasperation, "Damn that hurt—I said a fraction!"

"Sorry, sir—I swear I'll only go a fraction next time!"

"Ensure that you do, or I might commence to whooping on you the next time."

Baltor gulped.

Several moments later, the drill instructor stopped rubbing his no longer achy shoulder, and then he continued, "There's a similar technique to the one I just taught you, but this time, you will twist the wrist the other direction with both hands. This will minimally slam his back, possibly his head, hard onto the ground!"

They spent the next hour and a half very slowly going over this second technique.

Besides these two advanced techniques, Baltor learned one more that morning, which simply consisted of grabbing the opponent's thumb and then twisting it around like a joystick, which literally made the opponent's entire body roll the direction the joystick moved! Baltor was quite amused by this last technique.

Before lunch, the drill instructor promised that he had dozens of advanced techniques to teach; but instead of teaching his student any more after lunch, they spent the rest of the day practicing the first three techniques and always in slow motion.

At the end of the day, he commended his student with, "Good job today."

"Thank you, sir!"

"Tomorrow morning, I have several finger, hand and wrist stretches and exercises that I'm going to be teaching to you and from then on, you will be incorporating these movements into your morning routine, but only on an every-other-day basis.

"These exercises will not only help you to develop enough speed and power to effectively utilize any advanced technique against your quickest and most powerful of opponents, yet furthermore, they will drastically improve your own fighting skills with weapons...

"Why is the wrist just as important as the hand, you may be asking? Because the hand simply clutches the weapon—the wrist guides its direction and movement!"

"Yes, sir!"

Humonus said, "Oh—one last thing before I let you go for the day. Once you have finished learning most of the advanced techniques I know, I will then teach you the final and hardest step— learning how to re-unite your body as a whole. How much time all this takes is entirely up to you."

"Yes, sir!"

"Dismissed."

In the wee hours of the morning, Baltor tiptoed out of the bunkhouse and headed to the supply alcove. The only other usable item that he was able to find there was another coiled fifty-foot rope hidden in an old, dusty sack behind a small stalagmite—he did find it surprising that he hadn't noticed that sack before, but then again, supplies came and went.

He tied the one-hundred-foot rope and the fifty-foot rope together with several tight knots, put the rope into the bag, and then slung the bag over his shoulder. He also took an unlit torch with him, as well a piece of flint.

He soon made his way to the valley, wrapped the rope around the same spot, lit the torch, put the end of it in his mouth, and rappelled down as before. This time, he was easily able to make it to the bottom of the valley only a minute later.

He walked over to the crumpled figure, turned it over, and his mouth dropped open in aghast—it was indeed Vakshia.

After examining the body more carefully, he discovered that there was only one single bloodstain, spread out all across the front of her shirt. He lifted the blood-crackling shirt up, and discovered dozens of puncture holes in her chest and stomach by something needle-thin and razor-sharp—in ever-growing shock, horror and sadness, he no longer had any question in his mind: *Vakshia had not committed suicide ... she had been murdered*!!

Once he had overcome the shock and grief—perhaps hours later—he finally concluded that he would take the body now, and let the Guild decide what to do next in order to find the killer, so that justice could be served.

Therefore, he walked back over to the rope, dragging it over to the body. After tying the rope securely around her body, he climbed his way up to the top. Once there, two minutes later, he began to pull up the rope.

He had perhaps gotten the body about three-quarters of the way up, when he heard another boy's voice snarl, "I thought that you've been acting a bit funny as of late, Baltor! I mean, besides being a pathetic little worm, now I know why."

Baltor's head turned and he now saw Thesmul, who had just entered the perimeters of the torch's light.

With a bit of annoyance to his voice, Baltor asked, "Thesmul, what are you talking about? I'm just practicing some physical strength exercises—that's all."

"Oh yeah," Thesmul asked, who was still a dozen feet away but drawing closer by the second, "what kind of weights you using?"

Once Baltor saw the glint of steel reflected from the torch's light, he had no choice but to let go of the rope and turn to face his new opponent before it was too late.

Without any further delay, Thesmul leapt toward his enemy with a snarl and with stiletto already coming down in a strike— Baltor somersaulted to his left, just barely evading the attack.

Instead of waiting for his opponent to get another attack, Baltor leapt at Thesmul—but a second later his left shoulder smashed hard into Thesmul's upper legs, which caused not only both of the boys to crash into the ground, yet for the stiletto to fly out and land at the edge of the torch's light.

Within a foot of the cliff's edge, the two boys immediately began to wrestle on the ground, each vying for the upper position or the stiletto!

Now it is true that Baltor knew only a dozen or so less advanced-techniques than Thesmul, yet the elder boy had been training for a year-and-a-half longer, and he was still much stronger and bigger.

Therefore, within a minute's time Thesmul was on top, punching hard and repeatedly—although he had taken quite a few hard hits himself, especially the one in his left eye that was already black, blue and very puffy.

At first, Baltor blocked most of the hits that were coming in, but about twenty seconds or so later, Thesmul's punches finally began making full contact into Baltor's face!

Blood steadily poured from his nostrils and lips; his eyes were puffy but not completely swollen shut. He only saw shooting stars....

Thesmul continued to pulverize him long after Baltor was dazed—until finally, he leapt toward the stiletto. All the while, Baltor could only lie there on the ground and bleed.

After Thesmul had swiped up his stiletto, he turned back around, and while twirling it expertly between his hands, he asked, "You want to know what happened to Vakshia? I'll tell you. I promised her that I would help her succeed in this place. I even helped her all the way up to this point, but when I tried to seduce and have my way with her, she refused. At first, I was startled, but then I became upset and then angry. Regardless, she was a good girl until the end—except for the fact that she fought me the whole way through. Of course I couldn't have her report me, so..."

Thesmul made several sharp and quick jabs downward with the stiletto, but then he stopped. With a cluck of his tongue and a shake to his head, he added, "I'm sorry to say, but there truly is no honor amongst thieves!" He began to laugh sadistically at his little joke.

His semi-lengthy speech and laughter had given Baltor somewhat of a chance to recover his wits. Though he had only heard the last half of it—it infuriated his anger to rage!

Slowly and very unsteadily, he got to his feet and assumed the basic ready position.

This caused Thesmul to laugh even harder and through his laughter, he asked, "Do you—*ha ha*—do you want some more of me—*ha ha*—you pathetic worm? By the way, did you know that with all that blood all over you, you seriously do look like a worm? *Ha ha!*"

Baltor remained silent.

No longer laughing, Thesmul promised threateningly while beginning to approach ever so slowly, "I've got a little experiment I'm going to perform on you. I'm going to chop you into little pieces, beginning with your fingers and ending with your heart! We shall soon find out whether you, just like a worm, can regenerate."

Baltor said nothing, only waited.

With a mighty roar, Thesmul leapt at Baltor with stiletto jabbing in for the kill!

Baltor immediately fell backward, slapping his hands hard into the ground in order to do a reverse roll, and even though he propped his legs and knees tightly into his chest, he did not yet push himself backward onto his feet using his arms. Though the stiletto barely missed Baltor by an eighth of an inch, Thesmul was once again on top of Baltor and falling.

The split-second Thesmul's chest contacted Baltor's feet, only a second later, Baltor propelled his whole body backward with his back muscles, abdominals and arms, while extending his legs and feet straight out. These simultaneous motions caused Thesmul to propel back up into the air and scream as he flew nearly a dozen feet beyond the edge of the valley!

Unfortunately, neither did Baltor feel anything underneath him, except for thin air. Without pause, he reached out and forward with his hands, and luck was with him yet again, as his eight fingers barely clutched onto the edge of the cliff!

Ten seconds later, the echoing screams finally stopped—yet Baltor clung there for dear life.

Several times already, he had tried to dig his feet into the cliff face, yet always without success—the rock was just too smooth.

He next tried to pull himself up using his feet and fingers. Not only were his hands already too weak to pull him up, they were weakening even further by the second—he didn't know how much longer he could hold on.

Once the last remaining bit of strength in his hands was finally going away, he began to accept the fact that he would be falling to his death and joining Vakshia in the afterlife, as well his parents— until suddenly, an idea sprang to mind.

Thanks to all of his extensive leg stretches, he was just barely able to stretch his left leg over the edge of the cliff and hook his foot behind a small stalagmite. Gripping his fingers even tighter into the cliff's edge, he used mostly his leg strength in order to pull the rest of his body back onto solid ground. For an unknown amount of time, Baltor simply lay there too weak and tired to move.

When he found that his strength had begun to return, he slowly stood to his feet, and then began the unbelievably painful process, both physically and emotionally, of pulling Vakshia's body up.

After depositing her over his shoulders, he wearily bent to pick up the torch before he began to make his way back. It took him more than triple the time to do it, especially as his muscles were very exhausted and sore.

Once he had returned to the main cavern, an unknown amount of time later, he was so beyond the point of exhaustion that he didn't even assess that the other students and instructors had stopped in their training, now throwing strange and questioning looks.

His legs finally buckled and he collapsed to the ground with Vakshia's corpse still on top. When a female instructor had moved the body over a second later, she saw that Baltor was no longer conscious at all!

CHAPTER V

When Baltor first regained consciousness, an unknown amount of time later, he wondered why his head ached so badly. The second he tried to open his eyes, unsuccessfully, the throbbing pains in his head multiplied—he groaned in agony.

An unfamiliar woman's voice quietly soothed, "Relax—you need to get back your strength."

Once most of that pain had dissipated, he finally asked, "Where am I?"

"You are in the Guild's nursing ward at the moment."

"What happened to me?"

"Of that, we are not exactly sure—we have been waiting for you to wake up so that you can tell us."

Something about that voice only now began to sound vaguely familiar to him, though he could not recall her image or name, so he asked, "Who are you?"

"My name is Mistress Bayema," she introduced. "I was the one who first brought Vakshia to the Guild."

Once he heard Vakshia's name, many, many painful memories immediately began to surface. Not just the memories of Vakshia and Thesmul, but ones more distant like his parents' murders. With a deep sigh that physically hurt his chest, Baltor found tears pouring through his swollen eyelids.

"*Shhh*," Bayema said with that gentle voice, "Relax. Once you are fully healed, then the inquiry will begin before the High Council."

"That," he said, "may take many months, if not years."

After a few moments of silence, he heard her say, "Perhaps, but you're resilient, meaning tough. Do you mind if I ask you a question?"

"What?"

"Why were you so interested in Vakshia?"

After sucking in a deep breath and releasing it, he took yet another deep breath before answering, "She... she was the only other student that was ever nice to me, my Mistress."

"I see," Bayema replied thoughtfully.

A few moments later, he heard the sounds of silk sliding, and then he heard her say, "For now, relax and recuperate. I will be back soon."

He asked, "Before you go, I have one question that I'd like to ask you."

"What's that?"

"How long have I been out?"

"Three days," Bayema answered. "Your drill instructor has been here most of that time, patiently waiting by your side for you to wake up. He went to an important meeting about an hour ago, so I cannot say when he will be back. Relax and get some sleep, Baltor."

A few seconds later, he heard a door close and he was left alone.

Over the course of the next several days, he slept most of the time, while his body quickly recuperated. During one of those occasions that he happened to be conscious—though still temporarily blind due to the swollen-shut eyes—he had heard the door to his room open, and then he heard someone quietly sit down in a chair near the bed. As this person said nothing to him, he didn't say anything back either. During the times that he was sleeping, he had many strange dreams.

Finally, the time came when he could open his eyes into tiny slits, while noting that his body hurt a lot less. He first discovered that besides the bed he was lying in, there were more than a dozen other beds located on this side of the rather large room. On the other side of the room, a dozen operating tables with many drawers underneath—probably filled with medical tools, supplies, bandages, etc.

One such time that he had just awoken from one of his many naps, he saw Humonus enter.

His drill instructor immediately exclaimed, "Hey there, champ! How are you feeling?"

"A little better," Baltor tiredly said with a weak smile.

"Good, good," Humonus said. He then sat in the chair, leaned forward, and added, "I'm glad to hear it."

Baltor asked, "How are you?"

"Not bad, not bad," Humonus answered. "I'm just glad to see that you're looking a whole hell of a lot better!"

"How bad did I look?"

After chuckling with a few shakes to his head, Humonus confessed, "Whew. Let me put it to you this way—when I first came into work almost a week ago and saw you, I didn't think you were going to make it. Your body was beaten to a pulp and your face was redder than a beet from all the blood splattered everywhere!"

Baltor chuckled.

Humonus didn't laugh. Instead, he asked very seriously, "You know what's going to happen to you, right?"

Even though Baltor suddenly found himself getting very nervous, he still asked, "What, sir?"

"There will be a formal inquiry into the matter," Humonus said, "and you will have to report the entire incident, from day one, before the High Council."

Humonus gave Baltor about twenty seconds to contemplate before he added, "On the bright side of things, we are not only expert thieves, but we are also expert investigators, and the Guild has already done the investigating. That is a part of what makes a good thief, really. Anyway, to keep to the point, here is what some of us speculate."

He then explained the events of that night in relatively precise detail.

"That is exactly what happened," Baltor confirmed, nodding.

After another pause, a severe look of irritation crossed Humonus's face as he added, "There is one thing that I am severely peed off at you about."

Baltor asked, "What?"

"You specifically disobeyed a command that I made by continuing your own investigations into Vakshia's disappearance. Just so you know... you made me look like I have absolutely no control over my student!" Humonus said with ruffled feathers.

"Sir, please accept my apologies and my fullest assurances that I will never disobey you again," Baltor said sincerely.

After a few more moments to consider the apology, Humonus sighed, "Apologies and assurances accepted, I guess."

"Thank you, sir," Baltor said in relief. "Sir?"

"Yes?"

"Once I've graduated all my training, which I will, I have decided that I am going to find the culprits that murdered my parents and exact justice. I also wish to state for the record that though I have learned many valuable lessons from you, there is one that I am most appreciative of, sir!"

"What's that?"

"I have learned how to care for others, and for that, I wish to thank you, sir."

Humonus nodded and said, "I'm glad to know that I've been of service." He got out of his seat and revealed, "Just so that you can mentally prepare, your nurse has informed me that you will be ready for the inquiry tomorrow. I'm going to let you get your rest now—besides, I've some errands that I must finish."

He walked toward the door, opened it, stepped through, and was just about shut it closed behind him, but he stopped. Instead, he turned around, reopened the door a quarter of the way, poked his head around the door, and then added, "Oh, just so you know, Thesmul was not only a favorite amongst many of the students and instructors, but some believed him to have the potentials and qualities as a future Chief.

"Also, several of the High Council members suspect, based from your many nightly disappearances, that maybe it was you who raped and murdered Vakshia. And that later, you returned to finish the job, yet Thesmul caught you in the act. After all, no one is for certain who first held the weapon."

As Humonus said all this, he observed the ever-increasing look of shock and horror upon the boy's face. Just before closing the door behind him, he promised, "Make sure you have your facts all put together...

"If you don't and the High Council disbelieves your story in any way, shape or form—expulsion from the Guild may be the least of your worries. As for me, I believe your story and your innocence."

"Thank you, sir."

The door closed and Baltor remained alone to heal, and to contemplate.

The following morning, Humonus opened the door while carrying a duffel bag. "Good morning, Baltor."

"Good morning, sir."

Humonus first set the bag down onto the bed, and then he informed, "The time has finally come for us to leave. Inside the bag are some hand-me-downs. Please get dressed quickly, so that we can get some hot chow from the mess hall before we go before the High Council. Do you feel yourself ready and competent?"

"Yes, sir!"

"Excellent, Baltor. I'll be waiting for you outside," Humonus replied with a nod. He then exited the room, closing the door behind him.

Baltor opened the bag, and in less than forty seconds, he was dressed in clean underwear and socks, a gray tunic, brown pants and an old pair of tan boots, which all fit perfectly.

After he had opened the door and exited the room, he observed that Humonus was leaning against the wall, waiting in a very long hallway that had fourteen stylish doors in total—six on the far side, six on his side, and two at each of the far ends.

With another nod, Humonus gave a gesture to follow with one hand, leaned off the wall, and then ordered, "Follow me." He then turned to his right, walked down to the door at the far end of the hallway, opened it, and entered another magnificent hallway. Meanwhile, Baltor followed behind.

Three doors down on the right-hand side, Humonus opened the door and gestured for Baltor to enter.

This was not just any mess hall, but more like a fancy restaurant—indeed, this place was both beautiful and elegant. The dining room contained twenty large round tables with eight plush seats around each table—very classy people filled a little more than half of those seats, and even the waiters wore formal attire.

Even though Baltor was at first very self-conscious about the way he was dressed, his hunger took over once the delicious food had come, which Humonus had earlier ordered, and they feasted.

Once breakfast was over, Humonus led the way back into the hallway, and down two more. As Baltor followed, he presumed that the door at the end of this third hallway would lead to still another, but he was wrong.

After Humonus opened this door and gestured for the boy to enter first, Baltor discovered—with surprise—this to be a spectacular, throne room. The only sources of light came from four crystal chandeliers filled with lots of burning candles.

Within this two-hundred-foot-squared room, in which the walls were draped with red velvet, as were paintings of all types, there rested two rows of twelve golden thrones placed in a semi-circle. Every last seat was occupied, but no one wore a crown—eighteen males and six females. In the middle of the room was a plain wood chair.

Humonus led Baltor to the empty seat. After a physical gesture of beckoning with his hand for Baltor to sit in the chair, he stood behind his student and waited in silence.

Baltor took his seat and glanced through the crowd of onlookers. The only three people he recognized were Bayema at the far-left end of the first row, Lydia next to her, and Lupan behind Lydia. Today, he wore black robes and skullcap, and his colorful jewelry.

Baltor was very pleased to see them all here, especially Lydia.

Humonus began, "Masters and Mistresses of the High Council, as you know, my name is Humonus, and I have been a drill instructor here at the Guild for six years—a member for fifteen. In particular, I am the defendant's instructor.

"Wasting no more of your valuable time, I shall now introduce the defendant in question, who will present his side of the story, Baltor."

Baltor felt all eyes on him—his cheeks immediately flushed and his throat became constricted.

After clearing his throat several times, he began, "Masters and..."

He found that he had to clear his throat yet again, before he could continue, "Mistresses of the High Council, my name's Baltor. I have been a student, well I don't really know for how long, but for quite some time."

He paused for a few moments, so that he could recall the story from the beginning, and then he continued, "Okay, it all started several months ago, actually ever since I started here, because I wasn't very much liked by the other students, and so I became a bit lonely. One day in the training hall, I happened to observe this new student and overheard her name as Vakshia. Coincidentally, later that same day, my instructor released me for lunch at the same time as her lunch break.

"Vakshia introduced herself to me, but she sounded real scared and unsure of herself. In turn, I gave her the encouraging words of the one who inspired me, when I was real scared and unsure of myself. At the end, I told her that 'success is a road that must be paved.' And just like with me, these words seemed to hold merit and she seemed encouraged when her instructor called her to him.

"I wouldn't say that this was the last time I saw her, but it was the last time I ever got a chance to talk to her, for almost every night afterward, I did extra training to sharpen my own fighting skills.

"Well anyway, several weeks later, I observed that she was no longer around, but at first, I thought she was just doing her own extra training. Until finally the day came, I asked my drill instructor where she had gone. He told me that she had disappeared. I then asked him if he thought she had escaped. He told me that no one has ever escaped the Guild since its establishment.

"But that night, I asked another student, Thesmul, if he had seen her. He laughed in my face, but didn't answer."

After sucking in a deep breath through just his nose, Baltor continued, "I didn't tell anyone about my encounter with Thesmul, including my instructor, but I did begin to investigate into her disappearance secretly at night on my own. I borrowed a hundred-foot rope, and after securing it to a rock or something, I checked all of the crevices and holes near the obstacle courses and dropped a lit torch, just to make sure.

"For a month, I didn't find anything, until the very night before I fought with Thesmul. That was the night I had dropped a torch down the valley on the sixth course, discovered a body, and though I didn't know whose body it was, I had to find out.

"So the next night, I borrowed an additional fifty-foot rope, secured it to the hundred-foot rope, and then headed back to the valley. After I got to the bottom of the valley and sadly discovered that it was indeed Vakshia, my initial plan was to bring the body back for the Guild to investigate.

"However, after I had secured her body to the rope, climbed my way back up, and then began pulling her body up—that was when Thesmul arrived with a stiletto in hand. Sensing that my life was in danger, I had no choice but to drop the rope, and as my instructor had taught, I rolled backward in order to avoid his slash. I then rolled forward, collided with him, and the stiletto flew out of his hand.

"For the next several minutes we wrestled, but he got the better hand and began to beat the hell out of me! Once he thought I was beaten senseless, he picked up the stiletto and confessed to me that he had raped and killed Vakshia for refusing him!"

Immediately Baltor began to listen to the feverish whispers of the council members as he finished that last statement. Through the whispers, he continued even louder, "I got so angry upon hearing those words—I stood back up! That was when Thesmul threatened to cut me into little pieces like a little worm, and then he leapt at me with full intentions to do so.

"But just as my instructor had taught me, I turned my defense into an offense, and that was when I kicked him over the cliff face and into the valley. From the roll, I went over myself, but thankfully, I soon managed to get myself back onto solid ground. Sometime after, though I don't know how long, I pulled Vakshia's body back up and got her back to the training area. And that's what happened from beginning to end, I swear to it!"

Several of the High Council members began to mutter in angry tones yet again. Inevitably, one man's voice erupted from amongst the councilmembers, "How can you prove that Thesmul, who has a good reputation here in the Guild, was initially in possession of the weapon and not you?"

"I can't prove anything as I was completely alone. But let me tell you that he's guilty as sin," Baltor immediately shot back.

The man, after a short pause, asked, "Do you have any proof as to your innocence regarding the rape and murder of Vakshia?"

Lupan stood up, looked over at the man on the other side, and hollered over, "Do you have any proof that he's guilty?"

"No, I don't, Master Lupan, but I am trying to figure out all the facts. I have known Thesmul for quite some time, and I don't think it is possible for him to have done anything to Vakshia!"

Baltor could no longer hold back his own anger, and so he asked, "What I'd like to know is why you people didn't bother to check into her disappearance in the first place? And I mean check!"

The man stood up, outraged, and then challenged, "How dare you! It is us who ask the questions here—it shall be you who answers! Other than that, keep your mouth shut, boy."

At that, Lydia stood up and defended, "Master Salmot, Baltor has a point. Why didn't the High Council do a thorough investigation into her disappearance as soon as it was known?" Without waiting for his answer, she continued, "Baltor should be declared a hero for the risks he took and overcame."

"The High Council has many affairs to attend to, besides checking into the disappearance of any beginning students—you know this to be quite true, Mistress Lydia," Salmot answered. "But in my opinion, Baltor deliberately tampered with the scene to make it appear as if Thesmul was the aggressor, rapist and murderer."

Most of the High Council stood up and began arguing amongst each other, especially Lydia and Salmot. One voice, a feminine one, spoke out above the din.

The second she spoke, the din immediately quieted, "We should re-examine the area carefully and deliberate all the evidence in private, without having this student present. The Guild, our Shan-gri-La, has been in existence for nearly five hundred years! However, if you take a close look at us now, you will agree that we all need to stop acting like schoolchildren. I say we deliberate in private, without the defendant present. Agreed?"

"Agreed," said many voices in unison.

"Humonus, before you escort Baltor out of here, I have one more question for you," she said.

After delivering a low bow, he asked, "Yes, my Mistress?"

She asked, "What is your opinion? Do you think Baltor's guilty?"

"My Mistress... no, I do not believe he's guilty, but innocent."

"Very well. Keep him company in suite twenty-two until we have made our final decision and we call upon you again."

With another low bow, he replied, "Yes, my Mistress." He then rose from the bow, and gestured for Baltor to proceed to the door. He next escorted Baltor to the suite, which were quite a few more hallways and dozens of rooms later.

This room was not only very stylishly decorated, yet it contained two beds and a wide assortment of entertaining board games—only once inside with the door closed did Baltor ask, "So what do you think will happen now?"

"I don't know, Baltor," Humonus replied truthfully, "but I've never seen the High Council to be so heated up with one another."

After taking a deep breath through his nose, he said, "Well... Let's check out some of these games."

Three more days passed while Humonus and Baltor waited, yet simultaneously had fun. Mostly they played this strategic game called voo-span (thanks to Humonus's instruction), similar to four-dimensional chess—until finally the time came that the High Council called them back into their chambers.

As before, Humonus led Baltor to his chair, before standing behind him. Baltor sat down, nervously awaiting his verdict.

Once the boy was sitting, it was the mistress that had silenced the argument who spoke, "Though this decision was not easy to come by, it is in the rulings of the High Council that you are innocent. The Guild owes you a debt of gratitude for services rendered. Tomorrow, you shall recommence with your training. That is all."

Baltor breathed a deep sigh of relief.

The High Council stood out of their seats and most had begun to disperse—within a minute, only four people remained in the room, Lydia, Bayema, Humonus and Baltor.

Bayema spoke first, "I would personally like to thank you, Baltor, and I'm sure that Vakshia would have done the same. Good luck with your training."

"Thank you, my Mistress," Baltor responded with a bow.

Bayema then left.

Lydia added, "Baltor, you truly are a brave soul. We need more people like you in the Guild. I knew that I was right when my heart first led me to you. Oh, just to let you know, there is a reason I was gone for so long—it's because I found my way back home and let my parents know that I was still alive and well. Take care, Baltor."

Baltor repeated his words and act.

Lydia turned to Humonus and ordered, "Take good care of him."

"Yes, my Mistress," Humonus answered with a bow. He then turned to his pupil and ordered, "Follow me, Baltor."

He bowed one final time before Lydia and then he followed his drill instructor to their next destination.

CHAPTER VI

The drill instructor led his student through quite a few more hallways, until they finally returned to the room with the fountain in it. Along the way, Baltor silently remarked to himself on how gargantuan this palace really was!

Humonus turned the emerald and the trapdoor opened. He climbed down to the bottom of the ladder, and waited for his pupil to join him. He next led him back to the training hall and up to the weapons rack.

Upon completion of their regular stretching exercises, the drill instructor said, "Now, we shall go over all those wrist stretching exercises that I was about to teach you prior to your recent event, in which I want you to perform these stretches every other day. What you will ultimately develop is wrist control. Perhaps this afternoon, I will begin teaching you how to wrestle opponents—unarmed and armed. For now, watch me closely…"

Amidst explaining and performing the wrist stretches and exercises, he had his student perform them as well.

Ten minutes later, Humonus pulled two wooden sabers from the weapons rack as he said, "Now, I want you to observe some of my attacks that are based entirely from wrist control."

For the next minute, without having moved the trunk of his body even one inch, the drill instructor's sabers flew in a multitude of directions that seemed to combine both attacks and defenses. Baltor watched in awe.

Once Humonus had finished, he explained, "As you can see, my body did not move except for my wrists and arms. My arms simply followed the commands of my wrists—wrist control. Now you try."

With an instantaneous flick of his wrists, he flipped the sabers in his hands, now extending the handles out for his student to take. His student did.

For the remainder of that week and the following two weeks, Baltor not only practiced and mastered wrist control, yet he learned from his drill instructor how to wrestle.

The very next week on Charday, two days after Moonday, after he had already performed all his stretching exercises by himself, Humonus greeted him at the weapons rack with a "Good morning, Baltor."

The student stood to his feet and replied, "Good morning, sir!"

The drill instructor taught, "From here on out, and this is my final lesson to you, we shall begin to incorporate each of the individual techniques and skills that you have learned, re-unite your body back as one, and combine it all with the final element of speed."

"Yes, sir!"

"Once you have mastered all of this, and the both of us feel that you are ready, there will be a test with graders. If you should pass this 'special obstacle course,' you will be elevated to phase-three. If you should fail, you will most likely be dead, as the dangers are quite deadly."

"Yes, sir. Sir?"

"Yes, Baltor."

"What does this test consist of?"

The drill instructor revealed for the very first time, "There is another obstacle course that lies far beneath this chasm. It is not unlike the other obstacle courses you have already gone through, with ropes that you must cross and walls that you must climb...

"However, all of the swinging bags have sharp spikes imbedded into them. There are moving sword-wielding straw dummies that will strike at you, which you must take out. There will also be professional archers who will be aiming for your heart or head... and there is a time limit with which you must complete it. Oh, finally yet importantly, you must go through it all blindfolded."

He observed that through his explanations, an increasing look of worry crossed his student's face, especially the final part. Perhaps five seconds later, he added consolingly, "Relax, Baltor. Until both you and I feel competent, you won't be taking the final test. Besides, when you are finally ready, you will easily pass with flying colors."

"One more question, sir?" Baltor asked as his face visibly relaxed.

"Yes?"

Baltor asked, "If I am blindfolded, how will I know when I must jump up to a rope, dodge a spike-filled bag, evade an arrow, or even attack armed dummies?"

"Everything in life, whether a test or for real, will always contain signs," Humonus answered. "Once your body has become re-united, your senses will tell you how to interpret those signs, what to do, and when to do it."

"Yes, sir!"

Three more months passed as Baltor honed and perfected his skills, including learning how to wrestle like a pro, until his body finally acted as one, and with speed.

During that time, he only saw Lydia twice, and both of those visits were terribly short in his opinion. He had finally concluded to himself that the strange feelings in the pit of his stomach, whenever she was around, was the simple fact that he was "in love"—he wanted to see her more upon this realization, but it rarely happened.

Finally, the morning came when he asked his drill instructor, "Sir?"

"Yes, Baltor."

"I feel that I am ready for the final test."

Humonus's cryptic response happened to be, "What a coincidence."

"Why is that, sir?"

"Because last night, I swear that I had come to that same conclusion!"

Baltor asked with surprise, "Really?"

"Yes," the drill instructor confirmed, "I did. Still, I would like you to practice with me for one more week, just to be on the safe side."

"Yes, sir!"

"Tonight, I will inform the High Council that you shall be ready to take the test next week on Harrnsday."

"Yes, sir!"

"Just too properly motivate you—I will let you know what phase three is like," the drill instructor promised. After a short pause, he explained, "Phase three is called Education. You may take as many classes for as long as you wish, and as many subjects as you can handle...

"Just so you know, other instructors will be teaching all these courses to you, and not me. Of course, you can advance to phase-four without ever having stopped phase three...

"Certainly all thieves take the classes that pertain to thieving, like disarming booby traps and unlocking locks—they feel these to be the most important, especially for acquiring treasure and wealth."

"Unfortunately," Humonus taught, "most thieves greatly under-estimate the treasure and wealth that comes from other basic courses from reading, writing and arithmetic, to advanced courses like learning foreign cultures, customs and their languages. It is in my strongest opinion that all of these subjects are equally im-portant, as I still take courses to date."

The drill instructor paused for a good ten seconds to let the words sink in, before he continued, "During the times that you are free, you will either be allowed to continue training upon any of the obstacle courses down here, or you will be allowed to roam the streets on your own. Whether you wish to stay in the bunkhouse or eventually attain a place of your own is your choice, but you must never forget the vows you took when you first came here, especial-ly after I show you the secret location of the underground latch. And that's phase three in a nutshell."

Though there were a million other questions that instantly popped into the student's mind, such as what arithmetic was, to what phase-four consisted of, to how many phases there was in total, he also realized that he needed to pass his current phase first. Therefore, he simply responded, "Yes, sir!"

As if to confirm, Humonus said, "For now, let us continue train-ing."

For the next week, they trained longer and harder than they had ever done before, but by now, these elongated sessions had no ef-fect on Baltor's fatigue.

The night before testing day, he had gone to bed without being nervous in the slightest bit. Once morning came, however, he awoke to find that he was extraordinarily nervous—his adrenaline glands rushed like there was no tomorrow, perhaps literally!

Baltor anxiously waited for his instructor to arrive at the weap-ons rack while performing all his routine stretching exercises. Still, they did nothing to abate his nerves.

Soon after, Humonus arrived. After he greeted his student with a friendly smile and a "good morning," he asked, "So, Baltor, are you ready to take your test?"

"Sir, to be honest with you, I thought I was, but now I'm not so sure."

With a look of understanding, the drill instructor replied, "Baltor, that's just called nerves. In any potentially conflicting situa-tion, nerves will erupt and if uncontrolled, you will feel weak and helpless. But once you learn how to control them, they will be your greatest allies, ever! Take a couple of deep breaths."

The student did as instructed. He soon found that his nerves began to lessen though they did not altogether disappear.

"Sir, if I don't make it, then I'd like to tell you that I'm very appreciative of everything that you've—"

Humonus had placed both hands squarely upon his student's shoulders, looked him straight in the eyes, and then said emphatically, "Baltor, you must never think like that ever again! You are fully trained. You will make it. You will succeed!"

The student took a couple more deep breaths, and not only did he find himself relaxed but also ready—he finally replied, "Lead the way, sir!"

With a nod and a small smile, Humonus patted Baltor o n c e on the shoulder before ordering, "Follow me."

He led his student through several tunnels that wound themselves deeper and deeper underground.

About ten minutes later, they entered an enormous cavern that was twice the size of the training area.

Baltor first observed a large stadium to his left, already filled with a large group of onlookers—approximately seventy—pleasantly chatting with one another.

His eyes then scanned throughout the room, and observed a dug-in path that led through a myriad of obstacles from ropes, ladders, walls, bottomless pits, chasms, spiked bags and armed straw-dummies that were held taut by a thin rope.

Standing behind each dummy and out of harm's way was a man or a woman armed with a dagger ready to cut the ropes. He even observed that at random areas, archers stood with an arrow already hooked in their bow. He found himself becoming uneasy again.

Humonus allowed Baltor a brief minute to look at the area, and then he quietly ordered, "Follow me, Baltor."

He led his student to the beginning of the dug-in path, stopped, and turned around to face his pupil. Pulling a blindfold from his pocket, he said in a normal tone of voice, "Before I blindfold you, Baltor, I shall give you one last minute to scan your horizons."

With a frightened whisper, the student said, "Sir, this is a crazy-as-hell obstacle course and I don't know if I can do it blind—"

The drill instructor interrupted with his commanding voice, "Stop thinking about the things you can't do... and start doing the things you can. I know that you can do this, but you must have no doubts, as well. First, close your eyes and keep them closed, and then take some deep breaths. In through the nose... out the mouth."

Nearly thirty seconds later, the student finally answered with confidence, "I feel better, sir. I know that I can do this now."

Now with a loud and commanding voice, the drill instructor ordered, "Good—now open your eyes and scan your horizons!"

His voice immediately silenced the entire crowd of onlookers.

After sucking in one last deep breath, Baltor opened his eyes and scanned the path, from the first obstacle to the last, as well everything else in between.

Strangely, everything that he had to do became clear, even though his nerves remained a bit tense.

The student's gaze finally rested upon his drill instructor and with a nod he said, "I'm ready, sir."

"Excellent. I'll see you when you return."

The drill instructor securely blindfolded his student, walked over to the stadium, and took his seat in the front row.

It felt to Baltor that an eternity had passed before the word... "Go!"

Blindly, he bolted ahead, remembering that his first obstacle was a huge, circular, bottomless pit with a rope that he had to swing across to get to the other side.

With a leap, his hands found the rope—he grabbed it, and the momentum of the rope swung him to the other side. He let go of the rope, and continued to run at warp speed.

His second obstacle course was a seventy-foot high wall that he had to climb; however, just as he began to near the wall, he detected a whooshing sound.

He first rolled forward, just barely evading an arrow by mere inches, and then leapt up and forward, as his memory reminded him to do. Again, his instincts were right on—he latched onto the wall and quickly scaled his way up.

Once he had reached the top, and without any more arrows shot at him yet, he remembered that the path veered up and to the left. He also remembered that up here, it was possible for the archers to hit him.

As if to confirm, he heard two whooshing sounds back to back, and so he rolled forward, one right after the other. And one right after the other, both arrows missed, yet only by inches!

A few in the crowds had only now begun to clap and cheer. Paying them no heed, he was back on his feet as he booked ahead. His memory told him that at the end was a seventy-foot knotted rope that hung from the ceiling and led to the ground, but the rope was about twelve feet past the mouth of the tunnel! He also remembered that he would have to slide down real fast, as the archers would still be in range.

He leapt, and again his hands found the ropes: the rope began to swing back and forth from the momentum.

As he had begun to slide his way down, a good idea suddenly crossed his mind—he kicked his legs back and forth in order to keep the rope swinging.

He heard over a dozen whooshing sounds, but none of the arrows struck by the time he made it to the ground—and then he bolted forward! About a dozen-or-so more people had joined in with the applause.

Once Baltor had made it halfway down the dug-in path to his next obstacle, he recalled that there were several straw-dummies up ahead, yet fortunately, the archers couldn't get him over there.

As if to confirm this just seconds later, he heard the sound of a rope being cut, and then the sound of a sword slicing through the air to his left.

Instantaneously he rolled left, grabbed the sword that had just finished its swing by sound alone, and with an angular attack downward, he sliced the dummy in half.

He then bolted forward, and took out two more dummies with his newly acquired weapon. Approximately thirty people were cheering now.

His memory continued to serve him, for he recalled that the next obstacle in the course up ahead was a twenty-foot ladder that led into another tunnel. He also remembered that once he had begun to climb, he would once again be in range from the archers.

Despite the dangers, he climbed up the ladder and heard several whooshing noises. He held the ladder with his left hand; with his other hand, he swung his sword defensively. Baltor deflected three of the arrows, but the fourth struck him in his left forearm—quite a few people in the cheering crowds had oohed upon seeing that.

With the horrible pain, he barely managed to hold on to the ladder. Once he had made it to the top and into the tunnel, he heard several more whooshing sounds.

He rolled three times forward, which caused the shaft of the arrow to break off in his forearm and send shooting pains all the way up and down, but thankfully, none of the other arrows hit!

He dismissed the pain and ran, recalling that the path of this tunnel wound itself to the right. And that at the end of the tunnel that spanned for about two hundred feet, the next obstacle was another rope attached at the ceiling about twenty feet beyond the mouth of the tunnel, and that the ground was some thirty feet be-low.

However, what Baltor could not know was whether he would be in range of the archers at the tunnel's mouth and beyond. There-fore, he ran up to this edge and stopped.

He instantly heard a whooshing sound; his sword easily deflect-ed the incoming arrow; and now Baltor had his answer!

He quickly backed up twenty feet while deflecting still another arrow, and then he bolted forward. He leapt as hard as he possibly could over the side of the tunnel, extended his arms out, and then twisted his right wrist so that the sword was parallel with the ground.

As he rapidly plummeted downwards thirty feet to the ground, he only then remembered that there was a dummy waiting for him.

So the very second his hands contacted the ground, he rolled his body forward to break up the shock, and then he swung his sword up and out—this dummy was destroyed before the instructor had even the chance to cut the taut rope!

Most of the cheering crowd aahed.

While still running, Baltor remembered that there was only one obstacle left—the dozen spiked bags. As he drew close to his objec-tive, he next remembered that there was a railing about fifteen feet or so off the ground that secured all the bags.

He ran harder and harder while avoiding the many arrows shot at him. With a leap that literally caused the crowd to gasp, he grabbed the top of the railing before he actually managed to roll himself up to the top. He then ran the length of the railing, dropped to the ground at the far end, and then he continued running straight ahead.

A voracious amount of cheering was what he heard a few se-conds later; and with an ever-growing smile, he knew that he had completed the obstacle course ... passed the test.

From amongst the cheering, he unexpectedly heard a rather fa-miliar man's voice declare, Salmot's say, "Wait—wait—wait!"

Once the cheering had stopped, only a second later, Salmot con-tinued, "He didn't pass! Make him do it again—he cheated!"

Humonus challenged, "How you figure?"

Salmot explained, "He didn't go through the obstacles like he was supposed to! Baltor was supposed to go through the spiked bags, not over them! He probably also had his blindfolds loose so that he could see what lay ahead of him."

Baltor groaned inwardly.

He heard Humonus reply, "Well then, why don't you check the blindfold yourself to ensure that they are secure?"

After a minute had passed, the student felt his blindfold checked thoroughly. He then heard Salmot say in front of him, "Well, though he couldn't see, he still didn't go through the final obstacle course like he was supposed to—I say we put it to a vote!"

Baltor next heard his drill instructor dutifully reply, "Yes, Master Salmot, I totally agree! All those in favor that Baltor cheated and didn't pass his test, say 'Nay!'"

Only a few people replied to that.

He next heard his drill instructor enthusiastically roar, "All those in favor that Baltor has passed, say 'Aye!'"

Most of the people exclaimed, "Aye!"

Humonus exclaimed even louder, "The ayes have it!"

Baltor immediately heard a loud cheering and applause of the crowds—in fact, the volume of it all nearly deafened him. All the while, he felt someone untying the blindfold. Once removed, he observed that the crowd was literally on its feet.

The drill instructor proudly lifted his student's sword-bearing right hand, and again he stated louder than the crowds, "*The ayes have it!!*"

The crowd, yet again, roared its approval, punctuating the single greatest moment in Baltor's life!

CHAPTER VII

Several minutes later, once the last of the crowd had finished with their congratulatory applause, approximately half of the spectators began to disperse their separate ways. As for the greater half of the crowd that chose to linger around, they began to congregate and chat with each other in variously numbered groups.

Not surprising to anyone, Salmot was the very first to leave, without as much as a single clap or a word of congratulations. Only moments after his departure, half a dozen waiters rolled in carts containing finger snacks, delicacy desserts and fruity beverages. Some of those beverages even contained alcohol.

Meanwhile, a man who was in his early twenties, clean-shaven and dressed in a professional black jacket with a white-furled shirt, hurriedly approached Baltor and Humonus's location from the stands. Not only was he carrying a very large red backpack on his back, yet a plush black chair in both hands.

Once the young man had neared, he immediately stated with a smile on his face and excitement to his voice, "Congratulations to you, Baltor!" He promptly set the chair on the ground before him.

"Thank you, sir," Baltor said proudly.

After lightly patting his fist into his chest, the man introduced, "Oh, I'm not a 'sir' just yet, thank you very much—right now I'm a medic, and I am here to tend to the arrowhead still lodged in your forearm. My name's Racine, by the way."

Immediately, he pointed to the chair, and said, "So, please take a seat and be patient, while I pull everything I'll need out of my medical bag." He next began the process of pulling the heavy backpack off his back and setting it onto the ground.

As soon as the medic had reminded Baltor about his wound, his forearm had begun to get "really painful," coupled with the fact that his "adrenaline juices" had already begun to dissipate—he sat down while saying with a bit of pain in his voice, "Okay—thanks, Racine."

Racine opened his backpack, and pulled out a thin piece of wood that was a foot in both length and width. He next extended four legs from the bottom of the wood, and then he set the table on the ground right next to the chair.

He next pulled two bottles out of the bag, and set the larger bottle filled with a thin clear fluid onto the table. Still holding the other bottle filled with a thick black fluid, Racine extended it toward Baltor, saying with a smile, "Chug this all down—it tastes awful, but you'll be feeling awfully good in a minute!"

After Baltor had taken the extended bottle, and pulled the cork out with his teeth, he sniffed its very strong and unpleasing aroma.

"*Ewww...*" he said with a rather scrunched up face.

Humonus, who had been looking here and there, had also been listening to their conversation. He promptly looked back over to his student and laughed out, "Trust him—Racine knows what he's talking about!"

Baltor plugged his nose with one hand and with the other, he tilted the bottle and chugged the nasty fluids down his throat! Meanwhile, Racine had already pulled out several more medical tools, supplies and bandages. He began arranging them all neatly onto the table.

"*Uggghhhh...*" Baltor managed to say upon completion, despite the horribly tar-like substance that still clung to his tongue.

Once Racine was done a few moments later, he said, "When you no longer feel any pain in your arm, let me know so that I can begin, please."

Just as Baltor nodded, he began to feel a pleasant tingling sensation in his mouth, throat, and stomach. Not even a minute later, not only had his injured arm gotten numb, yet so had all his other joints, including his head—even though he felt wonderful, he said to Racine with quite a slur, "Yesss. Go 'head!"

Racine lightly grabbed the arm, and then began to pour the clear alcoholic disinfectant from the bottle and onto the area of the wound. Though a frothy substance appeared there, Baltor felt no pain or anything else, whatsoever.

Even though he had reached the state of oblivion, Racine remained quite busy. He first set the bottle back down onto the table, and picked up a sterile scalpel. He next carefully probed open the flesh around the arrow, and just as carefully so as not to damage any muscle tissues, he extracted the arrow.

Once done with this, he set the tool and the arrow back onto the table, picked up a primitive sewing needle with thread, and carefully sewed the wound back shut. Using a sterile cotton ball, he next applied a thick coat of some type of dark-green gel.

After dressing it up with a half-inch-thick sterile bandage, he wrapped a bunch more of the bandaging material around his entire forearm—the entire process took about fifteen minutes.

He turned to Humonus, because Baltor was still in the state of oblivion, before he revealed, "I'll be by every day to change his bandages and to remove the stitches in two weeks, okay?"

Humonus nodded.

Racine added, "Oh, and don't worry about the chair—I'll come back and get it later on today. Additionally, the elixir should wear off in about ten to fifteen more minutes or so, and then he'll be back to normal—nothing physical for him for the next two weeks...

"Don't get the bandage wet—and last but not least," he said, while pulling out a small bottle still in his bag and extending it to Humonus. "Here is some pain medication, but do not give him more than two teaspoons of it every six hours, okay? It goes down much better with juice."

"No problem... and thanks," Humonus said appreciatively, while taking the bottle.

"You're welcome!" Racine said just as appreciatively. He walked over to the backpack, pulled out another small leather bag, and began the process of packing all the bloody supplies into the bag.

By this time, Lydia and Bayema, who had been sitting in the bleachers with a group of seven others and chatting about all the incredible highlights of the show, next began the semi-lengthy process of exchanging their fond farewells to their friends.

Less than a minute later, after a quick farewell to Humonus and Baltor, Racine slipped on the backpack and left the area.

It was then that Lydia and Bayema stood up, exited the bleachers, and while still giddily chatting away with one another, began to stroll toward Baltor and Humonus.

At this time, Baltor had just begun to regain consciousness, approximately four minutes after Racine had left. He clumsily turned his head until he was looking at his drill instructor, and then he asked, "Sssirrr?"

Humonus, who had been observing Lydia and Bayema approach and were now about three dozen feet away, looked back to his student, and asked, "Yes, Baltor?"

"M I K?"

"Of course you are, Baltor," Humonus replied. "You'll just need to take things real easy for the next couple weeks. Relax—you'll be able to ask your questions in a few minutes."

"K."

A minute later, Bayema and Lydia arrived.

Lydia was the first to congratulate, "Excellent job, Baltor—I'm so proud of you!" She lightly gave him a hug.

Strangely, Baltor's mind suddenly became crystal clear as he said, "Thank you, Mistress Lydia."

Outwardly, he remained composed as he returned the hug. But inwardly, he could feel his heart beating hard in his chest, despite the fact that his body still tingled from that narcotic medicine he had consumed.

Once they had released the embrace, Baltor remembered his question, looked over at Humonus, and asked, "Sir, I was wondering. You said earlier that one can stay in phase three as long as one wishes. So what does phase four consist of?"

Bayema was the one to answer melodiously, "I can answer that question, if you don't mind, Instructor Humonus."

In acknowledgment, Humonus nodded his head humbly toward Bayema, and waited in silence for her to answer the question.

A moment later, Bayema answered, "Phase four consists of a mission that you must perform for the Guild—it is a mission of our choice and not yours. Once you have completed your mission and reported your findings and treasures to the High Council, we are the ones who determine whether your mission was a success or a failure, ultimately.

"If you are a failure, most likely you will have to wait about another year before you can retest—after all, there are plenty of other students waiting right in line behind you to take this ultimate test of all their thieving skills.

"If you are a success, then you graduate to your first official rank within the Guild—thief! Of course, there are thirteen higher grades within our organization, all the way up to Secret Chief, but we don't need to talk about this subject just now."

After taking in a deep breath through her mouth, she continued, "To keep with the subject matter, sometimes the missions the Guild has may initially seem simple and relatively easy only to become very difficult and complex in the end—or vice-versa. Seldom do these missions involve traveling to some faraway land in order to acquire a valuable treasure, and very rare is the occasion to try and acquire a supposed magical artifact."

Bayema added with a laugh, "As for me and my three-month-long mission, which is still labeled 'top secret,' I was pretty lucky twenty-two years ago. Because I trust you all implicitly, as you are all my valuable friends, let me say that my successful mission was to steal the legendary Shield of Ariakus from the third cousin of the Sultan, of who still resides in a heavily guarded palace here in Pavelus.

"Despite the fact that this valuable gem-and rune-covered golden shield bore no magical or combative capabilities, the Guild handsomely paid me 50,000 parsecs! Most importantly, my mission was deemed a complete success, and so I was officially promoted to the rank of Thief."

Lydia laughed, "You were lucky indeed! I had to sail north-northwest across the Sea of Albusina on a chartered ship, all the way up to the Ruins of Gravensky near the northpole, which journey took nearly eight months one way; my mission was to recover the Tome of Time. The sailors wouldn't even land at the nearby ice-covered docks, as they claimed the place was haunted and they were scared of the undead. Thankfully they let me use their rowboat and promised they would return in a month to pick me up.

"I found out—that very night—that the ruins were indeed haunted, but other than the loud, clanging noises the spirits liked to make and only at night, I was safe. After all, I donned an amulet necklace bearing their religious symbol, which I had painstakingly chiseled out of mahogany during the voyage and attached to my silver necklace.

"It took three weeks of diligent searching in order to finally locate the tome, made of a leather binder with papyrus parchment and buried within a secret library—one week later, as prearranged, the ship returned, so I rowed out to the ship with book in hand, and we sailed back to Pavelus. Upon my return, I delivered it to the Guild; they paid me 70,000 parsecs and promoted me to Thief. A year later, they informed me that although the Tome of Time had been deemed worthless in every way except for its value an ancient artifact, I could keep the money they had granted for all my efforts."

Bayema turned to Lydia and asked, "You were the one who did that?"

With a smile and a nod to confirm, Lydia said, "Yes—that was me!"

Humonus chuckled one time, just before he asked, "Oh, yeah? My top-secret mission was to infiltrate the Thieves' Guild in the Vaspan Empire's city of Mauritia, which guild members call themselves 'Ponchata'—a venomous-jungle snake that can kill a human in less than five seconds. In order to discover the top secret whereabouts of the kidnapped Princess of Thorium and rescue her..."

Both Bayema and Lydia wowed in unison, "*Ooooh!*"

Lydia asked with great interest, "You did that?"

After a quick nod, Humonus answered, "Yup."

Baltor looked confused as he asked, "Was that a really important mission or something?"

Bayema was the first to answer, "Yes. Just about every town and city has their own thieves' guild, including Mauritia. However, every guild, including ours, has double agents that also work for another guild, especially coming from our main rivals in more than one way—Mauritia! We have spent the last three hundred years trying to eradicate all of our double agents secretly working for any other guilds, yet this has almost always proven futile, despite our greatest oaths and measures, sadly."

Once Humonus realized Bayema was through with what she had to say, he next said with ever-growing excitement, "Anyway, to keep with my adventure, a little over a decade ago, the princess was kidnapped and held for ransom with an extremely hefty fee of 200,000,000 parsecs or she would be killed.

"Though this was a figure that was even impossible for the King of Thorium to pay, his love for his daughter was so great that he would do anything to get her back, even if it meant selling his entire kingdom piece by piece! That was exactly what Sedious Vaspan the Magnificent—ruler of the Vaspan Empire—counted on.

"For your information, Baltor, sedious is not a name, but a title that equates to an emperor, one rank above king, yet one rank below a sultan."

Baltor nodded his head once before he said, "Yes, sir."

Once again enrapt in his tale, Humonus said, "Continuing on, with only a little help from our Guild, I found out the *very, very* top secret location of Mauritia's Guilds' Chief's house. So that afternoon, I chartered a merchant ship that had a neutral flag to sail me to Mauritia. And once there, two-and-a-half weeks later, I went to the house, snuck my way over the fence and around all his masterfully designed security measures that ranged from booby traps to guards—ultimately I arrived within the Chief's personal bedroom, completely undetected."

After sucking in a deep breath, he continued, "The only thing my informant couldn't tell me was where his personal safe was in that bedroom—a safe that contained the map containing the exact coordinates of the princess. Therefore, once I arrived, I had to hide under the man's bed for two nights and three days with only the food and water I brought with me, until finally, the man *himself* entered, as well three 'drop dead gorgeous' females."

"About five minutes later," Humonus added with a chuckle, "both food and alcohol were dropped off; and several hours later, they all got pretty wasted. The Chief then began to brag about all his accomplishments, and of course, the girls were enthralled, so this made the man even more boisterous. So, after walking behind the luxurious white couch which the girls still sat in, he told them to stare deep into the heart of the fireplace that had been set ablaze just after their arrival.

"The girls did. He turned around to face the bed where I'm still hiding underneath, lightly tapped the base of the corner post with his right foot, which caused the entire fireplace to shift, and then he turned back around. What existed behind the fireplace was 'a secret passage' that led downstairs. The girls *oohed* and *aahed*, and immediately he invited them down. Let's just say that some adult-things happened—both down and upstairs—I will not get into!"

Even though Humonus paused to catch his breath, no one said a word. Finally he continued, "Hours after they had passed out in the bed above me, around midnight, I silently crawled out from underneath, kicked the same spot that the chief had kicked, and went downstairs. What I saw at the end of the passage caused my mouth to drool—tons of gold, jewels, paintings, you name it!

"But I had come there for one purpose, and so I searched all around this hidden room until I came to a ruby red box—this was the very same box my informant had told me contained the map to the princess's location. After disarming the trap and opening the box, which took about an hour, I took the map that I should have left for a reason I'll get into soon enough, closed the box, rearmed the trap, and exited the secret room. Once upstairs, I lightly tapped the same spot on the bed, in order to close the trapdoor, and stealthily exited the room, house, yard, etc.

"According to the map, as I discovered in my own hotel room that morning at sunrise, the coordinates of the princess's location was most surprisingly back in Pavelus! So not even an hour later, I chartered another merchant ship to take me back right away."

"And once back nearly three weeks later," he explained with a bit of excitement, "I arrived at the princess's location, which was in the northeastern section of the city at a boarded-up factory. There I found the princess tied and gagged up in the basement all by herself, and so I untied and un-gagged her, and told her to safely follow behind me out the building."

After coughing one time into the sleeve of his shirt, Humonus said, "What I didn't know was that the Chief had discovered that his map had been stolen the same morning I had left Mauritia, chartered a frigate ship with twenty master thieves aboard, and sailed to Pavelus only hours after me. He arrived six days before me!

"So it was just as I and the princess was about to walk out the front doors that the Chief and his henchmen finally revealed themselves to me in the lobby, armed to the teeth and ready to kill me..."

After a ten-second, hold-your-breath pause without interruption from anyone, he said with a whole lot of pride, "After the most ferocious battle I've ever experienced or even seen, I barely won by killing them all! Once it was over, I brought the princess back to Thorium by a merchant ship, and finally I dropped her off her city's doorsteps. Overall, this was a terribly difficult mission indeed..."

Bayema asked, "Isn't that where you got your battle scar?"

Humonus's hand went to the scar that strayed up and down his cheek, before he answered, "Yes, my Mistress. But if it hadn't been for my face, the princess would have been dead by the blade of the Chief!"

"Who is this princess, why is she so important, and what does she has to do with our Guild?" Baltor asked.

Lydia was the first to answer, "The now thirty-year-old Princess Calitta is the sole heir to the Kingdom of Thorium—amazingly her sixty-five-year-old father still lives today. His vast kingdom lays nearly fifteen hundred miles to the southeast of Pavelus, yet neighbors our own neighboring nation of Mauritia, which nation is half our size. Due to all the territorial disputes between us and Mauritia, and Mauritia with Thorium, the Sharia Empire and Thorium have become good friends and trading partners."

Humonus interjected, "And, if I hadn't rescued this particular princess, Thorium would have fallen under the rule of Mauritia and Pavelus might have been the very next to fall, as we do a majority of our trade and commerce with them.

"That is why I was called to this top-top secret task—that and I had already learned quite a few of the secrets of Mauritia's thieves' guild from that old friend of mine, whom shall remain nameless—the rest I figured out on my own."

"One last question, sir," Baltor said. "Why would Mauritia's thieves' guild want to kidnap the princess in the first place, and not Sedious Vaspan himself?"

With a very impressed tone in his voice, Humonus answered, "Good question! Even though Sedious Vaspan covets the wealth and lands of both the Kingdom of Thorium and the Sharia Empire, he's not stupid enough to do the act himself! After all, he has not the men or the supplies to do a two-faced war—literally! So, Sedious Vaspan paid the Chief of Mauritia's thieves' guild two million parsecs to kidnap the princess!"

Baltor breathed a sigh of astonishment.

Humonus added with his index finger pointed up, "That is just but one reason that I stress the importance of education."

Bayema extended her hand to Baltor, and once she had clasped it, she said, "Well, I have some errands to attend to. Great job on your test, and God's luck be with you for your future!"

"Thank you, my Mistress!"

Bayema then departed.

Lydia said with a warm smile, "Baltor, you have impressed me to no end. I know that you will go far in the Guild and make me proud!"

She then embraced Baltor with another tight hug.

Baltor felt his cheeks slightly burn, his heart flutter, and the words that he spoke came out stuttered as he said, "Tha-thank you very much, my Mistress!"

Lydia released the embrace and then she departed. A moment later, only Humonus and Baltor remained in the huge chamber.

"Sir, I shall make you proud. You have been an excellent drill instructor, and for that, I shall always be in your debt."

"You are very welcome, Baltor, but you may now call me by my name, as I am no longer your instructor. The only time I insist you use my title is when I'm with another student, or any other members of the Guild. Before I take you to the Hall of Education, let's first get you cleaned up at the bathhouse, and then go eat some grub. Okay?"

Baltor looked himself up and down and said with a smile, "Good idea, sir."

Before the two had climbed up the ladder that led into the fountain room, Humonus first showed Baltor the secret latch. He then ordered, "Ensure that you do not tell anyone where this latch is, okay?"

"Yes, sir."

Humonus next led him to the bathhouse, which happened to be currently empty. "There are some soap and towels on the shelf over there. While you take your bath, I have some things I need to get in my room, but I'll be back. Also, the medic told me to tell you not to get your bandages wet." He then left.

Baltor bathed and kept his bandages dry. By the time that he wrapped a towel around his waist, he saw that Humonus had just returned. His right hand held a pair of black boots. His left hand not only clasped some underwear and socks, yet a couple of metal hangers with some clothes hanging on them.

Humonus sang, "I purchased some brand-new clothes for you to wear!"

"Really? Thank you very much, sir!"

"No problem—I hope you like them." Humonus said as he handed over everything but the socks and boots, turned around, and waited for Baltor to put them on.

The t-shirt was blue and the pants were black—Baltor found that everything fit perfectly. Once fully dressed, he asked, "What do you think?"

Humonus turned back around, gave the up-down look for a few seconds, and said, "Nice! Now put these on." He proceeded to hand over the socks, as well the boots.

Baltor slid on the socks and then the black, knee-high boots that also fit perfectly.

"One more thing," Humonus said as he pulled a comb out of his pocket and handed it over, "There's a mirror over there, so you can comb your hair."

Baltor nodded, took the comb, walked over to the mirror, and combed his hair that reached halfway down his back, until it was nice and neat—this process took him about fifteen minutes, since he hadn't combed his hair in ages.

As he looked into the mirror, besides seeing himself, he also saw that Humonus now held a small golden ring in between his right index and middle finger.

Humonus informed, "With this, you can secure that hair of yours so it doesn't fly all around."

While turning around, Baltor asked in shock, "Is that real gold?"

Humonus smiled, and said, "Yes, it is. You earned it."

Baltor took the ring, pulled his hair together until it was tight, pushed it through the ring, and then pulled up the ring until it grew snug in his hair.

After Humonus had turned Baltor around by the shoulders until facing the mirror, and giving the boy a chance to admire himself, he concluded with a sigh, "Well. The time has come for us to head to the chow hall. You look great!"

"Yes, sir! I mean, Humonus."

After giving an understanding smile, Humonus next led Baltor to the fancy restaurant they had eaten during his trial, where they ate an incredibly delicious lunch.

While they were eating, quite a few of the other Guild members threw friendly smiles or waves at Baltor—he smiled or waved back.

Once done with lunch, they headed to the Hall of Education. Nearly five minutes later, they arrived.

Baltor realized that this "hall" wasn't a hall at all, yet a massive library containing thousands upon thousands of scroll-cases and books, all of which were systematically stored upon sturdy oak racks spanning from floor to ceiling throughout this room that was bigger than any room he had ever seen before.

Nearly a minute later, they came to stand before an old woman, who was sitting behind an oak desk that contained only three objects sitting upon the top.

One, a logbook bearing Baltor's name: two and three, a quill lying in a small bottle of black ink.

After gesturing to the woman with his left hand, Humonus informed, "Madame-Librarian Sharice will help you select your classes. As for me, I must get going. I've got 'a hot date' in an hour I got to get ready for."

"Sounds fun!"

"Oh," Humonus replied with a smile, "I'm sure it will be. Well good luck to you, Baltor!"

Baltor clasped Humonus's extended hand with his own, while jubilantly saying, "Thank you so very much for everything, Humonus."

After one last departing smile, Humonus released Baltor's hand, and he departed.

Baltor turned around, and asked, "So, Madame Sharice, what classes can I take?"

After listening to a very long list of introductory courses, which list took Sharice nearly five minutes to recite, he spent quite a few minutes to consider all his options—one course Baltor silently promised to himself that he would take very soon was archery, once his arm was fully healed.

Meanwhile, Sharice opened up his logbook to the first blank page, which was twenty-five pages after the beginning page; once so, she picked up the quill in her right hand, patiently waiting while Baltor inwardly deliberated.

Once ready, nearly a minute later, he said, "I wish to take the Pavelian language course, basic math, history, and unlocking doors and safes. That's it for now."

While writing his selections and weekly schedule down, she informed, "School for you begins tomorrow morning—do not be tardy to a single class, or it will count against you as a strike. Three strikes and you'll be expelled from that course. One unexcused absence and you're instantly expelled. Though all classes are one hour in length and conducted six days a week, the days and times will differ because of your other classes. Now, do you know where you're going to be residing?"

"Umm," Baltor said, "I've decided to stay in the bunkhouse until I can afford my own place."

"Okay, no problem," Sharice said. "You may stay in the advanced students' bunkhouse as long as you wish, as most students do until they make some money, but there are five rules that you must never break.

"One, you are allowed to leave the property whenever you're not in school, but never use the palace entrances—use the tunnels below. We'll even give you a fake ID, in case you ever have a run-in with city guards.

"Two, do not go to your former bunkhouse anymore.

"Three, do not chat with any other advanced students in your new bunkhouse, even if you become friends with another advanced student. Outside the barracks is fine.

"Four, if any beginning student tries to chat with you, do not say a word but instantaneously walk away, for there are twenty-four-hour monitors observing and recording everything.

"And rule number five; you are allowed to associate yourself with advanced students when you and they are not in class, but do not bother the instructors when they are with their students, beginning or advanced. Violation of any rule bears the minimum punishment of a whipping, or the maximum punishment of death, which punishment will be strictly enforced by the High Council! Any questions?"

Baltor replied, "No, ma'am."

"Good," Sharice answered. "Once our meeting is adjourned, I am going to have one of my many assistants show you the safe way to your new bunkhouse and how to avoid the booby-traps. Never disarm those traps, even when you learn how. And finally, for the next week, an assistant will retrieve you from your bunkhouse at 6:30 a.m., escort you to your classes throughout the day, and take you back to the bunkhouse after your final class. Any questions for me?"

"No, ma'am," Baltor answered.

"Have a nice day," Sharice chimed aloud.

She immediately pulled a bell out of her desk drawer, rang it six times, and only a minute later, an average-looking teenage girl arrived.

Baltor didn't know who she was, but he did see that she carried an unlit lamp in her right hand.

Sharice said, "Take this young man to the advanced students' bunkhouse, please."

The girl replied, "Yes, Madame Sharice. Follow me, boy."

"Thanks," Baltor said to Sharice, just before he followed behind the girl.

On the way there, which trip was without any conversation whatsoever, he silently decided that after he had finished all his classes each day, he would continue to train in the obstacle courses, just to keep up his physique—that is, after the two-week period to heal up until he got the stitches removed. Today he would take the day off, other than settling in. He also decided that he would firmly ignore everyone, except for instructors, medics, masters and mistresses.

It was shortly after making this decision that they entered back into the training cavern, about forty-five minutes later. She next headed for the second pitch-black tunnel to the right, and once inside, the girl made a right-hand turn at the first bend in the tunnel a hundred feet away, turned on her lamp, and turned around.

Once Baltor had arrived at her location, only a second later, she said indifferently, "As you will come to learn about this particular tunnel, there are seven natural pitfalls and four booby traps. All of them are lethal. For the most part, you will only need to stay on the right side of the tunnel. Only twice will you have to move your way to the left side. Memorize exactly where everything's at, because you are not allowed to carry torches or any other forms of light."

"Okay."

Baltor followed, observing where the pitfalls and traps were, and how to avoid them, by counting his footsteps.

Once they had arrived at their destination, about fifteen minutes later, the girl turned off her lamp, and left without a word spoken. He did not speak back to her either.

Baltor saw that this new barracks looked similar to his old barracks, but there were footlockers and/or wall lockers posted next to just about every bunk—thirty of them. Most of the beds were neatly made up with nice sheets, blankets and pillows. The remaining few had a green blanket that had been rolled up and placed at the head of the bed. Sitting on top of the roll was a thick, white pillow.

While eating some dinner that had been sitting in covered wooden bowls on the table, which dinner was a large turkey leg, some spicy mashed potatoes and some unknown type of cooked, green vegetable, he chose a bunk that sat in the middle of the room. After all, all the corner bunks were picked.

Following dinner, he made his way for his bunk, unrolled the blanket, hopped into bed, and lay his head down on the pillow.

While lying there and staring up at the ceiling trying to get tired enough so he could go to sleep, he decided to stay in the bunkhouse until he could earn some honest money and afford his own place. True he was technically learning how to become "a thief," but in secret, he thought of himself as "an adventurer!" Perhaps one day, he might even become "Drill Instructor Baltor."

It was upon thinking these last thoughts that he passed out.

The next morning, as Sharice had promised, a male assistant politely woke Baltor from sleep, and escorted him to all his daily classes. While the classes went on, that day and for the next week, the assistant took care of other daily duties he had on his list.

Ten school days later, after Baltor's final class of adding/subtracting had finished, he entered the training area. Surprise hit him upon discovering that Humonus had a brand-new student—this time a girl.

From a distance, Baltor watched in silent amusement, and recollection, as the hardcore drill instructor screamed insults in the young girl's face, while egging her on to do more pushups or sit-ups!

Baltor held back a laugh of remembrance as he watched her struggle, seconds before he made his way to the bunkhouse for some much-needed dinner. It was while he ate that he first wondered to himself if Humonus ever took a vacation.

Five days later, which was exactly two weeks after Baltor had first received the stitches, Racine paid his fourth visit to the bunkhouse. After cautiously waking Baltor up by wiggling a couple of his toes, Racine revealed that he had come to check on the stitches.

Baltor sat up in bed and extended his bandaged arm out, whereupon Racine used a pair of scissors to cut off all the exterior and interior wrappings.

After taking "a professional look" at the stitches, the medic informed that they were "good to go." He immediately began the process of cutting the stitches off.

Baltor not only expressed his appreciation during this painless medical procedure, yet he asked an important question, which was how much additional time he should take before taking archery?

Racine's answer was, "Two weeks."

Right before his departure, perhaps thirty seconds after his arrival, Baltor expressed his sincerest appreciations. Only seconds later, he lay back down in his bunk, closed his eyes, and quickly fell asleep.

The next morning, after having awoken and eaten a hearty breakfast of warm porridge with a mug of milk, he was at his first class of the day—reading and writing.

That evening, after his final class of arithmetic had concluded, Baltor painlessly trained through several of the obstacles courses before calling it "a day."

The following morning, Baltor visited the Hall of Education. There, Sharice granted Baltor the basic archery course in two weeks hence, as he was excelling in most of his classes.

And two weeks later at 3:00 p.m., Baltor began his first day of archery—quickly he found that he was getting the hang of it!

Several months passed and Baltor's level of education steadily increased. Not only had he just finished graduating the basic arithmetic and archery courses, yet he had just begun taking advanced arithmetic, archery, and the Mauritian language course.

As for unlocking door and safes course, this was another matter, as Baltor didn't have a whole lot of patience for the very complicated locks that Instructor Thaven would make Baltor unlock—after all, the student couldn't unlock any of them within Thaven's tight timeframes! It took him two semesters to graduate this course instead of one.

Those months turned into years, and Baltor had finally become a sixteen-year-old who stood at five-feet-nine-inches tall with a weight of one hundred and seventy pounds, had a peach-fuzz goatee, and possessed a slightly manly, crackly voice. He even had earned a week's worth of decent clothes (both outer- and underwear) that allowed him a hundred percent maneuverability—thanks to Humonus's kind generosities whenever Baltor received an "A".

Already, Baltor had graduated seven thieving-related courses so far! Moreover, he could now speak, write, and understand four languages—Pavelian, Mauritian, Thoriumite and Savekian. Just as impressive was the fact that he had graduated advanced algebra and geometry, and had just begun to take basic biology and chemistry, only one semester earlier.

As for where he lived, because he always put higher priority on his education over a job, he continued residing in the bunkhouse, though he now had his own private corner to himself, as well a large wall locker with a steel lock and key—also gifts from Humonus. The handle of the key looped around the silver necklace, which was always around Baltor's neck.

The evening after Baltor's seventeenth birthday, another two inches taller and ten pounds heavier, just after he had exited his basic-etiquette class and was heading down the hallway that led to the fountain room, he saw Lydia approaching from the other direction in the hallway.

As Lydia passed by Baltor, she did not recognize him because he had his hair pulled back into a ponytail, he had facial hair, and he kept his body washed and clean. As for him, however, he had never forgotten her image.

After all the years that he had known Lydia, he was still very much in love with her. Even though she was fifteen years his senior, he dreamt of her quite often.

He turned around and exclaimed with his manly voice, "Mistress Lydia—how are you?"

She turned around until she faced Baltor, and as she threw a puzzled look at him, she asked, "Do I know you?"

As his eyes squinted just a bit, a look of remembrance suddenly crossed her face, and she exclaimed, "Baltor—how on earth are you?" She then threw him a tight hug, but as she loosened her hold so she could look at him yet again, she added excitedly, "Woooow. You look spectacular!"

Even though his cheeks had been turning red from the compliment, he managed to answer, "Good, very good, my Mistress."

She gave him yet another tight hug, before saying, "That's sooo great to hear!" She pulled herself away for the third time to get an even better look at the young man, and said, "My oh my, what a man you have turned out to be!"

Suddenly gaining courage, perhaps from all her really nice compliments, he spoke aloud his heart and mind, "My Mistress, there's something I've been meaning to ask you for some time now, but I've never really had the nerve to do it before—until now. May I ask you that question?"

"Of course you may, Baltor."

Baltor was just about to pop the question, but unexpectedly, his throat had clogged itself up with phlegm, the nerves throughout his entire body felt on fire, and his head began to swirl!

Lydia's face instantly turned from happiness to concern, and so she asked, "Are you okay?"

He cleared his throat a few times, took a deep breath and slowly released it. After taking another deep breath, and feeling "calm, cool & collected," he asked, "Would you like to go out with me sometime... like on a date?"

She immediately looked away from him and toward the ground—only a second later, she completely released her hug, answering, "I can't, Baltor."

His eyes and face instantly betrayed shock and hurt, but he still managed to ask, "Why not?"

"Baltor..." she confessed with a pause, "I'm with someone else and am deeply in love with him."

With disappointment and sadness now clear in his voice, he asked, "What? Who?"

As soon as she saw the crushed look, she added sympathetically, "I have been for three years now."

With exasperation growing in his voice every single second, he asked, "Did you know what it really was that helped me through all my training and tests? It was you! Even though my mind didn't know it at the time, my heart has always known. I'm in love with you, Lydia! Who cares about our little age difference?"

She tried to console, "Baltor, you are so young and so obviously very handsome. There is no doubt in my mind that you can have your pick of any number of beautiful women your age. As for you and me, this can never be. Can't we just keep being great friends?"

With tears that had unexpectedly begun to pour out of his eyes and down his face, he said, "I... I've got to go."

"Wait, Baltor!" she called out, but it was too late, for he had already booked down the hallway toward the exit.

She was about to chase him down, but only after having taken a couple steps, she changed her mind. She decided that it was best if Baltor remained alone.

Two more very fruitful years passed as he continued to reside at the bunkhouse—Baltor was now nineteen, six-feet tall with a weight of one hundred and eighty-five pounds, and sporting a six-inch-long goat-tee that he kept braided. Typically but not always, he shaved off the mustache and three-quarters of the sideburns.

Diligently he pursued further into his education, especially his thieving-related courses—rare were the times he ever left the Guild, instead studying from a book, or two, or three before falling to sleep late at night.

Thus, he had already mastered eight different languages from all of the neighboring countries, as well learned their histories and customs. All of his teachers were highly impressed by the uncanny amount of intelligence Baltor possessed.

One particular subject that he had really enjoyed learning was world history, especially about Mauritia's history, the only city of the Vaspan Empire. And the fact that the legendary Sedious Vaspan, ruler of the Vaspan Empire, was actually the younger brother of Sultan Brishavo Helenus XI, ruler of the Sharia Empire.

The powerful family feud first started approximately twenty-five years ago, when Prince Vaspan Helenus had become so enraged when his elder brother had refused to share any of his empire. Therefore, he promoted himself to "Sedious Vaspan the Magnificent," stole one-third of the Sultan's troops while the Sultan was away, and without a drop of blood spilt, conquered another of the three cities of the Sharia Empire—the city of Mauritia. Of course, none of this information was listed in Pavelian history books, but it was clearly mentioned in Thoriumite history books.

Finally, regarding the feud, because of the lost wars and years that the Sultan spent trying to recapture his stolen city, which always ended in failure, he continued to have only two thriving cities—Pavelus and Lasparus. After all, Sedious Vaspan had quickly fortified his own beloved city with huge labyrinth walls that surrounds her to date—very effective defense for stopping massive armies!

Oh yeah, Baltor loved learning anything and everything in school! So perhaps because of this, the times were very, very, very rare when he saw Lydia, only twice, but that was okay by him, for knowledge had become his new passion and love.

Inevitably, Baltor and Humonus had become really good friends. Once or twice every week they would spar against each other in the training area, in order to improve their fighting skills. And on a rare occasion, perhaps once every other month, they would even go out to a bar for a few drinks of ale, for fun....

CHAPTER VIII

Finally, the day came when Baltor graduated ninety-nine percent of the courses he was allowed to take as an advanced student, which timeframe occurred days before his twentieth birthday. He pretty much looked the same as he did before, except that he had gained five more pounds of muscles.

Of course, there were a little more than fifty more courses he would be able to take upon achieving higher ranks in the Guild, which made him forty-seven percent of the way done. His two final courses had been equestrian combat, and its prerequisite course, equestrian riding. He had learned very well how to ride a horse, and to fight while riding at a full gallop.

The only course that he could have taken yet purposefully never selected was "picking pockets"—he felt this skill would undermine his purpose, especially as "an honorable thief."

In fact, he now felt so ready to undertake any quest that the Guild could ever ask, that he finally submitted the written petition for Phase Four.

Only one week did he have to wait until he was summoned before the High Council at nine in the morning. He stood before them, all of who were comfortably sitting on their thrones, and whose cast included Bayema, Lydia and Salmot, though not in attendance was the old woman that had silenced the group during Baltor's trial nine years ago, nor Master Lupan.

Sitting in that old woman's place instead was a middle-aged woman, whose long brown hair dropped halfway down her back before it loosely wove itself back up into a bun on the back of her head.

She was the one who pleasantly greeted Baltor with "Good morning to you, Baltor. My name is Mistress Tricia."

He extended his arms out until the entire High Council was within the reach of his arms, and as he bowed a moment later, he said, "Good morning to you all, Masters and Mistresses. Mistress Tricia."

A second later, Tricia went straight to the point, as she asked, "So, you are ready for Phase Four?"

"Yes, my Mistress," he answered confidently.

"In most cases, we do not give our candidates a choice to accept or deny the mission we select—however, in this particular and very unique case, we shall give you that option, Baltor."

He looked a bit surprised for a second at that piece of news. In the next second, he looked just as confident as the reply he gave, "No matter the mission, or missions, that the High Council wishes for me to accomplish, now or in the future, I shall succeed."

"Excellent," Tricia said, but after a short pause, she added, "But please make your final decision only after I've concluded with my rather lengthy briefing, okay?"

This time, the look of curiosity filled his face for a second. In the next second that look once again became poker-faced as he silently nodded his head twice in affirmation.

Tricia first cleared her throat. She began the briefing with a question, "Were you in Pavelus four months back when we experienced the major earthquake?"

"Yes, Mistress Tricia—I was in my chemistry class, which was nearly halfway over for the day. Actually, it was quite fortunate for everyone in the class that Instructor Qels had just begun reading from the next chapter on acid making, when everything and everybody got unexpectedly thrown violently about for nearly ten minutes. To explain the reason I say it's quite fortunate was because we had been experimenting with the powerful acidic solution taught and tested in the previous chapter, the very day before. We could have all been blown to bits!"

Even though Baltor's answer wasn't supposed to be funny whatsoever, several of the High Council members actually did find it to be humorous and began to chuckle quietly.

Not only did Tricia not chuckle, nor look amused, yet she looked sharply to her left and to her right at all seated around her, which silenced all laughers immediately.

Only then did she reveal, "As a result of that earthquake, not only was there a lot of structural damage to many of our buildings, as well our harbor, yet dozens of our underground tunnels had also become sealed or unsealed."

After sucking in a deep breath, she half-sang, "Interestingly enough, two and a half months ago, our clean-up crew discovered about a third of a mile underground, hidden behind a previously-sealed tunnel that became unsealed, a gigantic underground cavern with a lagoon within. The Guild did not know of this cavern's existence before. Located on the other side of the lagoon, there rests a three-foot tall white pedestal, which bears nine pictograms of stars that range from three to twelve."

She paused again, this time for about fifteen seconds so that he could digest all that information. Then she revealed, "Additionally, we discovered the top half to a very interesting map which rested on top of the pedestal. The Guild has already tested and determined that both objects are at least a thousand years old.

"As for the bottom half, someone had intentionally cut the bottom half off into a zigzagging puzzle piece right after the map's construction, most likely the mapmaker. Despite all our best investigative searches into all the surrounding tunnels, some that we had to purposefully unseal, we could not find any more pedestals, nor could we find the second half to the map anywhere.

"The first reason that this particular map is so important is because it reveals just about the entire upper half of the geographical world we dwell upon, which must mean that the second half reveals the entire lower half of the world.

"Before I continue with the briefing, Baltor, do you know why this type of map could be very useful and important to the Guild?"

"I believe I do, my Mistress," Baltor answered. "Because there has never before been produced a world map, or so we previously thought?"

She answered, "Exactly—more than two-thirds of the upper half of the map we currently possess is still uncharted, as the Sultan and his ancestral family have become extremely rich and powerful by focusing all the activities of the empire's cities only on trade with other extremely rich cities and seaports from other continents. They were certainly not doing any major conquests, or at the very minimum, the serious exploration of our own continent, which I think is quite sad and pathetic. For these reasons alone, we wonder often why he bothers to call himself a Sultan at all!"

Once she had concluded that question/statement/joke, most of the High Council began to chuckle.

This time, unlike the first time, she began to chuckle along with them, while looking highly amused at the other members—Baltor didn't laugh, look amused, or even speak.

A few moments later, Tricia looked back at Baltor with a serious expression. She continued, "The second reason that this map is important is because there is a small five-pointed star drawn on the map, which is typically indicative of a capital city, located exactly in the same spot as Pavelus. Though there are no other stars of any kind drawn upon the map, there are dozens of other dots, indicative of cities, spread throughout the entire continent. This authenticated map certainly proves that our city is much more ancient than historians have falsely presumed and taught for the last five hundred years."

Tricia paused yet again, clearing her throat. This time, instead of continuing, she turned her head to the left, and asked, "Will you please continue on in the briefing, Master Fargot? My voice is getting a bit tired."

"I'd be delighted to, Mistress Tricia," Fargot answered in a showman's voice. He continued, "The third and main reason why this map is so important to the Guild is because there is a pictogram of a tower within the center of an unnamed vast jungle far to the east, lying beyond both the equally vast Sharia Desert and Bospa Mountains.

"More than a thousand miles away, this tower supposedly exists. But that's not all—drawn within the tower itself, there is a drawn 'X.' If you're not already aware, 'X' typically marks the spot for a treasure on a map..."

Though Baltor nodded, Fargot still paused to let him digest that information for about ten seconds.

Fargot next revealed, "Finally, there is a message written just to the side of the map in an ancient script that has already been translated by one of our expert translators. For the last five years, he has had in his possession a poetry book written in the same runic language and era, and written by an unknown author. By the way, just in case you're wondering, this nearly-useless-and-tattered poetry book that I speak of is entitled *Love, Peace, and Joy*.

"Now, regarding the message on the map, it says, and I quote, 'The Rod of Ro'shain has unspeakable magical power, but it must be used wisely by only the chosen one. If one condition is not met, then the wrath of the gods shall utterly destroy.'"

After a short pause, Fargot then shrugged his shoulders and said, "As Mistress Tricia stated earlier, the other half was ripped long ago—therefore, the Guild regrettably does not know what else was said, Baltor."

Baltor remained silent.

Right away, Tricia cast a look over to Fargot, and asked, "My voice is much better now, Master Fargot—would you mind if I concluded the briefing, please?"

"I do not mind, Mistress Tricia. By all means, please proceed."

Tricia next briefed, "There are two more subjects we need to cover. The first subject is that you will most likely be traveling thousands of miles, which will take you many years until your return to Pavelus, if ever.

"The final subject is that there has never been any tangible proof that magic even exists, despite the centuries the Guild has sought, captured, and tested supposed magical religious artifacts and tomes out from all over the world, sadly enough. In my opinion, we should only be focusing upon treasures of gold and jewels instead of wasting our time on magical mumbo-jumbo."

Many of the other Council members were nodding in agreement, but a few shook their heads negatively.

Tricia concluded, "Therefore, even if both the tower and the rod should happen to still exist if what this mapmaker says is true, this unusual quest will most likely prove to be a big waste of your time."

With another nonchalant shrug to her shoulders, Tricia asked, "So now that I've concluded with my briefing, are you interested in such a quest?"

As Baltor scanned the crowd, he replied, "Not only shall I find this tower if it still exists, but I shall recover the rod, if that too exists." His eyes, a moment later, rested upon Lydia, noting that she had been silently looking at him without expression. He stared back for still another moment without emotions evident.

Tricia instantly drew his attention back to her, as she asked, "Even though this quest may literally take you years to accomplish?"

Baltor answered with a question, "Will I be allowed to take a good look at the pedestal, the map, and the poetry book? Will I also be given enough supplies to at least get me through the formidable desert: a weapon of my choice, some form of reliable transportation, plenty of water and dried rations, and one hundred parsecs, so I can buy all the other traveling supplies I'll need?"

She answered, "Yes, we shall oblige you in all those things you requested."

"Then my answer is yes, my Mistress, I shall take the quest."

Tricia replied with an elated tone of voice, "Excellent. Tomorrow morning at nine, Varce will meet you at your quarters. Varce is not only in possession of the poetry book and your duplicate copy of the map, yet he shall be your translator, teacher, and your guide to the guarded location of the pedestal. When he arrives, the two of you will arrange your busy schedules around each other for the next week—only when Varce is with you can you visit the pedestal, or view the book and map. Next Moonday, you shall depart with your own duplicate of the map. Show the map to no one and defend it with your life. Understood?"

"Yes, my Mistress," Baltor replied. He stood back onto his feet, bowed one last time before the High Council, and turned to leave. Once he had neared the double doors the guards had opened for him, he heard Tricia call out his name.

He turned around, and asked, "Yes, my Mistress?"

"Tell absolutely no one about the details of this top, top, top secret mission either."

"I won't, my Mistress."

For about thirty hours the following week in the library, Varce gave Baltor a crash course in interpreting the strange-looking runic language, though there wasn't a lot to work with. Just about twenty holding-on-by-a-thread pages of poetic material that contained less than a thousand words—for a language that could possibly contain millions.

The following week, Varce took Baltor to the cavern for the very first time—of course they had to pass the two non-uniformed guards, whose orders came from the High Council only to allow these two men to enter.

Upon entering, Baltor surprisingly discovered that this cavern was twice the size of the training cavern—its natural beauties mesmerized him for the first minute or so. Even more astonishing was the fact that not a single rock or stone within the entire cavern had dropped from the earthquake, except for right around the very entrance itself.

Also adding to the beauties was a very lush, green and crystal-like mildew spread thickly upon all the stalactites, stalagmites, and even the ground surrounding this large and obscurely shaped lagoon that nearly took up half the cavern.

Far out of reach of the potentially damaging properties of the mildew rested the white pedestal, which was exactly as Tricia had described.

The remainder of Baltor's time, when not sleeping, eating, training, or shopping, was spent in this cavern with Varce—learning, studying, observing, fiddling, and/or experimenting, though there were no secrets discovered with the pedestal, which was a bit disappointing to the both of them on their eleven different appointments.

Not disappointing at all to Baltor, he spent these occasions learning a whole lot of other useful information, besides the strange language taught by Varce, of who was an unbelievably intelligent man in his early fifties.

Near the end of their final appointment at the library, the day before Baltor's scheduled departure, Varce finally confided that he would have gladly taken the mission had he been twenty years younger. Baltor didn't know what to say, so he just shrugged his shoulders.

Varce simply laughed, and said, "Well, I must be off, young man. Good luck to you in your quest!"

"Thank you, sir, I sincerely appreciate the help," Baltor said.

"No problem. Take care," Varce said just before he bowed, turned around, and exited the library.

Baltor exited too, heading for the bunkhouse. There, he ate his dinner, lay down, and closed his eyes to go to sleep. After all, he had to wake up very early in the morning.

Only seconds before he had drifted off to sleep, a girl bearing a sealed-with-wax scroll in her right hand arrived at his bunk.

In a hushed voice, she ordered, "Baltor, wake up. I have an important message for you to read, which comes directly from the High Council."

By this time, Baltor had not only sat up in bed, yet he had his right hand extended. She handed him the scroll, and once he had firmly gripped it, she released it. Instantly, Baltor observed that the wax bore the official emblem of the Guild.

While she waited, he cracked the wax, opened the scroll, and silently read:

"We—The High Council—have voted and deemed, that because of your usage of the word "weapon" and not "weapons" during your "briefing," you are to only begin your mission with only one weapon—a weapon of your choice from amongst our massive arsenal. Sell or give away any other weapons you may have purchased, other than any knives with a blade of three and a half inches or less—do not try to sneak any other weapons. Once you have finished reading the last word of this letter, go to the weapons' racks, pick the weapon of your choice, and give that weapon to this delivery girl—she will ensure that it is strapped onto the mode of transportation we have selected for you, as well our other promised supplies. In part, we do apologize for any inconveniences this may have caused you, but really, you should think of this all as we do—a challenge! Good luck with your top-secret mission! Masters and Mistresses of the High Council."

The second after he had completed reading the letter, he nonchalantly folded it up and gave it back to the girl.

He next rose to his feet, put on his trousers, socks and boots, and unlocked and opened his wall locker. He pulled out a brand new bow and sheath carrying forty arrows.

After handing it all to the girl, he next pulled out two brand-new daggers, whose blades were six-inches long, and set those daggers onto the bed.

The second his wall locker was locked, two seconds later, he looked over at the girl, cocking his head toward the training area. Understanding the gesture, the girl nodded.

Upon seeing the nod, he turned around and exited the bunk-house—of course, she followed. Once at the training area, he first set the daggers into two empty slots at one of the weapons' racks. He next picked up another weapon lying nearby, which was his weapon of choice—a three-and-a-half-foot long saber with a dual-edged, two-foot long blade that was not only very sharp and lethal, yet perfectly balanced.

After testing out this weapon out for nearly two minutes and discovering that everything about this weapon was still perfect, he extended the handle to the girl. Upon taking it, the girl said with a flirty smile, "Have a good night."

As he headed back to bed, after having similarly responded but without emotion because he wasn't attracted to her, he strongly suspected who was guilty of making all this happen—Master Salmot.

Baltor also realized that there wasn't a damned thing he could do about it, so he might as well think of just about everything as "a challenge."

Before the break of dawn the following morning, he performed his morning routine of eating, showering, and dressing.

Once done, he next began the important task of neatly packing a week's worth of his clothes, socks and drawers into a large water-proofed backpack. It was "packed to the rim" with an extra pair of boots, flint, torches and other camping necessities.

The final stage of packing came upon filling one final medium bag that had hooks attached near the top, which bag contained all his living supplies like soaps, brushes, toothpastes & toothbrushes, a month's worth of dried rations, etc., etc.

After strapping the backpack on tightly, as well picking up the bag, Baltor made his way for the palace's front doors, where his mount was supposed to be located.

Upon exiting the main doors, nearly an hour later, he observed a larger-than-average camel standing on the granite path about sixty feet away.

Standing loosely around the camel and chatting happily away were three people he knew all—too—well. Thus was he sure that this camel was his mode of transportation.

The only one of the three Baltor expected to be there for his departure was Varce—the other two people who surprised the heck out of Baltor, because of their presence, were Humonus and Lydia. All three were unaware to Baltor's presence, of who was walking their way.

Only a second or two later, he observed that it was Humonus who loosely gripped the camel's reins. In between the camel's two humps, there rested a leather saddle topped with thick pillows. And firmly latched onto the sides of the saddle were four leather bags—two on each side—as well as a dozen medium-sized leather flasks. Finally, yet most importantly, he saw the leather sheath that securely held his saber—the one and only weapon in his arsenal.

Once Baltor had drawn to about thirty feet away, his eyes observed that Varce was the first to see Baltor, warmly extend his hand out, wave, and declare, "Hey Baltor! Glad you could make it. Now before I leave, which I must here in a second, I wish you good luck. I hope and pray that I have been of help to you in your most honorable quest, my friend!"

"Thank you, Varce, you already have," Baltor replied sincerely as the two men warmly shook hands.

Once released, Varce nodded one final time to Lydia and Humonus and departed off on his merry way.

Meanwhile, Baltor had already turned to Lydia with a slightly suspicious look, and asked, "So you came to see me off, as well?"

"Of course, Baltor," Lydia replied, throwing him a tight hug of her own. "You're a great friend of mine."

Not only did Baltor feel a little unnerved by the hug, he did not return that hug either. Instead, he asked with quite a bit of sarcasm, "Aren't you afraid that your boyfriend will become upset by your public display of affection?"

Without intending to spill his name, Lydia didn't let release the hug, as she defended, "Salmot has done nothing wrong."

"So that's who your boyfriend is?" was Baltor's indignant reply.

With a cluck of his tongue, he shook his head, answering, "Then I strongly suggest that you let go of me—especially with someone like that!"

Lydia grew visibly offended and hurt by his comment, and so she let go. She looked at Baltor for only a second longer—with that same look—before walking very briskly for the palace's front doors. Meanwhile, both men silently watched her until the guards closed the doors behind her.

Once she was gone, Humonus turned back to Baltor, and said, "You should watch what you say to people, especially to a member of the High Council. That was clearly a sign of disrespect!"

Angrily, Baltor pointed his index finger at Humonus and retorted, "It is my belief that she disrespected me by manipulating me and my feelings from the get-go!"

Humonus didn't immediately respond to Baltor's accusation but waited for him to lower his hand first. He then softly said, "Baltor, she didn't use you. She loves you, but not in that way—she looks at you like a little brother. Many times during your training, she came to me and asked about your progress, though she did not have to do this. In my belief, had it not been for her, you would still be a vagrant on the streets, and quite probably, dead."

With a clear look of anger still on his face, Baltor took off his backpack, tied it onto the other side of the saddle where there was some free room, climbed onto his camel, and grabbed the reins.

"Baltor, Baltor, Baltor," Humonus finally said, "you will have plenty of time to consider my words of wisdom. Perhaps by the time you return, you will understand."

Baltor was about to snap the reins, but Humonus also grabbed them before he could.

After another sigh of resignation, Humonus added, "Before you depart, there are two crucial things I need to tell you, which Mistress Lydia mentioned to me before your arrival. The first is that your map and new identification papers are safely tucked away within this here pouch."

Baltor asked with a sneer, "She told you about the map?"

"Only that there is one—"

"Why'd she tell you about something that's been labeled 'top, top, top secret' by the Guild?"

Humonus answered with both a shocked look to his face, and also a question, "Why—don't you trust me anymore?"

"Of course I do, Humonus, I'm just quite a bit surprised. The High Council did classify this mission: top-top secret."

"Maybe she's the type of woman who can't keep her mouth shut?" Humonus once again answered with a question.

After a short pause to contemplate his friend's words, Baltor said, "Maybe. So what was the second thing you had to tell me?"

"Something that was told to you long ago—there are double agents within every guild. You can bet that there are others besides me who also know about the map and shall attempt to steal it from you along the way so that they can take the treasure."

"Humonus, my friend, I'd like to thank you once again for your words of wisdom. I shall guard the map with my life."

Without another word, Humonus let go of the reins.

Baltor was about to snap those reins, but instead he looked back and asked, "Oh, Humonus?"

"Yes, Baltor."

"Would you please do me a favor?"

Humonus said, "You name it, my friend, and it shall be done."

"Would you please tell Mistress Lydia that I'm sorry for the immature way I've been behaving? I'm just, I'm just—"

Humonus interrupted, "You're just in love, Baltor. I shall tell her as soon as you are gone."

"Thank you, my friend, and goodbye."

"Goodbye to you, my friend."

Baltor looked ahead to the gates of the thieves' guild, and was about to snap the reins for the second time. But Humonus suddenly remembered something. "Oh wait—Baltor!"

In turn, Baltor looked back to his old friend. "Yes?"

After pulling something out of his front pocket, and holding it inside his closed left fist, Humonus said, "I have a gift for you."

"What?"

Instead of answering, Humonus extended his closed fist out in front of him and said, "Take it."

Baltor extended his right hand out, open-palmed, and took the golden object that had just fallen into his hand. As he looked at it closer, he could see an eighth-inch-thick gold necklace that even had a gold arrowhead as its ornament.

"Wow," Baltor could only say.

Humonus asked with a very cunning smile, "So you like it?"

"I love it—thanks, my friend!"

"Just so you know… there is something very special about that arrowhead."

"No way." Baltor realized with chills that ran up and down his body! His gaze strayed to the scar on his left forearm.

"Yup!" Humonus replied with quite a bit of excitement. He next said in a commanding tone of voice, "Let it always be a reminder to you that you can accomplish anything if you set your mind to it."

As Humonus had said his last statement, Baltor donned the necklace and gazed at it once again adoringly. It was just big enough where if he looked down, he would always see it!

Humonus concluded, "Goodbye, my friend. You come back soon now, you hear?"

With a single tear that streamed from Baltor's right eye and down his cheek, he looked back over, and replied, "I will! You know, in my opinion, I think the Guild should make you an official master! Hopefully long before the time I come back, which I will, they will see this as well and make it so... Master Humonus."

With that, Baltor looked back to the gates, and lightly flicked the reins on the camel to spur it on.

A minute later, the guards opened the gates to the thieves' guild, and then Baltor departed. Humonus silently watched until his friend was completely out of sight before he re-entered the main palace.

Five minutes later, Baltor approached the first of the inner checkpoints within the city. After he had pulled out the new id that stated he was an "upper class" man whose name was "Lord Poleax," he handed the paperwork to a guard.

That guard handed it to his sergeant, who then checked to make sure that it was still valid and official. After a bow, the supervisor said, "You may pass, Lord Poleax."

Baltor returned a nod of his own and passed.

About two hours later, which included a fifteen-minute shopping trip at the bazaar to get camping supplies and five months of dried rations, he passed through the final checkpoint that would lead him out into the vast Sharia Desert.

By this time, he was keenly aware of the fact that there were two riders on horseback following at a distance of about three hundred and fifty feet behind him, though he did not make this detection obvious. Without looking back once, Baltor continued to ride out the opened gates.

Almost another hour had passed, before he heard the galloping sounds of hoofs coming from behind—he knew that his followers were ready to attack.

Just as the galloping sounds began to draw closer and closer, he first tugged straight back upon the reins with both of his hands, which caused the camel to stop in its tracks.

Baltor, with his left hand, pulled the reins to the left, which caused his camel to begin turning in that same direction. As for his right hand, that had already drawn out his saber while raising it straight over his head.

Although they were still about eighty feet behind him, Baltor observed that it was the same two riders, still both wearing turbans and veils to hide their identities.

Only now, both riders had a sword raised high into the air; the one on the left held the sword in the left hand, while the one on the right held his sword in the right hand.

A few seconds later, just as the riders were nearing fifty feet, the rider on the right immediately pulled hard on the reins to the right, which caused that rider's horse to sharply veer in that direction. Meanwhile, the rider on the left pulled hard on the reins to the left, which caused his or her horse to veer to the left.

About twenty seconds later, both riders stopped their horses at the same time—the first rider was about thirty feet away to his left, while the second rider to the right was about forty feet—he was outflanked, but that was okay by Baltor.

Without fear, he turned his camel ninety more degrees, until he faced both riders out of the corner of each eye, and then he relaxed his grip on the reins, which caused the camel to stop—after all, he was quite aware that the horses could easily outrun his camel.

In unison, both riders snapped their reins while crying out, "Hee-yah!" Both voices, Baltor noted, sounded manly.

What seemed only seconds later yet at the very same time, the two unknown men drew their swords back in order to slice Baltor into tiny pieces! Meanwhile, Baltor had just risen up on his feet on top of the saddle though his body remained in a crouching position, and then he patiently waited.

At the precise moment, he twisted his body, before leaping off his camel and toward the closer of the two riders—the one on his left.

While still flying through midair, Baltor performed a quick roundhouse swing—the saber's very sharp edge not only chopped off the head of the first rider, yet it even caused his body to jerk back in the saddle, which in turn caused his hands to jerk back upon the reins. A moment later, the horse not only stopped galloping in its tracks, yet it then reared back and threw off the headless corpse!

Already had both of Baltor's hands met the ground before him, just before he performed a forwards roll with his sword paralleled to the ground—a moment later, he was back on his feet in the ready position with saber still clutched in his right hand.

Meanwhile, the other rider, due to Baltor's unexpected maneuver, had completely missed striking with the initial sword attack; this rider continued to ride in the direction he was going for ten seconds before turning his horse around.

Without pause, Baltor hurried over to the rider-less horse, hopped into the saddle, and then snapped the reins just in time; as his newly acquired horse bolted forward, he heard the sounds of the rider's sword zinging just inches near his left ear!

The living rider, being more cautious than his dead friend, did not pursue, but pulled back on the reins to stop his horse.

Once Baltor had gotten his horse about thirty feet away, he turned his horse around, and challenged, "You want some of this? Come and get it!"

Instead of the rider coming in as Baltor had anticipated, he saw the rider turn the horse around toward the direction of the camel, snap the reins, kick his feet hard into the stirrups, and cry out, "Hee-yah!"

The horse began to gallop hard and fast toward the camel.

Baltor now realized that the rider's goal was not himself, but the map. He immediately snapped hard the reins on his horse.

As the rider rode by the camel a few seconds later, his sword was extended; the very pouch containing the map was cut; in mid-air was the pouch caught, and again, his horse's reins were snapped.

Baltor was only about fifteen feet behind him, all the while continuously snapping the reins and kicking his stirrups into the sides of the horse, in order to get it to go even faster. Fortune smiled again upon him, as his horse ultimately turned out to be a bit faster, for with every passing second, he drew nearer.

The rider kept glancing back at Baltor, and once he saw Baltor only about four feet behind, he waved his sword high into the air in warning.

After one final snap on the reins, Baltor stood on the saddle. With one huge leap, he plummeted into the back of the rider, which caused their weapons to fly out of their hands, as well the pouch, and finally for the two of them to crash into the ground!

For several minutes, the wrestling was on. Just like before when he battled Thesmul, this opponent was more skilled and soon gained the upper position, this time with fingers already clutched around Baltor's throat and squeezing ... *murderously*!

119

This time, Baltor knew exactly what to do when this type of situation happened. He thrust his knee hard into his opponent's groin area, pushed the opponent off and then rolled right on top.

Baltor threw hard punches into his masked opponent's face, left and right, repeatedly—perhaps a dozen hits and a dozen seconds passed before he finally had his opponent knocked out cold...

Breathing raggedly, he removed the veil and hood, becoming completely surprised when he saw just whom this person was—Salmot!

At that moment, he could have picked up his saber lying in arm's reach, and easily killed this ruling member of the High Council. In his mind's eye, however, he saw Lydia's smiling face while her voice resolutely defended many years before, "I'm with someone and am deeply in love with him." For this reason alone, Baltor chose not to kill this vermin of a man.

Instead, he pocketed the veil and turban, before grabbing his saber and rising to his feet. It was only then that he observed with a bit of disappointment that Salmot's sword, which was also laying on the ground nearby, had gotten severely bent during the fight and was now unusable. After picking up the pouch, he shooed one horse away, hopped on the other and followed the trail back, all the while searching for his camel.

Perhaps fifteen minutes later, he located his camel traveling westbound toward Pavelus. Once he got near his camel, he hopped off the horse, shooed that horse, climbed into the saddle of his camel, and then the two made their journey east....

More than four months passed as Baltor and the camel that he had named Valuspo traveled their way through hundreds of miles of the "deadly" Sharia Desert, yet "Lady Luck" blessed them in quite a few ways, many times over!

For one, they ran across nearly a dozen oases, some bigger than others, each consisting of palm trees, shrubbery and a pool of water. There, they were able to replenish their water supplies though not always food supplies, except for the occasional fresh fruits which only lasted two days at the most, which was why he strictly rationed out his dried rations. Before they left each oasis, he always ensured that Valuspo had a chance to eat and drink, and that every water canteen was full before they left.

The second blessing was that even though his path crossed several times with different caravans of travelers, especially around the oases, all of them left him alone in peace. Though wary at all times, he never sensed anyone following, especially Salmot.

And the third blessing was, throughout this trip, there were only four mild sandstorms, which blew in from the west or north. Whenever one came about, Baltor covered his own head with the turban and face veil as quick as he could, before just-as-quickly using his blanket to cover Valuspo's head and wrapping twenty feet of rope over and around the blanket at the base of his camel's neck, so it wouldn't fly away. Standing in place, they would then wait the storm out; and once over, sometimes several hours later, only then did they continue on their "merry way."

On a geographical note, it was during the first five months and twenty-four days that they passed through desert terrains of all types, primarily rolling sand dunes. Throughout these last two days of travel, however, the sands had sharply rose in elevation, which became interspersed by small to large patches of rock or vegetation, and finally, replaced by rocky hills bearing small random patches of prairie grass, cactus and palm trees....

CHAPTER IX

Finally, the morning came when the sun rose, Baltor awoke and looked eastbound, observing tiny jagged mountain peaks throughout that entire horizon, approximately fifty or so miles away—the Bospa Mountains!

By noon, and another ten miles closer, he could even make out a very wide and fertile valley where he could safely cross. Without stopping his camel, he pulled out the map in order to check his co-ordinates, but after gazing at it for a few moments, he muttered aloud to Valuspo, "Hmmm. It appears that there is no exact way of knowing where I am on this map; the mapmaker just scribbled a bunch of angled lines to indicate the general shape of the mountain range, while certainly giving no clues as to the best route to pass them. But that's all good—all we have to remember is that we have to keep heading east, right Valuspo?"

Valuspo turned his head back and grunted in agreement. It wasn't until late that night that Baltor decided to stop and set up camp, which passed by without incident. The next morning, he happily discovered that he had halved the distance to the mountains.

Well into the afternoon a day later, they finally entered the fertile valley that mainly consisted of four-foot tall patches of prairie grass. Spread chaotically about in various-sized clusters were lush green trees. All the while, he listened to the songs of birds, primarily sparrows, as they played amongst one another just about everywhere up there in the clear, blue skies.

Up ahead and to his left, his keen eyes spotted several deer that had just started to bolt away from a small lagoon. He lightly tugged on the reins until his camel faced that lagoon.

After arriving nearly fifteen minutes later, he hopped to the ground, leading his camel by the reins to drink and refill. While his camel drank, Baltor pulled out all the water canteens in order to refill them.

Once he had hung the filled-up canteens back onto his camel, he pulled out some dried jerky from the bag, plopped onto the ground, and began to eat lunch and drink some water. After a thirty-minute break, he hopped back onto his camel's back, and they pressed on.

It was when the furious colors of the dusky evening set in that Baltor decided to make camp. After hopping off the camel and tying him to a tree stump, he compiled together a bunch of dead twigs and branches, collected some rocks while forming them into a complete circle around the twigs, lit the campfire with his flint, and then began to relax about ten feet away.

However, as Baltor continuously listened to Valuspo munch on some grass, his own stomach started to grumble yet again. He stood up, pulled out a piece of jerky from the bag, which he had a dozen pieces/meals left, and began to mindlessly gnaw on it.

Suddenly, "a brilliant idea" crossed his mind—hunt for some fresh dinner before nightfall!

Baltor therefore used all of his stealth skills, and only five minutes later, had caught an unsuspecting rabbit.

After snapping its neck, he headed back to camp, and once there, he created a poker from a stick, skinned the rabbit as best he could with his saber, stuck a poker through the carcass, sat down near the fire, and then held the poker over the fire. The rabbit slowly began to roast.

Night finally set in, and approximately forty minutes later, Baltor ate heartily. Once dinner was over, Baltor, who now had a full stomach, fell fast asleep. The night passed by without incident.

Just after sunrise the next morning, he packed everything up on his camel, eliminated all signs that there had even been a camp, hopped on his camel, and then continued on his journey deeper into the heart of the mountains.

He immediately noticed that the valley continued to escalate upward, as did the mountain peaks; and by dusk, he felt the temperatures had gotten a tad bit chillier.

After tracking another rabbit down and killing it, he set up a campfire, made and ate his dinner, and went straight to sleep—this time sleeping with the blanket wrapped over him.

The next morning, he awoke and they pressed on. The valley continued higher and higher; and by afternoon, he not only observed that there were small patches of snow here and there on the ground, yet most of the trees were now pine.

It was then that he decided to put on an extra layer of clothes and socks, after dusting off most of the desert sands.

Afternoon turned into night, but despite the campfire nearby, he shivered quite a bit underneath his thin blanket and two layers of clothes. Barely was he able to fit one final layer of clothes on.

Valuspo apparently wasn't happy with the weather changes either, as he kept snorting his irritations out. Moreover, a light snow fell from the sky for most of the night.

While they both fought against the below-freezing temperatures to get to sleep, he realized that the blanket and a small fire would simply not provide adequate protection for the nights to come, for he or for his camel.

Although it is true that two creative ideas sprang forth in his mind on how to attain that protection, he was dismally aware that he did not possess the skills to accomplish them. Those ideas were, one, make a bow and arrow in order to make a ranged attack upon at least one large animal: two, strip, cut, and sew together some cold weather attire for them both from the furs.

The furs from what? Baltor then silently asked himself. *I haven't, brrrr, seen any large animals around here, other than those two brown creatures that bolted like lightning away from me back at the lagoon, a couple days ago. Brrr.*

His last thought before falling asleep was, *I wonder why the Guild doesn't offer a fur-making course—I certainly would have taken it… Brrrr… ignore the cold, Baltor! Ignore the cold….*

The next morning, he awoke—cold, stiff and tired. While rubbing his hands briskly over his arms and legs in order to warm them up from the cold, brisk air, he observed that there was a good one-inch layer of snow everywhere. It had just stopped snowing several hours before he had woken up.

It was then that he heard Valuspo shaking his head, grunting out his irritations, and prancing around as far as the reins would allow him—all at the same time.

With a sigh of resignation, Baltor decided to let Valuspo go. He first set the backpack onto the ground, then the water canteens, then the two saddlebags and then the saddle itself.

He next opened his backpack, stuffing as much as he could into it—food supplies, a half-dozen water canteens, flint, map, ID, rations, fifty-foot rope, and of course, the other empty large bags. On the outside of his backpack, he tied two of his water canteens. As for his saber-carrying sheath, he tied that onto his belt using a piece of leather string.

After hiding the saddlebags, the saddle, and the remaining water canisters in a small grouping of trees, he marked the spot where he had stashed them in his brain. He next slung the backpack on, before heading up the trail.

A few minutes later, he laughed in amusement as he could still hear Valuspo following behind. He turned around to face his friend, patted him gently on the face, and then said, "Valuspo, you need to go, boy. Where I am heading, you would not want to go... it's probably going to get much colder than this. You are free." He turned back around and continued to head up the trail while his camel continued to follow.

Nearly five minutes later, Baltor laughed over his shoulder, "Well, I can't force you to leave my side, my friend, but I'm willing to bet that you will go soon enough."

Valuspo grunted with irritation, yet continued to follow.

By noon, snow had begun to fall again. Two hours later, two more inches of snow covered the ground and trees. Meanwhile, Valuspo continued to follow behind, even though he non-stop complained out his irritations.

Night came, but unfortunately, Baltor could find no dry sticks with which to build a campfire. Even though he tried to start one with the wet ones, all attempts ended in failure.

To make matters worse, the temperature had been steadily dropping all day long. But now that he was no longer moving, he soon began to shiver uncontrollably under his thin blanket. From the shivering and from hearing his camel's cries, it took Baltor many, many long hours to get to sleep that night.

About three hours before dawn, Baltor unexpectedly awoke from a light slumber. Now, the initial reason that caused him to open his eyes was due to some snow that had melted into cold water, which had seeped through his blanket and was dripping onto his bare hand.

Only seconds later, what really woke them both up was a howling sound that filled the night sky—sounding suspiciously like a wolf.

Immediately, Baltor was up on his feet with saber in hand, looking all around in a defensive posture.

Fortunately, due to the white snow that was coupled by the full moon and the quarter-waxing red moon, visibility was good; he estimated that he could see some sixty feet or so. Not surprisingly, he heard Valuspo making very frightened sounds from right behind him.

Suddenly, coming into Baltor's visibility was a pack of animals that were all circling in—dozens of them! Once they had neared to a distance of about thirty feet, Baltor could tell that they were wolves.

Strangely enough, the wolves didn't immediately come in for the attack; instead, they continued to slowly move closer and closer around Baltor and Valuspo. Twenty-five feet. Twenty-three feet. Twenty feet. Fifteen feet. Twelve feet. Eight feet.

Meanwhile, Baltor waited for the sign of their attack with his saber ready.

At five feet, just as the growling commenced, the two nearest wolves leapt in with fangs and claws exposed!

In the next split-second, he sliced off the head of the first wolf with a sideswipe, before rolling directly underneath the other flying wolf. While that wolf flew harmlessly over, he angled his saber up and sliced that wolf's guts open.

Without stopping, he leapt into another roll between his camel's legs, but just as he had gotten back to his feet on the other side, two more wolves were already in mid-leap.

Baltor swung his saber upwards into a wide arc, instantly killing one, but only slicing through the leg of the other. After twirling his sword once in his right hand, he plowed his saber deep into the crippled wolf, just before he rolled to his right to protect his camel's front side.

Upon killing two more wolves, Baltor next rolled back to the right side, killed one more, rolled back through Valuspo's legs, killed two more on the left side, and rolled again back to his rear! An eternity seemed to pass as he continued to take wolf after wolf after wolf out.

Finally, the last few remaining members of the pack retreated into the night.

After having inspected both himself and Valuspo, Baltor next gently patted his frightened camel on the neck to calm him down, remarking, "How lucky we were not to have even gotten injured, much less dead. Hey—maybe I could now fashion some warm fur coats for us!"

In response, Valuspo made another frightened squeal.

"Relax, Valuspo," Baltor whispered soothingly. "We're okay."

Valuspo relaxed.

Though untrained in the art of fur making, which was a course Baltor now greatly wished the Guild had offered, he immediately began to skin the wolves with his saber as best he could.

After he had skinned nine dead wolves to the best of his ability, he wrapped the meat-covered furs on top of Valuspo in order to get his camel warm first. Once done, he then cut slits for his arms and head into the largest fur, and then draped it over his body.

Overall, Baltor had tried to make sixteen furs—fortunately he had only mutilated six of them to the point of being unusable. Neither made complaints about the blood that completely drenched their bodies, especially for the fact that they were now both warm.

Just as he finished with this exhausting and frustrating task, dawn began to fill the skies with ever-lightening colors. Meanwhile, snow started to fall once again from the sky, which had already covered most of the wolf tracks.

Exhausted, he turned to face his camel, and yawned, "Well, Valuspo, I guess you'll be coming with me after all, huh, boy?"

Valuspo slobbered Baltor's face in response.

After he had wiped off all the drool, which took a few seconds, he hopped onto his camel's back, grabbed a morsel of hair on the back of his camel's neck, kicked his boots lightly into his camel's sides, and they continued. He steered by lightly tugging the hair whatever direction he wanted to go.

That afternoon, the valley abruptly ended with an ice-covered cliff face, certainly not climbable by a camel. There also appeared to be a fork in the road that split in two different directions—north and south.

Once they had arrived at the fork, Baltor stopped the camel, and looked in both directions carefully.

He saw that the path to his right that led south consisted of rocky terrain, which continued to escalate higher into the mountains. As he turned his head to look the other direction, he saw that the left path going north had a declining slope and that the terrain looked much smoother.

Without pause, he prompted his camel to the north. That night, he set up camp, and the very cold night passed by without incident.

It was shortly after dawn that they continued. Several hours later, the path switched from veering downward back to veering upward, while increasingly becoming rockier and colder.

By that afternoon, the temperatures had dropped to about twenty degrees Fahrenheit, and snow steadily fell. Despite the fact it snowed all night long, Baltor remained warm in the furs as he slept—Valuspo made no complaints either.

The following morning, despite the fact that there was more than a foot of snow on the outside layer of the furs, he happily discovered that the inside layer had remained dry and warm—that, coupled with the fact that he had slept so well, he felt wonderfully refreshed.

After eating a small breakfast of dried rations, they continued their journey north. The rocky path that they were on not only elevated higher and higher, yet the air got colder and colder still.

Late that afternoon, the blizzard winds had become so tumultuously strong that they began to lift the furs off their bodies— making them both quite cold! Valuspo had already begun to make irritated grunting noises, to confirm his displeasure.

An hour later with no sign of the blizzard stopping, which Baltor took that as an ominous sign, he breathed a sigh of exasperation, hopped off his camel in order to warm up his own legs by walking, turned the camel around, and then headed back south. They pushed on through the entire night without stopping.

The snow stopped by three in the next morning; and by six, the sun had even poked itself between two mountain peaks, creating a beautiful morning within this frigid environment.

However, Baltor's eyes, mind and body were so completely exhausted and numb that he didn't assess a thing—around seven in the morning, he tiredly hopped back onto his just-as-tired camel, and they continued onward.

A little over ten minutes later, and without any warning whatsoever, an unseen force slammed very hard into Baltor, which not only caused him to get completely knocked off his camel—a split-second later, he slammed even harder onto the ground.

While lying on his back, the only thing he initially knew in his dazed and starry state was that this creature was something very large, very heavy and as white as the snow around him.

When his senses came to, a few moments later, he saw that it was an enormous cat with two large fangs sitting firmly on top of his own legs, simultaneously tearing through the wolf furs with either both its razor-sharp claws and/or teeth, in order to get to the meat underneath—Baltor's meat!

He launched a hard punch into the cat's nose, in order to try to get it off him, but because he did not have the power of his whole body to back that punch up, the cat roared out in anger while throwing a powerful swipe of its massive paw into Baltor's head.

Instantly he was knocked "out cold," no longer able to fight against the ferocious and hungry cat!

CHAPTER X

An unknown amount of time passed before Baltor finally returned to the state of consciousness; already was he feeling a slight headache. After opening his eyes and s l o w l y glancing around with his very blurry vision, he discovered with surprise that he was lying under a very warm fur blanket in a giant-sized bed.

As his vision slowly-but-surely cleared, he next saw another bed of the same size adjacent to one he was currently in; the next objects he observed sat in the very center of the room, which was a massive rectangular wood table that had six giant-sized wooden chairs surrounding it.

A few moments later, just beyond the table, his eyes spotted a giant-sized, multi-colored/fur-covered couch that would have formed the shape of an equilateral triangle, except for the fact that one-third of it was missing. This opening was distanced about fifteen feet away from a roaring fireplace and chimney.

And hanging upon a stoker within the fireplace was a very large black cauldron with steam pouring out of the corners of the lid.

Within this giant-sized/one-room cabin whose floors, walls and ceiling were made of cedar, there were six frosted-up windows that revealed the winter darkness outside, as well thirty-eight silver mounted plaques hanging upon the walls—each plaque containing a different type of stuffed predator animal head.

Last but not least, there was one ten-foot tall cedar door, currently closed.

As he tried to sit up in bed, so too did he begin to feel the temples in his head pound rather painfully, so he lay back down while shutting his eyelids.

Several minutes later, just as the pain in his head was almost completely gone, his keen ears detected the approaching sounds of crunching footsteps in the snow.

About twenty seconds after that, those crunching sounds were replaced by the creaking sounds as that same someone now loudly stomped on a wood porch outside, fast nearing the door.

He shut his eyes into teeny slits, while ever so slightly turning his head toward the door—it was his intention to appear unconscious until he had fully assessed the situation, which could possibly turn dangerous at any given moment, as he had learned the hard way over the years.

Just after someone had turned the doorknob and the door pushed open, he saw the silhouette of a giant standing there—the top of this giant's head was a fractional bit shorter than the door-frame itself, making him or her nearly ten feet tall! And, Baltor observed, he or she was nearly as wide as the door too.

While the giant stood in place, he or she began to stomp his or her snow-covered boots heavily on the porch, and only a moment later, the whole place began to steadily vibrate from the powerful impacts by this potentially six-hundred-pound giant—so Baltor estimated.

As soon as the giant had completed getting all the loose snow off, nearly thirty seconds later, he or she then stomped into the room that still caused vibrations though on a much lesser scale, coupled with the occasional squeaks in the cedar floor.

Upon the giant's entry into the cabin, Baltor could tell through his slightly less squinting eyes that this male giant wore a very thick fur coat, pants and boots. The next thing to catch his attention were the very pale hands that were twice the size of his own hands, as well a clean-shaven masculine face, and finally golden blond hair that was so thick and wavy that it literally splashed its way down to just below his shoulders. Though Baltor wasn't interested in men that way, he still believed that this giant was actually handsome.

About five seconds later, the giant stopped at the table and turned toward it—he was as big from the frontal view as he was from the side. Baltor thought, *He will be extremely hard to take out if he should prove a threat, especially since I have no weapon.*

Even though his eyes soon discovered that the giant bore no visible weapons either, his mind asked, *What other weapons could he possibly need other than his gargantuan fists?*

A few moments later, a woman that was only half the giant's size entered the cabin, closing the door behind her.

She too had pale skin with thick, wavy and luscious blond hair, but her hair swam three-quarters of the way down her back. Her attire consisted of a black, brown and white fur coat that stopped just above her waistline, a shiny white leather pair of pants and shiny black boots—everything looking quite fashionable. In a way, she slightly reminded Baltor of Lydia.

After closing the door behind her, the woman took off her coat, revealing a furry v-neck shirt that snugly conformed to her athletic body frame.

Wow—she's hot!

About twenty seconds later, she joined the giant at the table, of whom was already in the process of emptying a bag that contained three giant-sized loaves of bread onto an even larger steel plate.

The giant looked to his left where the woman stood, and then he boomed something both short and foreign to Baltor's ears. Without warning, the giant shifted his head to his right, in order to look at the bed, but by the time his eyes had arrived two seconds later, Baltor had his own eyes closed, not moving a single muscle.

After hearing a rustling sound that lasted about two seconds, Baltor heard the sounds of thunderous footsteps getting closer to his position. A few seconds later, he heard those footsteps stop, and then he heard the giant's voice boom slowly and clearly, "Pasusco—sahu mao brevi!" (1)

Even though Baltor continued to feign unconsciousness, he began to doubt that he was being successful in his feigning, especially after the giant repeated his last statement—still Baltor did not move a single inch.

Two seconds later, he heard the giant's voice, now being angled toward the center of the room, boom out, "Ta hup gap's shatir lankia snet—bre pato semesa pasusco aspena crish Ta peusna gop retux Ta hatish, ven gap'd cher scarain lexum!" (2)

The giant next emitted very deep and booming laughing sounds that lasted about twenty seconds, and possibly because of the almost-deafening volume, Baltor couldn't hear if the woman was laughing or not.

It was then that he drew the conclusion that these people were most likely friendly, so he opened his eyes and revealed his conscious state to all, for better or worse!

The first thing he observed with clarity was that this extremely handsome, ten-foot tall and approximately five-hundred-and-fifty-pound giant had just taken off his thick fur coat and was now towering over him next to the bed.

He wore a fashionably designed brown leather pants and t-shirt that revealed his massively muscular arms, which were crossed just underneath his equally massive chest and torso.

Baltor silently wondered, *I wouldn't doubt it one bit if this giant is truly the world's strongest, biggest and tallest man!*

He also noticed the friendly and amused expression in the giant's blue eyes as he continued to laugh while looking at the woman. And a few seconds later, after Baltor had averted his gaze toward the woman, he saw that she was smiling kindly back at the giant.

Because neither of the two had yet noticed Baltor's conscious state, he purposefully yet lightly cleared his throat, which immediately drew their attention back to him.

The giant turned his head to look back down at Baltor, and repeated his earlier statement, yet this time a bit softer, "Pasusco—sahu mao brevi?" (3) He then shrugged his massive shoulders as his thick eyebrows raised.

As Baltor didn't understand the language, he simply shrugged too, even though he was still lying in bed. However, this simple act abruptly caused incredibly sharp pains to surge throughout his head and upper torso, and subsequently caused him to wince out in pain.

Suddenly, the giant broke out into a highly amused laughter, and while still laughing, he looked back up toward the woman, and said, "Ta'm pan fe tarisha semesa lankia pasusco's yamas fe grevant!" (4)

The woman glanced over and with a tender smile, she nodded her head several times in the affirmative, without saying a word. It was at that moment that two images and their fates crossed Baltor's mind—Valuspo, and even more importantly than his camel, the map.

Despite the pain he had felt earlier, Baltor tried again to get up in bed. This time, however, he felt too weak to prop himself up.

The giant uncrossed his arms, gently lowered his gigantic hands back down toward the bed, and said, "Vikshu sarmani."(5)

Though Baltor did not understand the giant's words, he did understand the physical action that clearly indicated he should lie back down and rest.

After he did so, he next looked back toward the woman and noticed that she was already walking toward the far corner of the room, now carrying a large metallic spoon and metallic bowl in her left hand.

About twenty seconds later, she picked up a poker tool that had been leaning against the wall next to the fireplace, turned to the cauldron, and pulled out the stoker with the poker, which simultaneously pulled out the slightly steaming cauldron from over the fire. Once done with the poker, she then set it back into its original place.

Upon shifting the bowl into her right hand, the woman used the spoon to scoop something *steamy* into the bowl, and once halfway filled three scoops later, she began to walk back over to the table.

Because Baltor had been paying attention to the woman and not the giant, he was not aware of the fact that the giant had quietly slid his heavy four-inch-heeled boots off his socked feet, making the giant nine feet seven inches.

As soon as the woman had begun to scoop, the giant walked with his very long strides toward the table, this time a bit more quietly, and grabbed two bowls off from the table. Meanwhile, the woman had just reached the table, and she handed the giant the spoon as he then walked over to the fireplace.

The woman picked up a much smaller spoon from the table, and then she began to move to Baltor's position—meanwhile the giant had already neared the fireplace with his very long strides.

With an inquisitive look on her middle-aged face, she extended the now-filled spoon containing a stew substance toward Baltor, and asked, "Sahu mao yar?" (6)

Baltor opened his mouth to accept the food, and found the slightly spicy flavors of the stew to be rather delicious—surprisingly perfect in temperature as well.

As she continued to spoon-feed Baltor, the giant walked over to the cauldron, scooped himself some of the stew, walked over to the table, sat down, and began to eat in silence.

By the time Baltor had finished eating the entire contents of the bowl, about two minutes later, the woman stood up, walked over to the table, and set the bowl down on the table. She then retrieved a mug, walked over to a large oak barrel, filled the mug up with the frothy beverage, and came back. She held the cup as he drank down the entire contents of the slightly bitter yet delicious ale.

Once done, the woman got herself a bowl from the cupboard, scooped a bowl and joined the giant at the table, who was on his third bowl of stew, and his second serving of ale.

Baltor listened as the two conversed at the table during dinner-time—but only moments seemed to pass until things grew dizzy, and he fell instantly asleep.

The following morning, due to a brilliant stream of sunlight that had managed to seep through the transparent glass window and into his shut eyelids, Baltor awoke. Without moving his head, he opened his eyes and quickly looked around, discovering that the giant was gone, though the woman was currently sewing something near the fireplace.

Without saying a word to alert the woman, while only slightly moving his head toward her direction so he could watch her work, Baltor noticed that the furs strikingly resembled the furs that he had acquired from the wolves.

Upon closer inspection, he confirmed that they were the same furs, except for the fact that all the extra flesh was no longer on the skin, and about half of them had been cut into nice, even squares. She was diligently cutting more squares.

It was then that Baltor heard the sounds of approaching footsteps in the snow, approaching the cabin. Fifteen seconds later came the sounds of the porch creaking and then the stomping sounds just outside the door.

Just after the giant had opened the door, he entered the cabin and closed the door behind him. During that split second the door was open, Baltor had observed only a few snow-covered pine trees, and way beyond those trees about a few thousand feet away, snow-covered mountains with dagger-sharp peaks.

Only a second later, he decided to sit up in bed and throw a friendly smile. In turn, the giant turned around, and as he observed that Baltor was wide awake, he boomed out, "Sahu mao anamos vrisha gabor blaka, pasusco?" (7)

Baltor assumed that the giant was inquiring to his health, and as he slowly nodded his head, he replied in Pavelian, "I'm feeling better, sir."

The giant's face bore an expression of confusion, but then he began to laugh. He turned to the woman and said, "Vesna gap prisha bagusaham, brim semesa pagor ana e pesanar vigi brevisto!" (8)

The woman's gaze fell to Baltor before she threw a warm and friendly smile, but she said nothing—only a second later she looked back down so that she could recommence with her sewing task.

The giant, on the other hand, tapped himself hard in the chest with his fist, which loud thumping sound immediately drew Baltor's attention back

With the index finger of that hand, he first pointed to Baltor and then toward the door, while saying, "Gaor tao." (9) He reopened the door, stepped outside, left the door open, and disappeared from view.

Understanding the hand gesture, Baltor almost got out of bed, only to notice he was neither wearing shirt nor breeches—fortunately, he was wearing his drawers that were now fresh and clean, though he wondered who had taken them off, washed them, and put them back on him.

Suddenly, Baltor heard the woman say, "Ooopsa dooopsa." (10)

As he looked over to the woman sharply, he saw her gaze falling away from Baltor, while her index finger pointed toward the kitchen table.

His eyes soon fell toward one of the kitchen chairs, where rested his shirt and breeches neatly folded on top of his boots—he almost found it funny he hadn't noticed his clothes sitting there earlier.

When he looked back over to the woman, he saw that she was once again looking at the furs and diligently sewing.

He slowly got out of bed, and it was then that he noticed—for the very first time—that his chest and shoulders had quite a few large and ugly bruises! Surprisingly, there were only a few minor scratches.

He walked over to the table, and as he put on the clothes and boots, he could instantly smell and tell that everything was now fresh and clean, including his socks and boots—even his gold necklace and arrowhead had been polished and buffed.

After he had put everything back on, he turned in appreciation to face the woman, but as she looked extremely busy, and as he didn't want to bother her, he simply cupped his hands together in a gesture of appreciation, bowed his head, and then exited the cabin.

Once he had stepped outside onto the porch and closed the door behind him, he was surprised that he was not cold, though there was a good foot of snow on the ground everywhere he looked. He also observed that this cabin had been built at the top of great hill inside of a gargantuan valley, surrounded by those dagger-sharp, ice-covered mountains.

At the base of the hill below, just beyond a small forest of pine trees, there were hundreds of other giant-sized log cabins spread all about in this gargantuan valley; a twirl of smoke puffed out from each chimney and up into the crisp blue skies above! He was so mesmerized by the quaint little town that he did not hear the giant with his heavy footsteps approach from behind and lightly tap him on the back of his shoulder.

Not only did this action startle Baltor, he instantly leapt into a sideways roll, only to land back on his feet in the basic ready position facing the giant—these actions caused quite a bit of pain to surge, especially in his head.

He confirmed his pains by cupping his head with both hands. "*Owww!*"

Even though the giant still bore a rather surprised expression on his face, he also began to bear an amused expression that was quickly overtaking the surprise—this became confirmed as the giant began to erupt with that booming laughter of his.

A few moments later, the giant stopped laughing, and with a serious look, he pointed at himself with his thumb, and introduced, "Yaush."

Baltor, in turn, pointed at himself, and then introduced, "Baltor."

With a cock of Yaush's head and his left thumb behind him, he boomed, "Baltor, pasant gaor tao, jaosaim. Gaor tao—gaor!" (11)

He turned around, waved for Baltor to follow, and then began to walk toward the backyard, which backyard consisted of a jagged mountain about five hundred feet away from the cabin.

Of course, Baltor followed, and upon the two reaching the backyard, he saw a giant-sized barn and more clusters of pine trees here and there—the giant had already reached the door to the barn and waited in silence for Baltor to near. And once this was so about thirty seconds later, he opened the main door to the barn.

After Baltor had entered, the giant closed the door.

Baltor saw six stalls, three on the left and three on the right. The first two stalls on the left had a horse sticking its head out, though the far stall looked empty, as well all the ones on the right.

Yaush saw Baltor turn his head toward him in confusion, and so he pointed with his index finger over to the last stall on the left.

As Baltor neared, he saw that these stalls were actually quite long, and that hidden in the last stall on the left—lo and behold there was his camel eating away on some hay!

Valuspo appeared to be as joyous to see Baltor, as the other way around. For when Baltor leaned over the stall, the camel marched right on up and slurped a big fat juicy kiss on his smiling face.

As Baltor spit out a few pieces of hay in his mouth, Yaush suddenly burst out into booming laughter—a few seconds later, Baltor joined him in the laughter, even though he had to spit a couple more times in between to get the taste of hay out.

Once the air had turned serious, nearly a minute later, Yaush again slapped himself in the chest, and again said his name, "Yaush."

He then pointed at his own eyes with both of his index fingers, and added, "kahusho." Finally, he pointed at Baltor and then said, "Baltor." (12)

Baltor nodded in understanding that "Yaush" had "seen" "Baltor."

136

A few seconds later, Yaush continued, "Yaush kahusho scarain—scarain." (13) He next physically demonstrated what "scarain" meant by baring his teeth, making a growling noise, and clenching his hands open and shut. Once done with his demonstration, he again said, "scarain."

Baltor again nodded in understanding that Yaush had also seen the giant white cat—scarain.

Yaush next said, "Yaush mansuon scarain." (14) He demonstrated what "mansuon" meant by fisting both of his hands right out in front of his chest, side to side. While keeping his left fist in place, he drew back the rear fist—once it had evened out with his chest, he opened that fist by spreading all his fingers outward and making a "zinging sound" with his mouth.

Instantly, Baltor nodded in understanding that Yaush had shot an arrow into the beast, and judging from the colossal size of this giant, most likely killed it in one shot.

Yaush confirmed Baltor's suspicion by pointing his index finger to his temple, and rolling his eyes into the back of his head for just a moment before saying, "Yaush banari scarain." (15)

Even though Baltor was only ninety-nine percent sure that Yaush had just said he killed the scarain—he was one hundred percent sure, and equally grateful, that the giant had saved his life.

Because Baltor didn't know how to say "thank you" in Yaush's language, he instead cupped his hands together in front of him at abdominal level and threw his head into a bow, in order to physically express his "sincerest appreciation."

A few seconds later, Yaush clamped his giant-sized right hand around Baltor's left shoulder, and said, "Gemne mao." (16)

Although Baltor didn't understand what Yaush had last said, he threw his gaze back from his shoulder and up, observing that Yaush was looking down and smiling—Baltor smiled back.

After letting go of Baltor's shoulder, Yaush first cupped both of his hands out in front of him, bowed for a second, and said, "Gemne mao, Yaush." When he said his name, he recommenced to smile.

Baltor now understood how to say "thank you," and so he confirmed, "Gemne mao, Yaush."

After nodding his head affirmatively twice, Yaush pointed his index finger at Baltor, and said, "Mao sahu vlaidim, Baltor." (17)

Baltor assumed that this meant, "You are welcome."

If he was right, besides the very few phrases he had learned, he had just figured out two really important keywords: "mao" meant "you," and "tao" meant "me."

Additionally, nodding your head means, "yes," and so he nodded his head a few times. He wondered if shaking the head meant "no"?

Nearly ten seconds of nodding and smiling occurred between the two men before Baltor strangely began to feel a little uncomfortable from Yaush's deep staring, and so Baltor cast his eyes back into his camel's stall, spotting three familiar objects sitting on the ground in the right corner—1) his saber resting in 2) his sheath. Both objects were resting on 3) his unopened bag!

With an elated expression, he looked back at Yaush.

Yaush, after a chuckle, walked over to the stall and unlatched the door, but only opened the door a sliver as he assumed that the camel would probably try to run away. Baltor, on the other hand, knew better.

He put out his hands in front of him, left hand in front of the right, and he next began to wiggle his index and middle fingers back and forth a dozen times, indicating a moving animal.

Two seconds later, Baltor stopped wiggling his fingers, clinched his fists, and shook his head negatively, in order to indicate that his camel wouldn't run away. Finally, he pointed at Valuspo with his right index finger while introducing, "Valuspo."

Understanding, Yaush fully opened the door to the stall, and tenderly he began petting the camel's face while cooing, "Visha blaka fe mao, Valuspo. Tai, mao sahu yuits e rescha chirsa, po larse eithen po vixtes!" (18)

While Baltor's mind assumed that Yaush's first statement was either "hello" or "good morning," the only clue that he had regarding the second statement was that it must have been "some sort of compliment," for Valuspo's head reared back quite proudly and happily, while his eyes equally reflected that "pride and happiness."

A few seconds later, the camel abruptly slurped Yaush in the face, which caused Baltor to burst out laughing; and a couple seconds later, Yaush joined in the laughter.

A few moments later, Valuspo looked a bit confused, and let out an excited "*Annhhhgggrrrrhh!*"

Valuspo's highly unusual sound caused Baltor and Yaush to burst out laughing heartily—meanwhile, the camel continuously made those really strange sounds, which in turn caused the two men to begin laughing so hard that tears were literally pouring out of their eyes! It took a grand total of three or four minutes before the out-of-control laughter finally subsided.

While still wiping the tears from his eyes and chuckling, Baltor walked over to the saber and bag, kneeled down with his back to

138

Yaush, who was still petting and talking to Valuspo. Baltor next picked up the sheath, set it down next to the bag, and opened it.

He was very relieved to discover that everything was set up exactly the way he had left it, and after sliding a bunch of items around in the bag, he was even more joyous to notice that the map was still in its original place at the very bottom.

He immediately slid the items back into their original place and shut the bag, and after setting the saber back down onto the bag, he stood back up onto his feet, and turned around.

Yaush noticed the furtive movement, turned his head to look at Baltor, and after pointing outside the open stall, he said, "Gaor tao, Baltor." (19) He exited the stall, walked to the outside of the stall door, and put his hand on the latch on the door.

As soon as he had seen Baltor exit the stall, which was only a second later, Yaush closed and secured the door before making his way for the entrance to the barn. Baltor followed.

By the time they were outside, a half minute or so later, he could see that Yaush was leading them back to the cabin.

Once they were standing on the front porch, another minute later, Yaush began to stomp his feet in order to get all the snow off, of which there was a lot. Baltor had barely any snow on his boots, so he was done first.

Once Yaush was done, he opened the door, entered the cabin, and gestured for Baltor to enter—after Baltor did, he closed the door.

After transforming his thick eyebrows into forty-five degree angles, Yaush said, "Baltor."

Baltor turned around. Meanwhile, the woman had just looked up from her task. Yaush pointed at his own nodding head, and said, "Gav."

As Baltor figured out that "gav" means "yes," he asked one question in all eight languages that he knew, "Can you speak this language?"

In the end, however, Yaush and the woman's confused faces and heads that shook "no" showed that neither understood a single one of Baltor's eight languages.

A few moments after Baltor had stopped speaking, Yaush stopped shaking his head, and said, "Busk." (21)

Even though Baltor had just begun to look frustrated, Yaush rubbed his stomach in tiny circles, while asking, "Yar?" (22)

Baltor nodded his head in the affirmative several times, as he understood that Yaush was asking him if he was hungry.

Yaush nodded his own head, while confirming, "Gav." He then shook his head from side to side and said, "Busk."

"Gav," Baltor replied.

Yaush turned to face the woman, who was still looking at Baltor. He then asked, "Pia, prisha maotaos casaom leama fe briska vas Baltor? Gaps yar, Jimnee." (23)

While gesturing to the fur coat, the woman replied, "Aprica busk, Ta've casaom optan suara vusko pren fretha rastuten vas gop sen gep chirso." (24)

After a short pause, she gestured outside with her thumb, and seemed to suggest something by the tone of her voice, "Yaush, nenso prisha't mao marsa gop fe *Peov Baeus*?" (25)

The woman's gaze then fell back upon Baltor; she pointed at herself and said, "Jimnee."

With a hearty laugh, Yaush lightly slapped himself in the head, and while rolling his eyes in head several times, he said, "Baltor, Jimnee. Jimnee, Baltor!"

Baltor nodded and smiled at Jimnee, and then walked over to her with hand extended—though she took his hand in hers, she did not shake that hand first before releasing.

At that moment, he remembered how to say "thank you" in their language, and so he said, "Gemne mao, Jimnee."

With a mild look of surprise, Jimnee promptly responded, "Mao sahu vlaidim, Baltor." (26)

He was sure she said, "You're welcome," so he nodded his head while still bearing an appreciative smile.

Meanwhile, Yaush was already waiting at the open door, and after another slap into his chest, which drew Baltor's attention back to the giant, he said, "Gaor tao, Baltor." (27)

Baltor followed him out the door, and the two made their way down the hill, through the forest, and toward the busy section of town, in which dozens of people walked here and there. Other than the children, he inevitably discovered that all the adult males were approximately 6 to 9 feet tall, while the females were all around 5 to 6 feet tall—most had pale skin with blond hair, but a select few had red hair. In all of his days, he had only seen one "blondie" before, and that was Lydia—and only once had he seen a "carrot top," Thesmul, and he had counted out four so far.

Though many of the townsfolk threw inquisitive looks at Baltor, none of them said anything directly toward him. Instead, they simply threw friendly smiles, and greeted, "Visha blaka fe mao." (28)

140

Each time, Yaush would respond back similarly.

Baltor's assumption was that they were saying "good morning" to each other. However, he didn't want to mess up and say the wrong thing, so he would simply throw friendly smiles and/or nods into their direction—always were those smiles returned.

Finally, they came across what appeared to be a restaurant, as there was a sign above the door written in a foreign language, and just above the writing, there was the etched picture of a roaring bear. The only reason that Baltor knew that this place was a restaurant wasn't from the sign, but from the smells of foods cooking and the chattering going on inside.

Yaush entered the restaurant with Baltor right behind, and as soon as the patrons saw "the stranger"—the chattering instantly died down and everyone stared in blank silence.

Yaush stepped to the left by Baltor's side, proudly clapped him on the shoulder with one hand, and with the other free hand, he extended it out amongst the patrons while his voice boomed, "Partastucia, caloph hup tai laka jaosaim, Baltor! Baltor, calophin sahu vusko tai visha jaosaims!" (29)

Even though Baltor didn't understand what in the world Yaush had just said, he did understand as the bulk of the patrons greeted back, "Visha blaka fe mao, Baltor!" (30)

Baltor felt a bit sheepish from all the attention, yet managed to respond, "Visha blaka ve mao."

Several in the crowd laughed at Baltor's mispronunciation, but even they then went back to business, eating and chatting happily amongst one another themselves.

Yaush gestured toward an empty table with four chairs nearby and said, "Baltor, haso." (31) He then walked over and sat down—two seconds later Baltor sat down on the other side of the table.

Within moments, this strawberry-blonde-haired girl approached the table with a serving tray in hand. In Baltor's observation and opinion, she was so cute, innocent, and adorable, all these wonderful qualities rolled into one, that his mouth dropped open a couple of inches.

The girl's gaze, however, was locked upon Yaush, and with this wonderfully soft and tender voice that made Baltor's heart pump even faster and harder, he heard her sweetly say, "Visha blaka fe mao, Yaush!" (32)

Yaush answered, "Po visha blaka fe mao, Yeea." (33)

He next introduced the two, "Baltor. Yeea. Yeea. Baltor."

They nodded at each other with a small, shy smile.

Only two seconds later, Yeea looked back over at Yaush and asked another question, "Mensa pagor Jimnee?" (34)

Yaush answered, "Sap pagor peov—gemnes vas bagusa!" (35)

Yeea then gazed at Baltor with beautiful eyes, and after throwing a quick but equally beautiful smile, she greeted, "Visha blaka fe mao, Baltor." (36)

Baltor's brain suddenly lapsed as his heart took all the blood— he had already forgotten how to say "good morning to you" even though she had just said it to him.

As if psychic, she repeated, "Visha blaka fe mao."

With an embarrassed smile, Baltor looked back down at the table. "Visha blaka fe mao."

Yeea's gaze fell over to Yaush as she asked, "Larsa Yaush, lamars trisha Ta eutra mao po maos jaosaim vas brasha?" (37)

Yaush responded after a point toward both Baltor and himself, as he said, "Trisha maotaos pasant casa cal barags vigi runags, paomche po richita, mentos oansa manati alasvo leeta, pasant?" (38)

Yeea replied with a very chipper tone of voice, "Onas lea!" (39)

Even though Baltor was completely lost as to what they were saying, as well feeling a bit embarrassed and shy, he silently listened anyway through their short conversation, while continuously looking at the table.

That is, until Yeea had relayed her last excited statement, causing Baltor to throw his glance back up at her. She purposefully threw another sweet smile directed at Baltor before leaving to place the order.

Once gone, he averted his gaze back toward Yaush, and noticed that the giant had already begun to look nonchalantly around the room—just in case he might have some more of his language to teach, Baltor mainly kept his gaze on him.

A minute later, Baltor observed a look of amazement and happiness suddenly cross Yaush's face. Only a second later, the giant abruptly stood up, which caused the sounds of his chair to screech on the floor, while calling out, "Salami!"

Baltor looked toward the direction that Yaush was looking and talking, and he saw a seven-foot tall, thin, and older-looking giant who had light-brown skin. The color of his neatly groomed facial beard and long braided hair was mainly auburn intermixed with quite a bit of silver. He wore old brown leathers throughout— why, even this giant's wide-brimmed hat and boots came from the same exact leather material.

With a gesture of his hand toward their table, Yaush asked, "Salami, tai aserti jaosaim, yosbe mao pasant sakti maitai vas brasha?" (40)

At this point, Baltor assumed that Salami must be this man's name—Salami's gaze fell to Baltor for a moment, and in the next, he looked back at Yaush while beginning to approach.

Once near, Yaush said, "Salami, caloph hup tai blaka pasusco, Baltor. Mit hrai semesa tai jaosiam trisha ara loots e valon otra illansis, sot gap trisha net ara Valakanese. Ta, lerta e breta oaste fretha yamika, trisha retis ara mautau wersa dravinsky. Yosbe mao pasant aserti po kahusho shari mao trisha ara cas vigi gap illansis, tai jaosaim?" (41)

Before the time that Yaush had finished asking his question, Salami had already gotten himself comfortable in a chair at their table.

Upon completion of Yaush's question, Salami puckered his lower lip out just a bit while scrunching his thick, auburn eyebrows. He next nodded, looked back over at Baltor, and tried speaking in three different languages, none of which Baltor understood. The only thing that Baltor did could tell was that they all sounded like a question.

Finally, on the fourth language, Salami asked with an extremely thick accent in the language of Thorium, "Do you perhaps know this tongue?"

Baltor beamed a smile that reached from ear to ear before replying with just as much excitement in the same language, "Yes!"

The man introduced with his own wide smile: "My name is Salami—what was your name again?"

"My name is Baltor."

In the next moment, Yeea came back with a tray of food that contained two filled mugs and two heaping plates of steaming food with forks stuffed into them—cheese and sausage omelets. As she began to set everything onto on the table, Baltor smelled a very pleasing and spicy aroma, which simultaneously made his stomach growl in desire.

Salami asked, "You are from Thorium, yes?"

Baltor looked from the food and back up to Salami, while answering, "Actually I'm from Pavelus, but I fluently speak this language, too."

Because Baltor, Salami and Yaush were all extremely excited at the breakthrough in the language barrier, none observed the desiring and wistful look in Yeea's eyes—her eyes had been firmly locked onto Baltor throughout the entire time she placed all the food and drinks onto the table.

Almost right after Yeea had completed her task, a slightly disappointed look crossed her face because Baltor hadn't even glanced at her once.

It was then that Yeea began to believe that the strange and unexplainable feelings she had for Baltor obviously weren't mutual. A moment later, it dawned on her that she still had one other table to tend to, so she turned to leave.

Just as she was about to head to that table, Yaush noticed the movement and asked, "Yeea. Al puor, pasant?" (42)

She turned back around quickly, asking with a bit of excitement, "Gav?" (43)

Yaush asked, "Salami, lamars yosbud mao jamir vas brasha?" (44)

Salami turned his head to look at Yeea, and answered, "Ta'll casa yani laos're casaoman."(45)

Yeea's eyes betrayed a bit of disappointment reflected in her voice, as she said, "Onas lea…" (46)

Her tone of voice immediately drew looks of confusion from all three men, as none understood the reason for her disappointed look. Neither could they ask because she was already rushing to the kitchen with her back to them, while bearing an embarrassed and rather disappointed look in her eyes and face.

In unison, the three men looked at each other in confusion while simultaneously shrugging, to which they began to burst out laughing from all the parallelisms.

About thirty seconds later or so, Yaush was the first one to stop laughing. Now bearing a serious look in his face, he asked Salami a question. Once done with what he had to say, several moments later, Yaush took a giant-sized bite of his food.

Salami interpreted seriously, but this time in Thoriumite, "Yaush wants to know what brings you through these parts."

Baltor answered, "I am on a quest." He took his first bite of the deliciously spicy sausage, and both his stomach and his taste buds craved more.

Due to Baltor's response, Salami bore a curious look but instead of probing further, he interpreted the response to Yaush.

With a nod, Yaush said something excitedly to Salami: In turn, Salami interpreted in the language of Thorium, "We are a people of peace, but we know that there are other people who are not for peace. Do you understand, and are you for peace?"

Baltor nodded while continuing to eat, and once he had swallowed the remaining bit of eggs and sausage in his mouth, he said, "Gav."

Immediately Yaush appeared to relax, for he picked up his fork and stuffed some food into his own mouth.

Salami added, "Even though Yaush has never left Valakan, I am a world traveler and businessman myself, and have even been to Pavelus several times on business. Had to hire a Pavelian translator to assist me, of course. Anyway, enough about me. My personal question for you is this: Is your quest for Sultan Brishavus Helenus, perhaps to expand the Sharia Empire this way?"

Baltor finished taking a long draught of the sweet juice. He then looked up at Salami, shook his head, and answered, "No—Busk. My quest is my own personal quest. I was trying to pass through these mountains and east toward the jungles before I was jumped."

With a very curious look in his eyes, Yaush tapped Salami, who in turn interpreted what Baltor had just said.

Yaush almost choked on his food as he had begun to laugh. After managing to get the food down the right pipe, yet still continuing to chuckle, he said something to Salami.

Salami then interpreted, "Yaush says that you were very, very lucky. He says that he was hunting for food when he saw you on the ground; a scarain was sitting right on top of you, already ripping and tearing into you with his claws and teeth! How do you say scarain in your language?"

"White tiger with very long fangs."

"Ah... white tiger with very long fangs."

Baltor threw his gaze over to Yaush, and after delivering a bow of his head, Baltor said, "Gemne mao, Yaush." (47)

Yaush nodded his head, and then he said something for a few minutes to Salami. Once done, Yaush took another bite of food.

Salami turned his head back to Baltor, and interpreted, "Yaush says that you can stay at his home as long as you like. He says that his wife Jimnee is making you and your camel the proper gear to travel safely through these mountains, though he does not know how long this task will take. He says that once you have finished your quest, you are more than welcome to come back at any time. He says that though he does not know why he likes you, he does."

Just then, a six-and-a-half-foot tall man who was wearing a dirty apron, obviously the cook, brought out a serving tray that contained yet another plate of an omelet stuffed with sausage and cheese, as well a mug of drink.

Just after having swallowed another mouthful of his own food, Baltor answered, "Gemne mao, Yaush." He took another large bite.

The cook not only placed this order in front of Salami, yet he even decided to stick around, beginning his own conversation with Yaush and Salami. (48-52)

By the time they finished this conversation, several minutes later, Baltor had finished everything on his plate—his stomach felt stuffed.

"Gemne mao, Paelsho." (53) Yaush and Salami replied in unison, and immediately the two began to roar out their laughter from yet another parallelism. Meanwhile, Baltor definitely looked confused at the "second bout of laughter" without him involved, and so he asked Salami, "What's going on?"

After Salami had stopped laughing about ten seconds later, he explained, "Oh—just a misunderstanding. Remember when we were all laughing a bit ago? Yeea, our waitress, thought we were all laughing at her right after she had taken my breakfast order, which was just a big misunderstanding. Yaush explained to Paelsho, the cook, that we were really laughing at ourselves!"

"That's true—by the way, gemne mao, Salami."

"For what?"

"For taking the time to explain to me what was going on."

"No problem, Baltor. You, I can tell, are a good guy!"

"Gemne mao," Baltor answered with a smile.

Though Yaush was nearly done eating his meal, Salami had only eaten a few giant bites himself—seven-eighths was still there.

Yaush said something for another thirty seconds-or-so to Salami, in which Salami took this opportunity to eat a couple more bites of food. Once Yaush had completed speaking, Salami nodded his head and looked over at Baltor.

Upon swallowing, Salami interpreted, "Yaush has changed his mind. There is something he definitely likes about you."

Baltor asked, "What's that?"

Salami answered, "The fact that you are willing to try to learn our tongue. Most foreigners never make that attempt." With that, he pushed back his chair, which caused his chair to screech on the floor. He stood up from the table and said in Baltor's tongue, "I will be gone for most of the day as I have important errands to tend. I will stop by Yaush's home this evening, and we talk more, okay?"

Baltor replied, "Gemne mao, Salami."

Just before Salami left the restaurant, he threw some foreign currency on the table, heartily waved, and said, "Taumaploth." (54)

146

Baltor figured this meant "farewell" and repeated, as did Yaush.

By the time they made it back to Yaush and Jimnee's cabin, the two men began to target practice in the backyard using a steel longbow and arrows—Yaush was quite impressed with Baltor's precise shooting skills! In turn, Baltor was just as impressed by the giant's incredible power and deadly accuracy!

That evening around eight, Salami stopped by the cabin, and the four of them shared a great dinner that Yaush had cooked in the cauldron for the last few hours or so—mutton and spicy potato stew. Jimnee had been taking a nice break, relaxing in her chair.

Once dinner was over, and mugs of ale were placed into everyone's hands, except for Jimnee's, they all talked long into the night—already had she begun to work like there was no tomorrow in the far corner of the cabin. Periodically, Baltor watched in amazement her sew like a pro, but not by hand.

Actually, she used a high-tech sewing machine, and by pumping her right foot repetitively onto the attached foot pedal, power was supplied that allowed the sewing needle and thread to sew the fur skins together. Never had Baltor seen a machine like this before!

Besides the "friendly and intelligent conversations" the men shared, in which Yaush later admitted he was the inventor of the sewing machine, as well a few other clever inventions he had made: Baltor pointed out—late, late in the night—that he needed to go to bed right away, as he had to leave early the next morning.

Once Salami had interpreted this news, Jimnee immediately made him interpret that she had only then just finished making Baltor his new hat, coat, pants, gloves and boot covers, and that she wanted him to try it all on, in case something had to be altered.

While Baltor stood in front of the mirror admiring his new clothes, which seemed to fit over his regular clothes for the most part, Jimnee visually scrutinized, saying something to Salami.

Salami interpreted right away, "Jimnee said she needs to make a few alterations still with your clothes. As for your camel, she will use the scarain's fur to make him a nice covering, which will be complete by the time you leave after breakfast."

Baltor looked right into Jimnee's eyes for a moment, and said, "Gemne mao, Jimnee."

"Baltor, mao sahu vladim, tai jaosaim," Jimnee replied happily.

He had no doubt she was saying, "You are welcome, my friend!"

Before they knew it, the night grew incredibly late, so Salami left—Yaush fell asleep in one bed, while Baltor slept in the other. Jimnee continued to cut or sew...

147

CHAPTER XI

At the crack of dawn, the three ate a warm, hearty, porridge breakfast that Yaush had whipped up in the cauldron—he smiled in between slurping down his porridge but said not a word to anyone.

Jimnee, totally exhausted from not getting any sleep whatsoever, as well from all the cutting and sewing, now appeared tired and haggard. She mindlessly stared at her bowl of food the whole time, while consuming hers slowly.

Baltor, on the other hand, hadn't slept this great in many, many months, thanks to the soft, giant bed, and breakfast was delicious. Because of the language barrier, all he could do was smile back.

Once breakfast was over, perhaps three minutes after it had begun, Yaush was the one to lead the pack on out to the barn.

And once inside, he began to pack two large bags full of hay for the camel to eat later. Jimnee, yawning all the while, lay the scarain fur over and around the humps of Valuspo's back. A perfect fit as it turned out, a minute or so later.

Already had Baltor made his way for the corner of the stall, where sat his gear. He then picked up his saber-carrying sheath, tied it onto his belt, knelt down on a knee, opened the bag, and confirmed that nothing in the bag had been tampered with.

After making sure he wasn't being watched by either of his friends at that moment, which he still wasn't, he quickly tucked the map inside his shirt, picked up the bag, and spun around.

By then, Yaush had just finished packing the two bags, so he tied each bag up at the top with rope, and then used that same rope to tie the two bags together.

Once done, five seconds later, "a look of remembrance" unexpectedly crossed his face, and after snapping his fingers once and pointing his index finger up into the air, he stomped out of the stall—Baltor understood he was to wait a minute.

Therefore he cast his eyes over at Jimnee, noting that she had just begun petting and cooing at Valuspo. His camel, he noted, looked and sounded quite thrilled at all this attention from a female.

Of course, only seconds later, Baltor had heard the giant stomp back into the stall. But as he looked over upon Yaush's arrival, he saw with surprise that the giant now carried on his right shoulder an extra-large leather saddle with very thick furry pillows sewn onto it. Hanging on his left shoulder were a bunch of thick leather ropes attached to a steel mouthpiece, appearing to be a new set of bridle and reins. And in his left hand he carried the very same longbow they had both used the day before, as well a wood quiver filled with dozens of arrows.

Without a single word spoken throughout, other than a chipper tune he began to whistle, Yaush first set the bow and quiver onto the ground, and then he began the process of strapping the saddle in between the camel's humps and the bottom of his belly. Because of the weapon, Baltor wondered if the giant had plans to go hunting wild game later that day, after of course Baltor had left the village. Of course, he didn't know their language good enough to ask.

Once Yaush had secured the saddle, he next took the bridle and reins that had been resting on his other shoulder, and secured them around the camel's mouth, which took a minute or so ... all the while whistling. It was then that Baltor walked over and attached his bag to the saddle, which only took a few seconds.

As for Yaush, he picked up the quiver of arrows, easily stuffing it into an equally sized pocket specially sewn into the side of the saddle. Not only did the right-side-up quiver fit perfectly, yet Baltor doubted that a single arrow would ever fall out, even if Valuspo and he were at a full gallop.

Yaush still wasn't done, with his tune or his task, as he secured the center of the longbow into a steel clamp that was clamped into the side of the saddle, which demonstration took only a second.

That is when he stopped whistling, looked over at Baltor, pointed at a little latch to the side of the clamp, made a low-to-high pitched whistling sound, and flipped the latch.

Instantly the clamp opened, and the bow dropped into the giant's ready hands—only a second later, he raised the bow back into the clamp, and without having to flip that little lever, the clamp secured the bow with a click, and Yaush released his grip.

Needful to say, Baltor was astounded by this high-tech mechanism: He had no doubt that Yaush was "a genius amongst geniuses!"

Only a second later, Yaush looked directly over at his new friend, smiled, and bowed his head for a second. The smile was still there when he looked up.

Baltor immediately smiled back in great appreciation for all the absolutely wonderful and useful gifts, so he cupped his hands together, bowed his head for a second, and then looked back up at this friend while declaring, "Gemne mao, Yaush, tai jaosaim!"

"Mao sahu vlaidim, Baltor, tai jaosaim!" the giant boomed back with equal appreciation. The two briskly shook hands. Yaush's were definitely twice the size as Baltor's!

Once the handshake was released, Baltor picked up the bags of hay, threw them right behind the saddle and right before his camel's final hump, which balanced out the weight of both bags so that he could have his hands completely free while riding.

No longer in the slightest suspicion of his trustworthy friends, Baltor pulled out the map from inside his shirt, held it right out in plain view, and cleared his throat several times loudly.

Yaush glanced at it for about twenty seconds. On the twenty-first second he pointed his finger at a spot in the middle of the Bospa Mountains, again saying the name of his town: "Valakan."

Baltor also noticed that the mountain pass from east-to-west was shortest at this town's latitude, as was Pavelus, due straight west—far more desert and jungle. However, there were no dots at all anywhere around here, which indicated that the mapmaker didn't know about Valakan, if it even existed a millennium ago.

"Gemne mao, Yaush," Baltor simply stated with a smile, before tucking the map into one of the large pockets in the saddle, mounting his camel and grabbing the reins.

Yaush snapped his fingers yet again and pointed his index finger up into the air—Baltor understood that he should wait yet another minute, for some strange reason, so he nodded affirmatively once.

Yaush ran out of the stall.

Seconds later he came back in, now carrying two steel water canteens, as well a full, leather bag that was the size of a watermelon. After shaking the canteens at the same to show that they were empty, he set them into another of the saddle's pockets. He next opened the bag at the end, showed the jerky to Baltor, sealed the bag, and put it in the same pouch.

Still holding the reins in his left hand, Baltor extended his hand out to Yaush, saying, "Gemne mao, Yaush. Taumaploth, Jaosaim!"

"Mao saaaaahuuuu vlaidim, Baltor. Taumaploth!" Yaush sang, while shaking hands again with his friend.

Once the handshake was released, Baltor looked at Jimnee one final time, saying, "Jimnee. Gemne mao, Jaosaim. Taumaploth."

She remained silent, except for throwing a cock of her head and a warm smile.

Baltor lightly snapped the reins, just before riding out of the stall, the barn, and finally the town of Valakan.

During this first morning of travel, which was spent in a hundred percent comfort and warmth for both he and Valuspo—thanks to the new fur clothes—he recalled all the hospitalities and wonders of these wonderful people, and promised that he would come back and visit, maybe even on his way back from the tower.

At noon, they ran across a small frozen lagoon. There, Baltor broke through the thin ice with his saber before filling up his canteens. While drinking a half canteen down, he led his camel to drink from the lagoon, but Valuspo refused. He next offered some hay, but as it was also declined, he climbed backed into the saddle, and they continued on.

That uneventful day turned into an uneventful week, and he continuously observed that the mountains and the valleys descended lower and lower at a rather steep incline, sometimes too steep—until finally they reached the base of the mountains, which heavily intermixed with the dense and lush jungle that lay just beyond. Frequently he heard the sounds of exotic birds singing somewhere up in the luscious trees, though rare was the time he actually saw them.

As soon as the weather had become "hot, humid, and sticky," he took off all of the furs and stuffed them, and the map, into the bags that had once stored the hay, as grass was once again plentiful—it all barely fit.

Even though he continued to sweat profusely without the fur on, he didn't complain. Nor did Valuspo make any complaints any longer.

That afternoon, they came across a pack of monkeys—some swung from tree to tree, while others played, while still others ate bugs off each other, or bananas. He had seen monkeys in Pavelus before, but they were almost always in cages. He watched them in silent amusement for about five minutes before he and his camel continued on their path.

Not even another hour had passed before they came upon a wide river, perhaps an eighth-of-a-mile thick. Fortunately it didn't appear to be deep anywhere, no more than waist height at certain places. Just to be on the safe side, Baltor hopped to the ground, kept a firm hold of the reins, and entered the river first—Valuspo followed.

Only seconds after having begun wading through the river, Baltor dunked himself completely underwater for a few seconds in order to cool himself off, before standing back to his feet—it felt great.

About five minutes later, they safely exited the other side of the river. Once on dry land, he quickly refilled the water canteens, and gave an opportunity for Valuspo to drink—he didn't.

As his hands were completely dry, he next pulled out the map from the bag, glancing at it for a minute.

According to the map, this jungle was even larger than the area of the mountains, and the tower appeared to lie somewhere in the smack center. Baltor said, "Indeed, it may take many years to find this blasted tower, if ever."

A second later, Valuspo turned his head back and snorted. Baltor laughed at his friend's response, patted him on the back, and after stuffing the map back into the bag, he climbed into the saddle. Together they headed toward what he guessed was the jungle's center.

After they had stopped for the night, an hour or so before sunset, and he had been in the process of compiling a bunch of dead branches for the campfire, he once again became very lucky—a tail from a giant green snake suddenly lashed down from the trees, in order to try and ensnare its prey.

Already had Baltor instinctively rolled out of harm's way just a millisecond before the tail could get its death grip. Only upon being back on his feet did he see that the very long tail was already halfway up and quickly rising back into those trees.

Because he didn't want to take a chance at throwing and losing his saber in the brush, he ran to retrieve his bow-and-arrows from his camel, about ten feet away. But by the time he had the arrow notched in his bow, the tail was already hidden away.

He said to Valuspo, "It appears that we are going to have to be extremely careful, my friend! Who knows what else lies around here?" This time, his camel didn't make a sound.

Once he had finished setting up camp, about twenty minutes later, he rested only eight feet away from the campfire with the sword and the bow and quiver at his side and ate his dried rations. Valuspo chewed on some grass nearby.

Just before sunset, he began to hear some unusual screeching sounds, though he could not tell what was making all the annoying noises; just in case, he had an arrow notched into his longbow and ready to shoot.

Over the trees, they flew—hundreds—no thousands of them, and the screeching grew irritatingly loud—small bats. Fortunately, none flew near.

By the time that the last one had passed, many minutes later, stars now twinkled in the darkening sky. The nearer of the moons was in the waxing position, though the other wasn't in sight.

With a yawn, he once again relaxed, sat back, and finished his dinner. Soon after, he fell asleep.

The next morning, he awoke, repacked the gear, and they continued their journey east. By noon, Baltor observed that the foliage was beginning to get too thick to ride through.

Inevitably, he had to walk ahead of Valuspo while slicing through the dense foliage with his saber, in order to pass. By sunset, the foliage had only gotten progressively worse. From all the hacking and slashing, he found that even his strong arms were getting seriously fatigued.

After he cleared a twenty-foot perimeter with his saber, he set up a small campfire, ate his dinner and then laid himself down to sleep, exhausted.

Sometime during the night when the waxing moon had just begun to descend, while the waning red moon had risen to about halfway up, he awoke to these painfully stinging sensations in about a dozen different areas throughout his body, including one on his forehead. From nearby, he could hear Valuspo snorting in irritation, as well.

With his eyes still closed, he slapped at the one on his left arm as it hurt the worst, thinking that it was just a mosquito. But his hand discovered a small bump that was both slimy and cold. He opened his eyes and looked at the spot. Though his campfire was already out, he could see a dark and wormy creatures sitting on his skin, due to the moons' light.

He tried to pull it off, but this only caused more pain.

"Ouch!" Baltor cried.

Again, he tried to pull it off, which only produced the same painful result—Baltor snapped, "Damn it!"

He stood up and working through the dizzy spells. He retrieved a branch, stuck it in the embers of the campfire until it was hot. He then took the end of the stick and pressed it into the leech.

It let go of his skin, and he flung it off. It took several more minutes for him to remove the remaining eight leeches, and then he began to work on removing the dozens of leeches attached to Valuspo.

Once done, he extinguished out the flames, hopped on his camel, and they continued to ride until the foliage had cleared out, which took until the next morning.

After the sun had arisen, Baltor first examined his wounds more carefully, and noticed a small stream of blood that had already dried up from each of his wounds. Fortunately, none looked infected.

He next looked up, observing an incredibly large prairie that lay ahead. Scattered throughout the hundreds of tall patches of prairie grass were large boulders chaotically stacked upon one another. Circling around this five mile or so long prairie, he could only see more jungle trees.

Interestingly enough, he saw to the north, about a half of a mile down, there was a pack of black and white striped horses grazing ... perhaps thirty of them.

After he had pulled out some dried jerky, as well his map, he began to nibble as he glanced at the map. However, there was no indication of this prairie being there, so he had no way of knowing where he was at, or if he was even going the right way.

For the first time since beginning his quest, Baltor got frustrated enough that he actually contemplated throwing away this useless map, but changed his mind in the next second because of the runes listed on it that may ultimately prove to be crucial to the success of his mission. He put it away in the saddlebag.

He next spurred on Valuspo, and the two began to cross the prairie. Halfway through, however, he began to get a funny feeling that they were being watched.

He stood in the saddle and looked all around for a minute, but there was no indication of a threat. It wasn't until they were three quarters of the way through the prairie that his sharp eyes first detected—and for only a second—some type of black creature rapidly running between two huge patches of tall grass to his south, about a hundred and fifty feet away.

Although he pondered using his bow and arrows, he also observed he would only get one shot or two before the creature would arrive and attack!

Therefore, he sat back down and snapped hard on Valuspo's reins in order to get his camel running at top speed. He chose to have his saber ready to strike, just in case there were more of those sneaky creatures around here. In his mind, he formulated an additional plan of defense. He figured that maybe he could use the horses as a distraction. That is, if he could get near enough.

He snapped the reins yet again as he screamed out, "Hey!"

Many of the horses stopped eating, now looking in his direction.

Again, Baltor peripherally spotted the creature darting between a different patch of prairie grass and a stacked group of boulders, this time much closer at eighty feet away. This time, he saw and knew exactly what it was, as he had seen them a couple of times before and always in cages. But this panther wasn't in a cage!

As he snapped on the reins to get Valuspo going still faster, he yelled out, "Hey you!"

By now, most of the horses were looking over at the intruder. Several started to prance around in order to warn away this new threat.

Baltor had gotten his camel seven-eighths of the way through, but observed that the panther was now directly chasing behind them on their path, about forty feet away, and drawing closer by the second!

"Hey you—yeah. I'm talking to you! You better start running!"

The horses had had enough—they began to run away, though the wrong way from Baltor's current position.

Still, the distraction worked for a second as the panther slowed its pace to look over.

In the next second, this predator decided that it would get its next meal from these two closer preys, and immediately quickened its pace back to full stride.

A few moments later, the panther thought it was near enough, so it lunged at the galloping camel. However, it was wrong as its claws missed Valuspo's rear legs by only a few inches.

Upon seeing this, Baltor realized that the only way to get rid of this panther was to get off the camel and fight it on foot—so he did. He lunged out of the saddle with saber in hand. When his hands hit the ground, he instantly rolled himself over into a defensive crouched position.

Surprised by the unexpected action from this prey, the panther slid to a complete stop in its tracks—only a foot and a half away from an unmoving Baltor! For five seconds, the two looked each other squarely in the eyes.

On the sixth second, however, hunger took over and with a growl, the panther threw a swipe of its paws and claws figuring to quickly finish off its prey, only to painfully discover that Baltor's saber had just sliced its arm in two!

155

As it roared out the excruciating pain, another painfully ripping sensation occurred as that saber quickly tore through its abdominal muscles and ripped all the way up to its throat. The panther died on the eighth second.

Once the battle was over, Baltor looked all around until he saw Valuspo, who had stopped about a hundred and fifty feet away, and whistled for him. He then sheathed his saber.

When his camel cautiously came back a minute later, he climbed back into the saddle—they rode east to the border of the trees.

About three minutes later, he discovered a very tiny path that was barely travelable with his camel's lengthy stride. The path loosely wound itself around thick barrages of interwoven roots that sprang out of the ground from gigantic trees—some trees were more than forty feet thick.

Just before he had turned around the bend that would take him out of view of the prairie, Baltor looked back one last time. He observed that there were now vultures slowly hovering closer and closer onto their treat.

An hour later, he began to suspect that *something* was not right. Though there was nothing to indicate something wrong, neither were there any of the traditional jungle noises.

Ten minutes later, he discovered that a twelve-foot thick tree had long ago fallen about thirty feet away and blocked his path and the view of what lay beyond the fallen tree.

When he drew closer, however, he saw that it wasn't a dead tree at all, but actually many exposed roots interwoven around each other, which sprang from one single living tree—a colossal tree that was at least sixty-foot thick and two hundred feet tall.

The nearest part of the trunk stood about fifteen feet to the south of the path, while its roots gradually extended and lowered themselves back into the ground, approximately ten feet to the north of the path.

He observed another cluster of roots that sprang in the southwestern direction, admitting, "Wow... I've never seen a tree this big!"

After having chosen to go around the northern end, he carefully steered his camel around all of the roots, which took them about a minute to get beyond.

What he saw on the other side of the stump caused his mouth to drop open in shock—for lying crumpled on the ground about forty feet away was a man whose skin color was black and whose attire considered solely of a grass skirt and sandals.

As he drew closer, he noticed that blood was still pouring from a large hole in the small man's hairy chest, dripping down the side of his body, and amassing into the ground—he appeared to have only been killed within the last hour by something or somebody!

Just as Baltor stopped his camel and drew out his saber, he heard the soft sounds of crunching leaves to his southeast; he looked up just in time to see several other black men running straight northbound. They were perhaps five hundred feet away.

None drew near or even looked his direction, and only a few seconds later, they disappeared back into the recesses of the jungle, and then the crunching sounds of leaves faded until the area returned to complete silence.

He scanned his immediate area more thoroughly, and noticed two other corpses to the south, partially hidden behind another large cluster of roots.

After lightly snapping his camel's reins, the two continued eastbound. All the while, he continued to listen for any other sounds, besides the ones coming from Valuspo's hoofs stepping onto the ground—all the while, his saber remained ready to strike.

A minute or so of silence passed, until, from deeper within the jungle directly to his south, a loud bird cawed, "Cee-cee-caw-caw!"

For a few more seconds, complete silence. Until suddenly, he again heard the sounds of crunching leaves fast approaching his current position. He first stopped his camel, looking over just in time to see another small black man also running northbound, probably in chase of those other men.

However, this man looked different from the others in the fact that he had chalky-white stripes painted onto his wicked-looking face—and the even more important trivia was that he carried a just-as-wicked spear that had colorful feathers attached underneath the spearhead! Additionally, he wore a few bone necklaces.

Upon seeing Baltor for the first time, the four-foot-tall man stopped in his tracks, and then he cawed using the same exact bird sounds Baltor had just heard, "Cee-cee-caw-caw-caw-cao-cao-cao!"

With his left hand, Baltor pulled Valuspo's reins to the left, so his camel would turn until his saber was clearly within the midget's sight, so as to intimidate him from coming closer.

However, the man didn't appear to care about the fact that this brown-skinned man was armed, for he began to run straight for him, cawing progressively louder, "Caw-caw-caw-cao-cao-cao!"

Once within throwing range a few seconds later, he cocked his spear back with his left hand and thrust it hard at Baltor.

Just before the spear could hit, Baltor's saber simply tapped the head of incoming spear, causing it to fly harmlessly away. He then rapidly twirled his saber several times more around in a circle, before stopping and assuming the ready position.

The man screamed in extreme agitation, but did not approach closer. Only moments later coming from out of the woodwork all around him, dozens more face-painted midget men came— almost all carried spears; quite a few carried foot-long bamboo reeds. The tallest in the entire group was perhaps five feet tall, while the shortest was about four feet tall: Most were in between these two heights, so Baltor observed.

He quickly put his saber away in the sheath and pulled out his bow and arrows. Before he was able to even notch the first arrow, however, he already felt a sharp stinging sensation in the back of his neck.

Instinctively, he reached with his free hand, discovering a thin needle poking out of it. He quickly pulled it out.

Seconds passed, but never did any of these savages draw any closer. Instead, they began to "caw!"

Baltor's head began to get dizzy, his vision became blurred, and the number of midgets that were now nearing tripled in number.

Two seconds later, he fell off his camel to the ground—no longer conscious!

CHAPTER XII

An unknown amount of time later, Baltor returned with surprise to consciousness, before squinting open his eyes. Prior to blacking out, he had worried that the poison from the dart might be lethal. Even now his vision remained blurry, and he had a headache.

Despite his partial blindness, he didn't have to move a single inch in order to figure out whether it was day or night, as he could clearly distinguish that the skies above were crystal clear blue, along with a hot and yellow sun hovering off to the right side.

Nor did he have to move to figure out that he was lying on the cold, hard and uncomfortable ground. What felt far worse were the venoms still coursing through his veins, especially around his neck area, feeling like a horde of scorpions had stung him!

Through the intense pains, he reached his left hand up to his neck to make sure the dart was gone. It was. He slowly turned his head to the right, in order to start to figure out his location.

As his blurry vision slowly but surely began to clear up, he first observed with great relief that no one had taken his golden arrowhead necklace, still firmly wrapped around his neck.

About thirty or so seconds later, he counted out twelve black midget men, all without white make-up on their faces—eleven wore grass skirts, while the final man in the far, left corner wore a black and brown skirt made of animal fur—neither did they move, but crouch on the ground and stare at it mindlessly. After all, they, and he, were obviously all prisoners within a roofless cage made of twelve-foot-tall bamboo sticks. No windows or doors that way.

As he slowly turned his head to look to his left, he counted only one entrance/exit this way, and no other prisoners. There was a bamboo door that had a rectangular window three quarters of the way up. And through this window he saw only the white-painted faces of two black men.

159

Baltor tried to prop himself up, but found that his head was just way too dizzy, and his stomach a bit nauseous—he slowly laid back down in order to collect his wits and his stomach.

When he finally began to feel a bit better, about twenty minutes or so later, he propped himself up into a sitting position. And after discovering that he was still feeling semi-okay a minute later, he slowly and cautiously rose to his feet until he was standing firmly.

Though a dizzy spasm did cross Baltor a moment later, he still found that he was okay enough to stand, but just to be on the safe side, he stood in place for still another minute.

Once that minute had passed, he quietly walked over to an old man, who sat by himself nearby, and whispered, "Hello."

The man completely ignored Baltor, as his eyes continued to look in the direction they had initially been looking at—the ground.

After another minute of silence had passed, Baltor next quietly walked over to the group of men huddling together—three of them—and whispered to them, "Hello—do any of you guys speak this language?"

All three responded in the same way by studiously ignoring him, just like the old man.

After his eighth attempt in all eight languages, he finally gave up, quietly walked back over to his spot, sat back down, and looked back out the window at the two guards. It was then that he first became aware that the guards were now chatting like birds, and it wasn't actual birds making the "coos" and "caws."

While still listening to the guards, he stood back up, quietly walked over to the wall that was his prison, found a small hole in between two of the bamboo stalks, and looked out that hole for a few minutes.

Outside this prison, he saw a whole lot of midget men, women and children, all with variously designed white make-up designs on their faces, as well dozens of other large bamboo huts. Some simply sat around and chatted in that foreign language, while others silently walked around and still others worked. None at all wore shirts, just those grass skirts and leather sandals. The women wore just enough bone necklaces to conceal their privates.

Once he had thoroughly scanned this side of the village as best he could, Baltor walked over to the other side of the hut, found yet another hole, and scanned thoroughly out that area.

On this side of the village, he observed that there were no huts, no living people and no camel. Instead, there was a huge fire pit still smoldering; hanging over the fire pit upon a dozen long bamboo sticks, there were half of a dozen human corpses with all skin removed, hanging by their arms and legs wrapped and tied around the sticks—turning to dried jerky. Valuspo was nowhere to be seen anywhere.

Obviously, even though Baltor had never before run across a group of cannibals, he had certainly heard of them and never forgotten, thanks to a bedtime story dramatically relayed by his mother's only sibling—ole' Uncle Baltor.

Because of the uncle's profession of choice, which was being a skipper on a merchant ship that sailed the "Eleven Seas," he had only two one-week-long opportunities to visit the nephew that had been directly named after the uncle.

Immediately the nephew began to get very nervous as the thoughts of his impeding doom swelled.

Before a minute's time had passed, Baltor suddenly began to feel very queasy, and a moment later he got so uncontrollably sick that he crouched down onto his knees so he could puke his guts out.

A minute later yet not feeling much better, he began to hear someone trying to speak to him quietly, though it was in that bird-like language, which sounded exactly like the cannibal guards.

He turned his head to see that young man standing before him, the man wearing the fur loincloth. Upon closer glance, Baltor observed that he stood at five-foot-six-inches and had powerful muscles. He was the tallest and strongest man out of them all.

Baltor slowly sat up, and then he shrugged his shoulders to indicate that he didn't understand what the young man had just said.

Again, the young man said something else, though what he said sounded just like an exotic bird.

This time, Baltor decided to ask in the language of Misharan, "Can you speak this tongue?"

The man said something else in his bird-like language that was completely unintelligible to Baltor's ears.

Baltor switched over to the language of Pagasian, while asking the same question for the second time—this time, instead of saying anything else, the young man turned around, walked back over to his buddies, and squatted back down into silence.

Giving up as well, Baltor walked back over to the hole in the hut that revealed the huts and the cannibals, and then continued to stare out of the hut as day slowly turned into night.

After all, there was nothing else he could do but wait and study his adversaries....

Once night had come, and still without any sign of
Valuspo, the tribe gathered at the fire pit. After a dozen or so
cannibals had taken the corpses to another location, the rest of the
tribe had begun to set up a large bonfire.

As soon as the last cannibal had returned, the tribe immediately
started with the ritual—a fast drumbeat commenced, whereupon
the cannibals simultaneously began to dance chaotically around the
fire while chanting in that exotic, bird-like language.

From amongst the crowd, a six-foot tall figure soon emerged that
was about two-to-three feet taller than all of the other midgets.
Even with the strange shadows cast by the fire, Baltor could see
that this was no man at all but a gorilla!

Almost amusingly, this beast joined in the dance as it continuously circled around the fire several more times, with everybody
now circling behind—until all of a sudden, everyone stopped at the
exact same moment when the drums stop, including the gorilla.

It then beat its fisted paws into its chest quite harshly, while
screaming something out that didn't sound ape-like at all, yet more
bird-like, "Chee-caw-chee-hee-choo-cha-ha-hoo-chaw-chee-caw!"

While screaming the chant back, the cannibals immediately began to spread themselves farther away from the fire, which soon
formed a twenty-foot circular perimeter around the gorilla.

Once again in that bird-like language, it screamed out,
"Caw-chee-chaw-hoo-ha-cha-choo-hee-chee-cawchee!"

Joining the gorilla from the crowd was a woman donning a
feather-covered costume, bearing a feathered hat that also bore the
head of a vulture seamed into the top. Meanwhile, the cannibals
screamed back the chant, their voices even louder this time.

The gorilla next screamed out, "Cha-ha-hoo-chaw-chee-caw-
choo-hee-chee-cawchee!"

As soon as the cannibals had finished screaming back the chant,
the two guards outside opened the door, and then cawed something to all the prisoners inside while gesturing with their spears to
exit the hut.

Within seconds, the other prisoners began to shuffle mindlessly
toward the door of the hut. Though Baltor appeared to be the only
one afraid, he too followed them.

Once he stood outside, his head and eyes quickly gazed left and
right seeking any possible escape.

One of the guards had been carefully watching and listening to
all the prisoners, especially this brown-skinned one, and immediately he slapped this prisoner in the back of the knees with his

spear very, very, very hard—this action caused Baltor's knees to crash hard into the ground, and simultaneously cause lots of pain!

A second later, the guard sharply cawed something out, while gesturing with the very sharp point of his spear in Baltor's face to follow the rest.

He slowly stood to his feet and then painfully stumbled toward the other prisoners that were already nearing the bonfire. The crowd had already made a small gap for them to pass toward the center.

When Baltor drew closer to the fire, he realized this was no gorilla at all, but a man in a gorilla suit that covered him from head to toe. That is, except for the gorilla's face that had been cut out, revealing a black-painted human face underneath.

Once the prisoners had all lined up near the fire that included Baltor, the gorilla-man then screamed out something like, "Choo-hee-chee-caw-caw-chee-chaw-hoo-ha-cha!"

As the crowds of cannibals closed the gap and any sort of escape, they screamed back the gorilla-man's chant.

The vulture-woman next screamed out, "Chee-caw-chee-hee-choo-cha-ha-hoo-chaw-chee-caw-caw!"

As soon as she had finished, the others slowly began to chant almost quietly at first, "Caw. caw. caw. caw! Caw! Caw! CAW!" The chanting grew progressively faster, as well louder and louder.

Suddenly and in unison, the cannibals stopped the chanting. Meanwhile, the gorilla-man and vulture-woman had made their way over to the first prisoner, and the gorilla-man growled out, "*Grrrooooooooowwwwwwwwwwwwllll!*"

Even though Baltor was the last of the thirteen total prisoners, he pondered any sort of escape options without averting his head. However, there were no options, as the entire tribe consisting of at least a hundred completely surrounded them.

Baltor picked up the sound of a shocked gasp, and he quickly gazed back over to see that two cannibals were holding the first prisoner firmly in place, and that the gorilla-man had just jabbed an extremely sharp ivory tusk into the center of the prisoner's chest.

As the prisoner screamed out his agonizing pain, Baltor could barely hold back his gasp of shock and horror as he observed the heart physically removed by the gorilla-man's hand—a heart that was still beating! He watched in ever-increasing horror as the gorilla-man extended the heart out to the vulture-woman, and the vulture-woman disgustingly crunched her teeth right into the heart, which caused blood to spray all over her white-painted face.

163

Shocked, horrified, and disgusted, Baltor bit back his own scream by biting his own tongue, as he watched the prisoner instantaneously drop to the ground while screaming out his anguishing pains and clutching his heartless chest.

As for the gorilla-man, however, he ecstatically raised the remaining portion of the heart into the air, and as he tightly squeezed it with his fist, which caused a whole lot more blood to pour down his arm—he screamed out, "*Ahhhhhhhhhhhhhhhhhhhhhhhhhh!*"

Baltor could no longer hold back his scream of shock and horror at the same time as the rest of the cannibals screamed ecstatically back in response to their leader, so no one heard his.

A moment later, he dry-heaved, and his eyes could not look away as the gorilla-man took a bite into the heart, which caused still more blood to squirt all over his face.

The second the gorilla-man casually tossed that heart into the fire as if it was a piece of wood, the prisoner finally died!

Meanwhile, Baltor could no longer hold back the remaining fractional contents of stomach juices that he threw up.

When he looked up about thirty seconds later with tears still pouring out of his eyes, he blurrily saw the gorilla-man and vulture-woman now standing before the next prisoner—the young man who wore the fur loincloth.

Already, the gorilla-man had recommenced with that strange and frightening chant.

Baltor realized that if he didn't do something quick, he would be the last to die this horrific and disgusting way, so he needed to use the element of surprise and fight his way through the crowd.

Without pause, he booked for freedom, and he even valiantly fought for it for the next several minutes. However, the masses immediately began closing in on his position like hordes of flies on a tiny piece of dung, as they began to leap at him with arms and legs extended completely outward as if flies without their wings.

Baltor knocked out or killed a grand total of fourteen cannibals, before the fifteenth such cannibal had successfully knocked him to the ground, with the rest of the cannibals piling right on top!

Only a moment later, the cannibals had completely pinned him to the ground. Baltor was unable to move with more than two thousand pounds of body weight on top of him, and for about twenty seconds, unable to breathe....

After the pile of cannibals had separated about a minute later, two of the remaining cannibals forcibly brought Baltor back to his feet. While breathing very raggedly and coughing all the while, he saw that the gorilla-man and vulture-woman were now standing in front of him.

Upon closer glance, he saw through his starry vision that both had bone rings that began from inside their nostrils that curled around the outside of their noses—even weirder than that, he observed that they bore friendly smiles, though all he could do was to gulp down his fears and wait.

The gorilla-man drew even closer, giving Baltor the up-down look, still with that friendly smile upon his face. Several seconds later, he scanned across the tribe around him as he said nicely, "Choo-hee-chee-caw-caw-chee-chaw-hooha-cha."

The vulture-woman also added nicely, "Chee-caw-chee-hee-choo-cha-hahoo-chaw-chee-caw-caw-caw."

Just as before, as soon as she had finished, the others began to chant quietly at first, "Caw. Caw. Caw. Caw! Caw! Caw! CAW!"

The chanting grew progressively faster and faster, as well louder and louder! Once again in unison, nearly a minute later, the chanting stopped.

The gorilla-man's gaze focused back upon Baltor, and his friendly smile turned diabolically evil a second before he growled at the top of his lungs, "*Groooooooooooooooowwwwwwwwwwllll!!*"

Baltor closed his eyes and awaited the plunge that would finalize his life.

It seemed that the gorilla-man had even given Baltor a few extra moments to live, as he was able to ask himself, silently, *What will life be like for me after I die? Oh—sorry God if I've done wrong, but I tried as best I could.*

Instead of Baltor feeling the tusk penetrate his chest as he expected, he heard the sound of a whooshing noise. The second he heard the sound of someone else's body crumpling nearby, however, he opened his eyes and looked around.

Even though the gorilla-man was now lying on the ground and completely unmoving, the vulture-woman had already begun to frantically push her way past the scattering cannibals who were rushing for their weapons located in their homes on the other side of the prison, while simultaneously raising a loud cawing alarm.

There were only a half dozen tribesmen still around, though they were all armed with either spears or blowguns, while looking all around the dark jungles for their enemy, or enemies. From all around, Baltor observed as several more of those tribesmen, including one of the two that had been firmly holding him in place, dropped to the ground.

Upon seeing his partner fall to the ground, the other unarmed cannibal that was holding Baltor let go, especially after having witnessed first-hand his very unusual and powerful fighting skills a few minutes ago, and immediately he bolted back for the village while screaming.

Baltor thought about chasing him down for a moment—yet he quickly changed his mind as he heard the screams of the returning cannibals get progressively louder.

From amongst the din to his right, he heard someone yell something like, "Caw-chew-chee-cha-cha-che-cha-cha-chew-Cheo!"(55)

Baltor looked over to see the young man with the loincloth that had tried to talk to him earlier that day, already about fifty feet away to his right. Not only was he directly looking at Baltor, yet he quickly gestured toward himself with both hands twice.

Without any further delay, the young man turned around and began to run toward the dark recesses of the jungle, which was still about fifty more feet ahead of him.

After immediately getting the idea that the young man wanted him to follow, Baltor booked north at full speed. With a spear that he had just scooped off the ground that a cannibal had just dropped upon falling unconscious from a poisoned dart, he quickly ascertained he would only have to fight his way past two more cannibals armed with spears. The nearest cannibal was twenty feet away from his current position, while the second nearest was thirty-five feet away.

He simultaneously observed that both cannibals were looking in other directions than his own running position—the further of the two cannibals had not only spotted the bolting young man, yet had taken off in hot pursuit.

The second Baltor had passed the bonfire which had been to his right about twelve feet away, his peripheral vision detected a female cannibal standing up on the northeastern side, who was now looking at him while placing the end of a blowgun in her mouth.

Baltor quickly estimated that the woman was about twenty feet away from his current position, while the male cannibal was only about fifteen feet away—meanwhile, the woman had just begun to aim carefully at the moving target that she had already deemed a dangerous threat!

The very second he had gotten twelve feet away from the male cannibal who, at that moment, turned his head toward Baltor's direction for the very first time, he first leveled one end of his spear into the ground while also firmly gripping the other end.

This action caused him to catapult high up into the air with both his feet kicking out straight in front of him for maximum thrusting power, all the while shifting his grip on the spear until he was firmly holding it in the middle with both hands.

Just before Baltor's feet made contact with his enemy's chest a second and a half later, he had already curled up his legs tightly into his own chest. The very second his feet made contact, he kicked his feet straight out with full force!

Not only did that cannibal fly sideways through the air for about a half dozen feet and not only did his head crash so hard into the ground, which instantaneously caused his neck to snap sideways and kill the man instantly, but his corpse even continued to roll sideways another half dozen more times before stopping once and for all!

As Baltor flew backwards from the propulsion, his legs instantly tucked themselves back into his chest; and not even a moment later he heard a whooshing sound from a passing dart that would have hit him had his momentum kept going forward.

The second he had completed his back flip back on his feet, he didn't pause yet cocked back the spear in his right hand, and rapidly flicked it toward the female cannibal who had just finished reloading her dart gun.

The spear plunged halfway through her before stopping—in both shock and pain, she dropped the blow dart gun, and then she grabbed the spear imbedded through her to try and pull it out. A second later, she collapsed to the ground dead!

He hadn't been watching her die, yet had already recommenced to bolting forward, while observing that even though the young man was just nearing the perimeters of the jungle, the last immediate threat was about twelve feet behind the young man and drawing nearer by the second.

Baltor slowed down his pace for but a second as he leaned over to scoop up another spear off the ground, which had been dropped by the first cannibal he had killed. After recommencing with his full running stride, he immediately cocked the spear back in his right hand, and then he heaved it with all of his might straight at the cannibal!

Though this cannibal was about forty-five feet away from Baltor's position, he was now only eight feet or so behind the young man.

Just as the cannibal was about to launch his own spear at the young man, no more than three seconds later, Baltor's spear not only sailed completely through the cannibal's midsection which caused him to capsize to the ground, yet the spear continued to fly straight toward the young man! Upon seeing that the spear hadn't stopped, Baltor began to grit his teeth in fear and frustration, as his feet came to a complete stop.

A split second later, the young man abruptly stopped in his tracks and turned his body, just as the spear zinged in front of his stomach by no more than a single inch.

Two more seconds passed before the spear finally sank a quarter of the way into a tree that was ten feet beyond of where the young man now stood—it was only then that Baltor breathed a deep sigh of relief, while wiping off all the sweat off his forehead with his left hand.

After the young man had glanced at the bloody spear forever imbedded into the tree, he slowly turned back around. Upon seeing Baltor breathing yet another sigh of relief while also shaking his head in disbelief, and also the mortally wounded cannibal who was screaming out his agonizing pains only six feet away, the young man once again excitedly gestured with both of his hands to follow.

Finally, he turned around and entered the dark perimeter of the jungle. Meanwhile, Baltor wasted no time and followed, though he was still about forty feet behind, yet slowly catching up to the young man.

As soon as the two had escaped the perimeters of the village, they suddenly heard many sounds of whooshing, fighting and screaming from behind them! Along the way, even though Baltor saw no one other than this young man, he continued to book.

After about twelve more minutes of running and Baltor had gotten to about ten feet behind, the young man suddenly stopped and turned around. Without saying a word, he immediately began pulling together a bunch of dead leaves off the ground into a pile, and then hid himself within them. Meanwhile, Baltor had already gotten the picture and followed suit.

Less than a minute after they had fully tucked themselves under the leaves, Baltor heard the sounds of approaching footsteps running by and the sounds of bird-clucking noises. He remained completely still, which included lightening his breathing up until it was virtually noiseless and undetectable.

Only seconds later, those footsteps receded. Nearly ten minutes later, the area became completely silent other than the sounds of grasshoppers and other jungle noises. Soon after, without meaning to, Baltor fell asleep.

CHAPTER XIII

Night turned into morning, and Baltor only awoke because he felt himself being shaken awake. Upon opening his eyes, he saw the young man squatting next to him.

This man gestured for Baltor to follow with a single wave of his hand, and without any further delay, he stood up, turned to the north, and began to jog that direction—Baltor got right up and followed at the same pace right behind him.

An hour before sunset, three days later, and with only about a dozen short pit stops the entire time to eat, drink, rest, etc., the two exhausted men finally reached the borders of another tribal village, consisting of a large number similarly-designed straw huts. On the far side of the village, there stood a single massive bamboo hut—at least thirty times the size as the rest.

Spread throughout this village were hundreds of midget villagers of all ages involved in daily tasks. The men either farmed his own little lot of land right next to his hut, or socially chatted with one another, while the women cooked or cleaned or chatted. The children played and laughed.

Thankfully, Baltor saw that no one around here wore that gruesome white make-up like the cannibal tribe. But like them, their clothes were the same, consisting of simple grass skirts and sandals; and these women also wore just enough bead necklaces to conceal their privates.

With the young man still in the lead, Baltor entered the perimeters of the village, noticing all the villagers stop in their tasks as this young man passed on by, bowing to the ground on their hands and knees.

Baltor instantly recognized the "universal sign" that the guy he'd been following for the last four nights was at least a very high-ranking member of society, perhaps even royalty!

Once the villagers looked up to see Baltor pass, however, their eyes remained firmly locked onto him—for never had they ever seen anyone with such light skin before, and especially such strange clothing.

Curious, all of the villagers soon began to follow right behind Baltor, while rapidly speaking amongst each other in that bird-like tongue—only moments later, he could feel hands touching his backside gently, but never did the villagers grab or stop him as he walked.

Baltor did his best to ignore the pesky annoyances, which certainly wasn't easy, but then unexpectedly, someone had just lightly poked his left butt cheek with his or her finger!

He was about to turn around yell out a reprimand, but when he heard the sounds of someone's hand being slapped and a woman saying something harshly that caused a young child to cry, he figured the culprit was that young child, so he just kept walking.

Perhaps ten minutes later, they—the young man, Baltor, and all the villagers who followed close behind—finally reached the big hut.

This three-story building even had outdoor patios looking out just about everywhere on all floors. Located at the only entrance Baltor had seen so far, there stood on each side a tribal guard in a semi-relaxed position, each armed with a feather-laced and very sharp spear.

The young man entered the hut first, while Baltor followed about five feet behind. The second his new friend had passed through the entryway, the guards immediately crossed their spears in front of Baltor, indicating that entry into the hut was forbidden, unless of course he fought his way through, which he was not about to do.

Instead, he stopped dead in his tracks and patiently waited. The instant the young man heard the sounds of the spears clicking, he turned his head around and said something in that very fast tongue of his to the guards. (56)

A moment later, the two guards drew back their spears into their original position, and Baltor assumed that that the young man had told the guards to allow him to enter the hut, and so he did.

Once Baltor had entered, the two guards re-crossed their spears, which forbade entry to all the other villagers that wanted to come in.

Even though there were no stairs in this hut, Baltor approximated that he was walking through a one-hundred-and-twenty-foot long hallway that escalated higher and higher into the hut, while bearing a dozen entryways decently spaced on each side. At each of the entryways, there was a large animal fur, which hung down from the ceiling. Baltor could tell from a passing look through the cracks around and underneath the furs that there was at least one room behind them.

After entering the third and final hallway and floor, Baltor surprisingly discovered that this hallway was very short—no more than ten feet in length it was.

At the end of the hallway, there stood another entryway that was much bigger than the rest, but this one was not covered by animal fur, and Baltor could see a lot of villagers inside this room, all facing the other way. Standing to each side of the entryway, there stood two more guards armed with spears.

The young man passed by the guards without saying a word. Just as before, as Baltor neared the two guards, they crossed their spears in front of him with that clicking sound.

This time, the young man said nothing as he continued his way into the room and without looking back once.

As Baltor patiently waited, he spent this valuable time examining this incredibly large room that he approximated to be at least one hundred feet in length, and six hundred feet in width.

There were also a large number of villagers, about sixty of them, who bowed as the young man passed—these villagers wore furs, tribal necklaces, golden hoop earrings and neck rings decked out with jewels.

Baltor observed—hanging upon the walls—the heads of an incredible assortment of stuffed predatory jungle animals—every single eye socket stuffed with a large jewel or diamond.

If that wasn't enough, he also saw a wide assortment of tribal shields hanging upon the walls, most bearing large and colorful feathers glued to the molten metallic substance underneath, which was obviously gold—underneath each shield were two crossed-spears, also made of gold, feathers dangling just below the spear-head.

Because all of the villagers were now bowing at the man who had neared the end of the room, Baltor could now see at the very far end of the room that there were three thrones adorned with furs, feathers, gold, and jewels, including diamonds.

Sitting in the throne in the middle was an elderly man, and in sitting to his left was an elderly woman. Both wore an actual panther's head ornamented with diamonds stuck in the eye sockets, as well animal furs covering the whole of their bodies, despite the hot and humid temperatures.

Once the young man had drawn near, he stopped. Without bowing, he began to rapidly talk to this king and queen. (57)

The young man turned around, pointed with his finger at Baltor, and added something else foreign to Baltor's ears. (58)

After a good seven second pause, he added something else. (59)

Once he had finished speaking this time, everybody in the room turned his or her head to look at Baltor—he had no doubt he was the center of attention, though he did not know why. What he did know was the fact that this young man whom he had been following must be royalty, because he hadn't bowed one time before this king and queen. Still, Baltor remained silent and unmoving.

The king was the next person to say something. (60)

A split second later, the guards pulled back the spears into their original at ease position. The king beckoned his hand for Baltor to enter—he did.

As he drew closer, he observed that both the king and queen donned an extensive amount of valuable jewelry around their neck and ears. About twenty feet away from the throne, Baltor stopped in his tracks and bowed in the standing position.

This king sharply said something (61) just before he began to gesture with his hand for Baltor to come closer, which words immediately drew Baltor's gaze back up. A second later, Baltor walked closer.

When he had gotten about five feet away, the king stopped the physical gesturing of his hand, while saying something else. (62)

Baltor stopped in his tracks.

The five-foot-tall king stood up from his throne, and as he walked around and around Baltor, he gave the up-down look for about twenty seconds.

About the tenth time around, the king stopped right in front of Baltor and as he patted Baltor's chest, he said something rapidly and excitedly. (63)

Even though Baltor didn't have a clue as to what had been said, everybody else in the room did as they began to loudly "caw" in unison; that is, except for Baltor, the king, queen, and this extremely important young man.

Baltor began to turn his head around in order to look at the still-cawing crowds, but felt his jaw gently pulled back toward the king. He saw that the king bore a very happy smile, though Baltor did not know why.

Out of the corner of his eye, he next saw the young man take the seat upon the left throne—this prince, as he obviously was, was now gazing and smiling at Baltor, which smile was the exact same as his father's.

After the king had excitedly said something else, the crowd stopped cawing, and then they began to shuffle their way out the throne room doors—the king, meanwhile, sat back down in the middle throne.

Nearly a minute later, only the royalty remained in the room, and of course, Baltor.

It was then that the prince stood up from his throne, walked over to Baltor, pointed at his own chest with his left index finger, and identified, "Cheo-Sucanamo-Chaosnam-Casaman-Namao."

"Cheo." Baltor only repeated the first part to his friend's name, and after pointing to himself, he said, "Baltor."

Unexpectedly, the queen said something (64). After she was done speaking, Cheo cocked his head from side to side.

Without any further delay, the prince grabbed Baltor's hand, led him out of the throne room, and took him down to the next floor. After passing three fur-covered entryways on the right-hand side, he opened the fourth entryway, and after entering, held open the fur so his new friend could enter.

Just before entering, Baltor already observed that it contained a five-and-a-half-foot tall stand-up tub made of wood, and filled with hot, steaming water—heated from a large pit of burning charcoals underneath. Leaning against the near side of the tub was a ladder.

After Baltor had entered, the prince said something in his way-too-fast-to-comprehend language, (65) climbed the ladder into the tub, took off his loincloth and threw it over the side.

Baltor figured Cheo had been telling him to get into the tub, so he took off his shirt, and then kicked off his boots and socks.

Just as he was about to take off his pants yet leave his underwear on, two beautiful girls came in from another fur-covered entryway, each holding a sponge in hand.

Cheo was already sighing deeply as the hot and medicinal waters soothed his aching muscles all the way up to his neck. As for Baltor, he continued to stand there, completely unmoving and watching, as the two girls also hopped into the tub with the prince.

As soon as Cheo saw not only that Baltor wasn't even getting undressed, yet standing there with a beet-red face even with his tanned complexion, he began to laugh in a cocking fashion, "Ca-ca-ca-ca-ca-ca-ca-ca-ca, etc., etc." With his hand however, he gestured for Baltor to enter the tub. Meanwhile one of the girls began sponging the prince's back underneath the water.

Baltor got undressed, and quickly entered the tub, which water proved to be very hot.

As soon as he stood within the tub, which water reached the very bottom of his neck, his entire body immediately began to relax—both from the heat and from the tribal medicine that had been specially intermixed into the water.

In under a minute, he could no longer feel those aching muscles that he had long neglected. As the girls massaged and scrubbed the two men within the confines of the bathtub, Baltor and Cheo spent the next ten minutes trying to learn to understand each other's language, but all for naught.

This prince's language was not only far too fast for Baltor to comprehend, even when he spoke it very slowly, yet it was too repetitive with all the *chaw's* and the *chew's*!

One perfect example was when the prince said Baltor's name alone, he pronounced it this way, "Ba-cha-cha-cha-al-chu-chu-chu-tor-chew-chew-chew."

On the eleventh minute, the girls smiled at Baltor and Cheo in turn, and then they exited the tub. Baltor became quite surprised and relieved that they had never touched his private parts, not even accidentally.

For the next minute, neither said a word to each other but simply smile at each other, which was all they could do. At the end of that minute, Baltor cleared his throat and then exited the tub.

As soon as he had stepped back onto the floor, he saw that the two girls had neatly set onto the floor two pairs of fur loincloths and two pairs of jewelry-laced sandals. Quickly he threw his loincloth on.

Just after the sun had set twenty minutes later—language or no language—the partying commenced.

Though Baltor didn't understand the slightest bit of what any of the villagers said, other than his or her name, he understood their kind faces and friendly pats on his back.

He also rather enjoyed the roasted boars that they had cooked over an open fire. Not long after his food had begun to digest, the prince came back to Baltor with a long tribal pipe in his hand.

After Cheo had lit it and taken a couple of puffs, he then extended it out for Baltor. He took two hits, and for the rest of the night, that was nothing but a blur ... the only thing he could remember for sure was that he was up until right after sunrise.

That afternoon, Baltor awoke to find that he was lying on a blanket of furs—what really startled him was the fact that he wasn't alone, for curled up next to him was a beautiful young woman— fortunately still clothed.

Only seconds after he sat up in bed, an old tribeswoman was entering and carrying a green leaf with some funky green substance. It wasn't until she patted her stomach that Baltor realized this was food.

When he took a taste of the nasty stuff, it took all of his willpower not to spit it back out.

The old woman, however, wouldn't leave until Baltor had eaten the entire contents of his bowl. Unfortunately, in the end, she did not give him something to drink, in order to wash down the very bitter aftertaste. The young woman continued to sleep.

Once breakfast was over, only a minute later, a tribesman entered the room, approached Baltor, and with a gesture of his hand to follow, led him up the hallway until they reached the throne room—the king and queen were not there this time.

The prince was sitting in his throne, now adorning a black, fur coat and loincloth, some golden earrings and other types of tribal jewelry. He stood up and approached Baltor with a kind-hearted smile. Baltor smiled back.

Over the course of the next several hours, they tried very hard to learn the other's language, but again, all their best attempts proved futile.

Just after nightfall, and the feasting and partying had once again recommenced with the prince, his parents, and the villagers by the large bonfire outside, Baltor knew that he must continue on his quest and soon, but now he no longer had his camel, and even worse, the map!

It had always been in his hopes that maybe Cheo might at least have some sort of clue about the tower, especially since it's supposed to be in his jungle. But due to all the previous failures in communication, he was about to lost hope ... until suddenly, a brilliant idea crossed Baltor's mind!

After picking up a nearby stick off the ground, he drew the picture of the camel into the dirt.

Because the prince had a clueless look in his face, Baltor realized that he didn't know anything about his camel.

Therefore, he scribbled out the camel with his foot, and began to draw the picture of the tower. He looked up to see a fearful expression upon Cheo's face, and a moment later, for the prince to obliterate the drawing with his foot, while excitedly clucking something incomprehensible for a few seconds. (66)

Baltor, realizing that the prince did know something about the tower, drew its picture for the second time—and for the second time the prince scribbled it out with his foot, while clucking his tongue repeatedly again. (67)

Baltor slapped his chest, said his own name, drew the tower into the sand for the third time, wiggled his index and middle fingers back and forth a few times to indicate that he was traveling that way, and then pointed at the drawing with the stick.

The prince was about to obliterate the drawing, but then he stopped that foot only an inch away. A second later, he placed it back where it originally had been, which was next to his other foot.

Baltor looked up. Cheo sighed in resignation, pointed at Baltor and then the drawing, point to the night sky overhead, and then extended four of his fingers.

Baltor nodded his head in understanding and agreement that the prince wanted him to stay four more nights. But as the prince looked confused from the nodding gesture, Baltor cocked his head from side to side, to indicate the affirmative. Cheo smiled.

During the next three days and nights, even though verbal communication had proven impossible so far, both refused to give up. Despite this setback, fortunately, Cheo and Baltor learned how to communicate in other ways—sign language and drawing.

It was through drawn pictures that Cheo was able to explain that his culture was not the culture of the cannibals. In fact, the two tribes were hated enemies for centuries, having warred too many times to count. They, Baltor and the prince, learned quite a few other things about each other as well, though not a whole lot.

He also noticed that the villagers really loved to party every night, including Cheo's parents, and every night was a great old time. And during the days, he and the prince spent just about every waking moment exploring all the natural wonders and beauties of his kingdom, from cascading waterfalls to unusually shaped rock formations. Very little sleep did either of them get through this whole time, but neither were they tired.

Finally, the fourth morning came, a tribal guard arrived, and after a prompting of his hand for Baltor to follow, he then led the way into the throne room. This time, the king and queen were there as well, in order to see him off before his scheduled departure.

Once near the thrones, the prince beckoned Baltor to approach closer with a hand gesture. Once he had drawn to about five feet away, the prince stood up from his throne, walked over to Baltor, and clasped his friend tightly. When he pulled back from the hug, Baltor observed that a teardrop had formed at the corner of his friend's eye.

Instead of just simply wiping it away, however, Prince Cheo extended his pinky out, swiped the teardrop before it fell, and rather surprisingly, rubbed it in a little circle right on Baltor's forehead.

Baltor didn't know or understand why the prince had just performed this very unusual action—nor could he even begin to ask with only the fractional bits of sign language they had painstakingly co-developed.

A moment later, he found it even more unusual that his mind's eye suddenly began to relive these last few days spent with all of the villagers, which included smiles, laughs, and fun, of whom had become his newest collection of wonderful friends.

Upon completion of all the happy recollections, a few seconds later, Baltor sadly realized he was going to miss everyone once he was gone, and he could feel his heart begin to tighten up in his chest. A tear mysteriously formed in his own eye, so he repeated Prince Cheo's very unusual act.

A moment later, Baltor's eyes held even more curiosity and surprise after he had glanced up to the thrones and observed that the king and queen were proudly smiling at the two, though he had no clue why they seemed so proud and happy.

Meanwhile, the prince looked over to a tribesman that was standing idly by, and then said something to the man (68)—the tribesman cocked his head from side to side, bowed down on his hands and knees, and then hurriedly exited the throne room to carry out his orders.

Prince Cheo reassumed his throne, smiled yet again at Baltor, and pointed one finger up in the air.

Baltor understood that he was to wait a minute.

Exactly one minute later, that tribesman reentered the throne room carrying three very recognizable objects in one hand, 1) his saber 2) inside the sheath, and 3) the map. In his other hand he carried a pear-shaped/sized bag made of black fur.

Baltor was quite surprised and delighted to see that they had miraculously retrieved his prized objects, most likely from the cannibals—he delivered both an elated smile and a respectful nod of his head to the prince, queen and king.

The tribesman, just as carefully, placed all objects onto the ground before him, bowed once again, and went back to his former post.

Already had Baltor begun to pick everything off the floor—in turn, stuffing the map into his shirt, tying the sheath to his belt, and then picking up the bag.

While feeling on the bag that was very soft on the outside, yet hard and shifty on the inside, Baltor's mind's eye once again saw and thought of Valuspo. His camel, companion, and friend.

He drew the picture of the camel into the air, but as before, Prince Cheo rolled his head around in a circle, indicating that no, his camel had not been found.

Out of curiosity as to the contents of the bag, Baltor looked down and just about to open it up when Prince Cheo unexpectedly whistled, which he had earlier taught the prince how to do.

He looked up to see the prince gesture around his throne room, and then at himself. He next pointed toward Baltor, pointed around the throne room again, and then pointed at the bag.

A moment later, Baltor shook his head from side-to-side in understanding that the prince wanted him to open the bag only after he had gotten home, and so out of respect, he tied the end of the bag securely around his belt loop.

As he looked back up, he saw that Prince Cheo was smiling as he for the very first time said his name right, "Baltor." He then pointed at the tribesman that had just brought all his possessions to him, and then pointed out the door.

As Baltor looked over, that man prompted for him to follow—he followed the man out of the throne room.

After he stopped and looked back one last time into the throne room, toward the three thrones, he saw the prince trace the outline of the tower into the air. He then pointed eight fingers in the air.

Baltor cocked his head from side-to-side to indicate he understood the prince's message. He next dropped down onto both hands and knees and bowed, as he had seen the villagers do out of respect.

He stood back onto his feet nearly ten seconds later, before casting one final smile and one final farewell wave of the hand, and then making his way for the palace's main entrance.

Once outside, he discovered that there was a caravan of twenty tribesmen waiting around in loose formation, all armed with feathered spears and blowguns. Shockingly, the tribeswoman who stood in the very middle held onto the reins of a giant, grey, saddled animal with long ivory tusks that had just knelt down onto it knees, so Baltor could climb up. This animal, as his memory reminded him, was called an "elephant"!

And the reason it was *so shocking* for Baltor to see an elephant was because he had seen them only once before in his life yet never forgot, when he was six-years-old—thanks to his mother who had taken him to the bazaar. Along the way, they had been stopped by a short parade of visiting royal dignitaries; their guards rode either on horseback or on elephants. While waiting, his mother had told him the name of this animal. Never, ever, ever had he conceived he would get to ride one ... until now!

He climbed up into the elephant's comfortable, multi-pillowed saddle and relaxed. After all, per Prince Cheo's message, the journey to get from the village of Chao-chu-sha-maen to the tower would take approximately eight days....

CHAPTER XIV

About thirty minutes-or-so before the sun was about to set, eight days later, and surprisingly without so much as a single encounter through this trip through the vast jungle, Baltor's eyes finally gazed upon a tower far to the east. Hanging just above it in the skies was the full, gray moon, as well a dozen twinkling stars.

This tall, black and lonely tower rested at the top of a great, grassy hill without any trees. Even from this distance of two miles, he could tell that parts of this ancient structure had collapsed, and were in severe ruin due to the harsh elements. He could also tell that his tribal escorts had been quite nervous, especially after these last few days as they drew nearer to this taboo area.

So after climbing down off his elephant, he pointed them back to their village, although he knew they knew the way better than he.

After the tribeswoman had given him a lit torch and a quick smile, they quickly departed back for home.

Only once they were completely out of sight, about five minutes later, lost behind a thick cover of jungle trees, did Baltor turn around to face the tower that had just begun to blend into the ever-darkening sky.

He simultaneously observed that, amongst this prairie containing mostly two-foot tall patches of grassy rolling hills, there were quite a few clusters of grouped trees here and there, for possible predatory animals, robbers, or even cannibals to hide.

As his mind considered his options of whether to stay or head to the tower, he mused aloud, "Well, how much safer am I here?"

At a good pace, he began jogging toward the tower. As he drew nearer, his eyes could clearly see, even with the darkness that was quickly consuming the skies, that this tower was definitely in a very serious stage of decay—more than half of the tower's extended rectangular-shaped building had long ago collapsed.

Perhaps three minutes after the sun had set, he finally reached his destination. While throwing another quick glance westbound into the last of the furious colors of dusk, it was only then that he noticed for the first time that the red moon was also in the western skies, also full.

After cautiously circling around the perimeters, which took about an hour, while examining everything carefully with his torch, he soon realized that the only real entrance to the tower was a lop-sided door that hung solely by its bottom hinge. Inside, he saw that the wooden floors had been exposed to the elements, as there were large gaping holes in the floor, the walls and the ceiling.

The next problem that he had to solve was where the rod could be, but only one option surfaced on where to start—the front door. By this time, a luminescent night consumed the lands, thanks to all the reflected light shed from both moons.

After entering into the tower, his right foot accidentally kicked a very small rock that flew down into one of the dark holes in the floor, which in turn caused a whole lot of echoing noises below.

Subsequently, he heard loud, screeching and echoing sounds as hundreds of small bats flew their way around him and out the front door.

He quietly mused to himself, "So much for the quiet way." He drew his saber and then scanned a wooden staircase with lots of gaping holes that led both up and down—he first decided to check downstairs before the upstairs.

After walking over to the staircase, he mentally prepared to jump over a very large and gaping hole between ten missing wooden steps. After all, he knew that if he didn't make it to the steps on the other side, he would most likely plummet deep into the base of the tower, and die—he, now prepared, jumped, and made it.

Three more gaping holes right below the first did he have to jump across, before finally reaching the bottom of the stairwell, which took nearly ten minutes.

At the base of the stairwell, he observed three doors, one to the right, one to the middle, and one to the left—he sheathed his saber.

In the next moment, he chose the one directly in front of him, opened the door, and was about to walk through. However, he stopped the very second his "warning senses" had begun to ring.

He scanned down the dark hallway that ended with another door at its far end, which was about hundred feet away from his current position. Though these floors were extremely dusty, he could still see hundreds of slight bumps that elevated from the ground in many various spots. On each side of the wall, there were thousands of little pinprick holes.

Though he had little doubt that this hallway was rigged, this minor setback didn't stop him, even though it took him quite some time using all his agility skills to cross over to the other side, while always ensuring that his feet never touched any of the bumps.

Nearly a half an hour later, he finally reached the door at the far end of the hallway. After having carefully checked for booby traps all around the door and doorknob, yet discovering not a single one, he slowly cracked open the door a smidgeon before checking just as carefully for any traps on the other side.

Once he detected no booby traps upon, near, or around the door a minute later, he pushed the door halfway open, and to the best of his ability, he checked around the floors, walls and ceiling of the room for still more booby traps.

Ten more minutes passed before he felt confident enough to enter; he carefully walked up to the pedestal that was the only object lying in the center of the room—a pedestal that looked exactly like the one in Pavelus, except for the fact that this pedestal was black.

Strangely enough, about a dozen feet away, he observed a soft, white light that had just begun to beam down from some unknown source through the ceiling, and sparkle down onto the pedestal.

As he slowly and cautiously drew closer, he could see that just like with the other pedestal, there was a small, hollowed-in pit at the top.

In the center of this pit, he discovered a rod within the borders of this pit, resting on top of the bottom half of a map!

He excitedly leaned in to gaze at what he now believed to be the Rod of Ro'shain, as well the bottom half of the world map, but touched neither. They might be booby-trapped.

Upon closer inspection, he first realized that there were absolutely no markings upon this boring-looking rod. Except for the handle that was made of stone, most likely granite, the rest of the rod was made of a dark-stained pine.

Only seconds after the inspection had begun, Baltor came to realize that this rod was monetarily valueless.

Because of the fact that the map lay underneath the rod, he first pulled out the top half and positioned it a half a foot directly over while comparing the jigsaw patterns—it was a perfect match. However, as the handle of the rod lay directly over the first portion of the runic writing on the map, he could not begin to try and decipher the second half to the message.

Once again, he stepped back to gaze more carefully at the engraved symbols, in hopes that this pedestal might tell whether or not this thing was booby-trapped or not, or at the very least reveal some sort of puzzle, riddle, clue or story.

Just like the pedestal in Pavelus however, all of the symbols on this pedestal were chaotically placed pictograms of stars, whose points ranged from three to nine. In other words, the pedestal revealed absolutely nothing.

Deciding to do, or die doing, he reached his hand over the edge of the pit in order to grab the handle of the rod. Within inches from grabbing it, however, he heard a man's hollow voice say in Pavelian, "I wouldn't touch that if I were you."

Baltor immediately stopped moving his hand toward the rod, but neither did he move his hand any farther away.

Approximately ten feet away on the other side of the pedestal—a very small yet brilliant prismatic light suddenly sprang into the middle of the air! The dazzling glare was already so bright that it immediately caused Baltor to squint his eyes.

Yet that very magical light seemed to grow bigger by the second—not only was he forced to close his eyes, yet he had to then shield them with his right arm—his left hand still had to hold the torch safely away from his body.

Not even fifteen seconds had passed before the diamond-shaped prismatic light grew to ten-foot tall by eight-foot wide, though Baltor was not aware of the dimensions.

From the depths of the portal, a figure stepped out: The portal and its light slowly dissipated away into nothingness, which just as slowly brought the room back into its original state, except for right around the pedestal, of course.

That same man's hollow voice said, "Open your eyes."

Ever so slowly Baltor did—he next began to study the masculine being that now stood before him, of whom strongly resembled a man in his mid-twenties with a pale complexion, a perfectly contoured face without any sign of facial hair, and shoulder-length brown hair that was thick, lush and curly. This being's simple attire consisted of flowing gray robes and nothing else like rings, necklaces, etc. The only strange thing at all were his green eyes, whose pupils still magically glowed with that same prismatic color as the portal!

For this reason alone, Baltor believed he was meeting God. Immediately he bowed to the ground on both hands and knees, while simultaneously lowering his head and eyes to the ground.

This being crouched down, just before gently grasping Baltor's chin and lifting it until they were looking eye to eye. With a look of amusement, his voice no longer sounded hollow but normal, he said, "Stand up there, young one. I am not God."

Baltor slowly stood up, as did the being.

Baltor asked hesitantly, "You're not? Who—what are you then?"

The being tucked his hands into the sleeves of his robe, laughed, and answered, "I was once a human like you, Baltor, but now I am something else. As for my name, I was once called by mortals Trendon Harrn."

"How—how'd you know my name?"

"I know quite a few things about you, young one, besides just your name," was Trendon's elusive answer.

"So tell me what you are now, if you're no longer human."

Trendon suggested, "Consider first all the legends and tales you've been exposed to throughout your very short life. Then consider that which is far, far greater—this is what I have ultimately become after nearly ten thousand years of existence."

For a moment, Baltor wanted to believe this man, and all his cryptic talk, but what he had to say sounded way too good to be true. *Ten thousand years of existence!?*

Trendon laughed and said, "That is okay there, young one. I do not expect you to believe me, yet. In Time, you will learn that I speak only Truth. For now, consider your legends and tales, please."

Even though Baltor was actually becoming a little annoyed with all the elusive answers he was receiving, his eyes squinted as he began to think long and hard—legends of dashing heroes and diabolical villains. Dozens of people on both sides popped up in his mind. Okay, tales ... well, he heard a lot of those. Folklore of there being other races like elves, goblins, dwarves, mummies, genies, angels, sea serpents, dragons, ghosts and other undead. Devils even.

Meanwhile, this being continued to wait in silence, and without moving a single muscle, including his unblinking eyelids.

After a few more minutes of contemplation, yet with nothing else springing forth, Baltor began to give up.

Trendon appeared to have read his mind yet again, as he explained verbally, "In order to fully explain and understand exactly what I am will in fact take many centuries of your time. So let me surmise all my successes that I have accomplished within my immortal existence into a tiny nutshell. I have traveled through hundreds of worlds and dimensions, and mastered them all!"

Though Trendon's lips did not move, Baltor still heard the man's voice say inside his head, *Yes, Baltor, hundreds of worlds and dimensions! In some worlds, I have discovered that magic seems to come from nature alone; in others, it comes solely by the mystical powers that the gods (sometimes false) or the Creator of the Multiverses (never false) bestow.*

Why, there are even some worlds I've mastered where there seems to be no need or belief for spirituality, magic, or religion, as their technological advances seem to rule quite effectively, or so they think! They, however, are quite mistaken, as these are the easiest of worlds to conquer... if that was my destiny, I could be their master, but it is not. Instead, I like to watch. And if necessary, defend the innocent from the worst of the villains out there in this universe.

Now verbally speaking, Trendon said with a smile, "Oh yes, magic does exist in many forms. And in this world, in particular, it primarily comes from within."

At that moment, a strange look crossed Baltor's face. Trendon answered the look, "I know. Now that you realize I'm neither human nor a god, you want to know what I am—correct?"

Baltor nodded his head to indicate the affirmative.

Inside his head, he heard Trendon's voice say, *I call myself "A Watcher," and like you, I'm one of the good guys.*

On the other side of the coin, there is a whole race who shares the same physical forms and magical powers as me, but they are Chaotic Evil and classify themselves "Vompareus!"

Their single mission is to control the entire universe with them as the sole masters. These are the villains I still fight against, ever since I first become a Watcher nearly ten thousand years ago.

Although Baltor wanted to know exactly what a watcher and a vompareus were, the first question that suddenly sprouted forth within his mind was: *What would have happened if I had touched the Rod of Ro'shain?*

Still looking intently, Trendon answered verbally before Baltor could ask it aloud, "You would have opened the portal between the hundreds of worlds and dimensions called, 'The Dragon's Realm.'

"Some of the things that could have come out of the portal might be awesomely beautiful sure, but other things that might have come out could be disastrously deadly!"

Now telepathically speaking, Trendon added, *To name off just a few of the endless examples if the Rod of Ro'shain is wielded by the untrained user—wizards or other magically-gifted humans, elves, dragons, vampires, demons, devils, or even the most powerful type of undead creature of all, the vompareus... You named quite a few of them yourself, Baltor.*

"Of course," Trendon added verbally, "this would not be a problem to the fully trained user."

A moment later, Baltor said, "I see. Well, the map said that only the chosen one could touch the rod, or the gods would befall their wrath, and utterly destroy... Even though I don't know what the second portion to this message, am I this chosen one?"

"Perhaps in time." Trendon continued to speak verbally, "For now, you have way too much to learn, young one, before such an esteemed position could be bestowed. And that is, only after you've proven your mastery over the rod, and its many powerful secrets."

Baltor said, "I see. Well, can you tell me who created the pedestals, the map, and the rod? And what their purposes are for?"

Trendon answered aloud, "Yes. First, let's get rid of that torch. We don't need its light."

Before Baltor could think of where to put the lit torch that he had been holding in his left hand, it had instantly disappeared! For a few seconds, he looked at his empty hand with disbelief.

"Now," Trendon interrupted, "in order for me to properly answer your questions, you are first going to have to hear this relevant and important piece of history that I'm about to teach. So please sit down and get comfortable on the chair I have provided. It's right behind you."

Baltor turned around, and amazingly, there was a white chair only two feet away! But it wasn't just any chair, looking more like a very comfortable one-man couch with some plush, white cushions. He sat down, and indeed, it proved to be very comfortable.

As soon as Trendon saw that he had Baltor's complete and undivided attention, he answered, "Simply put. A little over nine thousand years ago, I created the rod, which took nearly a millennium to create... no joke.

"Two thousand years ago, I created the world map, the tower, and both pedestals—with but a willed thought. I next cut the map into two pieces. With the top half, I placed it upon the pedestal underneath Pavelus, which at that time was the imperial capital city to a completely different dynasty called the 'Elysian Dynasty,' coincidentally enough!

"Back then, Pavelus used to be called by its original citizens, and royalty, Taumasha."

At this point, Baltor couldn't help but make an interested humming sound...

After an affirming nod, Trendon revealed, "As for the bottom of the map, as well the rod, I hid them both upon this very pedestal right here, which area was also ruled by the Elysian Empire.

"In fact, this whole continent took only four centuries for the Elysian Empire to conquer and command, and for six more centuries, the Elysian Dynasty ruled nearly unchallenged! More than a millennium they lasted.

"That is, until six hundred and fifty four years ago, the 'Helenus Invasion' began. The Helenus were, back then, a clan of seafaring barbarians consisting of more than fifty thousand strong, originally stemming from a neighboring continent, and seeking to conquer this continent, as well. After a century-long war with no winner, the barbarian leaders set sail for Taumasha, who, with a white flag rose on the bows of their ship, proposed peace.

"While peace negotiations were being discussed in the palace between them, and the last living royalty, a naïve eleven-year-old boy named Sultan Rotan Elysian XIV, your ancestor, the rest of the fleet quietly sailed into the undefended harbor in the middle of the night, and attacked the city.

"Before morning, the Helenus conquered most of the city against the thirty thousand unprepared and disorganized soldiers. Regarding the sixty thousand citizens, the barbarians mercilessly impaled all the men and boys, and took the girls as slaves.

"Moreover, it was presumed that someone else within the ranks of the Elysian Empire had murdered Sultan Rotan the very night of the invasion, or so the Helenus believed when they kicked his bedroom door open in order to kill him! After all, they discovered the burned-up body of an eleven-year-old boy who had been wearing the pajamas of the Sultan, and lying in his equally burned-up bed."

Baltor looked a little shocked, and horrified, to learn this information about his ancestor.

"What they did not know," Trendon added, "was that the body was merely an illusion. I had taken the Sultan and delivered him to a family I could trust, in another city far away from Pavelus. I told Rotan to keep his mouth shut about his true identity and even change his name, or the Helenus would find and kill him. In the end, I promised him that one of his offspring would rise up in the future and redeem the family name of Elysian. He agreed."

After clearing his throat, he said, "Because the Elysian Empire was without a leader, the rest of it quickly fell apart. Almost all the historical artifacts, statues, coins, books, and even symbols that identified the Elysians were eradicated by the Helenus Empire, whose name soon changed to the Sharia Empire, due to the neighboring desert and the fact that they lost their homeland to still other invaders."

It was at this point he stopped teaching, in order to ask, "Are you following me so far, Baltor?"

"Yes, I am. So far, yes."

With an affirming nod, Trendon replied, "Excellent. Let me continue. What the Sharia Empire did not know either was the fact that the Elysians had many cities spread throughout the entire continent. Yet without any strong leaders governing them, they inevitably grew weak and transformed into other nations, like the Kingdom of Thorium and the Vispano Province.

"Ultimately, it was I who caused the earthquake a year ago and turned visible the pedestals. Yes, I am the one who arranged for you to come here two thousand years ago, though it was you who ultimately made all the right choices along the way."

It was at this point that Baltor looked at Trendon in both surprise and quite a bit of disbelief.

He could only ask, "Why me?"

Once again speaking telepathically, Trendon answered, *I have searched millenniums for the right person to come along and assist me. Though there are very few in this universe that can single-handedly stand up to the power of my might and magic—they, my throngs of enemies, do exist.*

Together, they continuously try to destroy me, so that chaos an disorder can rule over all of the ordered worlds that I currently protect… and watch!

Baltor begged, "Take me along with you. Train me and I will learn. Together, we can fight these atrocities—"

"No, young one," Trendon answered verbally, "you have way too much to learn, and I have far too little time to train you. For now, you must first master this realm before I shall take you to any others."

Baltor asked, "What do you mean, master?"

"Even that answer," Trendon replied, "must you decipher in your own time—but let me give a little hint. When you have truly discovered, and mastered, the truest law that governs this world and realm where you currently exist, then that very discovery shall also lead you right back to me—though I can guarantee you that we shall not meet again in this tower."

It was then that Baltor became seriously exasperated at all of Trendon's cryptic answers, and replied with frustration clearly evident within his voice, "Well—if everything that you say is true, then it will take me literally centuries and centuries to get where you are at! In fact, I'm sure I'll long be dead before I'm even close to being ready—"

Trendon interrupted, "In a sense you will be, and yet not."

"Huh?"

After sighing, Trendon explained, "Even those elves who dwell upon other planets, and whose lives literally span two to three thousand years, only get a fractional glimpse of what really lies out there, due to the fact that most are stuck on one planet—I'm not, thanks to the rod, and my immortality."

With irritation seriously brewing now, Baltor asked, "So you're saying that it will be impossible for me to learn everything in this lifetime, in order to become the chosen one. Am I right?"

"Yes and no." Trendon answered back quite calmly, "In order to truly live, one must have first died."

Baltor thought in disbelief, anger, and frustration, *This man is insane! His claims are impossible—even ridiculous—no way can any of this be true! Maybe I'm the one who is either hallucinating or insane.*

Trendon appeared to have read his mind yet again, as he verbally confirmed, "No, you are not hallucinating or insane. Now listen carefully, as my time grows short. What I am about to offer to you is a choice that I was not given a long, long time ago."

Baltor asked, "What's that?"

Trendon answered, "If you should accept, I will make you an immortal, though the costs and demands of this powerful type of immortality will be extremely high at first, much higher than any other type of immortal races.

"You must learn how to curb them all through your own wit and resources—should you accept!"

Sounding like a pouting toddler, Baltor asked, "Accept what?"

Trendon telepathically answered, *Becoming a vompareus... or in your best understanding of the word, a vampire!*

As for the word "vampire," Baltor did comprehend. He had read an ancient, compilation scroll on undead creatures only about two years back in the Guild's library. The semi-zany author who lived four hundred years ago claimed that the undead once walked this world millenniums ago, but were banished into hell by the good-aligned god Titus, so that humanity could be tested for its value, whether good or evil.

Seven types of undead did the author list and illustrate: ghosts, skeletons, zombies, wraiths, specters, mummies, and vampires.

Regarding vampires, the author mentioned about how vampires were the only undead creatures who still looked alive, were blood suckers, and preyed only at night upon living creatures, preferably human beings—for, during the day, they slept in coffins, grave-yards, or at least someplace underground. Sunlight was the only thing that could permanently destroy them. Yet they also hated religious symbols and holy water. Oh, and there is always "a head vampire."

Just after he had looked away to the ground, only a few moments later, he asked, "So your plan is to make me a vampire, let me master this world and realm completely on my own, and once mastered, you will then teach me about all the other ones?"

"If that is your destiny and your will."

"I don't know," Baltor replied quite reluctantly, as his mind flashed upon his recent encounters with the cannibals, and of course, their disgusting rituals. He didn't want to hurt anyone, much less drink his or her blood!

Again having read his thoughts, Trendon added, "As I have already explained, you must use your wit and resources to help you overcome all your weaknesses, and upon every level—even with the initial need to feast upon human blood! Even in the beginning, be selective by removing only the human vermin from the earth and feasting upon the blood of your enemies.

"Ultimately, in order to understand the future, one must also learn from the past; in the same way, in order to understand absolute good, one must also understand absolute evil. If that's not enough of a hint, then let me put it in a way you will understand— in order to beat your enemy, you must first become that enemy!

"And since we're now talking about you, young one, let me confirm that there are many obstacles in your past that prevent you from clearly seeing the potentials for your future! But, the signs are also clearly there."

Despite the fact that Baltor wanted to learn and discover all that this man had to teach, he still was quite reluctant in the heavy price tag involved, and so he replied, "I don't know."

Trendon pointed his left index finger up, and then said telepath-ically, *You have one hour to decide, as I have other affairs that I must tend to presently. During this hour, you are not to touch the Rod of Ro'shain for the reasons I've already specified.*

He verbally added, "Should you choose not to accept what I have to offer; that is okay, but you must leave and never return. If you do and/or you bring others, I will be forced to destroy you all, for the rod must stay upon one of the physical planets, and I have chosen this planet for a very specific reason! Should you accept, then you will soon find a whole new world of opportunities and powers that were previously unfathomable, here."

Trendon abruptly switched back to telepathy, as he said, *Once you have fully mastered this world and realm, I will next commence to take you to other worlds and their boundless opportunities. That is, of course, if you still want to know the mystery behind all of the other mysteries, then this is the only path to go! This is the way toward absolution and the absolute truth, where the very Heavens and the Divine co-exist!*

Baltor nodded his head a few times, and then proceeded to sit back in the chair so that he could contemplate in silence.

Trendon asked, "Do you have any other questions?"

Still looking away, Baltor shook his head negatively.

"I shall be back in one hour."

As soon as Baltor nodded his head, Trendon snapped his fingers and instantly disappeared.

Baltor stood up, walked over to the pedestal, looked at the rod again, and shockingly noticed that there were now hundreds of tiny emerald teardrops in the mahogany wood—not only that, but the handle was no longer made of granite, yet a perfectly smooth gray, white, and black marble!

As he took a closer look at the marble, his mouth dropped open upon seeing that the marble patterns were continuously shifting around! *Beyond priceless!* Because Trendon said not to touch it, he didn't, but sat down back in the chair and thought.

For the next hour, he considered the fact that he was now standing on the crossroads of life—on one hand, he didn't want to become a vampire, forced to drink people's blood in order to survive.

On the other hand, he wanted to know the mysteries of the universe, and maybe Trendon was right that this was the only way to go about it, yet he had also said that this would be his one and only chance to decide! Baltor admitted that he had always been curious about the truths behind life and death.

At the end of the hour that only felt like minutes to Baltor, Trendon reappeared.

Even though Baltor still looked quite uncertain, Trendon revealed, "Now is the time for you to make your choice, young one."

Baltor asked a couple whiny questions, "Why can't you just train me to be a watcher now? Why do I have to become a blood-sucking vampire first?"

Trendon sighed before answering this question, "Just as I explained before, in order to beat the enemy—one must first become the enemy. Let your heart and mind continuously be your guide as you have always done before, Baltor, and you shall never fail again. This is the very reason I seriously believe that you have the potential to be the chosen one."

With fear, Baltor looked to the ground. After swallowing back the saliva that had accumulated in his throat, he asked, "Will it be painful?"

After considering his question for a few moments, Trendon replied from his own experiences, "It is always painful when one wants to know the truth, but I can guarantee you this. Once one has ultimately discovered and united with the 'Truth of Truths,' there shall never be pain again, only utter joy and peace. Even I, after nearly ten thousand years of existence, have not yet found it, though I believe that I am very, very, very close!

"But I know exactly how your question referred, Baltor—yes, the physical pains are just as excruciating as the emotional, mental, psychic and spiritual pains."

Baltor looked up into the compassionate eyes of Trendon, and then slowly nodded his head up and down a couple times.

Almost as an afterthought, Trendon snapped his fingers just before he stated, "Oh... something else you need to know right now. Within the cosmic heavens, souls are continuously generated that ultimately spread out throughout the multi-verses and beyond, while filling new life forms. Yet for each powerful soul that takes a physical or spiritual form, there erupts from the furious planes of hell an anti-soul to taint and destroy its counterpart!

"You have not had the opportunity to meet your 'anti-soul' just yet, but when you do, you'll know it, and so will that other person, when he or she meets you! In other words, Baltor, you have had since before your birth an enemy whose sole mission is to destroy you, an enemy of equal power! Only once you have destroyed your counterpart can you truly transcend to the next stage!"

After a ten second pause so that Baltor could digest all that crucially important information, Trendon promised, "As for me, I am here to help you, Baltor, to fulfill your rightful destiny... if you should accept my proposal."

Baltor nodded.

"Do you accept my proposal?"

Baltor nodded again and confirmed, "Yes, I do."

Trendon telepathically concluded, *Before we commence with the transformation, I have two rules for you. One, never reveal what you're about to become to anyone. Two, never create another vompareus without my expressed consent, even if you learn how— break these rules, even once, and I will destroy you and your creation back into oblivion in the next moment! Do you understand and agree to my two rules?*

With ever-growing fear, Baltor nodded a few times, but not so much because of the verbal threat.

It was because, as soon as Trendon had finished asking his question, his figure had quickly begun to transform *from a human and into something else*—at first, it was the fingernails, which transformed into foot-and-a-half long claws, and then it was the hands, which tripled in size, and turned to onyx. The human face had already nearly completed transforming into the face of an onyx-black gargoyle beast; along with a set of vampire fangs pointing down from its mouth, a set of curvy horns protruding up and outward from its forehead, and of course, the glowing red eyes!

Abruptly, Trendon's gray robes disappeared, revealing a crystalline/muscle-packed chest, arms and torso that had already been growing quite rapidly, along with everything else. If that wasn't enough, erupting from behind the abominable beast that now stood at twenty feet tall—two very large sets of clawed wings spreading themselves out into the heavens!

As the creature drew closer, only a few seconds after the transformation was complete, Baltor managed to stammer out, "Why me?"

IT answered in a hollow whisper, "*Because you have been found worthy.*"

Before Baltor even had the chance to flee, which he was about to do, the horrifying monster thrust a razor-sharp claw deep into Baltor's lower-abdomen, and the claw broke off! Not even a split second later, IT disappeared back into oblivion.

The room around Baltor instantly began to swirl between reality and darkness, and agonizing moment after moment passed as he slowly and painfully felt that razor-sharp claw slowly yet continuously claw its way up through his abdomens, and into his chest cavity. Just as the claw ruptured into his heart, what felt an eternity later, he released one final scream, only a moment before Death overtook his life!!

CHAPTER XV

Not only was it quite a surprise for Baltor to wake up again, as he thought he was now dead-dead-dead forever, yet even more surprising was the fact that he was completely buried under solid earth without any air, which meant that he didn't need to breathe anymore, which meant that he truly was undead!!

Despite this rather uncomfortable situation of sand almost everywhere, he was happy that his eyes, his mouth, and yes, even his nostrils and earlobes had strangely remained closed throughout his entire slumber time, and even now as he furiously pulled himself out. Never before could he shut his lobes and nostrils.

Even without a single clue as the time, date, or location, he greatly hoped to discover that he had been buried underneath the sands of the Sharia Desert, for obvious reasons.

Though he did not expect anything to be easy, there was the slight hope that these might even be the very sands near the city walls of Pavelus, as this was his home and final destination. And soon enough, he would be able to report to the High Council about the seven-month-long quest to date, so his analytical mind revealed to him just then.

After digging himself out of the ground, a dozen-or-so seconds after having awoken, he first began the lengthy process of dusting off most of the sand, before trying to figure out where he was through sight—the sounds, however, clearly revealed that he was by a raging ocean—perhaps the Sea of Albusina. Additionally, he could feel a piece of parchment tucked inside his shirt, as well his necklace with arrowhead pendant, but not his saber on his belt hook.

Once he had cleared enough of the sand to see, he looked all around the sandy dunes for his saber, just in case there was danger nearby. Yet as his saber wasn't to be seen anywhere, he next threw his gaze up toward the sea, which began about twenty feet away and was very vast and very dark....

Though Baltor saw neither moon this direction, he did see thousands of stars that radiated over that sea alone—a few seconds later, he sighed aloud, "Perhaps this is the Sea of Albusina, and if I simply turn my head one direction or the other, I will see Pavelus."

Now patting off the sand from his clothes to make himself look presentable, he turned his head to look both directions, yet his eyes spotted no signs of civilization at all anywhere.

With a very confused look on his face, Baltor spun a one-eighty—he glimpsed the last fractional bit of sun disappear behind the trees. A dense lair of both palm and jungle trees that lay just beyond the last of the sandy dunes about three hundred feet away.

A second or two later, he realized that the direction he now faced was west, which meant that the sea behind him was to the east, which meant that this wasn't the Sea of Albusina at all.

Suddenly, Baltor's mind began to ask him these series of questions, *Am I even on the same continent? Maybe I'm on a completely different planet, or maybe even another dimensional plane of existence, but then if this last possibility were true, why would I be buried underneath the sand?*

Only a second or two after these series of questions had finished, he said, "Obviously if any of these answers are true, then that means it would be pointless to go west, as there is no Pavelus in that direction. So where should I go?"

It was only then that Baltor observed half of the all too familiar large moon that was just starting to wane in the northeastern skies, as it rose above the sea's horizon—the other moon wasn't anywhere in the sky. He was on his planet.

A few more minutes passed, yet never was a solid answer given for his last question of which way to go, internal or external.

Several minutes later, and still without any answers, not only did he slowly become frustrated and upset, yet he screamed out his last question out to the sea, "So where in the hell should I go?"

Other than the continuous sounds of the waves crashing into the coastline, still another minute of silence passed.

Baltor, in frustration, shifted his body to look to the north in order to scream out his question yet again. Before he had the chance, he felt a piece of parchment still tucked in his shirt also shifting.

He stopped in mid-shift, pulled out the parchment, blew off the excess dust, and then gazed at it carefully with his right hand—it was the original bottom half to the map. After lightly slapping himself in the head with his left hand, Baltor's eyes mysteriously began to translate the second half to the message.

It read, "all that this Chosen One has created, so that Law and Order will prevail until the End of Time within these Universal Realms, which the chaotically evil Vompareus—otherwise known as the 'vampiric beast overlords'—seek first to conquer and then to utterly destroy through Chaos!"

Just as he finished reading the final word, he heard Trendon's voice say within his mind, *Go west, young man. Go west!*

In what was obviously a western direction, Baltor turned around, tucked back the parchment into his shirt, and then surprisingly ran almost as fast as the speed of light—the speed of shadow.

He was not only extremely delighted about his incredible and inhuman speed, yet he became even more delighted to discover that he also had the dexterity and the agility to easily maneuver his way past the sandy beaches, and into the border of the thick, lush and dark jungle forest!

Approximately five minutes and a dozen miles later, he suddenly stopped at the edge of a large prairie harbored by thin trees all around. The only reason he had stopped was that he had felt the map slip out from underneath his shirt, and fall to the ground.

Before Baltor had the chance to run back, pick up the map and tuck it back into his shirt, he both heard his stomach grumbling from hunger pains, and his nostrils detected the smells of something living nearby!

He sniffed the air again, and turned his head over toward the direction where he caught the odor of a whole pack of animals.

As his night-vision eyesight dramatically increased like binoculars, he was able to see all the way up to the animal pack that stood about four hundred feet away from his current position.

These animals appeared to resemble deer, but they had large, curved horns that wrapped around their head several times. His human mind faded to black only a moment later, as his beastly mind fully emerged and dominated. Before the animals even had a chance to react, the beast had already crossed the extensive distance, ripped into the animal's neck, and ravenously feasted.

Though the fresh blood ever so slightly quenched the predator's hunger, *it* did not like the taste of this prey's blood at all, and found it very unsatisfying. Yet all the other animals were long gone, so it was too late to get more.

The very second after the feasting had concluded, Baltor's human mind regained control, and he discovered—with a whole lot of shock—that there were no traces of blood anywhere. The rest of the animal was intact. And just as shocking, his clothes and boots were on his body and completely intact!

He raised his hands into the skies that had only just begun to lighten up to the east and screamed into the heavens, "What, oh God, have I become?"

After a dozen or so minutes that passed without any sort of external answers, he began to shoot for the internal answers. He first reflected back toward his conversation with Trendon, specifically to the part when Baltor had been told that he was about to become "a vompareus," or as he would understand, "a vampire."

Once again, he began to think long and hard about everything that he knew about these evil, undead creatures, especially now that he was one himself. But other than that one book, there was no other useful information in his deepest of memories....

Due to all his contemplative thoughts, he hadn't been paying to the fact that not only had the skies seriously lightened up, yet the sun was only a dozen or so seconds from rising to the east.

As he squinted quite painfully, just from the sun's first indirect ray that poked into the morning sky, he quickly scanned his horizons, noticing that at the southern end of this prairie, there stood a massive hill covered with lush jungle trees, perhaps a thousand feet away.

He next saw the map still lying on the ground four hundred feet away in a slightly different direction, and as he looked up one more time to the hill, he saw a cave leading underground at the base.

Immediately he booked, and only a second later, he had already picked up the map, and a second after, reached the entrance.

A split second after having entered the cave, he turned back around and looked out—the sun's rays had just burst over the eastern horizon, shedding their powerful light onto the land.

As his eyes already had seriously begun to hurt from the incredible light, he turned back around, tucked the map under his pants and shirt, and then proceeded deeper into the darkest recesses of the cave.

A moment later, the fresh smell of animal crossed his nostrils, and he suspected that he was not alone in this cave. That confirmation came as a giant black bear stood up from its sleeping spot in another part of the cave, with teeth bared and a low-pitched growling noise coming from its throat.

Due to the low height of the cave, the bear could not stand up on its hindquarters, but it did slowly begin to approach him on all fours. Once it drew nearer, it began to kick up dirt with its front paws, stirring dust into the air.

He instinctively reached for his saber, only to realize again that it wasn't there, yet from that simple movement alone, he felt very weak. And as the seconds passed, he came to realize, quite exhausted.

With his peripheral vision, he quickly looked around the cave in search of a weapon, though the pupils remained locked on the bear—other than a few bones scattered throughout the cave, there wasn't anything useful.

Better that than nothing. He thought, before rolling backward away from the bear, while simultaneously picking up a jagged bone.

Only once he had gotten back to his feet did he realize that this bone actually had a rather sharp point at the end, and that this might turn out to be a decent weapon after all—he readied it for the bear that had neared to eight feet away.

The bear growled ferociously, swept both of its paws into the dirt yet again, which caused a lot more dirt and dust to fly in the air, and immediately it charged toward him.

Though he could no longer see, he heard the stampeding approach of the bear—he rolled to his left and jabbed the bone ahead of him.

The bear first roared in pain, lunged right for him, and then bit its sharp teeth deeply into his shoulder!

He yelped out in utter pain, but did not stop his desperate jabs into the bear with the bone.

The bear finally received a fatal jab in his neck, fell right on top of him, and died!

Despite his best attempts, he could not squeeze his way out from underneath the immense weight of the bear—he was just too weak and exhausted.

Without even realizing it he immediately fell asleep; and only moments later, a dream began to form.

Within this dream, at first Baltor could only see that he existed within a black area of unknown proportions, floating in the middle of the air. Though there were no sources of light at all, he, upon glancing at himself, could surprisingly see himself as if he was standing out in broad daylight.

Just after he had physically pinched himself to be sure that he wasn't dreaming while surprisingly feeling substance, he began to suspect that maybe he wasn't dreaming at all, but more likely, fully conscious in another dimension!!

As he looked around one more time, he confirmed yet again that there are absolutely no sources of light, or anything else, anywhere else.

It was then that he purposefully yelled out a question, "Is this all a dream, or am I really awake?"

His own voice repeatedly echoed the question around the void for about a dozen moments or so, until the area once again immersed into complete silence. Meanwhile, he waited patiently for the answer.

Another dozen or so seconds of complete silence passed, until suddenly, his eyes spotted the prismatic twinkle of a tiny light far off in the distance—a brilliant twinkle that only lasted but a nanosecond.

He squinted to try to scan in on the area that was once again utter dark, but all for naught.

A few moments later, that twinkle unexpectedly re-emerged, but it remained for another split-second.

Two seconds later, he began to suspect that maybe he was seeing a flickering star, though it did seem to get bigger and bigger each random time it flashed.

Seconds later, once the star had drawn much closer, Baltor soon realized that it wasn't a star at all, yet a glowing sword that was floating in the middle of the air, twirling and spinning around in a slow and chaotic fashion.

Once the sword had neared itself to five feet from Baltor's position, its pommel pointing straight up and its blade straight down, it stopped twirling and spinning, though it continued to float.

The moment the sword stopped, he instantly recognized and remembered that this very sword had been his father's most-prized possession.

The dream did not end there with this trivial discovery, yet instead added the complete backdrop of his father's workshop behind the sword, where it once again rested within his father's trophy case.

Even though Baltor was still aware that he was within the parameters of a dream and that his father was dead, he surprisingly saw and heard the very man walk into his field of vision with that all-too-familiar limp, unlock and open the glass trophy case, and then carefully pull the sword out.

Now lovingly holding the sword in both hands, Baltor's father turned back around, and then he proudly declared, "Countless hours of meticulous work has my father, your grandfather, invested to create this masterpiece I consider priceless—you've never met the man, as he died five years before you were born. Despite the fact that Grandpa Veran spent most of his life trying to make another, all his best attempts ended in failure."

For some strange reason at that very moment, Baltor gazed down at his own hands and surprisingly discovered that they were youthful in appearance, like when he was nine years old.

"Baltor, you need to pay attention to me when I'm talking to you. Now please look at the sword, okay?"

Almost surprisingly, Baltor heard his boyhood voice saying, "Yes, Popa."

He then saw his eyes averting to the blade that his father was gesturing toward with his left hand.

Once the father saw that he had his son's attention, he continued, "As you can clearly see, boy, a whole lot of valuable materials were used to construct *her*—gold, diamonds, ivory, and of course, the platinum. Don't be deceived in thinking that there's even an ounce of silver in there, which tarnishes so easily. Platinum is worth twice what gold is, and rarely ever needs polishing.

"*She* was not created to kill, or to combat against other swords, but simply be an artistic masterpiece! Not even on his dying day would he tell how he got the money for these materials. Or for the materials to make another sword, which I had no choice but to sell about six years back, in order to keep this shop running when business was really slow and rent was due.

"I—we—still don't have to worry about paying rent for the next ten years, and business is doing good. So after I teach you everything you need to know, and I retire when you're twenty-one years old, you will be able to keep the shop efficiently running on your own. Okay?"

"Okay, Popa."

"Son, let me talk a little more about this sword and what *she* can do... *she* can chop off a man's head with but one light swipe! After all, this three-foot long blade of steel was folded hundreds of times over, in order to make the entire blade, as you can clearly see, paper-thin! As for the tempered and very sharp edges that run up and down both sides, they've been measured at $1/1000$th of an inch—in other words, very few blades in the entire world can match this one."

After his verbal explanation, he pulled an apple out of his pocket, and tossed it up into the air. Once the apple had risen to its maximum height of a foot and a half, he rapidly flicked his sword-bearing wrist back and forth one time. This action caused not only the sword to sing loudly for a moment, yet for the very apple to fall to the ground in three pieces.

"Whoa."

"Now, my son, feast your eyes upon the pommel, but please do not touch the sword," his father added, while carefully flipping the sword around until he was gently holding the blade, and the hand was facing Baltor.

The first thing he saw looking back at him was a golden hawk's head that served as the pommel—a hawk that had two large diamonds representing its eyes.

The next thing was the foot-long/vanilla-colored leather grip, which leather had been tightly wrapped around the handle, before it was wrapped and secured by leather string.

Finally came the defensive bracers, which not only had a golden sun disk on one side, yet a platinum moon-disk on the other—on both sides were masterfully chiseled two ivory hawks, safely tucked inside the curvy defensive bracers, made of solid steel.

His father continued, "Again, you can clearly see the countless more hours that your grandfather placed just into the design of this sword, eh?"

Baltor's head nodded up and down in complete agreement, both then and now.

His father twisted the sword around until the very top of the sword was facing Baltor, and with excitement adding to his voice, he said, "On the top of the hawk's head, you can even see our family's royal crest, which according to Grandpa Veran, originates back more than a millennium.

"He told me, as his father told him, and so on and so on, that our ancestors once ruled a great Province that was larger than the Sharia Empire! Our ancestors went by the name of the Elysians. But something happened where we lost the entire empire."

After a short pause, he added, "Grandpa Veran told me that, as a youth, he had found the design on an old parchment located in an old trunk, and then showed the design to your Great-grandfather Pabs. That was when your great grandfather explained the meaning of the crest, and our ancestral heritage, to your grandfather.

"Ironically enough, it was right after he had married Grandma Blasa that, while in the process of making this very sword, he had a horseback-riding accident that ultimately caused both of his legs to become paralyzed. You never met your grandmother before, as she died a year before you were born..."

After taking a deep gulp of air through just his mouth, Baltor's father continued, "And when I was about your age, just after I had first discovered the sword and mentioned to Grandpa Veran, that was when he told me all that I'm telling you now. Even way back then, however, it was too late for me, as I had literally popped my knees out several years before, after having accidentally fallen out a tall tree that ended any and all chances for me to ever become a hero."

He had to swat away a fly that had been buzzing near his ear, before he added, "As for the reasons why no other of our family members has tried, I do not know, but I'm sure there must have been a good reason in every case.

"Your grandfather even believed in a chosen one, but I do not—I keep my head firmly rooted in the ground, so that I can make ends meet for our family. As you well know, we may not be rich, but we certainly survive."

His father concluded his spiel with this: "So, who knows? One day, this sword and everything it represents will be yours; that is, if you can beat the family curse...

"But now is not the time. For now, we must keep our heads firmly grounded in reality, as we have lots of horseshoes to repair before dinner tonight. Okay?"

"Okay, Popa."

Once Baltor had gotten one final look at the crest, his father carefully placed the sword back into the trophy case, and locked it back up.

Without warning, the parameters of the dream changed into "utter darkness," which darkness snuffed out the view of the sword— when he next opened his eyes, still in the dream, he saw that his hands were only a little bigger and still youthful, and that he was lying in his old bed back in his parents' house!

Just like the night when his parents had been murdered, he was once again extremely terrified for some strange reason.

He suddenly had his explanation, as he heard his father's outraged cries of protest, and even though Baltor knew what was about to happen, he even now could do nothing except for lie there frozen in bed.

Just as before, he heard his father's death scream, and moments later, his mother's, as well!

At that moment, just like that fateful night, his body became unfrozen, and he managed to get out of bed, put on his clothes and shoes, and crawl out the window—that was all he could do.

It was while climbing across the roof that he observed something moving on the ground that he had not seen that night, perhaps due to his fearful, shocked, and devastated state, though those fear and shock levels were on a slightly lesser scale. This time, he saw a horse parked out in the back of the shop.

In particular, Baltor observed that this horse was a powerful white stallion, and hanging from its youthful neck, it bore a gold crest on the front with two crossed sabers—the crest of the Sultan!

It was then that the dream faded back into nothingness, and it seemed that only a second or two later, he woke up.

Even where he lay inside the cave, and the seven-hundred-pound bear still lying on top of him, he knew that it was night.

He immediately tried to squeeze himself out from underneath the bear, yet this time, he surprisingly found that it was like removing a featherweight!

He stood up onto his feet, and then examined his shoulder where the bear had bitten him.

Interestingly enough, even though he saw that his shirt was torn, his skin was not; in fact, there was no evidence of damage in his shoulder at all, not even a bruise!

As he moved his painless shoulder around and around to confirm, he noticed that the leech scars had completely disappeared, as did his forearm scar, yet these little movements caused his stomach to grumble.

A second later, he left the parameters of the cave, looking for something alive to eat. Not only was he hungry, but quite famished!

He scanned the prairie out, but there were no decent-sized animals to be found anywhere—right away he began to run westward, back into the thick clusters of trees.

Even though Baltor immediately discovered that his speed and powers had diminished from the night prior, he was still quite aware that he was running about a mile every two minutes.

It seemed only minutes had passed before his nostrils detected the smell of fresh meat.

His beast mind once again took over for some time. Once his human mind had come back, an unknown amount of time later, he saw that he had just finished feasting upon the blood of an ape.

Though he heard the alarmed sounds of other apes screaming from within the trees, he no longer felt famished, as well feeling a bit repulsed from his vampiric act, so he continued in his voyage, ignoring those light hunger pains.

By dusk the next morning, he was on the brink of starving, feeling oh so weak and hungry. Even though he had been diligently searching for food halfway through the night, there was no other game found, nor could he find any caves.

Only minutes before the sun was about to rise, he furiously dug a shallow grave in the dirt and buried himself in it. He had just finished covering himself under the dirt when the sunlight penetrated the area.

The next night, he awoke due to an excruciating hunger—moreover it had actually become intensely painful in his entire midsection!

Through the agony he pulled himself out of the dirt, just before scanning through the thick forest of trees while sniffing the air trying to find some living creature with blood. Unfortunately nothing was nearby, and so he hightailed it west—running just a bit faster than the fastest human can on the entire planet.

About a dozen or so minutes later, he ran into another small clearing, just as the cloudy skies above began to pour down rain.

At the far end of the clearing, there were several long-necked animals with orange and black polka dots feasting on the leaves at the top of tall and lush trees.

Never before had he seen such an animal, but his bestial mind did not comprehend, or even care. The only thing the beast knew was that *it* was going to feast! In the blink of an eye, the beast was on one of them, and gorging away on the blood.

Even though it felt to the beast that *it* had drunk a ton of blood before this large animal turned dry. By the time the beast was done, *it* didn't feel very satisfied at all, as if it had only been an appetizer.

Before his human mind had the chance to come back, *it* had already tracked down another species of the same animal and consumed it as well—by the time his human mind had returned, he felt much better though not full, and so he continued along his way.

It was on the fourth night of his journey back that he discovered that his powers and speed had faded to normal. No game at all was to be found anywhere this night, and Baltor nearly starved to death!

During the last two nights of Baltor's trip through the jungle, he had to dig shallow graves, as he could find no caves whatsoever—the only good thing about these nights was that he was able to find enough animals to keep him barely alive.

As for the two reasons he seriously hated sleeping under the dirt—not only because he hated getting the dirt off and out of him after having awakened, yet more so because of all the underground bugs and worms that loved to crawl on his body, too.

Upon reaching the borders of the mountains, he chose to head north and cross the mountains via another path. After all, he did not want to eat any of the friendly folk from Valakan, even accidentally.

So north is where he headed, and he took the next valley entrance. Though the blizzard-like weather conditions and freezing temperatures would have frozen to death the unprepared traveler, he startlingly noted that it had no effect on him, whatsoever.

It took him a week to cross through the mountains in a southwestern direction, while always luckily finding caves to sleep in, and wolves or other small animals to quench his thirst, but never had he, during this last stage of his journey, run across a single human. That was about to change.

CHAPTER XVI

Just after sunset the following night, Baltor found and sucked the blood from a rabbit, though it did absolutely nothing to curb his thirst and hunger, and though he did not orally voice his complaints, his stomach certainly made up for the silence through its continuous whining and grumbling.

After having traveled through the valley of the very last mountains, he saw that the mountains here nearly abruptly transformed themselves into the Sharia Desert.

As he gazed out at the sandy dunes, he realized that he must still be an unknown distance north of where he had originally entered the mountain pass, though his initial goal had been to reach the fertile valley. Therefore, he began walking southwest.

After having traveled halfway through the moonless night without any encounters at all, animal or otherwise, he finally saw a large fire up ahead in the distance, perhaps a dozen miles away.

As he drew nearer to about two hundred feet away, he could see that this bonfire was located within the confines of a rather large oasis, which also contained a large lagoon and a half-dozen or so parked wagons with men and women camping all around it.

As he drew to about one hundred feet away from the oasis, he counted a little over two-dozen people within his field of vision, while noticing that three-quarters of them were still engaged in a celebratory party.

Of course he was aware that this number did not include those possibly sleeping in the wagons or those perhaps hiding on the other side of palm trees—all those outside of Baltor's field of vision.

Fifty feet away, he observed as a bald-headed man unexpectedly jumped onto the top of a wagon and began to make beep-box sounds with his mouth—a very harmonious tune and beat, as it turned out.

Another man with shoulder-length blonde-hair joined the bald guy on top of the wagon, and he began to sing in a deep-bass voice to the tune. Of course, everyone else joined in with the singing as well—a song sung in the language of Pavelian.

"Yo—ho—ho,
I've got this song I know!
You—hoo—hoo,
I've got some news for you!

I was alone and lost,
Being pulled, whipped, and tossed!
It wasn't until just yesterday,
That I joined my family at play!

And we sang, yo—ho—ho,
We've got this song we know!
And we sang, you—hoo—hoo,
We've got some news for you!

Family is my number one goal,
Harmony is what makes me flow!
You wanna mess with the best,
You gonna die like the rest!

And we sang, yo—ho—ho,
We've got this song we know!
And we sang, you—hoo—hoo,
We've got some news for you!

We have come, never gone,
We're just hidden in this song!
Strike that bell and make your ding,
Imagine the treasures that we will bring!

And we sang, yo—ho—ho,
We've got this song we know!
And we sang, you—hoo—hoo,
We've got some news for you!"

At the same time they finished with their song, Baltor casually emerged from out of the depths of the darkness, walking into the perimeters of the oasis—feeling unbelievably thirsty.

Several of the members, mainly men, glanced at Baltor as he walked by their current positions, but said nothing. He had begun to near the campfire, when a large, fat man with a thick, black beard and a drunken slur raised his mug toward Baltor, and called out, "Who are you, stranger?"

Baltor calmly answered, "I am Lord Poleax from Pavelus."

Someone nearby, whose gender was unknown due to a hooded cape that cast his or her face into shadow, attempted to stand up from the sitting position, but collapsed back to the ground, most likely due to his or her drunken state.

The man with the beard either did not notice or care, as he declared, "Lord Poleax from Pavelus—well then, come and join me for a drink! My friends call me Big Bear." He then began to chortle in laughter.

Baltor smiled, but found that his gums were already sticking to the roof of his mouth—he was indeed getting rather thirsty, but not for alcohol!

He sat down next to Big Bear, but found that he had to clear his throat.

Still after several attempts, he could not speak. To make matters worse, his chest began palpitating very hard, and he found his breath to be short.

Unnoticing, Big Bear extended his mug to him, and said, "Drink, Lord Poleax."

Baltor took the mug and tried to take a long swing, however, the moment that the fluids touched the insides of his mouth, he couldn't help but spit it all back out—it was repulsive to say the least.

Big Bear laughed, patted him on the back, and said, "Sure it takes a bit of getting used to, but it'll get you feeling nice and cozy once you do—take another deep swig!"

Baltor shook his head and barely managed to muster the words, "No thanks."

Big Bear patted him heartily on the back again, and suggested, "Come on! What'll it harm you? It's just some wine!"

Baltor extended the palm of his hand out that held the mug, and rasped, "No really."

Big Bear looked quite offended as he stood to his feet, pulled out his dagger, and growled, "I said, *drink!*"

"Are you threatening me?" Baltor somehow managed to ask through his dry mouth, while simultaneously rising to his own feet and assuming the ready position.

Surprisingly, Big Bear shook his head, dropped the dagger to the ground, and sighed, "I'm sorry. I don't know where that came from. It's just that the wine takes a bit of getting used to, but once you do—you'll love it! My wife spends a lot of time preparing it for—"

At that moment, the hooded figure rose from the ground, and said in a strangely familiar man's voice Baltor had not heard in a very long time, "The brat's obviously not going to drink the wine! Let's just kill 'em now and get it over with, Big Bear. Surely, he's got to have the rod or the map on his person somewhere, probably hidden somewhere the sun don't shine! We'll just have to find out now, won't we, boys?"

Quite a few of the men laughed—meanwhile, Big Bear chuckled while nodding and picking up his dagger from the ground. Baltor didn't laugh at all, nor even smile.

Just then, the hooded man pulled back his hood, so that Baltor could see his face—it was indeed Salmot!

In turn, Baltor no longer contained himself as he instantly lunged toward Salmot. Before Salmot even had the chance to draw his sword, Baltor had not only clotheslined him to the ground, yet had already leapt on top of him and bit deeply with his vampire fangs in Salmot's jugular vein.

For the very first time, Baltor's body began to rapidly transform from man and into the twenty-foot tall beastly vompareus, all the while ravenously feasting upon his hated enemy's blood. Every previous time he had remained in human form.

The moment everyone saw the physical transformation, all freaked out—those that could run into the desert, including Big Bear, did!

Those that couldn't move, due to being too intoxicated, watched in pure shock, horror and disgust as Baltor continuously feasted on Salmot—not only did quite a few pass out from fear, yet several more became violently sick and retched all over themselves.

Besides the physical transformation, a mental transformation also occurred—for the very first time, Baltor surprisingly found that his bestial side and his human side had just become connected. Simply put, he had the instincts of an animal combined with the intelligence of a man—actually, two men.

For, Baltor even saw Salmot's life flash before his own eyes, and learned all of the man's master thievery skills—as well many more personal things! Salmot was the one who had brought Thesmul to the Guild. He was also a double agent with the thieves' guild in Mauritia. He was also the one who had ensured, for the last six years, that Humonus had been passed for promotion to Senior Drill Instructor three different times, and all because of what happened between Thesmul and Baltor. Salmot evilly hated Baltor and Humonus!

Just as evilly, Salmot was the one who had secretly arranged and bribed three-quarters of the other High Council so that Lydia became a Mistress Thief at such an early age. The underlying reason why he spent nearly ten million parsecs wasn't because he believed she was High Council material, but because he wanted to hook up with her, which actually worked out that way.

The whole time, he deceivingly made it appear to Lydia as if he really loved and cared about her. Up until the last second of his life, everything that Salmot did in his life was to satisfy his own lustful desires, because he really only gave a damn about himself all along, and certainly not about Lydia, the Guild, or anyone else!

Though the night skies previously had been cloudless, from across the western horizon, they came and quickly—deep, dark thick and angry clouds filled with dazzling bolts of green lightning—a very, very tempestuous thunderstorm it looked to be.

Once the very last drop of Salmot's blood and life force had entered Baltor's mouth, he slowly rose to his feet.

From all around, the winds picked up and howled out into night skies like screaming banshees, causing dry sand to fly everywhere through the air. Only a few moments later, large drops of rain splattered down, fast drenching all those around!

He didn't care about the sand or rain but tilted his head back, and roared a beastly roar that literally filled the stormy heavens!

A moment later, his roar was answered back by a loud clapping of thunder that rolled across the fast-moving clouds, while thousands more green lightning bolts zigzagged everywhere above!

Only seconds later, Baltor came to discover, ecstatically, that his two sets of wings were allowing him to fly higher and higher into the air. Just below him on the ground, thirty feet below, he could see the fearful expressions of the people gazing up.

He flew up to the height of fifty feet; and through the pouring rain, his eyes scanned all across the deserts—a few moments later, his vompareus eyes found exactly what he was looking for.

With but a willed thought, Baltor flew toward Big Bear, who was hightailing it across the desert sands at top speed—the one who had pretended to be his friend in order to get him drunk, so that he could easily kill Baltor after he had passed out.

Seconds later, he caught up and engulfed this man's blood from his jugular vein, as well, his memories. He learned that Vamen a.k.a. Big Bear was no nice guy at all either, although he pretended to be such to his unsuspecting victims whom he then typically robbed. Yes, "victims" was the appropriate pluralistic word.

If that wasn't enough, there were dozens of times during his life that Vamen had sadly backstabbed those that called him a "friend" or "family member."

From all the intoxicating bloods and knowledge that now flowed through his veins and mind, things became quite a bit distorted and blurry, as if he was again flying through the skies. Several moments later, he blacked out.

The next night, Baltor awoke to find himself buried underneath the earth, with no knowledge of how he had gotten here, or where he was. Now, he only knew that it was night, and for the first time in a very long time, he wasn't hungry.

He pulled himself out of the sandy ground, noticing that he was still wearing his clothes and boots. And once he happily discovered that he still had the map tucked underneath his shirt, he looked all around his terrain.

The first thing he noticed was that both half moons were now in the sky above, although the larger moon was to his northwest while the other was to his southeast. This not only cast distant shadows all across the sand dunes, yet made it look like the sky was actually late evening, and not night.

The next thing that he noticed—with surprise—was that the city walls of Pavelus lay about a mile or so to his west.

As his eyes gazed to the south-southwest, he discovered something that he hadn't seen when last he left Pavelus. There was now, under construction, a megalithic coliseum about a half-mile to the south of the city. Three-quarters of this structure was still incomplete.

As he glanced back over to the city itself, he remembered that he had been able to fly the night before, so he jumped straight up to get some air, in order to fly again. Even though he jumped more than forty feet high into the air, there was obviously no flying power within him now.

Just then, all of Salmot's master-thieving skills again resurfaced within Baltor's mind—he used those very techniques to work his way around shadowy parts of the sand dunes that rendered him nearly invisible from the passing formations of marching guards, until he finally neared the six-hundred-foot wall.

Once he was ten feet away from the wall, he made a springing jump for it and again got forty feet high.

Perhaps nine seconds later, Baltor was already at the top.

As a safeguard, he first scanned the lengths of the guards' walk-way to make sure the coast was clear. Once he saw that it was, but only for a few seconds, he quickly snuck across the one-hundred-foot span in only a second, and then he scaled his way back down the other side and into the heart of the city.

Once he stood upon the streets, a strange sensation occurred as if his eyes were yanked out of his body. His "gaze" moved ahead two more blocks, then to the right, moved three blocks ahead, and then went to the left—deep inside the scummy sections of Pavelus.

The "gaze" stopped in its movement, and focused upon a very-familiar-yet-much-older-looking white stallion that bore the crest of the Sultan, just like the one he saw in his dream.

The stallion snorted a bit as it returned the gaze back, and the image instantly dissipated.

He knew exactly where to go. And only a few seconds later, he saw the same stallion with his very own eyes, though he was quite a bit in shock that his vision actually had been true.

He looked up from the horse, as well the two-dozen other horses also parked outside, and then to the bar that bore the sign, *The Rusty Pipe*. Even from outside, this bar sounded packed full of drunkards. Without fear, Baltor entered.

Indeed, the bar reeked of stale beer and sweaty people, and to confirm, ruffians, sailors and fat-old women occupied this dismal environment. Of course shady-looking people sat in the dark corners.

As he scanned throughout the crowd, he thought to himself, *Now why would someone who works for the Sultan want to come to a putrid worm-hole like this?*

He next walked to the far end of the bar, observing a concrete staircase that led down into a basement—already could he hear the loud cheers and jeers coming from below, for some reason.

From the depths of this smoky environment, two drunken patrons clamored up the concrete steps; the man on the left was excitedly telling the man on the right that he had just won five hundred parsecs. Thankfully both men ignored Baltor.

Upon nearing the bottom step, the answer to Baltor's earlier question came as he saw exactly what was going on down here within this concrete basement, whose parameters were about ninety feet by sixty feet. Not only was it filled with more than a dozen large circular tables, though only three had a single lit candle, yet there were nearly sixty chairs surrounding all those tables. Nearly half the chairs were filled with drunk and loud patrons. A liquor bar without stools sat in the far-right corner; behind the bar, there was a middle-aged man dispensing drinks to the ugly waitresses who dispensed out the drinks to the customers.

Of course, can't forget to mention the dozen-or-so drunk patrons standing around a well-lit forty-foot circular pit located in the center of the room, calling off bets and swapping money. It was solely because of all the light emanating from the pit that prevented this basement from being very poorly lit.

As he walked over to the edge of the pit, and leaned over on the safety steel railing in between two sailors, he saw four torches spread halfway between the top and the bottom at each of the four quadrants. At the very bottom, about thirty feet below, two dogs viciously tore into each other with fangs and claws! Currently, this pit had two small entryways on opposite sides that were both open, as well a human-sized gated door that was shut.

Baltor thought, *My parents' murderers either come to watch things fight and kill, or do it themselves, for violence is their nature.*

From the other side of the pit, a beam of light flashed in Baltor's eyes, though only for a split second. His eyes quickly scanned in that direction, but saw nothing out of the ordinary, except for a large bunch of the Sultan's soldiers—two of them were now leaning slightly over on the far side of the pit to watch the fight close up, while the rest sat behind them at two tables, drinking and laughing away. There were no signs of anything glinting.

Even after several more minutes that he spent watching them, and counting fifteen soldiers in total, he still didn't see anything else glinting. However, he knew one of them had to be the owner of the white horse outside, though he didn't know which guard.

He next started to check out another group of people sitting near the far left corner of the room. In that corner, there was another concrete stairwell leading down, this once spiral. Yet another flash of light caught his eye, and he gazed back over.

His binocular-vision instantly zoomed in on the source of the light, observing that it was actually two prismatic lights that reflected off two diamonds set in a golden hawk-headed pommel. With growing excitement and anger, Baltor realized that this s w o r d had to be his grandfather's sword!

Just then, his vampire hearing radically increased, and he listened as one of the two guards leaning over the pit looked back over at the man who donned his grandfather's sword, and say with excitement, "Major Briggs, you've got to check this out! I told you that the pit-bull was going to take out the rottweiler, and I was right. I mean, please, sir, come and take a look-see!"

This Major Briggs, a rather powerful-looking officer with angular eyebrows and a thick, graying goat-tee, finished drinking a swig from his mug of ale, laughed, and then said, "I'll be right there, Lieutenant Harshem. I'm kind of in the middle of an important discussion right now with Captain Lowell."

Baltor immediately began to approach, but upon drawing several feet from them all, this soldier turned to look at him with great suspicion.

Without a word, he walked past the first, and was about to pass the remaining soldiers in order to reach Briggs, but found swords pointed at him from all directions.

"Identify yourself and state your business," Harshem was the first to say though he did not have his weapon drawn.

"My name is Baltor. I am a messenger from the Sultan, and I bear a message solely for Major Briggs! I shouldn't be saying this to you, but I think that he plans on promoting him to colonel."

Harshem asked, "How come I haven't seen you before?"

"I have just started, good sirs. May I please speak with the major so that I can be on my way, sir?"

"Lower your swords, men," Harshem ordered. He next looked over at his major and stated, "Major Briggs, there is a man here who says that he bears a message for you, directly from the Sultan."

Briggs stood up from his seat, approached a bit closer until he was about fifteen feet away, and then asked, "What is the message?"

Without hesitation, Baltor answered, "You have a possession that belongs to me—you must give it back, or else."

Looking confused, Briggs asked, "The Sultan said this?"

"No... I did!"

Briggs laughed, put his hands on his hips, and in a mocking tone, asked, "Well then. What possession do I need to give back to you, and what are you going to do about it if I don't?"

Despite the fact that Baltor once again had swords pointed in his face, he still calmly said, "Give me back my grandfather's sword, or else I will be forced to kill you."

Briggs straightened up with a serious look to his face, while his right hand cupped very protectively over the sword's pommel. He ordered, "Men—"

With a wag of his index finger from side to side, Baltor interrupted, "I wouldn't issue that command if I were you!"

Even though Briggs had just about enough, he still asked with an incredulous tone of voice, "Why not?"

Baltor answered, "According to the law of the Sultan, thievery and murder are not crimes to be tolerated within this city, all here knows these laws to be true—yet it was you, Major, who stole my family's sword more than a decade ago and murdered my parents!

"If I were you now, however, I'd fight me in the dog pit below. After all, who am I but a skinny punk pitted up against an ultimate warrior like you?" As Baltor had asked this question, his voice had not only gotten very sarcastic, yet snotty sounding.

Seething with uncontrolled rage, Briggs roughly shoved his way through his men—the soldiers hurriedly moved their swords out of their major's way.

Without pause, Briggs grabbed and yanked the front of Baltor's shirt with both of his fists, which caused both Baltor's body and face to be less than an inch from his own, as well make him quite unbalanced: The major hissed, "Let's go!"

Abruptly, Briggs let go of Baltor's shirt, which caused Baltor to drop to his knees, and then he stared at the boy who did not try to stand back up onto his feet, while mentally daring him to do so.

After a short chuckle, Briggs looked back around at all of his standing around.

He then ordered almost pleasantly, "As this snotty punk and I are about to fight to the death, I'd like to place my entire life savings on the duel—eighty five thousand parsecs for me to win! Anyone want to match my bet?"

Briggs then began to look around the room, but not a single person said a word, especially for the fact that Baltor continued to remain on his knees.

"Come on—is there not one single person amongst you who wants to take on my bet against... What was your name, punk?"

It was only after he had asked that question that he looked back down at the kid who remained on his knees.

Baltor apparently loved to push buttons, as he first smiled up at the major, and answered, "My name's not important. I've got a very good suggestion that would make this fight even more interesting."

After a short laugh, Briggs then asked, "What would you suggest?"

"Let's add some fresh dogs to the pit, during the course of our battle to the death," Baltor suggested quite calmly.

For a split moment, Briggs looked quite a bit nervous at that suggestion, but he could also see the eyes of his men, and everyone else, looking directly at him, so he nodded confidently while answering in the form of a question, "Why not?"

Even though Baltor had just slowly stood back onto his feet, he heard an unrecognizable, old woman's voice declare, "I'll match your bet, Major Briggs. The house knows I'm good for it!"

Everyone in the room turned to look at the woman who said it with quite a bit of surprise. All, except for Baltor, knew that the old crone's name was Sessy, and that she was indeed good for it. After all, Sessy not only owned the gambling house, yet the entire bar.

Briggs looked over at her in surprise, as well with some agitation. Instead of displaying any emotions that might make him seem a coward, however, he glanced over at his captain, nodded his head, and said, "You heard Sessy."

Lowell replied, "Yes, sir."

Briggs then began to walk toward the stairwell in the corner of the room. Baltor followed right behind.

Two soldiers followed behind them, and Harshem and Lowell followed behind them in the rear of the formation—all made their way down the stairwell, just in case Baltor should try to do something underhanded to their beloved major.

Baltor observed—in the basement's basement—there was a door open to his left that led into another room filled with various-sized dog cages of all sorts, mostly filled with yapping dogs. He also observed that the remainder of this room surrounded the entire perimeters of the pit, which also lay to his left.

From where he stood, he could see one human-sized door and one of the doggy doors. Seconds later, a dirty old man with a whip in his hand walked out of the room to his left, and then closed the door behind him.

Without pause, Briggs ordered the old man, "Remove the two dogs in the pit, and prepare three fresh dogs to enter three minutes after we commence with our battle to the death."

After delivering a toothless smile, the old man nodded his head, opened the door he had just come through, re-entered it, and then closed that door behind him.

A few seconds later, Baltor watched as the old man came back with his whip, followed by two of his assistants carrying beating sticks.

The three entered the pit through the human-sized door, and once inside, they beat the dogs senseless, and then they quickly cleared the unconscious bodies out of the pit. Only a few of the betting people groaned from up above.

Once done, Briggs entered the pit, walked to the far side of the pit and turned around. With a wicked-looking smile, he quickly drew out the hawk-headed sword from a special sheath attached to his belt that caused the sword to literally sing for a moment!

Meanwhile, Harshem turned to one of the two guards, and ordered, "Give this man your sword, Private Simons."

Even though Simons said, "Yes, sir," he still reluctantly extended his sword to Baltor—Baltor took the sword, and without a word of thanks, he entered the dog pit.

Lowell next ordered the other guard, "Shut and lock the door, and only open it once the winner has declared his victory over the dead loser, Corporal."

After the corporal had replied, "Yes, sir," he then shut and locked the door.

Upon completion of this task five seconds later, Lowell ordered his three underlings including Harshem, "I want you all to stand guard here—understood?"

"Yes, captain!" all three men snapped. Lowell turned and proceeded back toward the staircase.

At that moment, a slight look of hope crossed Harshem's face, just before he asked, "Sir? Can I please watch the fight upstairs?"

Lowell turned around, and said, "Sure, but you two other men must stay here."

"Yes, sir."

Lowell and Harshem next headed back upstairs to watch the fight—all the while Baltor had been gazing up to see a packed crowd leaning over the side of the edge, and looking back down.

This was a show, and the bets were on, though all but one was betting on Briggs to win.

With a cocky smile, Briggs looked over to his opponent that was still looking up at the crowds, and then he asked, "So should I say ready-set-go, or should we just battle?"

Without waiting for a response, Briggs angled an attack with his sword—Baltor easily deflected the incoming sword away, by taking several steps back.

Baltor replied nonchalantly, "Just battle."

"Have it your way," Briggs growled as he jabbed in with his sword—however, Baltor had already rolled away and resumed a defensive position.

Briggs delivered quite a few more thrusts and slashing attacks, though he was never able to get one in, nor had his opponent made a single offensive strike.

Briggs finally stood back, and while breathing a bit heavily, he commented, "You're pretty quick, aren't you?"

Upon seeing that Baltor hadn't even broken a sweat these last couple of minutes of combat, several of the patrons began shifting their betting from Briggs to Baltor. For, despite the fact that they hadn't seen Baltor make a single offensive strike, they were quite aware that he was extraordinarily handy with the sword.

As for Baltor, he did not respond, but listened as the dog gates had slowly begun to rise up on both sides, and after throwing a quick smile, he made his first offensive strike throughout the whole duel, which was a roundhouse type of swing with his sword.

Briggs not only parried with his own sword, yet he immediately launched an offensive counterstrike—only by an inch did Baltor manage to roll safely out of the blade's way!

As for the crowd, they were seriously getting frenzied and quite loud, as some were booing while others were cheering—the remainder of the crowd was screaming their bets to the man taking all the bets, as they wanted to ensure that their bets were set before the climactic part of this duel was over!

Just a nanosecond after the gates had opened at the very same time, three violent dogs rushed into the pit with fangs bared, and the roar of the crowd from up above became deafening!

Baltor was the first to leap at Briggs in order to make a sword attack, but found out "the hard way" that a dog had already grabbed a hold of his right pants leg with its teeth—his sword flew out of his hands and slid across the floor!

As for his knee, that also crashed hard onto the ground, though it fortunately only caused pain for a single moment!

Taking the advantage of the situation, Briggs began to swing his sword directly for Baltor's neck, figuring to end the battle quickly. However, he discovered with frustration and anger that the second dog's teeth had just ensnared the sleeve of his shirt, and that he couldn't deliver that attack!

Only a split second later, the third dog slammed hard into Briggs's side, which caused his own sword to fly out of his hand. As for Briggs himself, he fell smack on top of Baltor!

Without pause, Briggs reached for the dagger in his boot, but found that Baltor had already firmly locked that wrist into place, preventing him from reaching the dagger at all, even from underneath!

Briggs had his other hand free, however, and so he began to pummel punches into Baltor's face!

The two men continued to fight and wrestle, mainly with Briggs on top who had just yelped out his first cry of pain from one of the dog bites. The dogs, meanwhile, climbed on top and all around while continuously snarling and biting away into both combatants. The crowds above were going freaking ballistic!

Although the dogs were biting and tearing into both men, Briggs was no match at all against his opponent, nor did he understand Baltor's underlying reason for having the dogs brought in, nor that Briggs was actually the one meant to be on top in the end.

For Baltor used both the dogs and Briggs as shields to prevent the onlookers from seeing what he was about to do. Immediately after grabbing Briggs's neck from underneath, he sunk his vampire fangs deep into this man's neck!

Even though Briggs had already been screaming from all the painful dog bites, he really screamed out in horrific pain from Baltor's bite. At that very moment, such a strong gust of wind blew throughout the basement, and the basement's basement, that even the torches in the pit went completely out, enshrouding the entire bar in complete darkness!

Meanwhile, after Baltor's body had transformed into the beastly vompareus, he began to feast upon Briggs's blood, and knowledge!

In a flash, Baltor saw a much-younger enlisted soldier who was unquestionably Briggs enter his father's shop sometime during the day, but as no one was currently in the shop, he began to stroll around the shop while glancing around.

As Briggs walked by the trophy case, he glanced inside, and a look of envy crossed his face as he gazed at the sword adoringly.

It was but a second later that Baltor's father entered the shop from the attached house, as he greeted in a chipper tone of voice, "Good afternoon, sir. I was just on my lunch break. Is there something I can help you with?"

"Yes, my stallion outside needs his horseshoes replaced, and I heard from my troops that you were the perfect man for the job."

"Of course I am, sir! If you can just bring your horse in here, I will get to work right away—only twenty parsecs, sir."

"No prob. By the way, is the sword in that trophy case for sale?"

"Sorry, but it isn't."

"Why not?"

"Because, good sir, it is the only one of its kind," Baltor's father politely explained. "And my father made it, so for these two important reasons, it is very sentimental to me and my family. So, in answer to your question, no, this sword is not for sale."

"Can you make me a sword just as good, if not better?" Briggs asked with a lot of hope in his voice.

"It'll be very tough to beat my father's work, good sir, but I can give you my best!"

"How long will it take for you to deliver your best?"

"At least six months... more likely a year."

"One last question—how much?"

"That really depends upon the materials used and the time spent—after all, my father's sword has been appraised at sixty thousand eight hundred parsecs."

Briggs first whistled in admiration, and then said, "Well, that's too bad. I'm only on a sergeant's pay, and not a general's, yet. Thanks for the info, but I'll just bring in my horse."

"No problem, sir."

As Briggs went to retrieve his horse, Baltor even heard him think, *There were quite a few valuable treasures in that case, besides that sword! I think I'm going to take a little trip here after work tonight. Why wait six months when I can get the whole package tonight—for free? Even better, I can come back tomorrow morning to thank this blacksmith for his excellent work, write down his report about the stolen sword and other valuables, but never turn in that report... yeah!*

The vision ended, just as Baltor had swallowed the last drop. Briggs was now dead.

A moment later, Baltor's body instantly changed back into human form, and so he took Brigg's sheath, strapped it on his belt, and then psychically commanded the dogs to feast— they obediently feasted upon the remains of the dead major!

He walked over and picked up grandfather's sword, holding it in his hands for the very first time in his life, while calling out, "The battle is over. Turn on the lights and open the door!"

About two minutes later, several of the workers finally re-lit the lights in the basement, and a minute later, the guards opened the door to the dog pit. By this time Baltor had his sword sheathed.

As he nonchalantly left the bar, many of the patrons clapped him on the back while congratulating him, especially Sessy whom had just made a fortune. She promised him free drinks for a year.

Not a single soldier stood in his way, or even said a word to Baltor: five minutes later, he stood before the gates to the Guild.

One of the two posted guards, upon seeing Baltor approach the entrance, informed, "Let me see your papers, please."

It was only then that Baltor realized he no longer had the identification papers. Still, he identified, "My name is Lord Poleax. Unfortunately, I've lost my papers, but I do know Lady Lydia and Instructor Humonus very well, as do you."

Sounding just like a snob, the guard replied, "Well, without papers, we cannot permit you to pass, no matter who you claim to know or be. This is, after all, the Ambassador to the Sultan's palace, and this place is restricted access, except for those who have their authorization papers."

Baltor nodded his head in understanding, made his way back along the main street, and then climbed over the wall near the corner. Quickly he hid within the bushes, just as some guards were walking by and chatting.

Once gone, he knew exactly where Humonus's apartment lay from here, and that's where he stealthily proceeded.

Not even a minute later, the man himself opened the door, only a second before his mouth literally dropped open in amazement—excitedly, he replied, "Come on in, Baltor! Come on in!"

"I'm sorry about waking you up at this hour, Humonus."

With a nonchalant wave of his hand, Humonus said, "Not a problem—I don't have to be at work until nine in the morning. I'm so glad to see you're alive!"

"Thank you."

"Please take a seat, Baltor. Would you like some food?"

"No thank you, Humonus. I just dined on a seven-course meal, thanks—it was delicious."

"Well how about a glass of ale, or some water?"

"No thank you, Humonus. Please relax and I will tell you my tale."

"Okay, let's hear it!"

For the next hour, Baltor began his tale starting from day one. He was truthful with Humonus when he revealed all of Salmot's underhanded plots, and he was truthful with everything that happened until he came across the rod. That part he lied about, saying that the pit only contained the bottom half to the map.

However, he also added that besides the map, he had also acquired "something else," though he didn't know what was in it.

When Humonus looked confused, Baltor simply pulled out the sack that Prince Cheo had given him, and sprinkled its sparkling contents onto the bed—dozens of small-to-midsized emeralds, rubies, sapphires and diamonds spread all about!

"Whoa," Humonus and Baltor both said in utter amazement.

Only a second later, Humonus was the first to pick up a diamond from the stack that was the size of an acorn.

He first closed one eye, and with the other eye, he gazed at the clarity of the diamond within the lamplight. It was so crystal clear without a crack anywhere that his mouth literally dropped in shock. He then asked with growing excitement to his voice, "Do you, can you, imagine how valuable these treasures are? The quality of this diamond alone is exquisite! You are a rich man, my friend, a very rich man!"

Baltor replied, "I am a very rich man, but not because of wealth. It is because of my friends, and you are one of my richest and wisest of them all—so half of all this is yours!"

Humonus began to get puffy eyed, as he sobbed happily, "Thank you, my friend!"

Baltor indifferently said, "No problem, but back to business. I have some interesting findings to report to the High Council, as soon as possible, and I'm sure that they will love to hear it. Can we have this arranged?"

A few moments later, Humonus forced himself back under control over his emotions, and said, "Of course, Baltor. It might take some time, so you'll have to be patient."

"I have one more question, really a favor to ask of you."

"You name it."

"Can I get my bed in the advanced students' bunkhouse back for a while?"

"Why in God's name would you want to live in a place like that now that you have all this treasure? You could easily buy your own house with this diamond alone!"

"Let's just say I miss it. I'm sorry if I don't sound excited now, but I'm really tired!"

"I definitely know that there's a bed for you then, even if I have to make another student sleep on the floor!"

With a yawn, Baltor asked, "Good. By the way, why hasn't the Guild promoted you to Master yet?"

After shrugging his shoulder, he answered, "Well, there have been a few rumors these last couple of months."

Baltor countered, "In my opinion, as I've said before, they should've promoted you long ago."

Humonus then asked, "Say, do you want me to help you find a new place tomorrow?"

"Maybe tomorrow night, but for now, I must be off to bed, Humonus. I'm very tired."

"Well," Humonus said, "let me get you inside the main building, before I bid my final goodnight to you, my friend."

"Thank you, my friend," Baltor replied with a very appreciative smile.

CHAPTER XVII

Baltor awoke the next night in the bunkhouse—his hands clasped protectively over the hilt of his grandfather's sword, which rested upon his chest. Fortunately, there had been an empty bed for him to sleep on.

Upon deciding to spend some time in order to examine the sword more thoroughly, he sat up in bed, noting that he was alone. For the next hour or so, he studied the magnificent beauties of his grandfather's sword, which was now his family inheritance.

Just as he was finishing his examinations, his super hearing detected the sounds of soundless footsteps, and so he immediately stood onto his feet with sword in hand. When he saw that it was only Humonus, he relaxed the sword back into its sheath.

Humonus had a warm smile plastered upon his face, as he greeted, "I hope your day was a restful one, Baltor!"

"Indeed it was, my friend!"

"That's good news, but I do have some bad news, as well—I talked to one of the High Council members today, and he said that it might be a month, or maybe even longer, before they shall be able to convene and hear your tale."

"Why's that?"

"Yesterday, the Sultan has decreed twenty percent higher taxes upon all of his residents, and for two reasons. Not only does he want to re-conquer Mauritia no matter the costs, especially since it really costs us, yet he also has called us to assist with the finances for building the coliseum, so that we can draw more foreigners to the city with gladiator games, which he promised he would pay back in full, once the profits start pouring in! Yeah, right."

"Hmmmmmm," Baltor replied.

Humonus added, "Regardless of what we think about it, the Sultan has his men going door to door, in order to retrieve his tax money, or properties. Most in the Guild are still stashing away their most-prized possessions, just in case they decide to resort to probing around the upper-class neighborhoods again."

Baltor's simple response was, "I see."

"I'm sorry, but there's no way to swing around this—you'll just have to be patient."

"I have learned much about patience from my quest, Humonus."

Humonus congratulated, "That's great to hear. Oh, by the way, I've got some really great news to deliver!"

Curious, Baltor asked, "What's that?"

"Well, this afternoon, I had the jewels appraised. Do you know how much they're worth?"

"How much?"

"One hundred and eighty thousand parsecs!"

With a whole lot of shock, Baltor asked, "Are you serious?"

"Oh yeah. Once I heard that astronomical number from a trustworthy source, I immediately sold the jewels to the guy, because I figured you would be happy. After I divided it up evenly between you and me, I decided to check out some houses for you within the fifty thousand bracket—I found one with an incredible view of the city not too far away from here! But, before you and I go to check out this house, how about going out for a couple of rounds of ale first? I'm thirsty!"

"Of course I'd love to accompany you, Humonus, but I'm not much of a drinker anymore."

"Fair enough." Humonus said. As he laughed aloud, he added, "Then I'll do the drinking!"

Mere seconds after they had entered the training area, Humonus pointed at Baltor's sword before saying, "Wow. That's a beauty! Don't think I didn't notice it before, but I just had too many other things going on in my mind. So, where on earth did you find that?"

Baltor replied as he glanced down to his sword, "This—this was created by my grandfather, long ago. But we can talk about that at the bar, right?"

Humonus laughed and said, "Sure."

The two then made their way out of the Guild, and toward the local bar that they used to drink at occasionally called, *The Hurried Wind.*

After having entered the packed tavern, and taking the only two empty stools that sat next to the bar, a fat man with long, greasy black hair and an apron approached from behind the bar, a man that Baltor remembered as Kerrick.

225

Kerrick greeted enthusiastically, "Hey there, Humonus and Baltor! Long time no sees either of you guys, especially you, Baltor—how's it going?"

"Good," both men replied.

"So what can I getcha'?"

Humonus replied, "I'll have a mug of Bolinksy ale."

Baltor added, "I'll have the same, Kerrick."

"One minute, guys."

Once Kerrick had gone to retrieve two mugs, Humonus asked, "So tell me more about that sword—I'm dying to know all about it!"

Seconds later, Kerrick returned with the drinks, collected the two parsecs from Humonus, and then went to serve the next customer.

Baltor then recalled all the stories and legends of the sword that his father had passed on to him; meanwhile, Humonus held on to the sword and gazed at each little part adoringly.

Once he had completed with the saga, Humonus then returned it back—Baltor sheathed his sword.

Humonus took a deep draught and sighed, "Whew. So, it's really because of this sword that is how you ended up orphaned and destitute, am I right?"

"Yes, sir."

Humonus sucked the last drop from his mug, and then said, "Wow!" He then observed that Baltor had not touched his drink, and asked, "You're not going to drink that?"

Baltor shook his head negatively.

"Well, you don't mind if I have that, do you?"

"Not at all, my friend, not at all."

Humonus took the mug and began to consume it. He had finished his third round when his eyes first spotted a large group of the Sultan's guards entering the door—there were at least nine of them. Both Baltor and Humonus turned their eyes toward the guards, but not their heads.

The captain held out a rolled-up scroll in his hand, and declared, "The Sultan has decreed that all inhabitants are to pay twenty percent of whatever they own to him—we have been sent to collect! All of you are to pay at this time, or we will immediately execute you. Are there any questions?"

One skinny man stood up and said in a whiny voice, "I have one—I was at home not even an hour ago when the Sultan's guards came to my door stating the exact same thing, and I paid! My question is: Do I have to pay again?"

The captain laughed, "Yes, you do. You should have stayed at home where you belong. If you're coming to bars, then that means you must have plenty more to give for charity."

The man exclaimed, "That's bunk. I already paid once, and I'll be damned if I pay again!"

A couple of other grumbles filled the tavern. However, before this man's words of defiance could carry throughout the crowd, the captain hurriedly walked over to the man, and without hesitating, he chopped off the man's head—many gasped in horror and fear at being the next.

The captain then asked, "Does anyone else have any questions or problems?"

No one said a word.

The guards began to extract from the patrons whatever goodies they wanted—meanwhile, Baltor and Humonus sat where they were at, and said nothing.

It appeared obvious that Baltor's sword had no less of an impact on this captain, for he soon approached and asked, "Well, what's this?"

Baltor looked over at the man, before he casually replied, "It's my ancestral sword."

"Hmmm." the captain said. He gazed adoringly at the diamonds that brilliantly reflected the lights in the room.

"I think I'm just going to take—" he said as he reached for the sword, but became interrupted in two different ways.

"I don't think so," Baltor interrupted—at the same time, his hand had physically interrupted the captain by grabbing the man's wrist, twisting, and locking him into an inescapable position by the time the word "so" had crossed his lips.

The captain yelped out in pain, "Guards! Kill him!"

From Baltor's peripherals, he saw that Humonus had his hand on the hilt of his dagger, but had not pulled it out just yet.

Meanwhile, the other guards slowly drew nearer.

Baltor felt the urge to sink his teeth into this man's neck, but resisted—after all, he didn't want Humonus to know the truth about what he had become.

Instead, he simply twisted more upon the wrist, causing the captain's face to mesh even farther into the disgusting floor. He then called out, "Stop! If any of you come any closer, I will literally rip your captain's arm right out of his shoulder!"

Meanwhile, the captain screamed in horrific pain, "Stop! Stop! Please, I beg of you, quit hurting me!"

The guards stopped, though still with swords drawn.

"Drop your swords, or this man dies," Baltor commanded.

The guards reluctantly did as instructed.

"Now, clear away so that my friend and I can safely depart. Only once we are outside and clear, will I then let go of your captain. Oh, don't even think of following us either, or you will regret it, I promise you that!"

The guards shuffled their way so that there was plenty of room for them to depart.

Baltor twisted the captain's wrist the other way, which caused him to jerk back onto his feet though still off balanced, and still firmly locked by his grip! Humonus silently noted with pride in his eyes, regarding his former student's "outstanding performance."

The three made their way outside, and the rest of the guards stayed put inside.

Once outside, Baltor slammed his elbow into the back of the captain's neck, knocking him out cold.

"Forget the house for now. Let's go back to the Guild," Baltor hissed, "before they come out."

Humonus and Baltor wasted no time in getting back to the Guild, via the back routes.

Once they were safely in Humonus's room, he said, "You know, Baltor, there will be a high price on our heads by morning. And you know that there were plenty of guards who will be able to identify us—they will comb this city seeking us out!"

Smacking a fist into his open palm, Baltor replied, "Let them come!"

Humonus extended his hands out in front of him and said, "No. The Guild must be kept top secret!"

Instead of pushing the subject, Baltor said, "Fine—still, I would suggest that you find any High Council member, and tell whomever, that we need to conduct a meeting first thing tomorrow night. As I said before, the quest I went on taught me a lot of useful information about our past, present, and especially about our tomorrows!"

Even though Humonus still looked both nervous and unconvinced, he still said, "I shall try to do what I can. As for tonight, I suggest we both sleep in the underground caverns, just in case."

"I agree with your suggestion," Baltor replied.

For the rest of that night, they slept hundreds of feet below ground.

The following night, Baltor awoke to find that he was alone in the cavern; he could still see clearly in the dark, as it was only his second night since he had last feasted.

Baltor made his way back up and toward the surface.

Even as Baltor passed by the training area, he could not see Humonus anywhere. However, after entering the main foyer to the guild, Baltor's eyes first rested upon Lydia, who was sitting on one of the lush couches alone.

Her eyes gazed up from oblivion and toward Baltor as he approached, and said pleasantly, "Good evening to you, Baltor."

Baltor bowed low and replied, "Good evening to you, my Mistress."

Without waiting for any more cordiality, he asked, "Has the High Council determined whether they will see me or not?"

Lydia answered, "Yes, we will. In forty-five minutes from now, we will convene to hear your story. However, you will only be given five minutes of our most-precious time."

After a nod, Baltor replied, "Fair enough. I need to tell you something really, really important, but I need you to listen to me until I'm done and don't say a word. Okay?"

Though looking very confused, Lydia answered, "Uh—sure."

For the next forty-four minutes to pass, Baltor explained to Lydia about his two separate encounters with Salmot, and the fact that Salmot had tried to kill him both times.

During the second encounter, Baltor really had no choice but use self defense and kill Salmot, who was hell-bent on killing him. Before she could react, he explained that "this worm" had never gave a damn about the Guild or about Lydia, yet greedily used everyone for his own profitable gain.

At the end of Baltor's explanation, he again reiterated that he had no choice but to kill Salmot in the end.

As he had gone through his story, Lydia looked in disbelief, shock, then horror, and finally grief! Her body began to tremble, and then she tried to run away and escape, but Baltor was ready as he clutched on to her tightly.

He sighed, "I'm sorry, my Mistress! I didn't want to kill him, but seriously, I had no other choice."

After a couple of more minutes of struggling had passed, her body finally began to relax—even though there were still the flowing tears and sobs.

A minute or two later, he released her, and looked at her dead in the eyes, as he gently confirmed for the fourth time, "I had no other choice. Besides he only used you anyway."

Lydia's teary eyes continued to meet his, and after a few more moments, she shook her head in disbelief, flatly stating, "I don't believe you. You never saw Salmot the way I did, especially during our intimate moments—he was like a little boy! I don't even know why I just told you that!"

"Most likely you told me because you are upset, my Mistress! You must believe me—I swear that all I've said is true!" Baltor swore.

A masculine voice suddenly interrupted their little heated conversation in the hallway, by calling out, "Are you ready to join us, Mistress Lydia? The remainder of the High Council is quite anxious to see Baltor after his quest."

Lydia turned away to face the man, and said, "Yes, we'll be right there, Master Jensa." She then turned back to Baltor and said, "There are always two sides to every story, Baltor. You have your viewpoint, as would Master Salmot, if he could have given his side."

Without another word, Lydia escorted Baltor into the room of thrones, and then she took her place in the High Council. Instead of Baltor taking the offered wooden seat that sat in the middle, he chose to stand up.

He began, "Masters and Mistresses of the High Council, I have been given five minutes to explain a mission that took nearly a year to perform... a three-fold mission, really, that all began because of the top half of an ancient map found in our underground labyrinth due to a major earthquake.

"Number one, locate the tower; number two, retrieve the Rod of Ro'shain, and number three, retrieve the bottom half of the map!

"As for number one, the tower itself does exist, though it is in such a serious stage of decay that I doubt it'll last too much longer, maybe several years, tops. As for number two, yes, I did explore everything possible in and around this tower, but no, the Rod of Ro'shain could not be found anywhere; that is, if it ever really did exist in the first place."

"Mistress Tricia," Baltor said, while pulling the map out, walking over to her, and extending it for her to take, "as for number three, here is the bottom half of the map, which obviously proves my claims that I did indeed make it to the black tower."

After a pause, he added, "Regarding the map I just handed you, you will soon find that it is as authentic as the top half of the map, which should still be in your possession."

"Thank you, Baltor, it is," she said happily.

He continued, "Even though one-third of my mission was a failure by retrieving the rod itself, the other two-thirds of my mission were a complete success, which makes me feel like my mission was a success, ultimately.

"Especially if you were to consider all the trials and tribulations I overcame through my adventure, like barely surviving through deserts, blizzards and jungles, even escaping from a vicious cannibal tribe! Of course, my story would take far more than five minutes to explain. More like five hours, or maybe even five days!"

After a short pause, he asked, "So... do you all—Masters and Mistresses of the High Council—find my quest to be a success, as well?"

After Tricia had looked to her left and her right, and saw most of heads nodding with pleased smiles, especially because of the recovery to the bottom half of the world-map, she confirmed, "We of the High Council do find your quest to be a complete success. As a result, we are promoting you to your first official rank: 'Thief.' Congratulations!

"As for the monetary reward that you will receive from the Guild for all your efforts, we—the High Council—will award you that amount in the next week or so, once we've decided how much this map is worth."

Baltor said with a low bow, "Thank you, my Mistress. Before I go, may I be allowed one more minute of the High Council's most-valuable time?"

After Tricia had looked to her left and right and saw that most of the High Council was shrugging their shoulders nonchalantly at the one-minute extension, she said, "Sure, go ahead, Baltor."

Baltor first cleared his throat before he spoke, "During my journey, I learned many other important things that pertain to the past, present, and toward the future—very relevant things that simultaneously pertain to the Guild."

After a short pause, he revealed, "The Guild, from what I have ultimately learned, is nothing more than a secret rebellion against the Sultan's tyrannical dictatorship!

"Moreover, the time has come for us to unite the people of Pavelus and overthrow him for good! I believe that this can easily be done once—"

A feminine voice interrupted, "Overthrow the Sultan? Are you out of your freaking mind?" The High Council began furiously whispering amongst one another; that is, except for Lydia, who still had a distant and sad look in her eyes.

Baltor did not answer either question, but continued in the speech, "Once the Sultan and his imperial forces have left Pavelus in their attempt to conquer the city of Mauritia—this is when we shall make our strike. I can guarantee you that he certainly will not be expecting an attack to come from within his own beloved capital city at the very same time!"

Another voice, this time masculine, questioned, "I, for one, do not think that we can afford to take that chance—mutinying against the Sultan! What makes you think that you stand a chance in hell?"

Baltor answered confidently, "We will only be successful once the peoples of Pavelus have been secretly united, and we overthrow him together as one, and together we create a new republic!"

"Preposterous!" screamed one.

Another one yelled, "I'm not taking that chance of exposing all that we have worked so long and hard!"

"Agreed," said another.

Still another cried, "I have a family to think about!"

Lydia continued to remain quiet the whole time, though she had just now cast her eyes to the ground.

Baltor had already turned around to leave, but before he did so, he stated, "If the answer's no, then I shall go about the task alone."

Tricia's voice said from behind, "If you do decide to undergo this task, you will go through with it without the assistance from the Guild. If you should become captured alive, you must remember your oath, no matter how they might tease them out, Thief!"

"I understand, my masters and mistresses," Baltor said before exiting the room.

CHAPTER XVIII

On his way to the Sultan's palace, Baltor was able to extract the blueprints, thanks to Briggs's visual memory banks that revealed a map: The only part of the palace Briggs had never visited or seen on any map was the top floor. Still, Baltor reasoned to himself that the Sultan's bedroom had to be on this floor, as it wasn't located anywhere else.

It only took him five minutes to near the palace's external walls—thanks to his superhuman speed and sticking to the shadows the entire time. By the time of his arrival, he had already formulated a simple yet effective game plan.

First, he would sneak his way passed the tons of guards until arriving at the Sultan's bedroom. Next, he would hide under the bed, wait for the man until he had arrived and gone to sleep, assassinate the Sultan, and escape.

Indeed, it turned out to be "easy as pie" for Baltor to sneak past a large group of guards that were all drinking, chatting, and laughing away by a roasting fire. He next passed between two of the many bodies still impaled upon spears around the palace walls—slightly less than a third of those impaled were still alive.

Only seconds later, he made it to the eighty-foot palace walls, themselves.

Once he saw that no guards were looking, he rapidly scaled the wall, and only seconds later, cautiously poked his head over the top. Once he saw that the coast was clear right on the other side, he climbed over the wall, dropped the eighty feet to the ground, rolled out his body to spread out the shock, and then hid in the middle of the nearest large and thick bush.

Only then did he take a good look at his surroundings. He first observed that around him lay an extremely huge and lush garden that made the Ambassador's garden pale in comparison.

Before being given a serious chance to marvel in this beautiful, tropical paradise, his eyes had already locked onto a breathtaking five-story palace, lit by a golden lamp on every corner that literally made the gold walls illuminate.

A pair of palace guards, obvious by the purple capes and the silver chain mail armor bearing the Seal of the Sultan, guarded every set of double doors that led into the palace on the first floor. There were also a whole lot of palace guards patrolling the paths, every few minutes passing near Baltor's hiding position. In total, he counted more than a hundred guards stationed within the palace's perimeters.

He sat in his position for a grand total of thirty-two minutes and fifteen seconds.

Until finally, the palace guards that stood by the doors looking outward acted in unison—they each took a step forward and then toward each other, walked to the center of the double doors, turned toward their respective door, opened them, entered as one, and then closed the doors behind them.

He bolted across the garden in the blink of an eye, and in the next blink, he had already leapt onto the first-floor balcony. Quickly he hopped from balcony to balcony, until he finally hung by his hands on the balcony of the top floor.

After poking his head up over the ledge, and discovering that the room was dark and void of occupants, he rolled over the ledge and crouched onto the balcony.

He was about to enter the room, but he stopped in his tracks upon unexpectedly hearing Briggs' voice say in his mind, *Only royalty, their guests, and officers with the rank of colonel or above ever visit this floor. Including of course, the Sultan and his beloved daughter, Princess Brishava, whose bedrooms are located here.* Briggs actually had sounded nice and respectful, Baltor startlingly noted.

He was just about to enter the empty room, but Briggs's voice stopped him yet again, as he added, *Even though I've never been on this floor myself, of which I've heard that there are a dozen rooms, including a harem room, I am sure that the Sultan has four bedchambers. Each of these four bedchambers is continuously guarded by two colonels, except during the changing of the guards at night. The princess has three bedrooms, also guarded.*

This time, Baltor waited a few extra seconds to see if Briggs had more to say.

Sure enough, he did, *Only the Ruling-General Glacius knows exactly which room the Sultan will sleep, which becomes randomly se-*

lected by the Ruling-General earlier in the day. It is during the night shift change that he and the Sultan walk the halls alone—the Ruling-General leads the Sultan to the pre-assigned room, and selects one of the other three bedchambers to spend the night before the guards have returned, so not even they know who sleeps where....

Without replying, Baltor waited another minute to see if Briggs had any additional thoughts, but none surfaced, not even an apology. All the while, his night-vision eyesight had been scanning the room—a regal room decorated with very exquisite valuables and furniture, including an emperor-sized bed that lay in the center of the bedroom, surrounded by hundreds of silky purple veils that hung down and around the overhead bed frame.

There were more of those same veils loosely hanging from the corners of the walls. Also fashionably hanging on the walls was a wide assortment of beautiful scenic portraits. A gold chandelier with dozens of unlit candles dangled from the center of the room, above the bed.

He didn't stop to adore the room, but immediately headed over to a double set of mahogany doors—doors elegantly designed with gold vines, and set with diamond-studded knobs, probably real.

He was just about to turn the knob on the left door when he heard a little girl's voice whine from the hallway, "But it's not fair, Daddy!"

After letting go of the door handle, he positioned himself behind the door while leaning up against the wall, just in case the door should happen to open.

"I don't care what you think, Brishava. You will not wear that dress at dinner tonight, and embarrass me in front of everyone!"

"Fine then, be a butt-head."

"You will not call me names either, young lady! If any of my subjects ever heard you talking like that way to me, they'd instantly be rebelling! Remember that I am not just your father—I am foremost the Sultan! Now, I will be back to check upon you in thirty minutes, so go change!"

Baltor heard a few sniffles as she said, "Yes, Popa."

Two seconds later, he then heard the sounds of a door closing to his right. Fifteen seconds after that, he finally heard the sounds of another door closing farther away to his right.

He wasn't sure which of the two rooms to his right that the Sultan had just entered, but he was cautiously determined to find out. He opened the door a split crack and peeked out into the hallway.

235

The floors of this rather long hallway were constructed from some type of dark-stained wood; covering only half of the floor's width was a royal-red-interlaced-with-gold carpet, whose length appeared to span the entire hallway.

Additionally, there were abstract three-dimensional designs artistically chiseled and polished into the shiny marble walls on both sides.

Hanging from the ceiling above each set of double doors was a crystal chandelier filled with burning candles. An artist who loved to portray angels in a variety of acts had masterfully painted the ceiling, and the prismatic reflections from those crystals caused the angels to appear rather mystical.

Finally, the end of this rather long hallway turned left while continuing down in that direction—he could see through the crack on the other side of the door that the hallway turned right at the opposite end, and that there were no doors at all in that direction.

What really drew his attention, however, were the two guards stationed at the other two other sets of double doors in this hallway, though he did not know the reason why his own bedroom was currently unguarded.

Unexpectedly, the door to Baltor's immediate right reopened, and stepping through that door out in to the hallway was this "Lady" wearing a shimmering white evening gown—he strongly suspected she was Brishava, the Sultan's daughter. Fortunate for him, she had begun to walk toward the room at the far right, instead of having turned his direction.

As he continuously watched her from behind, he thought, *I don't see anything wrong with that dress.*

His binocular-vision scanned in, and he could now see small, prismatic diamond studs sewn into the dress; as well, studs sewn into her jet-black hair ran down her back in thick weaves, while being pinned down at the base by several diamond barrettes. He couldn't tell, despite his superhuman powers, just how old or young she was from this angle.

She turned toward her father's door and neared it—only when she turned did Baltor observe that she also donned a white silky veil that perfectly concealed the lower half of her face, a veil filled sporadically with tiny prismatic diamonds.

As for the upper half of this girl's face, who he guessed to be sixteen years old, it looked flawless in every little detail, or so Baltor's opinion immediately became—this breathtaking woman unquestionably bore the face of a *true princess.*

A few moments later, she raised her hand up as if to knock upon the door but didn't—a few more moments passed, but still she didn't knock.

Instead, she abruptly turned around and walked back up the hallway, back into his direction! Baltor closed the door until it was but a tiny sliver, just enough to allow him to glimpse through.

"*Ah..*" When his eyes really scanned in, he now understood the reason for the Sultan's disdain—the front of the dress had been cut semi-low, revealing a fractional portion of her cleavage. What competed for this area's attention, however, were several varying lengths of platinum necklaces interjected with small yet brilliant diamond studs.

That wasn't the thing that really captivated this thief's attention—it was again her face. Moreover, there was one thing about it all that stood out in particular—it was her doe-brown eyes, which sparkled ever so radiantly.

The more that he stared, the more he found himself not wanting to look at anything else, until suddenly, something else grabbed his senses, but this time, it came from his sense of smell.

As he took a concentrated whiff, a scent fully penetrated his nostrils and his brain—thanks to his superhuman powers, he had the full opportunity to learn that it was exotic, wonderful, and a flowery fragrance, making him want to sniff the air more and more.

She had just turned toward her room, but suddenly, her head and face stopped directly into his direction, her hands cupped lightly over her mouth.

After giving a slight gasp, she breathed out the word, "You."

It was only because of his super-hearing that he was able to hear this word from more than one-hundred-feet away!

One of the guards that stood closer to her current position by her bedroom door asked after a low bow, "Yes, Your Highness, is there something that you want from me?"

The princess quickly looked over to the guard, and stammered, "No, no, there isn't, colonel. I was just, uh, talking to myself again, sorry. I forgot my, uh, my favorite comb in the spare bedroom, yes. I need to go get it, right away."

As soon as the princess said the two words "spare bedroom," the colonel unconsciously looked in that direction, but saw nothing out of the ordinary—Baltor had just closed the door a split second before.

"No problem, my princess. Would you like me to accompany you?"

"No, thank you—I can handle it on my own, thanks." She said just before she proceeded to the spare bedroom.

Meanwhile, as Baltor strangely continued to wait in the room, his curiosity began to swell as to why she had uttered the word "you" and, most especially, why she had not alerted the guards to his position.

Despite all his curiosities, however, he refused to forget his mission here: Restore justice and freedom for all Pavelus by assassinating the tyrannical Sultan.

What seemed an eternity passed, until finally, she opened the door to the guest bedroom, entered, closed the door behind her and slowly began to approach Baltor. Meanwhile, he waited at the other exit of the room, which location was only feet away from the balcony.

A few moments after she had stopped in her tracks about five feet away from Baltor's position, he began, "Why did you say 'you' like that to me?"

As she began to giggle like a little schoolgirl, both of her hands covered her veil—still, this act did nothing to stop the giggling underneath.

He threw up his hands in slight exasperation, and asked, "Well?"

In between the giggles, she answered, "You—*hee-hee*—wouldn't believe me—*hee-hee*—if I told you."

He asked with a bit of exasperation, "Can we get serious for one moment please?"

"Fine then—you want me to be serious?" the princess asked, while straightening out her composure until her back was arched straight back, lifting up her chin until it was parallel with the floor, and placing her hands delicately by her sides while lightly grabbing the folds of her dress.

She even asked with the eloquence of a princess, "Is this much better for you, kind lord?"

"Yes, thank you," Baltor said seriously with a nod. He then asked, "Now, please tell me why you said 'you' like that to me, and why you didn't alert the guards to my presence?"

"Well, I dreamt about you coming and rescuing me when I was a little girl," the princess informed just as eloquently and seriously.

"Come on," Baltor said in exasperated tones, while extending his arms and hands up in exasperation, "That's preposterous! You obviously have no clue as to the reason why I'm even here at all, much less do you know who or what I am. So—why don't you tell me the truth?"

Both of the princess's jet-black eyebrows rose into sharp angles at that. She sucked in a gasp of air through her nose, walked over, leaned her face until it was inches away from his face, and then gently snapped, "In my dream, you weren't so mean."

His heart had strangely begun to flutter—perhaps by those gorgeous and angry eyes of her that strangely captivated him so—and for a few moments, he didn't know what to say at all.

Finally, as a question popped into Baltor's mind, so too did it come out of his mouth, "How old are you?"

Suddenly that look of anger was completely gone from the princess's face and that what replaced it was a look of shyness—she, after looking at the ground for a few moments, looked back at Baltor, and evenly replied, "I'm seventeen, almost eighteen."

"What's your name?" After having asked that question, Baltor suddenly remembered the answer, but thought that he would sound foolish if he abruptly called out the answer now or asked a better question that had just popped into his mind, which question was, "Why didn't you alert the guards?"

"Brishava" was her expected response a few moments later. "So how old are you?"

"I'm twenty-one," Baltor said just before his eyes scanned over toward the door for a second, in order to ensure that it was still closed and everything was still okay—it was, even if for a moment.

Immediately Princess Brishava began to look around uncomfortably herself, but before Baltor could ask if there was something wrong, she said, "Listen, my father's going to be looking for me soon—believe me when I say that he's very protective of me. Right now, I need to go and get ready for dinner, but I can guarantee you that there will be no royal dignitaries coming into this bedroom tonight, so you will be safe right here until I get back."

As soon as the princess saw the confused look on Baltor's face, she explained, "Right after dinner is over, I will tell my father that I'm rather tired and wish to go to bed early, and then I can come back here, and we can talk some more, okay?"

Instead of answering the princess's question, Baltor finally asked the first real question he now had the opportunity to ask, "What makes you think that I'm here to 'talk?'"

As she had already arrived at the door, but before she opened it to leave, she said rather confidently, "I have my strong suspicions why you're here. Please, before you do anything rash, talk to me one more time first. Promise?"

While sighing very reluctantly, Baltor said, "Fine—I promise."

Without another word, she left.

Just to be on the safe side, he hid himself in a closet, and patiently squatted. His patience seemed to pay off, as it seemed that an eternity had passed until he heard the door reopening. He looked out the closet doors, and was quite relieved to see that it was the Sultan's daughter and not some roaming guard.

He observed that she now donned a silky-blue gown intermixed with reflective-gold fabric that was much more concealing, and a matching veil that covered her face. Additionally, he saw that her hair was now pulled tightly into a bun, which then delicately splashed down around her shoulders, and finally curled back up into the air about another inch.

"Hello?" she asked a bit timidly.

He opened the door to the closet and took a step out. "I'm here, just like I promised. Now, what do you want to talk about, your Highness?"

Most unexpectedly, she ran over to him and leapt into his arms, giggling all the while.

Though he was a very powerful man, physically and otherwise, he was not ready for her abrupt move. Subsequently, he took a few steps back.

"What are you doing?" Baltor asked in shock. A different type of vanilla-smelling perfume wafted up his nostrils, no less exotic or wonderful than the first perfume she had donned—actually, it was an even better smell.

She ripped off the veil, revealing a perfect button-shaped nose, and a full set of prominent lips already posed to pucker. Her kisses spread throughout Baltor's face and neck—all the while giggling like a little girl.

He asked, "Why—why are you kissing me?"

The princess didn't answer the question, but began to kiss his lips again—he found that he was actually beginning to enjoy all of the sensuous feelings that were coursing through his masculine body. Never before had any girl kissed him like this!

Suddenly, she stopped kissing in order to gently grab his face, guide it to hers, and profess, "I love you."

That brought him to reality, and he asked, "What in the hell are you talking about? You don't know the first thing about me."

"But we shall have our whole lifetimes to learn about each other, while exploring our infinite love."

He realized that this princess's head was seriously lost in the clouds, and therefore, he decided to show her the real Baltor. He confessed, "You want to learn about me? Well, there's not much to know about me, woman, except that I am an orphan, a thief, and a killer. I do have friends, yes, but they're all thieves and killers too."

The princess's mouth dropped open, aghast, just before she put her feet back onto the ground. Her mouth had begun to form a frown, and her eyes then quivered.

The moment that the first tear had poured down her face, he found his own heart struck, and so he tried to apologize, "I'm sorry if the truth hurts you."

"But in my dream—you were not only a mighty hero, yet also a true leader, Baltor," she revealed.

His mouth dropped open in astonishment that she had somehow known his name—he had specifically not said it for an easy-to-figure-out reason.

"You—you know my name?" he finally stammered.

The princess's only answer was to wipe away the remains of the tear with that pretty hand of hers first, and then turn to leave.

He grabbed her hand before she could escape however, and then he asked, "How do you know my name?"

She tried to shake the embrace off, while answering, "Maybe I do, but from what you just told me, then even dreams do lie! Please, just let me go."

He released his grip, but requested, "Please don't go yet. I made my promise to wait, so you owe me one. Let me talk to you for one more minute, and then you can go one way while I go another, okay?"

She slowly turned around lightly while nodding her head— Baltor observed that her mascara had slightly spread out from underneath her tear-stained eyes, which were still gazing at the ground.

As he gently wiped the mascara stains off her face with both of his index fingers, he thought, perhaps aloud, "More and more beautiful every single moment."

"What?" she asked, just before her head looked back up into Baltor's still-staring eyes.

A moment, or an eternity, later, he turned away to look to the ground. Instead of repeating his earlier statement, he muttered, "Well, Princess Brishava, it appears that I'm in quite a predicament."

"How so, Lord Baltor?"

"I'll be blunt," Baltor replied. "My purpose for coming here was not to meet you but to assassinate your father—he is a tyrant that needs to be stopped! He doesn't care about his citizens, taxes us at ridiculous rates, robs us, or tortures or kills us if we can't pay him—my parents were murdered by his men! But now, there's you, and I no longer know what to do."

Even though this princess was four inches shorter than Baltor, she first gently lifted Baltor's chin until they were looking eye to eye. Once they had made eye contact, she said, "Even though my father tries to hide the truth from me, I too know that he is a ruthless tyrant... but for you to kill him makes you no better!"

"Great," Baltor said with a bit of frustration and certainly not enthusiasm, "so what do you suggest?"

Drawing closer with a seductive smile still wrapped upon her delicate face, she had once again tightly wrapped her arms around his waist. Just before he felt their lips touch, she answered, "There are better ways to become the Sultan."

This time, he could no longer resist her kisses, and for an unknown amount of time to pass, the passionate kissing commenced!

CHAPTER XIX

Even though quite a bit of time passed as the two continued to kiss, it was certainly not enough time in the princess's opinion—Baltor was the one who forced the kissing to stop so he could ask, "Like what?"

"Silly," she answered, "that's the easy part."

"It is?"

She then propped herself forward onto her tiptoes, so that her lips were a half an inch away from Baltor's ear, and then she whispered seductively, "Yes, run away with me, tonight. Marry me tomorrow. As far as I'm concerned, our honeymoon can go on for many months, or years."

Due to her bold marriage proposal, Baltor could only stand there in shocked silence! While still clasping his arms, she abruptly rocked back onto her heels, which allowed her to playfully swing away, so she could give him the up-and-down look.

A second or so later, once she was again looking directly into his eyes, she cooed with a very pleased smile, "After all, you are the finest thing, my eyes have ever seen... and that is what I truly mean, you gorgeous muscle machine!"

The shock inside of Baltor instantly became replaced by the feelings of being flattered, due to her "exceptional poetic compliment!"

After all, he had never really thought of himself as good or bad looking, just average. In fact, the only person who had ever complimented Baltor on his looks, besides his mother, a few other girls in the Guild, and this princess, was Lydia. And even though Lydia had once told Baltor that he could have his choice on any number of women, he couldn't have the one woman he had wanted for so long—Lydia herself.

Now there was this girl he didn't even know one iota, except for the fact that she's the daughter of the man he had been planning to kill. And now she was asking him to marry her!

All the while, this princess gave a light sigh of content, wrapped her arms delicately back around his torso, and leaned her mouth in until it was an inch from Baltor's ear. Once this was so, she then whispered, "Only when the time is right and we are ready will we come back. It will be then that I declare to my father that you are my husband, and the next Sultan of the Sharia Empire!"

Baltor thought her plan preposterous, pulled away, and said in an almost-too-loud tone of voice, "Your father will never concede to this—never! I am an orphaned peasant... literally!"

"Not once you've married me. Once you are my husband, you will become the royalty that I have always been since birth! Regardless of whether my father accepts us or not in the end, one day soon he will pass off into oblivion, and you will be the Sultan. And I, the Sultaness."

"But—"

She gently cupped her hand over his mouth, which immediately silenced him, and then she whispered, "Shhh. You are making things far too complex! I know that I have always loved you ever since my eyes first beheld you within my dreams as a little girl, but can you grow to love me? Do you want to take the chance and be with me—to tease out all my girly secrets, while simultaneously exploring all my womanly secrets? I have many, I can assure you of that, and they're all very good ones."

She then removed the hand that had been cupped on Baltor's mouth, placed it lightly upon his muscular shoulder, and silently gazed into his eyes with absolutely no doubt.

Baltor responded, this time much quieter, "Yes, I feel something for you. But I, we, don't even know what love is, nor do we even know each other at all."

A curious expression crossed her face, certainly no less beautiful than any of her other looks, as she began to study every contour of his face. Except for a manly-looking nose and a neatly braided goatee, she realized that the rest of Baltor's facial features resembled that of a hawk!

She then looked back into his eyes, and sighed, "Baltor, Baltor, Baltor. To me, love begins as a simple feeling, yet ultimately ends as a unified state of mind, heart and soul. Never will those feelings end, not even death... unless you want them to! And trust me that we'll have plenty of time to get to learn about each other. That'll be half the fun."

Baltor stood in silence for a lengthy amount of time and pondered her words, especially, "not even death." Finally he spoke, "I hear your wonderful promises, but—but you don't know the first thing about me. Until you do, marriage is out of the question."

"Why?"

"There are some things about me that you may not like discovering."

"Like what?"

"I... I have an unusual and mysterious illness that prevents me from bearing sunlight, so I live by the night and sleep during the day. My illness also prevents me from eating the same foods as you—my meals have to be specially prepared, and I have to eat alone! If that's not enough, I also don't think that I'm ready to get married, just like that. Now do you understand my three very important reasons why?"

"Then I will become nocturnal myself, and you can eat whatever you want on your own whenever you're hungry—as for the marriage, I will patiently wait until you are ready, okay?"

"Just like that?"

"Yes, just like that, Baltor. So please relax."

"I'll try."

"Will you also try things our way, and if they don't work for you, then you can go back to your way?"

"What do you mean?"

"Instead of killing my father, take me with you, and let's run away."

"As you wish, Princess Brishava."

"Just like that?"

Baltor smiled. "Just like that."

"Great!" she replied enthusiastically. "There is one last thing. My father will check on me before he goes to bed at midnight. Afterward, I will come back, all packed and ready to go. The only problem we will have is how to escape from this room and floor of the palace."

"Escaping will be no problem, my princess. Actually, I've a better idea—why don't I simply climb onto the roof, walk over to your balcony, hop on down, and hide in your room until after your father checks on you, and then we can leave right after? After all, I am a professional thief."

She squealed, "That sounds like a great idea!" She turned to head out of the bedroom; however, she stopped in mid-stride, turned around, and jumped back into Baltor's arms while exclaiming, "I love you! I love you! I love you so much, my beautiful Baltor, my beautiful soon-to-be Sultan!"

This time, Baltor was ready for her leap and even happier about the ensuing kisses.

The second that she left, an unknown amount of time later, he headed out to the balcony, and while reaching for the ledge above, he jumped.

After he grabbed the ledge and climbed onto the roof, he quickly made his way to the princess's balcony, and dropped down behind a patio chair.

Upon observing that no one was in this room either, he then entered, and took a seat in a plush couch. Just then, the door opened and in she walked.

After the guards had closed the door behind her, she turned around and nearly jumped five feet into the air when she saw him already there, and looking quite comfortable.

"My," she hummed, "you are quick."

He threw a humble smile, yet instead of commenting about his quickness, he asked, "Where would be a good place for me to hide?"

"Under my bed, but give me a quick kiss first! My maidens will be here momentarily to assist, so you must be extremely quiet after they've arrived."

He obliged the princess with a quick kiss, climbed underneath the center of the king-sized bed, closed his eyes, and strangely drifted off into a light sleep.

About a minute later, two young women entered the room. They first removed the barrettes out of the princess's hair, causing it to splash halfway down her back, and then they combed it thoroughly for several more minutes.

Once done, they next carefully removed the makeup that donned her face with a sponge. Five minutes later, they assisted her out of her formal attire, and into her pajamas. Once done, they gave a low bow, said their good nights, and left for the night.

The princess immediately began the process of packing her belongings into a medium-sized backpack.

Once done about a half an hour later, she hid the backpack in her closet, and then hopped into bed. A few moments later, she whispered from above, "Hello, my love."

He immediately awoke from his nap, and whispered back, "Hello. Are you now done with everything?"

"Yes, I am."

"Good...."

Perhaps a dozen seconds later, she whispered with excitement, "Hopefully my father will soon come so that we can go! I don't like not being able to look at you—not one bit."

"Well, at least it's not too uncomfortable down here."

After a short giggle, she added, "That's good to hear. If you like, later, I could give you a back massage?"

Baltor hummed, "Hmmm."

"Shhh. I think he's coming."

The sounds of muffled voices slowly grew louder as they approached the room, and one of those voices that he could hear was the Sultan's, though he strongly suspected that the other man's voice was Ruling-General Glacius.

About fifteen seconds later, both double doors were opened by the guards, and in walked the Sultan, himself. Meanwhile, still under the bed, Baltor heard the sliding sounds of the Sultan's feet, which were wearing slippers.

Once inside, the Sultan turned back around, and said, "I'll be right out in a minute, Ruling-General Glacius. I need to say good-night to my daughter."

Glacius's snappy reply was, "Yes, my Sultan!"

The guards closed the door behind the Sultan, who then approached the bed—the only thing that Baltor could see was a pair of man's gold-embroidered velvet slippers, each bearing the symbol of the crossed-sabers on top.

"Good night, my Princess" were the Sultan's first words to his daughter as soon as the slippers had stopped in front of the bed.

"Good night, Daddy," she responded.

Now sounding apologetic, he said , "I'm sorry that I yelled at you earlier, Brishava, but you must ensure at all times that the attire you wear is appropriate. After all, one day, you will become the next Sultaness, and I do not want any of our subjects thinking of you as a slut!"

At that, she grew angry, and retaliated, "Just because I decide to show a little skin does not make me a slut, Father! Now if I was inviting all the hunks in our empire to have a sexual fling with me, then I would understand why our subjects would think of me as a slut that I'm not and never will be."

Upon realization of her retaliatory statement, the Sultan became quite angry as he snapped, "Brishava! I would suggest that you keep your mouth shut, especially once you've married the Duke of Vispano in nine months from now. He may not be as forgiving of a man as I am, and I shall not live forever to protect you!"

After releasing a little sigh, she agreed, "You're right, Father. I'm wrong. Okay? For now, I'll keep my little mouth shut, except to swear to be the obedient wife to the man I ultimately marry before God—I swear that on everything. Okay?"

"Okay."

"Goodnight, Daddy—I love you!"

The Sultan chuckled, and said, "Good, now maybe we can have some peace around here. I love you too—goodnight!" He then leaned in, gave his daughter a kiss on the cheek, turned around, headed toward the door, opened it, exited the room, waved at his daughter, and then closed the door behind him.

About four minutes later, Baltor heard the sounds of the guards outside the door retaking their post.

As soon as he knew that the coast was clear, he climbed out, and then asked, "Ready to go?"

"No, I'm not. I have to change," she answered just before she went behind a three-piece stand.

When she came out a minute later, she wore a silky black tunic, pants, black leather boots, and even a black silky cape. She then opened the closet, pulled out the backpack, and strapped it on her back.

Despite her camouflaged appearance, Baltor could make out her perfectly formed curves, and confirmed that she was indeed quite a beautiful woman, no matter what she wore!

He first stepped out onto the balcony, scanned the area thoroughly, and then informed, "Hop on my back, and hold on tight."

Without hesitation she did, and once he saw the coast was clear, he hopped down from balcony to balcony, until he landed back onto the ground.

In less than two seconds, he had already made it to the exterior palace walls, even with the princess on his back.

Though she wanted to wee out from the fun ride, she silently continued to watch with exhilarated eyes, as he quickly and easily climbed the eighty-foot walls, even with her added weight. Instead of hopping down, as he had done before, he simply scaled his way back down the other side.

Fortunately, the coast remained clear throughout these whole eight seconds.

As soon as she had hopped off his back, she pulled the hood over her head to conceal her face. As she continued to walk by his side through the streets of Pavelus, she asked with awe, "How is it that you are able to do such amazing feats with such amazing speeds?"

"I'm a trained thief, remember?"

"I see," she said with her voice in awe. A few seconds later, she added, "Well, as for me, for some time to come, I'm just an ordinary peasant girl wishing I was a princess, right?"

"Right."

They had just been drawing near to a small T intersection that had buildings to their left and right as well in front of them. Most unexpectedly, however, a squad of guards marched around the corner from the right, and headed directly for them.

Even though Baltor was very shocked that he hadn't heard them marching, especially with his vampire hearing, he still managed to count a leader who led two columns of six guards that were now about eight feet away.

Upon drawing to five feet away, this leader called out to his troops, "Halt."

The leader and the guards halted in unison a step later. In that same nasal tone of voice, the leader called out, "Who goes there?"

Baltor had already been using his peripherals to scan his area quickly, while simultaneously trying to formulate a plan of escape.

Even after having scanned all around, which only took three seconds, he couldn't think of a way to safely get Brishava onto his back and scale any of the walls of these neighboring buildings without giving the guards at least one opportunity to hurt her during the first escape option.

The only other type of escape that he could think of was taking this road back toward the palace, but would he be quick enough to grab Brishava, and then safely hightail it out of there, he wondered?

Meanwhile, Brishava was the one who answered, "We have been sent on a top-secret mission by the Sultan."

As for the guards, even though their leader hadn't issued the order, they had already begun to semi-quietly move forward and encircle the two, which had only taken them about three seconds after the time their leader had asked, "Who goes there?"

Once surrounded, Baltor then realized that his second and final escape route was gone, and that the only other two options were talking or fighting.

"Really," The leader sighed nasally. "Then I don't suppose you have top secret proof to your supposed claims?"

She answered, "That's why it's called 'top secret,' dear."

"Are you trying to get smart with me? I'll take you in for that alone!"

"No, of course not, officer," she answered humbly.

"There's something oddly familiar about your voice—let me see your face, woman."

The hope that she would be persuasive enough to get by them without a fight was beginning to disappear within Baltor's mind. He again began to look around with his peripheral vision at all the possible routes of escape just in case, yet there were still not a single one found.

Meanwhile, Brishava answered, "I really can't do that."

"Why not?"

She answered in a haughty tone of voice, "My identity must also remain top secret, Lieutenant—the consequences for revealing my identity could be disastrous to the Sharia Empire!"

"Yeah, right. Take off the hood now. Or I'll have my troops do it for you!"

Slowly but surely, Brishava complied.

Out of the thirteen men, only this lieutenant had ever seen and heard the princess once before, which happened at the only military ball he'd ever attended shortly after his commission a little over a year ago.

When the lieutenant's major had first introduced him to the princess in the greeting line, he had never forgotten when her incredibly beautiful eyes met his own eyes for the very first and last time. She had acknowledged his existence with the words, "Nice to meet you, Lieutenant Cuffins."

Ever since, even though Cuffins believed that he had a rat's chance in hell of ever hooking up with Brishava—he never stopped secretly wishing that maybe he'd be the one to rescue this princess one day, and now maybe that day had finally come.

"You're Princ—" Cuffins tried to say—Baltor's sword, however, had just cleanly sliced off Cuffins' head!

Even though the troops had become quite confused as to what was going on, they did recognize that this other man was a serious threat as he had instantly killed their lieutenant, while also figuring out from their lieutenant's last words that this woman was the princess.

Immediately all but one guard drew out their swords and came in for the attack, though the guard who hadn't drawn his sword had instead grabbed the princess by her hand and quickly yanked her out of harm's way.

Fortunately, for Baltor, due to the rather narrow street, only five guards could come in for the attack at once, and this is exactly what they did. Still, his sword arm was so incredibly fast that he was able to deflect every single attack, occasionally landing in a finishing blow of his own, one after the other.

One minute later into the battle, the very guard that had pulled a non-fighting Brishava back to safety, soon observed that all of his buddies were slowly but surely being slaughtered, and he promised her, "Come with me, your Highness, and I'll get you to safety!"

She said, "No way."

The second she said "no way," he decided to take it upon himself to get her to safety anyway, so he picked her up, threw her over his shoulder, and began to run.

This time, Brishava began to scream and fight back—however, his grip on her was quite tight and secure as he ran toward the palace's main entrance about three blocks away.

Baltor heard her screams, and he quickened his offensive strikes. Ten seconds later the four remaining guards were dead.

Immediately he booked with his superhuman speed, and ten seconds later, he had nearly caught up to the guard that was seconds away from rounding the last corner before the palace's main entrance about fifty feet where dozens more palace guards were stationed, and hundreds more inside.

Before the guard could get round the corner however, Baltor lunged and plummeted hard into the back of the guard, which caused the guard to crash hard onto the ground with him on top. As for Brishava, she flew to the ground a couple of feet farther away, and not only landed hard on the ground, yet was now in visible range from the palace gates about fifty feet away.

Without pause, Baltor snapped the guard's neck, ran over to Brishava, quickly picked her up, hightailed it back out of visible range a second later, and then gently set her down onto her feet.

After giving her the up-down look, he asked, "Are you okay?"

She nodded her head, and said, "My shoulder hurts a bit from slamming into the ground, but other than that—yes, I'm okay."

His eyes glanced furtively around as he said, "Brishava, we've got to get going and quickly—more guards may have seen us! Hop on my back."

She did, and he again used his super speeds to get them back. Never before had she astonishingly ever seen anyone move so fast.

Less than five minutes later, he slowed down his pace a quarter-block short of the Guild, and said, "We'll be there in a moment. Until we find my friend and I say it's okay, we're going to remain completely silent without a single word spoken, okay?"

She tightened her grip even more, and sighed, "Okay."

A second later, they stopped in the shadows of the thirty-foot wall that contained the Guild.

After glancing from side to side to ensure that the coast was still clear, Baltor climbed almost to the top of the wall, gripping the edges with his fingers. Slowly he pulled himself up until just his head peeked over the wall.

When he saw that the coast was clear on the other side, he dropped back down to the ground, told Brishava to climb on his back, scaled back up the wall, and then climbed back down on the other side.

They made their way stealthily to Humonus's apartment, and once they had arrived nearly ten minutes later, Brishava stood back on her feet. Meanwhile, Baltor tapped the door quietly several times, but no one answered. He knocked again, this time louder, but still no response.

With frustration to his voice, he growled, "Damn. There's no way for me to get underground before morning!"

"Why not?" she asked.

"Because," Baltor quietly explained, "there are guards who watch the main entrance at all times, and I don't have a pass."

Just as he had finished saying that, a good idea crossed his mind. He snapped his fingers as he said, "Better yet—climb on my back and let's just go to my other friend's apartment, and see if she's there to get us in."

She nodded her head, and said, "Okay."

With her once again on his back, he snuck them to Lydia's onsite apartment, which took several more minutes.

Once there, he knocked on her door, but no one answered there either.

Clearly frustrated, he cried, "Damn. Now I don't know what to do—I have to get underground soon! See? The skies are seriously beginning to lighten up. Dawn will be here soon!"

"There's got to be something we can do," she came back. "Are there any other side entrances that lead underground around here?"

He snapped his fingers upon thinking about the spa, and said, "Yes I do."

"Which way do we go?"

"Damn it—forget it! I don't know how to get there from above ground—damn it!"

She sighed, "You must seriously relax. An answer will reveal itself before it is too late!"

"The answer to what?" Baltor asked with frustration.

"The answer to the problem of how to get you underground before the sun rises."

"The only other answer I can foresee is fighting my way inside, even though I do not want to go this route!"

She didn't say anything, though a deep look of concern was clearly there upon her face.

Grimly shaking his head, he said, "Let's go—we're just going to have to fight our way in, and hopefully we'll be able to hide ourselves way down there where no one can find us until tonight."

Once they had gotten to the side of the main building, a minute later, they then began to hurry for the front doors.

It was right then that he knew it was too late to fight, as the sun had just risen, for he instantaneously felt both very weak and tired. The only thing that worked in his favor was the fact that the shadows here would block the sun's rays, but for only a couple of hours.

Only seconds after the sun had risen, he instantly found his weakened legs give out beneath him, causing him to stumble and crash into the ground.

In turn, she flipped him over onto his back, laid his head upon her lap, and began to rub his hair.

His eyes wanted to shut from sheer exhaustion, but neither did they want to close and no longer look upon her lovely face.

From out of the corner of his very sleepy eye, he noticed a furtive movement, and looked over to see someone jogging upon the winding cobblestone path. A few seconds later he realized that it was Lydia.

"Lydia," he tried to call out but found that the only sound produced was a hollow whisper.

Brishava had heard the name, however, and yelled it out way too loud.

Lydia instantly stopped in her tracks, but saw only two shadowy figures, one sitting and one lying on the ground by the side of the building. She next observed that one of the guards by the door had heard the sound as well, and had begun to hurry toward the source of the noise.

A moment later, she said while slowly approaching closer, "Who are you?"

"Tell her that it's Baltor," he whispered, his eyes now closed.

"Baltor," Brishava repeated a bit louder though not too much.

Lydia walked closer, and upon seeing Brishava, she asked, "Who—who the hell is that with you?"

"I'll explain in a minute. Right now, I need to get inside," Baltor whispered as loud as he could, hoping Lydia heard.

The guard asked as he neared the group, "Is there a problem, Mistress Lydia?"

"No, there isn't. I know them. They're with me."

"Yes, ma'am. Would you like assistance?"

"No, thanks, I've got him," Lydia said. She then assisted Baltor by draping one of his arms over her shoulder, while Brishava draped the other one over hers. They led him inside and past the guards.

Once seated inside on the lush couches, Lydia probed, "Who is that with you and why is she here?"

Even though all Baltor wanted to do was sleep, he explained, "She's just a friend—I brought her here—*yawn*—because there were guards chasing us and I had no other choice."

"You know the rules, Baltor," Lydia replied, "The High Council will not be pleased."

"What they don't know—*yawn*—won't hurt them." he sleepily replied.

Lydia was about to reply to that, but Brishava interrupted, "Please, Lydia, we need a place to sleep, for now, deep underground. We'll be out of here by tonight, I promise!"

Lydia scanned from Baltor to Brishava, and back.

From an immediate glance, she could tell that this young woman was deeply concerned for him, yet suspected more. She could also tell that he was already seven-eighths asleep on the couch—Lydia's sympathy got the best of her.

A moment later, she said, "I don't know what the hell's the matter with you Baltor, but you two can sleep down in the underground caverns, but only for today. Do not leave tonight, as I will come down so that we can talk further before you go."

"You got it, and thank you," he said, just before he yawned real deeply.

The two girls assisted Baltor into a deep, underground tunnel. Once Lydia had stopped in her tracks, and said, "This place will do. But remember, before you leave tonight, I need to talk to the both of you."

After nodding, Baltor plopped down onto the ground, and was already sound asleep...

CHAPTER XX

Once the sun had just set, Baltor was the first to wake from the depths of unconsciousness—he felt something very warm curled up within his arms and chest, and heard something else. It was the sound of two hearts beating almost as one—for the very first time since his transformation to an undead vampire did he become aware that he still had a heartbeat!

He opened his eyes, and through his night-vision, he clearly saw Brishava sleeping contentedly away on him; his mind was greatly relieved that his stomach hadn't accidentally gotten the best of him.

Perhaps from his ever-so-slight movement, she sighed.

He asked lightly, "Are you awake, Brishava?"

After a pause, she asked back, "Hmmm?"

"I said, are you awake?"

"No, I was sleeping. The first time you asked that question, I thought I was dreaming—I was afraid to wake up and find that it was only a dream, my love!"

From her response, he could only deeply sigh. Never in a million years had he ever imagined that he could be so happy.

Even in the utter darkness, she turned over so that she was facing him and began to cradle his face with both of her warm hands.

"My—your skin is a bit chilled. I wish I had a blanket to keep you warm, my love."

"I—I can't believe it."

"What can't you believe?"

After a moment to formulate the right words, Baltor answered, "I can't believe how happy I am! I can't believe that I've been lucky enough to meet you."

"Really?" she cooed. She then began to kiss his cheeks and forehead with her lips in an effort to warm them up.

He laughed confidently, "Yes!"

Despite the utter darkness of the tunnels, her lips soon found his and they began to kiss, softly and gently. A minute later, their kisses began to intensify as their passion began to rise!

Only seconds later, however, *someone* interrupted their built-up passions—he stopped in mid-kiss to look toward the direction of the virtually soundless sounds, and he could clearly see Lydia approaching through the pitch-black tunnel.

Brishava whispered, "What is it?"

"One moment," he whispered back. He then spoke aloud, "Mistress Lydia, I'm over here."

"Good, I'm glad to hear that you are," Lydia answered—her voice was strangely without emotion.

"We shall be leaving immediately. As for where we're going, we plan to let the tides—" he tried to say before he was interrupted.

Lydia interrupted irritably, "You can't go anywhere! The High Council needs to speak to both you and your girlfriend, who just happens to be the Sultan's daughter!"

He asked, "How'd you know about her?"

She snapped back, "Who doesn't know?" She then added, "The Sultan is tearing Pavelus apart in search of her. It will only be a matter of time before he finds our headquarters. Please come with me."

"Listen, Mistress Lydia, we can escape out a back entrance or something. And then we'll be gone forever!"

"No, Baltor, I've been given strict orders to take you two before the High Council, as soon as possible," Lydia insistently replied.

He stood in front of Brishava, before he replied, "No. Please— you must let us escape out a back entrance—just report to them that we were long gone by the time you got here!"

"No," Lydia snapped, just before she snapped her fingers—six other people came from around the bend behind her. Two of them bore flaming torches, while the other four bore weapons.

Baltor quickly drew his sword and assumed the ready position.

Lydia then added, "Do not fight us but come voluntarily."

"We will not come—after all, we need to get as far away from here as soon as possible," Baltor declared.

Nearly six seconds later, Lydia finally spoke by promising, "If you will not come before the High Council voluntarily, then the majority have already voted that you are to come involuntarily, alive or dead! So if you insist on fighting, I'd have the princess take some steps back, as she'd become absolutely worthless to the Guild if she were to accidentally die."

At the thought of Brishava dying, Baltor said, "Step back, Brishava."

She took several dozens of steps back until she was outside the perimeters of the torchlight, and then she stopped so she could watch.

"Baltor, before I have my thieves take you down, I am going to declare the charges brought against you by the Guild, just in case you should happen to die while we're trying to apprehend you...

"Number one—you showed a non-member the secret location of the Guild. And number two—you revealed the secret identity of another member of the Guild to a non-member, especially a member of the High Council! You know the penalties for such violations of your most sacred oath."

To the thieves behind her, Lydia replied, "Kill Baltor slow, piece by piece—but keep the princess alive! She'll be worth a hell of a lot of money upon her safe return!"

As the four-armed thieves moved in front of Lydia and took their positions, the first held out a steel quarterstaff, the second pulled out his stiletto from his boot, the third drew out two of her daggers from her belt, and the last unsheathed the long sword that had been hanging on his back.

Because of Brishava's presence, Baltor dared not let loose the beast within—after all, he didn't want to accidentally kill her.

Therefore, as he began to take steps forward, he simultaneously began to twist and twirl his sword rapidly around his body using one or both hands—the speed and the song of the sword was so astonishing that three thieves had stopped in their tracks to watch in awe. Even Lydia looked mildly impressed.

Only one thief continued, the thief with the stiletto, but immediately found that he was looking at his own headless body for about twenty seconds after his head had stopped rolling for ten seconds.

The man with the quarterstaff slowly drew closer, as he expertly twirled the staff around his own body with one or both hands nearly a dozen times, and then stopped it in the ready position, with the quarterstaff resting four inches in front of his body.

With pure wrist control, that man flicked his quarterstaff straight down in front of him, intending to make it slap the top of Baltor's head and knock him unconscious—Baltor, however, had already safely rolled to the right, along with an upward slice of his sword.

Baltor's sword had completely sliced through that man's entire left side in the mid-section area! As blood began to gurgle from the man's mouth as he unsuccessfully tried to say something to Baltor, so too did blood and guts spill out from his wound. A second later, which was a second before his body and his metallic quarterstaff crashed hard into the ground, this man was dead.

Loud, ringing sounds continued to reverberate throughout the cave tunnels, thanks to the quarterstaff that continued to roll away. Meanwhile, the woman twisted and twirled both daggers around her body quite expertly, as she taunted, "You think you're quick? I'll show you quick! Come on!"

Baltor smiled sweetly in response to her threat, yet remained in the defensive position.

Without warning, the woman threw herself into a forward roll, and even before she had risen back to her feet, she hurled her first dagger perfectly aimed for his heart.

Baltor simply slapped the side of the dagger with his sword at the very last second that caused the dagger to stick into the ground—his sword was once again in the ready position.

Even though he heard the woman growl, he also saw her flick the last dagger in her hands at him, as if it was simply a dart—a dart that was flying straight toward Baltor's right eyeball.

A nanosecond before this dagger penetrated—Baltor again slapped his sword into the incoming dagger, which caused the second dagger to deflect off the wall to his left.

He threw her another sweet smile, and asked, "Would you like to throw that third dagger you've got in your belt at me? This time, I must warn you, you will painfully find that very dagger plunging into your own heart—without it even so much as having touched either of my hands even once!"

Without pause, the woman ran away, along with one of the thieves who bore a torch. The two remaining thieves, one being Lydia and the other a man bearing a torch, did not approach closer—they were both in shock.

"Leave, or I will be forced to kill you all, even though I don't want to," Baltor promised.

After a short pause, Lydia said with quite a bit of anger, "Even if you should happen to kill us, the rest of the Guild will eventually track you down and—"

Baltor interrupted, "Perhaps, but I seriously doubt that they'll be able to take me down, much less kill me. After all, I lied to the High Council about one thing my quest—I did find the rod. And not only is it very magical, yet it has even given me the strength, speed, and power of four men!"

Lydia's face looked in total disbelief, as she asked, "What are you talking about? When I saw you not even twelve hours ago, you were weak as a baby!"

"Ah," Baltor replied, "but that's because I have only had it for a very, very short time. Yet every day and night that passes, I become that much stronger and more powerful!"

As Lydia didn't believe even one of his words, nor did she want to hear anymore of what she believed were lies, she said, "By the order of the High Council, I command you to surrender both your weapon and yourself! I will give you one more chance."

He replied, "No." He then slowly began to take steps backward while always remaining in the ready position. Without looking back, he soon found Brishava's wrist with his free hand and said, "Let's go, my love."

As he began to head down the tunnel, still facing his enemies the whole way through, he observed that though they kept their distance, they continued to follow.

Before long, out of his peripheral vision, Baltor spotted a ladder that led up. He told Brishava, "Climb up first. I'll be right behind you."

She did.

Just as he had reached the fifth rung, he stopped, looked over at Lydia, and said, "My Mistress, you turned my life around many years ago. You gave me direction where I had none. It has all led up to this date—this moment in time.

"Please, just let us go, and you'll never see me or my beloved around here again, though you'll always have my gratitude and friendship for everything."

As Lydia pulled out her own dagger, she barked, "I can't let you do that! You violated your oath and brought none other than the daughter of the Sultan here, and told her who I am—you must be punished for your crime... by death!"

Immediately she leapt at Baltor. Even though her speed was exceptionally fast—his speed was much faster, as he had already jumped off the ladder and safely rolled out of harm's way.

Lydia's target wasn't Baltor, however, it was the ladder—immediately she yanked hard on it, which caused it to collapse to the ground. Fortunately, Brishava now stood on the street above.

Meanwhile, Lydia said, "Let's see how your little princess behaves on her own, for once in her life. It is now time for you to die!" With a look of hatred firmly implanted upon her face, she leapt again at Baltor, while arching her dagger in for the attack.

259

He easily defended the attack, and though he could have just as easily turned the defense into an offensive strike and killed her, he didn't. Instead, he rolled several times backwards, and once he had regained the ready position, he pleaded, "Please don't fight me, Lydia. Don't make me unleash the power of the rod upon you!"

She paused.

"All we wish to do is leave and go far—far away. Forever!"

Most surprisingly, Lydia immediately tucked back the dagger into her belt. Still facing him, she sighed and then ordered the last thief still standing nearby, "Put the ladder back up."

Right away that thief began to lift the ladder back up to the grate. Meanwhile, Lydia's face had turned sympathetic, as she sighed, "I'm so sorry, Baltor. I don't know what came over me— you're right. Am I forgiven?"

She began to walk closer to Baltor and extend out her arms, waiting for a hug.

In turn, he notched his sword back onto his belt, extended his own arms to hug her back, and then said, "Of course you are."

It wasn't until they were fully in that embrace that Baltor felt her dagger plunge deep into his back!

Instantly the "vompareus beast" fully emerged with a howl that seemed to shake the very foundations of the city, causing a gust of wind so strong in the tunnel that the torch the thief was holding literally went out, enshrouding the area in utter darkness.

It grabbed Lydia, pulled both her and the dagger even deeper into him and then bit just as deeply into her neck—Lydia screamed in horrific pain. Meanwhile, the remaining thief, after having heard the echoing howling, became scared of the lurking monster and jetted as fast as he possibly could through the pitch-black tunnels, while stumbling quite often in the process.

As Baltor drank, he heard the sounds of footsteps coming down the ladder. He stopped drinking and then quickly looked up—it was Brishava, and from somewhere up above, she had somehow acquired a lit torch.

Before she had the chance to look below, he had already thrown Lydia's body over his shoulder and zoomed into the darkness. About one hundred feet away, he stopped, but as he watched the blood continue to flow from her jugular vein, and he felt his stomach growling for more—he continued to feast. Lydia's memories and knowledge continued to surge into his brain.

He not only learned all her master thievery skills and personal history that was exactly as she had told him, surprisingly enough.

Yet he also became quite surprised to learn that she had fallen in love with Baltor upon his declaration and challenge to the High Council to overthrow the Sultan two nights ago. Yet when Lydia had first seen Brishava and Baltor yesterday morning, she became confused by Brishava's feelings for Baltor, though he was obliviously out of it.

If that wasn't enough, when the High Council had convened and made the vote regarding Baltor and Brishava earlier this afternoon, Lydia, Tricia, and Bayema were the only three who voted that Baltor only be brought in alive to explain his actions, but as always, the majority won.

As Baltor came close to finishing feasting on Lydia, he came to discover the most shocking piece of information about her, which news also made him feel very sad. Only a few minutes earlier, when Lydia had heard Baltor call Brishava "my love," Lydia realized that Baltor was now in love with Brishava and no longer with her—she felt hurt, betrayed, and worst of all, unloved. Except by the Guild, with whom she was going to continuously lead and obey the order to kill Baltor if he resisted.

Baltor, at the end of dinner, actually began to feel quite a bit guilty that it was too late to save Lydia's life—every bit of blood was gone.

Brishava had apparently not seen Baltor, or his vampire act, or his vompareus body, as she timidly called out, "Baltor, my beloved, are you still there?" For the next minute or so, she kept calling out his name with fear growing in her voice each time.

He, while also trying to sound weary even though he felt incredibly strong, answered, "I'm coming. Hold on a minute, please."

He dropped Lydia's body to the ground, pulled out his sword, chopped her head off precisely over the bite marks, and then put his sword away.

Her memory banks had also revealed to Baltor that she carried her identification paperwork on her at all times, underneath her shirt—he immediately took those papers that fortunately didn't have a drop of blood on them.

He then took off his own shirt and looked over his shoulder at his back—the dagger wound had not only healed up, yet there was no evidence of even a scar, at least a physical one.

"I'm on my way," he replied, just after he had tossed the bloodied shirt onto the ground and then proceeded back to the entryway.

Once there, he could see that Brishava looked awfully frightened, and that there were tears that had just stopped flowing from her puffy eyes upon having just seen him emerge from the darkness.

Her fears appeared to be only semi-relieved, as she cried, "Baltor! Are you all right?"

Baltor answered, "Not really."

She hurriedly checked all over his body, yet after having found no visible wounds, she asked, "Where does it hurt?"

"In my heart, really."

She walked around him twice more before she said, "But I see no wounds on your chest or back."

"The wounds that I speak of are not physical—they are emotional," he said with quite a bit of sadness.

"Why?" Brishava asked, "Were you close to Lydia?"

"Yes, I was," he answered with a deep sadness to his voice. "I've known her longer than I've known anyone else, including my own parents!"

Before she could ask any more questions, he shook his head, and then he added, "I will explain later. For now, we must get going, as there are already others looking for us."

The two then made their way out of the tunnel and into the city streets—they were easily able to escape the city walls of Pavelus, with Lydia's paperwork in Brishava's hands.

Shortly before the next morning, they had located a cave just north of the city, and they camped in this cave during the daylight hours.

CHAPTER XXI

When Baltor awoke the next night in the cave, he saw that Brishava was no longer sleeping on his belly—he skillfully searched the pebbly ground for her tracks, a brand new master thief skill, noticing that her last set of footsteps led outside.

Upon exiting the cave and seeing the last of the dusky skies to the west, he saw that her tracks continued to go the same direction.

After looking up from the ground, he saw that she was standing about four hundred feet away on the sandy beach, while looking westward across the Sea of Albusina, presumably having just watched the sun set below the darkening waters.

A split second later, he was right behind her, and he wrapped his arms loosely around her waist while nuzzling his chin into her neck—immediately her petite hands came to rest comfortably up-on his muscular arms.

He whispered in her ear, "Are you okay?"

She sighed, "Yes, I am, my love."

After a short moment of silence, he dared to ask, "Are you sure you don't want to go back home?"

She turned around to face him, and after studying his face with a very serious look for a moment, she then asked, "And take a chance at losing you?"

He didn't answer.

After another moment, she sighed, smiled, and then declared, "Never. I love you too much!"

"How can you love me so much when I don't even love myself?"

She caressed his cheek with one hand and sighed, "The only thing that I know is that the first time I saw you in my dreams, I fell in love.

"And now that my dreams have come true, my greatest fear is that I will wake up and find out that all this was only a dream...."

From her comment, or maybe it was her touch, or maybe both, he didn't know, but he found himself beginning to chuckle.

Even though her hand never stopped gently caressing his cheek, she did stop to ask, "Why are you laughing, mister?"

He didn't relinquish his chuckling, but said, "I don't know, miss."

"I do."

"Oh yeah? Then why am I laughing?"

"Because you love me!"

Once realization hit, he stopped laughing and confessed, "Yes, I do love you. I am in love with you—I want to marry you tonight!"

"But where can we go, and who will marry us?"

"Good questions," he answered. He turned his head to the right and left while he scanned the horizons, yet no answers formed, internal or external. "I don't know."

She wrapped her arms around Baltor, clasped him tightly, and then lightly whispered in his ear, "I have an idea."

He whispered back, "What's that?"

"First, before I tell you of my idea, I need to know something about you. Do you believe in God?"

He pulled back from the hug so that he could see her entire face, and then he asked, "What kind of a question is that?"

"Just answer it, please," she said in kind.

"I... I have never met God, if that's what you mean. But I do believe that it takes intelligence to create intelligence."

"So, is that a yes?"

"Yes," he said slowly. He was still unsure of where her line of questioning was leading.

She said, "I don't know that any of us have met God, either, but I choose to believe that He exists. It is in my beliefs that God started the scenario of this universe, and that He is watching us to see what we do with it—for good or for evil, while always hoping for the good."

He listened attentively to every word she said. Despite her interesting religious beliefs, and despite the common knowledge that it had been her own grandfather who had banned all religions in the empire, he didn't understand where all of this was leading, so in silence he waited for her to finish.

Her gaze dropped down to his powerfully built chest, and her little hand soon followed where she then began to draw little imaginary circles there.

A few moments later, she looked back up and suggested, "Maybe it'll take us many days, months, or even years before we can find a

Justice of the Peace who will dare to certify our marriage. So with vows that stem from our hearts, minds, and souls, why don't we marry ourselves before God, right now?" With her piercing brown eyes, she looked back up at his face, and waited for an answer.

He sucked in a deep breath and then asked incredulously, "We can do this, ourselves?"

"Why not?" she asked. A second later, she added with both of her eyebrows rising into those sharp angles he found so very attractive, "Later we can have an official wedding that is best suited for the heir and the heiress to the Sharia Empire!"

He cocked his head slightly to the right in confusion, and asked, "Right here—right now?"

"Only if that's what you want."

He confidently stated, "I do—I really, really do!"

"Me, too!"

In unison, the two slowly released their hold of each other, yet they continued to face each other.

Before he could start, she did as he she swore, "I, Brishava Helenus, do love you, Baltor, with all of my heart, mind, and soul!"

She raised her arms toward the heavens, and with growing excitement to her voice, she exhaled, "I declare unto this world, unto this universe, and most especially unto God—from this day forth, and until eternity's end, I shall always be your loyal and loving wife."

He took from her impending silence that it was his turn, and he said, "I, Baltor Elysian, do love you, Princess Brishava Helenus, also with all of my heart, mind, and soul."

Following suit with her physical gestures, he added, "I declare unto this world, unto this universe, and most especially unto God—from this day forth and until eternity ends, I shall always be your loyal and loving husband!"

The two, on cue, joined hands.

She ever so gently added, "I also promise that I shall always be supportive of whatever decisions that you make, in the present and in the future. I only hope that you will always be supportive of me, and mine."

He similarly responded, "I also promise that I shall always be supportive of whatever decisions that you make—in the present and in the future, and I only hope that you will always be supportive of me, and mine."

He then began to chuckle as he added, "Even though I haven't ever had the privilege of getting to dream about you, I think that the reason for this is because you are beyond my wildest, imaginable dreams!"

She laughed at his comment for a moment, and in the next moment, she asked, "Really?"

He answered very seriously, "Really."

After a moment, she then asked with a soft, tender, and very sensitive voice, "Well? Aren't you going to kiss your bride, Lord Elysian?"

He dutifully responded, "With pleasure, Lady Elysian."

A gentle kiss began between the two, and only moments later, the gentle winds of the sea had begun to pick up, as if to confirm their mystical marriage by lifting both of their long strands of thick hair into the wind, whose hairs soon became as one.

Once the magical kiss was completed and their hair had settled back down due to the dissipating winds, she then asked, "Aren't you going to carry me inside our honeymoon suite, my husband?"

"Yes, my wife," he answered. He picked up his wife and escorted her back into the cave—the rest of the night was filled up with incredible and wonderful passions between the newlyweds....

CHAPTER XXII

The following night, after he had woken from sleep, an idea slowly began to form as he lay there—all the while, she continued to sleep contentedly upon his stomach.

At first, he recalled from his geographical studies that the Sea of Albusina continued northbound for a little over a hundred miles before it angled northwest. He also recalled that the Bospa Mountains wrapped around the Sharia Desert, on both the eastern and northern borders, and about twenty miles northwest inside the mountains, there was another seaport called Lasparus, which also belonged to the Sultan.

Because his newlywed wife needed food and water to survive, of which he had neither, his best idea was to head north alongside the coastline until they reached the mountains, make their way east through the mountains, pass through the jungles, and ultimately make their way back to Chao-chu-sha-maen.

Once she had woken up, he suggested his plan to which she immediately agreed, and the two began to travel north on foot. By day, they slept deep in caves, and by night, they continuously hoofed it, so that they could easily hide from other passing caravans, and most especially, the Sultan's troops.

Throughout this trip, he found it strange that she never questioned him on his unusual eating habits, especially for the fact that he would always leave shortly after having made dinner for her so that he could scrounge for his own food.

Also throughout the trip that took a little less than a month, he first talked about his youth and his ancestral sword. He also talked about the tragedy that befell his parents because of that very sword, and his subsequent destitution. He then talked about his running into Lydia and the Guild. In addition, of course, he talked all about his recent quest, including the world map, but never did he talk about the Rod of Ro'shain, or Trendon Harrn, or the fact that he himself was an undead monster.

Her love for him only flourished from his words. In turn, she talked about her own youth, and the fact that only four months prior, her father had involuntarily engaged her to wed the Duke of Vispano, who she said was only younger than her own father by nine years—almost three times her own age.

After all, these two men had concocted the plan to unite the two massive kingdoms into one ultra-powerful nation via the marriage ceremony. Following a week-long honeymoon spent between bride and groom, both leaders would march/sail their armies and navy, approximately 110,000 forces total, down the coastline to Mauritia, and not only easily conquer this city, yet the entire Vaspan Empire.

Though she mentioned many hobbies she liked to do, she said that her favorite hobby was riding on horses, equestrian style. From all of her precious words, he found himself falling in love with her more every night that passed.

Once they had reached and entered the tree-filled mountains, they turned east, traveling through the valleys. Three more nights passed without incident; but on the fourth night, when he awoke, he realized that his wife had once again left the cave.

He followed her footsteps northbound for about eighty feet, noticing that they had stopped at a bush filled with ripened raspberries. He also saw several other horse tracks that had come from the north. From the looks of it, she tried to escape, but one of the horse's riders had grabbed her in mid-stride and thrown her onto the horse!

Since he realized that Brishava had been kidnapped, anger and rage quickly set in—he immediately followed the tracks, yet found that they ended at a thin, gravel road that led both east and west. There was no indication on which direction her captors had gone.

As he was unsure of which way to go, he then began to contemplate what he did know, which would probably become his only options. He pretty much assumed that going west on the road would lead him toward the city of Lasparus, though he didn't know where the path to the east ultimately led, as there was no indication of this road being there when the map was made.

He then tried to rationalize on who her captors could be, *Was it the Sultan's troops who got her? If it was the Sultan's guards, they'd surely take her to Lasparus first, but if it was anyone else, then there'd be a fifty-fifty chance that they'd head to Lasparus, right?*

He decided to take his chances and run west as fast as he could upon the road that most likely led to Lasparus. After about eight miles, the road started veering northwest, which confirmed his suspicions.

About an hour before morning, he spotted a cave to rest, and that's where he slept without incident.

The next night, he continued his journey. Even though hunger had set in, his love for his wife prevailed, and he chose to ignore his hunger pains. Three more nights passed until he finally observed the lights of Lasparus. Throughout this trip, he did not run into any passing caravans, guards, or his wife. But upon the second night of his trip, he did cross upon a beaver that temporarily eased his hunger.

During this time, he focused his mind not on his pains, yet contemplated on all the possible locations his wife could possibly be in this city, if she was there at all.

The best possible solution seemed to infiltrate Lasparus, find and kill a "vermin" in order to reacquire his vampire abilities, and locate the palace.

He had long ago learned from his schooling that there was a palace built for the Sultan in Lasparus, though seldom, if ever, did this man come here to visit.

Once at the palace, he would locate his wife, assuming that she was actually there. If she wasn't there, he had no other clues of where to look for her.

Fortune smiled upon him once he arrived, as he saw only a single line of guards patrolling around the perimeter of the one-hundred-foot walls. He quietly knocked out the very last guard in the column, of whom he suspected was "vermin," dragged his unconscious body into a large group of bushes, bit into his neck, and then drank from this man's blood though limited amount of knowledge, mostly about farming and a sliver about soldiering. In the end, Baltor found out his suspicion about Vushna being vermin was true—he had raped a girl only a year earlier.

The second that he pulled his lips back from the man's neck, he felt incredibly powerful, once again—this time Baltor had the power to remain in human form the entire time.

After concealing the body in the bushes, with the speed of shadow, he ran toward the wall and leapt over to the other side.

A man and a young girl happened to see him land in the middle of the street, only a dozen feet away in the very direction they were walking.

The man cried out as he stood protectively in front the young girl, "Leave—leave me and my daughter alone! We have no money if that's what you want!"

Baltor replied, "I do not want your money or anything else from you. Say nothing of what you just saw for I am a phantom of your imagination. Go about your business."

After a very short pause, the man still answered nervously, "Ok. Jonish, come with me."

"Yes, Popa," the girl said with fright—they departed away at a rather brisk pace.

As Baltor watched them disappear around the next corner, he wondered for a moment if he might ever be a daddy one day. But then the present hit him, and he realized that he must find his wife first.

He combed out the seaport and soon located the palace walls. After waiting for the right time, he leapt to the top of the sixty-foot walls, and while standing on top of the wall, he looked over to the other side.

There he observed a truly magnificent two-story palace and gardens, but nothing even close to the one in Pavelus. With but a willed thought, he literally flew across all of the guards and landed on the deck of a balcony on the top floor.

After Baltor looked into the interior of this room from the balcony, he observed that this wasn't a bedroom, yet a huge royal banquet hall, containing more than two-dozen elongated tables, all covered by red tablecloths heavily interwoven with golden threads.

Seated around the tables were gold chairs that had red velvet cushions upon the seats and backrests, and hanging from the ceiling were more than a dozen gold chandeliers that filled the cozy room with their lustrous lights.

All but one of the tables was empty—sitting at this table was a group of ten nobles, six men and four women, lightly eating away upon their dinners and socializing.

The rest of the room was empty, except for two guards who stood by a set of large gold doors at the far end about fifty feet away from his current position.

Without fear or caution, he walked straight in, and boldly called out, "Any of you happen to know where's Princess Brishava?"

At that comment, the group all looked toward the direction of the voice—with a lot of surprise and shock. Strangely enough, none of the guards apparently had heard the comment, nor seen Baltor's bold entrance right in front of where they stood.

An old bald man dressed in ridiculously rich purple garments asked, "Who—who are you?"

"It doesn't matter who I am. Any of you know where she is?"

The obese man slowly stood and then said, "To answer your question, no one knows where the princess is, nor have they for over a month...

"Why—do you know where my betrothed is? Or should I say was? Now you will answer my question, as I am the Duke of Vispano!"

Baltor didn't answer, but instead turned back around to leave out the way he had come in ... the balcony.

The duke also had begun to run that same direction as fast as his fat old body possibly could, while screaming, "Guards! We have an intruder! Get him and bring him before me!"

Before they could even react, Baltor had already flown across the grounds and over the entire height of the wall. As he continued to fly out of the seaport, he could hear guards trying to alert all of their other fellow guards, but he was already long gone.

In fact, with his vampire speed, it took him less than a minute to depart the perimeter of the seaport and travel the southeastern road.

For the new few hours to pass, Baltor flew the forty miles or back to the cave where his wife had been kidnapped. However, he arrived back at the cave with a few more hours to spare before the sun would rise over the eastern horizon.

As he sat still in the dark and lonely cave, his worries and frustrations increasingly began to get worse while contemplating the fate of his beloved, especially for the fact that her kidnappers could have gone any direction at all!

About thirty minutes later, his agonies exploded into a fit of rage as he screamed, "Trendon Harrn! It is I, Baltor! Come to me! Look at what you've made me! A worthless creature by day, and a powerful creature at night, and only when I've feasted on a human being!

"I could not even protect my wife, Brishava, when she needed me the most! Come to me, damn you! You told me that when the time was right, I would know when, where, and how to find—"

He stopped in mid-sentence, as he saw that brilliant prismatic light appear in the middle of the air.

This time, however, his eyes could handle the intensity of the light as the portal opened up to its full size, and without so much as a squint, he watched Trendon step through it. Not unlike the sun whose indirect rays greatly hurt Baltor's eyes.

271

"Well there, young one," Trendon said, sounding sympathetic, "it appears that you have quite a dilemma on your hands now, doesn't it?" The portal shut behind him.

Baltor screamed with a c t u a l bloody tears flowing out of his eyes, "Yes, I do!"

Trendon extended his arms in front of him, and then slowly lowered them until they were by his sides. He then soothingly said, "Shush there, young one, and listen carefully."

Trendon pointed one finger in the air. After shaking it from side to side only once, he said, "Baltor, I am going to assist you this one time, and that's it. Next time, you can beg, rant, or scream all you want, but you will entirely be on your own. I will not help you again until I am sure that you are fully ready to begin your training with me. Do you understand me clearly? One time only."

Baltor nodded, almost in shame.

Trendon began, "Good. As you are already aware, several members of a rather large caravan kidnapped your princess. The caravan itself was heading east from Lasparus. What you are not aware of is the fact that there are fifty-eight of them to be exact. What this caravan does for a living is to travel from town to town, stealing young and attractive girls, and then selling them off at the next—basically, your run-of-the-mill slave traders...

"It is quite fortunate for you that they do not know who she is, or they would have altered their route directly toward Pavelus and the Sultan. As I speak, they are camped about eighty miles southeast of us within the desert, and have just woken up to prepare for their journey today...

"Tomorrow night, take the path east. You shall soon find that it veers off into two different directions, one going northeast and the other going south. Take the southern route, which shall lead you straight into the Sharia—"

Before he could continue, Baltor interrupted like a little child, "But—but how am I supposed to find her in the middle of such an enormous desert?"

Trendon shook his head and sighed, as he had been about to forthright reveal that answer. Instead, the cryptic bit of advice that Trendon had been given nearly ten thousand years ago and now gave to Baltor was "Will it and you shall."

Baltor was about to ask, "What the hell is that supposed to mean?"

However, Trendon, with a snap of a finger, had already disappeared into oblivion.

In the next moment, Baltor could feel that the sun had arisen, and he fell instantly asleep.

CHAPTER XXIII

Just after Baltor had awoken the next night, and was about to exit the cave, he looked back around one last time. For the very first time, he noticed that his wife had left her backpack in the far right corner of the cave.

Therefore, he walked over, picked it up, donned it, and then began to trek eastward, still with that speed of shadow. As he shot through the night, he also began to think long and deep. He first realized that the way he behaved last night toward Trendon was rather childish, and he began to feel sorry for it. He then began to think about his beloved wife, and of the immense amount of love that he had for her, and that anyone else probably would have reacted the same way.

The more that he meditated, the more memories of his past victims began to surge through his consciousness, as well. He saw the relationships and twisted love affairs that Salmot, Big-Bear, Briggs, Lydia, and of course, Vushna.

He also saw that even though each one of them had their own unique share of tragedies when it came to losing loved ones, they each had their own particular way, some were bad and some were good, when it came to dealing with their losses.

His thoughtful conclusion to all of this information in the end was, "Yes, I did act rather immature. But that was not an unusual response from my part, either, especially given my history."

By the time he had come to this conclusion, he had just entered the desert, and could see that the skies were lightening. He pushed on for another fifty minutes, dug himself a hole, and then completely covered himself with the sand.

The following night, after he had pulled himself out of the ground, he asked himself, "Now how am I going to 'will it and it shall'?"

As an idea popped into his head, he recalled the entire world map with his physical eyes shut. In his mind's eye, he first saw the perimeters of the desert pitted up against the mountains or the sea—he next shifted his focus upon the image of Brishava.

A minute or so later, her image formed, and he could see that she was sitting in a very large cage with a dozen or so other women—it was sometime during the daylight hours.

A moment later, he saw two horses pulling that cage at a decent pace through the desert. He next saw that there were many other men, before and after the horse-drawn cage, riding on horses themselves.

Still in the parameters of Baltor's mind, this entire image of the caravan began to shrink, until it had shrunk into a dot upon the world map he had earlier conjured within his mind—by now, they were already one-quarter the way through the desert, and still going southeast.

Excited he knew her location, he hurriedly ran in that direction with that speed that was slightly faster than the fastest runner in the world could.

As he continued to travel, yet with nothing else to do, he began to think more. His thoughts first reminisced back to the time when he had first met this Trendon Harrn.

Specifically to the point in the conversation when Trendon had informed, "As I have already explained, you must use your wit and resources to help you overcome all your weaknesses, and upon every level—even with the initial need to feast upon human blood! Even in the beginning, be selective by removing only the human vermin from the earth, or feasting upon the blood of your enemies.

"Ultimately, in order for anyone to understand the future, one must also learn from the past; in the same way, in order to understand absolute good, one must also understand absolute evil first. If that's not enough of a hint, then let me put it in a way that even you will understand—in order to beat your enemy, you must first become that enemy!

"Now, since we're talking about you, young one, let me confirm that there are many obstacles in your past, which prevent you from clearly seeing the potentials for your future! But, the signs are also clearly there."

Baltor thought aloud, "What parts of my past could possibly be preventing me from seeing the future?"

He immediately began to think about his days of youth, prior to his parents' murders, which thoughts came to dwell yet another of

275

his Uncle Baltor's exciting, bedtime tales. This tale revolved around a very famous sea hero named Captain Percos.

In it, a giant sea serpent hungrily erupts from the bosoms of the sea, swims to a nearby river, locates a nearby village, and slowly begins to stalk and eat the villagers at night and on land.

The villagers, in response, send a large hunting expedition to kill the serpent, but Percos becomes the only survivor of the hunting expedition, as the surprisingly clever serpent has taken out the rest of them, one by one.

During the first of many battles between Percos and the serpent, Percos slightly wounds the serpent with his spear, and the serpent retreats back to the river. Percos does not let it get away, but immediately takes a rowboat, and follows the serpent back out sea.

"The eleven seas" is what it ultimately becomes, as Percos chases the serpent all across the world; meanwhile, he visits other towns, cities, nations, and cultures, and even earns a galleon-class warship and crew that ultimately destroys the sea serpent in the end of the tale.

The following day, just as eight-year-old Baltor clamped a horseshoe down onto the anvil for his father, he then informed his father that he wanted to become just like Percos.

Instead of getting the congratulatory reply as he expected, his father yelled at him, and said, "There are no sea-serpents, there are no heroes; there is only reality. You and your uncle need to get your head out of the clouds. And you, boy, need to hold that horseshoe still right now!"

That memory faded, yet another one surfaced, an earlier one. He remembered watching his parents arguing shortly after Baltor had just turned seven.

This argument came about because his mother had wanted to continue babying him, while his father insisted that he was big and old enough to begin the family practice.

The seven-year-old Baltor didn't know which parent was more right during this argument, so he silently watched as they heatedly argued and yelled for over an hour—not surprising, his mother finally ran off toward her room while crying.

His father, apparently the winner, looked down at him and pronounced, "Baltor, I know that it's time that you become a man, even though your mother sees otherwise. You must trust me on this. One day, you'll be thanking me for it."

That memory faded yet still another one surfaced—an even earlier memory. It occurred when Baltor was about five years old. He was sitting in his mother's lap, while they lounged on the porch outside.

He listened as she spoke, "My little baby boy, Baltor! I know that I should probably let you do things more on your own, but I need you by my side. Your father works so very hard and long to keep us alive, but I get so lonely because I have no one to talk to during the day, except for you."

Baltor heard his own childish voice say back, "I'll always be there for you, Moma!"

That memory dissipated, but when another memory didn't surface, the twenty-one-year-old Baltor thoughtfully asked himself, *So what do these memories mean?*

When no answers came from the heavens, he rationalized aloud, "Perhaps these are the very reasons that have been keeping me from seeing the future. Perhaps there's even more!"

Just then, his eyes scanned to the south, spotting a single column of lights moving east to west.

About thirty seconds later, his night-vision was able to count out twenty-two of them all on camels, while the one in the rear was riding on a beautiful, black warhorse—neither was there a cage filled with slave women, as he had seen in the vision.

For all of these reasons, Baltor realized that this wasn't the right caravan—he stopped jogging, though he wasn't out of breath or sweaty.

Unfortunately, he had none of his money with which to purchase that horse, and even though he was a "thief," he no longer wanted to steal, and so he contemplated for several minutes whether to trade his grandfather's sword for the horse. After all, the sword was very valuable to him, yet so was his wife, Brishava.

Once he had finally made his decision to sell the sword, he yelled out, "Hey—hey guys!"

Meanwhile, he began to sprint toward the caravan. Within moments, the caravan had already formed a complete circle with each member facing out of that circle, clearly a defensive position.

Baltor called out, "I am alone, and I mean you no harm."

Despite this assurance, the caravan remained in their defensive position.

It took another minute or two before he finally neared the circle, all the while holding out both of his hands in a symbolic gesture of peace.

"Listen," he said upon entering the perimeters of the light, "I would like to purchase that horse you've got."

A woman's voice, presumably the one with the horse, asked back incredulously, "What could you possibly have in exchange for my prized stallion? This horse is a pure breed and could easily go for eighteen thousand parsecs."

Baltor began, "I have this." He stopped through three-quarters of the sentence, just before he was about to utter the word sword, but at that split moment, he remembered Brishava's backpack hanging on his back, and his mind stopped his mouth.

Curious, he pulled the backpack off, opened it up, and looked in. He pushed aside several other pairs of tunics and pants, and angled the backpack so that a little of the lights could shine inside.

What he saw made his mouth drop open in shock—besides a bunch of small-to-midsized precious stones, there were two huge diamonds inside. The larger was the size of an apple!

He pulled out that v e r y diamond and then said, "I have this diamond here, which I'm guessing is worth more than five times the asking price, maybe even six."

The woman saw the reflections of the light off the diamond, and though he could not see her excited facial expression, he heard it as she gasped, "Let me check it out first, to make sure it's not a fake."

With a wave of his hand toward the diamond, Baltor said, "By all means."

As the woman handed the reins to another caravan member, still another member handed the woman a torch; she then drew nearer.

The woman took the diamond in both hands, examined it for a moment against the light, and said, "Give me some glass, Bonsu."

Bonsu gave her a piece of transparent glass, after having re-trieved it from his backpack. She set the glass onto the ground, held the diamond in both hands, and then drew a circle upon the glass. After handing the diamond back to Baltor, she picked one end of the glass off the ground, and then tapped the center of the glass one time—this caused the circle to pop out.

Immediately, she replied with quite a bit of excitement, "Deal!"

Baltor nodded his in relief. He glanced up into the skies briefly, and noticed that they were beginning to lighten up, and he realized that he would need to care for his horse during the day, somehow.

The woman said, "Opsam, give the warhorse to the man, please. You can ride with me on my camel."

Baltor gave the woman the diamond. In turn, Opsam handed over the horse's reins to Baltor, before climbing onto the woman's camel.

Baltor said, "Listen, the day is nearly upon me, and I have no water to care for me or my horse. Is there anyway that you guys can
hook me up with some water?"

"What else do you have to barter?" the woman asked.

"Hey—I just gave you that diamond which is worth far more
than the horse, and you're going to ask for more?"

"Well I guess you're right, but that deal has already been concluded. Pity, without water, neither you nor the horse will be alive
by tonight."

Baltor pulled out a small ruby, handed it over, and said, "Fine ...
a week's worth of water."

"Deal—we'll even graciously give you a water bowl for your
horse."

Opsam set two sets of large, water bags—tied shut at the ends—
across the horse's back. At the same time, Bonsu handed Baltor a
large bowl made entirely of brass.

"Anything else we can do for you?" the woman suggested. "Maybe some food for you and your horse?"

"True," he replied. After pulling out a slightly bigger sapphire
and holding it out, he asked, "Do you have fresh food to sell, as
well?"

The woman answered, "No—we currently carry only extra dried
rations, hay, and water, as we sold all our other goodies. Currently
we're enroute to Pavelus for more."

"That's fine," he replied. "A week's worth of both."

The woman again exclaimed out the word, "Deal."

After he handed her the sapphire, he watched as another large
bag was tied to each side of his new horse's saddle, and he began to
inwardly wonder whether or not this horse would be able to move
swiftly with all of the added weight on it, not to mention his own.

The woman appeared to recognize the dubious look on Baltor's
face, for she said, "Oh. You got a good deal, don't you worry about
that—this is the most powerful warhorse my eyes have ever witnessed! Took four men to tame her."

The skies had turned another lighter shade of blue, and Baltor
took a second look at his new purchase. Indeed, this warhorse's
legs were twice the normal size that he'd ever seen on any other
horse, and her height was about seven feet tall.

He turned back toward the woman with an appreciative smile—
but they had already begun to continue on their journey.

After putting the bowl into the right saddlebag, he climbed into
the saddle, grabbed the reins, and spurred her on. He decided—in

the next moment—that he would name the horse after his mother, "Grasha."

Within moments, he had rapidly snapped her reins several more times, which in turn, caused her to pick up a speed that was breathtaking.

It wasn't even a minute later when he happened to look into the eastern sky—the sun would be rising within the next fifteen minutes. So about five minutes later, he pulled back on the reins and she halted.

After hopping down to the ground, he pulled out the bowl, put it under the tap at the base of the water bag, filled it up to the rim, and set it on the ground in front of his horse. She immediately began to drink.

Nearly a minute later, after having consumed a quarter of the bowl, he picked it up, refilled it to the rim, and again set it before Grasha. He next pulled out a very large chunk of the hay, laying it down on the ground.

With only seconds left, before the sun would rise above the eastern horizon, Baltor furiously dug into the loose sands, while firmly holding onto the reins in his right hand. Once the sun had risen, he instantly fell asleep.

CHAPTER XXIV

The moment after the sun had disappeared behind the western horizon, Baltor returned to consciousness. Even though he could see and hear absolutely nothing, due to the fact he was still buried under the desert sands of the Sharia, he did experience a minute amount of relief as he still felt his warhorse's leather reins in his right fist.

However, that relief lasted but a moment, as three serious worries from this morning immediately began to flood back.

One, Grasha might not have enough water to survive the extremely long and extremely hot desert day. Two, someone might see her, cut the reins, and steal her. Three, a ferocious sandstorm might come along and kill her!

None of these possibilities would prove very fortunate for him at all, which is why he worried, though those worries wouldn't be there much longer—already he was in the process of pushing himself up toward the surface, and as quickly as possible.

Once his head and neck had finally cleared the sandy ground, a few moments later, he shook his head to clear away a bunch of the sand.

About ten seconds later, he stopped shaking his head, and then he opened his eyes.

Not two feet away stood Grasha, chewing on the last bit of hay that he had left out, though he unhappily discovered that dry sand halfway filled her water bowl.

"How ya doin', Grasha?" he asked.

He next had to spit out a bit of sand that had accidentally gotten into his mouth, and then spit again to get out the additional sand that followed right behind.

She threw her head back with a bit of irritation, coupled with the sounds that came along with it!

After spitting another time, he replied, "I know you're thirsty, Grasha. Before you know it, you'll be drinking some delicious water, okay, girl?"

She made a *Hhhhrrrrmmmmppppphhhhh* sound.

It took a grand total of twenty seconds to get free of the sandpit, until he was standing again on solid ground. Once so, he walked several feet farther from his horse, and then began to shake himself around vigorously in order to get as much sand off as possible, without getting any on her.

After clapping his hands together several times, he used his dusted off hands to wipe off the remaining particles of sand that still clung to his ears, face, neck, as well, his other personal areas.

Once complete, and feeling relatively comfortable, he walked back over to the bowl, emptied it of sand, filled it up with water, and set it before her—without haste she began to drink deeply.

As she continuously drank, he released his grip on the reins. He then began to groom her face gently with his fingers, while talking to her in soothing tones.

About a minute later, just after she had finished drinking the whole bowl, she snorted her nose back into the air, but this time, it was a much shorter *Hrrrmmppphh* sound.

He lightly laughed, and while refilling her bowl with seconds of water, he said, "Of course you can have some more, girl! You truly are a magnificent creature, but you already know that, don't you?"

She darted her head up and down several times in the affirmative, and then she dunked her head back into the bowl to continue drinking.

"And smart too," he concluded with a laugh, as he pulled out her brush out of the saddle so that he could give her a quick grooming.

By the time she was finished, several minutes later, the bowl was about a quarter full.

He, not wanting to waste anything, most especially water, poured the rest of it back, while mentally noting, *Brishava can just drink from the other water bag—once I've gotten her back from those slave-trading, wife-stealing bastards! They're soooo dead meat.*

As he reflected upon this last thought yet again, despite the anger that was firmly etched onto his face, only pure determination was revealed through his squinting eyes.

Several moments later, he grabbed a hold of the reins, climbed into the saddle, sharply snapped the reigns while kicking his feet into the stirrups, and roaring out at the top of his lungs, "*To Brishava!!*"

His words echoed for miles across the lands and the skies. Despite all the weight from the nearly full water containers, Grasha instantly charged into such a furious gallop that it felt more like flying—the scenery rapidly passed them by, not the other way around.

"And so powerful too," he whispered aloud in awe.

Perhaps a minute later, once the adrenaline rush had finally tamed, he called forth his wife's image in his mind's eye.

This time she was standing outside the cage and stretching out her body's limbs, as were the other women—only a few moments later, he saw that the entire caravan, currently camped at a small oasis, was guarding them and preventing their escape. Still in his mind's eye, he then called forth the world map, and the two separate images quickly merged into one.

Even though it was impossible to tell exactly how far the caravan was from his current location, he happily observed that he was indeed catching up really fast, though he needed to steer his stallion a bit more to the southeast.

For most of the night, he pushed her hard that direction through the desert sands, and it turned out to be a night without any encounters.

An hour before morning, they came across the single largest oasis Baltor had ever seen, consisting of hundreds and hundreds of palm trees, dozens of them filled with coconuts or bananas. Filling the gaps between the trees was a myriad of other lush vegetation like berry bushes and tall grasses. And in the smack middle of it all, a large lagoon.

He believed that this strikingly beautiful oasis would require dozens of sandstorms back-to-back to cause it to disappear into oblivion. Yet before he had even arrived, he had already decided not to stay—only to refill the water canister, which was now nearly empty, and then leave. After all, oases are the "saving graces" of the desert for lost travelers, and he didn't want any lost traveler to find and steal his prized stallion during his sleeping hours.

Therefore, after all the refilling had been complete about ten minutes later, he pushed his horse hard for another thirty minutes.

Five minutes before sunrise, he halted her, hopped off the saddle and back onto his feet, pulled her bowl out, and refilled it with the water container.

Grasha immediately dunked her head into the bowl, and drank about three-quarters of it before she stopped drinking and turned her head away from the bowl.

By this time, Baltor had already set down a very large chunk of hay onto the ground. He next refilled the bowl back to the top, and while gripping tightly onto one end of her reins that he had just unsecured from her bridle, he dug himself back under the sands only seconds before sunrise.

The next night, he discovered with relief and happiness that his stallion had survived yet again. As she consumed her dinner and water, he used that time constructively to locate Brishava's position, as before.

From the merged images, which happened only seconds later, he happily discovered that the caravan had not traveled this day at all, as he easily recognized the small oasis, though for what reason they did not travel, he did not know.

In fact, the only notable difference with this mental vision from the last was that the women were either standing, sitting or lying down inside the cage. He also saw that he had halved the distance on the map!

About five minutes later, once she had finished drinking yet another bowl of water, he climbed back into the saddle and pushed her back into a full gallop.

Three in the morning, or so, and still without a single moon in the sky, he observed a small bonfire to his southeast, perhaps a mile away. Perhaps the light from this fire would reveal his lovely wife's image in real life, so he greatly hoped.

About ten minutes later, once he and his horse had begun to draw near the perimeters of the bonfire's light, though still protected by the darkness of night, he pulled pack on her reins, which caused her to stop in her tracks.

It was only then that he carefully looked all around at the small oasis, which housed this bonfire. This was the same oasis he had seen twice before, in his mind's eye.

Besides the dozen-or-so palm trees that surrounded a very small lagoon in the center, there were dozens and dozens of parked horses and setup tents, as well as a horse-drawn wagon that had a covered top.

Lying thirty feet away on the far side of the bonfire was the cage filled with women—they were all sleeping. Standing at each corner of the cage was a nomadic guard, each wielding a sword strapped onto the belt. The rest of the caravan was obviously sleeping in their tents.

As soon as he spotted the cage, but not yet his wife, he spurred his horse to a prance directly into the encampment.

About three seconds later, the nearest of the four guards looked over, saw the stranger, and loudly called out, "Halt! Who goes there?"

Several more members of the caravan woke up out of their sleep, and quickly came out of their tents to find out what was going on with weapons in hand—so Baltor observed out of the corners of his eyes. The other three guards united into single file with the guard who had spoken.

Baltor immediately brought his horse to a halt, before he said very casually, "Evening—my name is Lord Poleax from Pavelus. I just, ah, came to this here oasis to replenish my horse's thirst, refill my water canteens, and ah leave, if that's okay with you."

"Well, okay, but be quick about it," the guard informed.

Most of the members that had come out appeared to relax their stances, as well the grip upon their weapons. None returned to their tents.

Meanwhile, Baltor, who made it seem that he was oblivious to what was going on, innocently hopped off Grasha and led her by the reins to the nearby pool of water; whereupon, she immediately began to drink.

Just after he had pulled off the three-quarters filled water bag, he dunked it under the water. While it began to fill, he simultaneously began to stretch himself around into weird contorted positions, all the while yawning.

What he was really doing was scanning out the area for the worst and biggest threats, and there were about nine that Baltor counted out so far. Four were equipped with bow and arrows.

Purposefully, about a minute later, he turned around until he made it look accidental that he even faced the cage at all. And after casting an astonished look onto his face, he turned back to the nearer guard and asked with a point of his thumb, "What are those in that cage?"

That guard said quite loudly, "None of your business! I think it's best you be on your way now, stranger!"

Besides the members who were watching the spectacle, and had once again tightened the grips on their weapons, a half dozen more came out to join them, also armed with weapons.

Despite the fact that he was now mostly surrounded by the caravan members, he still asked in casual tones, "Are those women in there?"

The guard yelled at the top of his lungs, "*Everyone—wake up! Intruder alert!!*"

Within moments, the entire caravan of fifty-eight was there—all but one was armed.

Even though the caravan members had pretty much surrounded Grasha and Baltor, except for the lagoon that was behind them, he waved his hand down nonchalantly, and replied, "Relax—I was just curious."

"Well, you best be on your little way before you get hurt there, boy," threatened the guard menacingly.

While pointing his index finger at the guard, Baltor cried, "Now hold on there just one minute. As I said earlier, I am a lord from Pave—"

A fat man wearing a wrapped red turban and matching robes, the only one not armed, stood out from the bunch, and interrupted, "Nay—ye hold on just one minute. I give the orders round here, not ye!"

After gesturing around him with both of his arms, the man in the red turban added, "As ye can see, we ain't exactly in Pavelus, are we?"

Several of the caravan members laughed.

Baltor raised his hands up in both a gesture of peace and surrender, and said, "You're right, sir. You give the orders."

The man shot back, "Me first order be that ye mosey the hell out of here 'fore I have to give me second order, and that be have ye throat cut!"

The rest of the caravan began to laugh raucously.

Through the laughter, Baltor asked, "Fine, but can I ask one question first?"

In unison, the group immediately stopped laughing.

With the snap of his finger, the man snapped aloud, "One question then ye be gone—one way or the other!"

Seedy chuckling immediately erupted from several of the members.

Baltor nicely asked, "My question is this: May I buy one of those lovely girls from you? After all, though I'm an extremely rich and powerful lord, I'm currently in need of some human companionship, and I couldn't help but notice that at least one of your fine ladies look good enough to keep me nice and warm, especially during these cold desert nights!"

"Ye ain't look like ye no lord nor got no money," the man with the red turban glowered skeptically. "Lords don't travel around the desert alone."

"I don't look like I have money? Oh but I do!"

286

That really piqued the red-turbaned man's interest. With his right eyebrow fully raised and his left eyebrow half squinting, he slowly nodded his head while saying, "Show me what ye've got first—then we negotiate."

"Okay, cool!" Baltor said with excitement, as he hurriedly pulled off the backpack. After opening it up, taking the clothes out, and dropping the clothes to the ground, he then angled the bag so the man could make out the contents of what lay inside, though the man would have to come quite a bit closer to Baltor's position to do so.

The man in the red turban had already taken a couple of steps closer, as his eyes had spied some glittering objects within the bag, yet those eyes then caught sight to Baltor's very glittery sword!

Simultaneously, the man stopped in his tracks, crossed his arms defensively, and implanted a very suspicious look onto his face. Voicing this look, the man asked, "How do I know ye won't strike me with ye sword once I draw near?"

With that, all of the caravan members prepped their weapons, or aimed their arrows right at Baltor!

"Sir," Baltor promised, "the only thing I'd like to do is to buy at least one of them girls off you—that's all! If you like, I can holster my sword onto my horse, which is my only weapon, and we can go talk by the fire? How about that?"

"Fair enough... and I promises that me and me men won't lay a single finger on ye, if ye be tellin' me the truth. But if ye be wastin' me time, or tryin' to trick me, then ye be a dead man!"

"Fair enough." Baltor next holstered his sword onto his horse's back and then indifferently walked toward the fire.

Meanwhile, one of the members had already placed a sinister-looking dagger into the right hand of the red-turbaned man, who then walked toward the fire himself, about ten feet ahead of Baltor. As for the caravan members, they continued to stay encircled around the two the entire time.

Less than a minute later, both arrived at the fire.

The man with the red turban turned around, and with his un-armed arm, he extended it out toward Baltor's direction.

While extending and drawing his left fingers into the palm of his hand, he said, "All right. Now, give me the bag. Don't ye be worryin', me lord—I won't steal it from ye."

Without pause, Baltor drew to about two feet away, and handed the man the bag.

As the man began to peer inside the bag, while shifting it

around with his left hand, the other hand cautiously held the dagger straight out in front of him.

A moment later, his mouth dropped open in pure astonishment, especially at the size of the large diamond. With a happy smile on his face, he first looked back up at Baltor, and then he looked around at all his underlings while declaring with happiness, "Aye, what fine treasures ye have!"

He looked very happily at Baltor, until they were eye to eye, and then he added, "Kill—"

The man was about to say "him," but looked down in surprise to see that Baltor had just firmly grabbed his right hand with both of his hands, the very hand wielding the dagger.

While still firmly holding the man's hand and wrist, Baltor expertly twisted both of his own arms around in a big wide circle, which caused the dagger to stab deep into his fat gut! All the while, the man was quite shocked that he had been holding the dagger almost the whole way through.

Even though blood gurgled a moment out of his mouth before he and the backpack dropped to the ground, the red-turbaned man did manage to way the last word of "him" before he died. As for the dagger, that was now firmly in Baltor's right hand.

It was actually fortunate for Baltor that the caravan members had surrounded him, because the archers didn't want to kill their own accidentally.

Fourteen fighters, however, stood out from the rest of the bunch, and formed yet another circle around Baltor.

He waited in silence, until one huge man bearing a long sword came in close. He leapt into a roll just off to that man's side, and while coming out of the roll, he angled his dagger outwards, which caused a slice to rip the man open from abdomen to shoulder—that man collapsed to the ground dead!

Baltor was already in the defensive position, and waiting.

An even larger man, who was seven feet tall with a weight of about three hundred pounds of pure muscle, bore a large double-edged axe, thought he now had the advantage over the now-crouching enemy that was facing in the opposite direction as him.

After the man had begun his charge, he began to swing his axe downwards with all of his might—so that it would split Baltor right down the middle into two pieces!

What he didn't count on, however, was for Baltor to twist his body ever-so-slight out of the axe's way, nor did he think that the axe would suddenly fly out of his powerful hands, solidly imbedding itself into the ground several feet away from his position.

Lastly, this man could not have begun to anticipate that Baltor would simply extend his foot and leg out, tripping him in mid-stride, and that a split-second later, he himself would land hard upon his axe and become split down the very middle of his torso, and die!

Over the course of the next four minutes, a huge and fierce battle was waged as Baltor took out fighter after fighter—fourteen more to be exact!

Despite the fact that he was still severely outnumbered, he saw the remaining caravan members fleeing into the dark desert night in all directions.

Once the last of them was gone, he took one last cautious look around, and once satisfied they were indeed gone, he looked back to the cage, so as to try and locate his wife.

However, due to the blood that drenched his body and his sword, he became exceedingly hungry from all the intoxicating smells, and he knew that the beast needed to feast.

No longer able to hold the cravings back, he immediately hopped onto Grasha, and pursued one of the fleeing members.

After leaping off the horse, perhaps a minute later, he slammed into that man which caused the two of them to plummet hard into the ground, with Baltor on top.

As soon as he sank his vampire fangs into the man, who in turn screamed out his agonizing pains, his body instantly transformed to the beastly vompareus, as he ravenously feasted! He soon came to learn that this man's name was Ciaro, yet another piece of vermin—a whole hell of a lot of vermin around this world, Baltor sadly realized near the end of his feasting.

Fifteen minutes later, when he had ridden back to the camp completely quenched, extremely powerful, and again in his human form, he happily discovered that none of the other caravan members had returned either.

A little more than a minute later, he then opened up the cage and watched as all the young, attractive, yet dirty women poured out. Already they had begun to congratulate, hug, and even to kiss him, despite all the blood that soaked and caked his entire body from the earlier battle.

From amongst the voices, one voice stood out from the rest—Brishava's most beautiful voice!

She fought her way through, gingerly pushing off the young women who either clung on to or kissed Baltor, and then squealed out as she hugged him tightly, "Baltor—Baltor—Baltor! You rescued me!"

As he hugged her just as tightly back, he first chuckled for a couple of moments before he replied, "Yes, I did! But it was because of my love for you that I was able to find you, my wife."

At that comment, the rest of the girls immediately realized whom he had come to rescue, and many of them began to look disappointed.

One particularly attractive woman, a brunette with sea-blue eyes, soon asked, "Now what are we going to do?"

Without looking away from his wife for one second, he replied, "Go back home. You're all free!"

This brunette looked all around as she replied, "I have no clue where I'm at now—originally, I came from Pawshen. Do you know where my town's from here?"

Looking over for the very first time, he sighed, "No, I don't. Actually, to be honest with you, I've never even heard of that place before." Not even Brishava had heard the name of Pawshen, so she could give no directions.

A few moments later, the brunette asked, "So what in the world are we supposed to do?"

He thought for a minute, until suddenly, a good idea hit him! He said his idea aloud: "I have a good friend of mine named Yaush who lives in a town not too far away to the east, called Valakan. Unfortunately, I can speak very little of his language or he mine, but I am in high hopes that he will be able to help us all find accommodations there; that is, until you girls decide what you're going to do, okay?"

Other than Brishava, the girls talked amongst one another for a minute, and then they all said at the same time, "Okay."

Over the course of the next ten minutes, they had quickly thrown almost everything they could find into the covered wagon, goods, supplies, parsecs, and other valuables. Specifically they made sure including seven two-person tents.

By the time they were done packing everything into the wagon, which even included two of the water bags that originally had been on his horse, the wagon was three-quarters full.

Two of the girls elected to drive and/or sit upon the wagon— both had previous experience. The nine others, not including Brishava, would ride upon their own individual horse. The rest of the horses, except for Grasha, were left at the oasis, as there was plenty of water and shrubbery for them to eat.

The newly formed caravan began to ride east toward the mountains—sitting on his warhorse, he led the way with Brishava sitting r i g h t on his lap. Nearly right away they began kissing...

Another hour or so passed as they continued in their journey at a trot, but he was so obliviously happy to have his wife back, and vice-versa, neither of them had been paying attention to anything else—both had been kissing each other with eyes closed nearly the whole time.

Brishava was the first to open her eyes, notice that the skies had long ago been lightening up ahead of them, break the lip-lock, and then exclaim, "Baltor—the sun is about rise!"

That statement brought him back to reality!

Quickly he looked around all across the sandy dunes, and even with his binocular-eyesight, he saw no oases or caves, or anything else whatsoever to protect him from the sun, except for the desert sand, itself.

He also realized that if he dug himself a hole in the sand and completely buried himself under it, it would seem very odd and maybe even obvious to everyone that he was actually a vampire, especially his wife.

He got quite upset, especially after having gone so far and through so much just to get her back, but he tried not to let it show. He looked back at his wife, while grimly saying, "There's nothing to protect me from the sun's furious rays—it's soon going to be over for me."

She asked with hope to her voice, "Can't we at least wrap some clothes over you? Maybe that would help. We could also fit you into the wagon too."

He believed that he had to be underground, and that the clothes would do absolutely nothing to protect him. He finally sighed, "I doubt it. In only a few minutes, my love, I may no longer be alive."

"No!" Brishava cried out, "I will not let Death tear us apart after having overcome such incredible struggles and adversaries, especially now that we have been reunited, my husband!"

Tears began to pour down from her eyes as she gripped onto him desperately.

Several of the other women behind them wondered what the problem was, and why Brishava was crying instead of squealing in delight, as she had been doing almost the whole time since being rescued. And so they rode up on their horses to find out why.

After having seen the tears, a young woman with wavy blonde hair asked, "What's the matter?"

From that little question, Brishava began to bawl yet again. She could see that within a minute or two, the sun would rise over the eastern horizon.

A bloody tear began to pour down his face as well, but no one saw it as he quickly wiped it away.

Even though his heart ached painfully, he also began to wonder what lay on the other side of life, even though he was an undead creature.

Strangely enough, probably due to all the intense emotions, he realized that he did not feel tired in the least bit.

Brishava somehow regained her senses, and through her tears, she yelled, "Do any of you girls have some extra clothes that we could throw on top of my husband? We need to hurry—he has an unusual illness that prevents him from tolerating the sun!"

He and his wife hopped off the now-stopped horse, and onto the ground. The rest of the caravan had stopped upon seeing their leader stop, though the brunette with the sea-blue eyes immediately asked from near the rear of the caravan, "What's going on up there?"

"Ladies," the blonde yelled out, "we need as many clothes as possible! Can one of you please check in the wagon to see if there're any more clothes, and bring them up here?"

Meanwhile, Brishava had already opened her backpack, pulled out the two extra outfits that she had stuffed back in there while packing the night prior, and then she began to try and wrap them around her husband's face and neck.

Even though he was completely covered by the time she had wrapped both outfits around him, it didn't seem as if the wrappings would be secure at all. Any bump, and they could easily and fatally fall right off.

Moments passed as the women passed along any extra clothing that they were wearing though there wasn't much! A couple of them had even begun to think about going in the buff.

But the red-headed passenger riding in the wagon had just discovered a sack within the wagon that contained something quite useful—a large roll of a black, silky material.

While trying to drag the heavy sack out of the wagon, the red-head yelled out to the front of the caravan with an unusual twang, "I've found some black silks for Baltor—someone quickly get over here and help me get this sack to him, please!"

The driver of the wagon, a woman with jet-black hair and piercing brown eyes, volunteered—the two women drug the bag of silks up halfway to the front of the caravan, which nearly took a minute, as the sack weighed about seventy pounds—there was indeed a lot of silk.

Meanwhile, he had already taken off the extra clothes, and then he and Brishava met the two women in the middle of the caravan, as they had heard the redhead yell out that information.

In under a minute, the women had thoroughly wrapped the silks around Baltor's hands, arms, legs, torso, and even head, and with that sinister-looking dagger, they then cut the rest of the roll off. Even though he could still walk and move his arms around, he couldn't see a thing—he looked just like a mummy wearing black attire.

Once done, they then guided him to the back of the wagon, where several of the other women had already cleared a spot that was just big enough for both he and Brishava to either lie or sit down.

They then assisted him into the cleared spot in the wagon, and Brishava joined her husband in the wagon, a moment later.

The woman with the jet black hair, the one who had been the driver of the wagon, said, "Baltor, my name is Poila, and if you like, I could ride your horse today, while my new friend Chelsea drives the wagon. Is that okay with you?"

"No problem... thanks!" he muffled through his silks, unsure of whom Chelsea was.

As the caravan began to move forward again a minute later, Brishava then held onto her husband as tightly as she could, ready to fight Death himself if he should come.

Even though he could no longer see, he still knew that the first rays of the sun had risen over the eastern horizon, for he had become very sleepy. He turned to face his beloved, and muffled through the silks, "This may not work.—*yawn*—Just remember, I shall love you for all eternity, my Brishava!"

In the next moment, the sun's rays hit the wagon and continued to rise up. Meanwhile, Brishava held tight her husband, and whispered, "I shall love you for all eternity, my Baltor!"

Despite all of the layers that included his clothes and boots, the silks, and even the covered top of the wagon, he could still feel the sun's heat penetrate first over his legs, his thighs, his abdomen, his chest, and finally his face and head. As he lost consciousness a moment later, he doubted that he would ever return....

CHAPTER XXV

When Baltor did return to the state of consciousness the second after the sun had set, he was quite surprised and relieved that his body had not turned into a pile of ashes, though he could not see a thing even after he opened his eyes.

Still, despite his temporary blindness, he knew that he was alive and well because he could feel the soft and silky wrappings throughout his entire body and head; he simultaneously felt the ground beneath him continuously shifting around him, most likely the wagon in motion. Finally yet importantly, he felt somebody's warm-and-soft arms tightly wrapped around his waist, most likely Brishava's arms.

Just to make sure he was alive, he asked in a much-muffled voice, "Am I alive?"

"Yes, you are, my beloved." she sighed from behind, as she nuzzled her face into the side of his neck for a moment.

In the next moment, she released her grip on her husband, sat up in the wagon, and then added, "Yes you are."

A moment later, he sat up—he next allowed his wife to begin removing first the clothes, and then the silks that covered his head, face and neck.

Once done, nearly four minutes later, he saw that she was the only one sitting in the back of the wagon with him.

He also saw that the last of the sun's rays had left the sky, as was revealed through the sole opening to the covered wagon that looked west across the sandy dunes.

About ten seconds later, he called out to the driver of the wagon, "Hey—I'm both alive and awake now. Can you please call out to the rest of the girls that we need to stop, so that we can set up camp for the night?"

He heard that woman with the unusual twang to her voice, yell out, "Hey, girls—stop the caravan! Guess what? Our hero Baltor's alive, awake, and well!"

As soon as he heard the accent, he strongly suspected that the driver was Chelsea, unless someone else with a twang voice had volunteered to drive the wagon during the course of his sleep.

As the caravan slowly brought their horses to a halt, including the driver of the wagon, the girls all whooped out their sighs of exhilaration and relief at all the great news, which relieving news included stopping the caravan because of their sore bottoms from riding horseback all day.

Once everyone had come to a complete stop, the girls had already gotten off their horses, and the driver of the wagon had hopped onto the ground—they all then began to stretch and walk around, while trying to look around in the night skies.

The last of the silks were finally removed off of him, about a minute later, and both he and his wife hopped out of the back of the wagon, looking all around.

As he scanned from west to north to northeast, his eyes came upon the jagged peaks of the Bospa Mountains far off in that direction, and a few moments later, he recognized the very peaks that existed to the southeast.

His gaze then fell to the south-southeast, he soon saw the very same fertile valley that he had passed through the first time. All of this was due, of course, to his vampire ultravision.

Brishava, who was now standing to his left side, however, didn't see a thing other than the darkness of night for obvious reasons.

After he looked back at his wife, he asked aloud in shock and wonder, "How can this be? How can I still be alive?"

"It could have been a number of factors," she answered. "Perhaps all you needed were the silks and the wagon to protect you from the sun, perhaps it was our strong love for each other, perhaps it was God..."

She gave him a kiss on his cheek before adding, "Most likely, it was probably a combination of all those factors."

"I'm alive!" he exclaimed with glee. He grabbed a hold of his wife tightly, and kissed her in exultation—she was just as joyous, especially from the flood of positive emotions that poured from her husband!

Once the kissing had abated, perhaps a minute later, she lightly drew her finger down her husband's cheek and said, "I love you."

"And I love you!" he exclaimed—they began kissing yet again...

Poila was the one to ask a minute later, "I hate to break you two lovebirds up, but is there any way we can get camp set up soon? None of us knows how to set up a campfire, much less the tents. Chelsea volunteered to cook, but we don't know what we've got just yet."

"Of course," he replied as soon as he had stopped the kissing a moment later. He then asked, "Will you ladies please oblige me by gathering up as much firewood as you possibly can find into a pile. Say, right over there? While you do this, Brishava and I shall begin to set up all our tents, okay? Oh, by the way, can one of you please get my flint that is located in my stallion's front left saddle, please? It looks like a rectangular piece of rock about oh so big." He then gestured with his hands to indicate the size of the flint.

"Sure," the women agreed, and immediately they began to make things happen. Meanwhile, Baltor and Brishava began the semi-difficult process of learning how to set up the tent for the very first time—it took about ten minutes to figure out how to set the tent securely into the ground that theoretically would last the night.

About twenty minutes and three tents later, he saw that the women had gathered enough wood, and a blond-haired woman had just handed him his flint. He immediately stopped putting together that fourth tent in order to safely set up the campfire, and light it with the flint.

Meanwhile, Brishava continued to follow right behind her husband, and assist whenever he asked her to do something.

As for the redhead, she surprisingly found enough components in the back of the wagon to conjure up a month's worth of dried rations, and a week's worth of nice breakfasts and dinners, as well some pots, pans, plates, silverware, glasses, etc.

As soon as the redhead had excitedly informed everyone about her discoveries with that unusual twang, he realized for the very first time that this was Chelsea—the only redhead in the group of women. However, he was too busy setting up the tents to do an introduction, right now.

Chelsea immediately began the process of mixing a salted ham and vegetable stew, and about ten minutes later, she then began cooking it in a pot over the open fire, which she realized would take about forty-five minutes to cook. As for Baltor and Brishava, they continued setting up the tents, one after the other.

About forty minutes later, just as they were just finishing setting up the last of the tents, they heard Chelsea calling out to everyone with that twang, "Dinner time, everybody—time to eat!"

He kissed his wife, informed her that he will be back soon, and without any further delay, immediately headed out into the darkness to forage for his own food.

Once Brishava had arrived and picked up a plate, Chelsea approached while asking, "Why isn't Baltor eating any of my stew—it's absolutely delicious!"

Brishava explained, "He's got his own special type of diet. By the way, just to let you know, my name is Breeze."

"I'm Chelsea—nice to meet you!"

"Nice to meet you!"

After the two girls had given each other a couple of squeezing hugs, Brishava then asked, "So, where are you from, Chelsea?"

Chelsea answered, "Oh—I'm from Lochas, which is a very small town located in the Vispano Province. You?"

"Oh. As for me, I'm from here and there."

Chelsea replied with a wide smile, "Oh, well nice to meet you. Well, go ahead and enjoy your meal, Breeze! I'm sure you're hungry."

"Thanks—I will!"

The girls spent the rest of the meal in silence, as most were far too exhausted to stay awake—Baltor and Brishava had no problems staying awake all night long, even though there wasn't a single incident to report. She also told him that he should call her Breeze, her childhood nickname, for at least a little while—even around these other girls. He agreed.

Just before he was wrapped up into the silks the next morning, he pointed toward the southeast and informed Chelsea, who had volunteered to ride his horse that day, "Hey Chelsea, make sure you keep leading us all southeast, okay?"

With that twang voice, Chelsea replied, "No problem, Baltor!"

Two evenings later, the caravan had left the last of the desert, and entered the fertile valley of the Bospa Mountains.

The women, including Brishava, could no longer take the continuous riding on the horses or on the wagon, due to their very sore fannies.

After he had awoken the third night, he immediately discovered that all his vampire powers were once again gone—as he was finishing setting up the campfire, he began to wonder if he would only have his powers in three-day bursts for all eternity.

Once the entire camp had been set up with the girls' assistance, they soon ate a great meal consisting of a large deer that Baltor had hunted, killed, skewered, and cooked.

Later that night, while they all sat at the campfire, ate, and relaxed, he informed the girls, "In about three days or so, we will come to a major fork in the path that goes both north and south. Make sure, if I'm sleeping, that we choose the southern route, even though it looks easier to go north—trust me on that.

"Also, things will be getting colder from here on out, so I would suggest that you find whatever extra clothes you can find, and be ready to put them on. It will soon get cold enough to snow, even during the middle of the day—okay?"

Meanwhile, the women, including Brishava, agreed to all his suggestions by either nodding or saying "okay" in between his pauses.

Almost immediately after, the women fell asleep, though Brishava was the last to fall asleep as she cuddled with her husband by the fire.

As for Baltor, he remained on guard all night long, which night passed by without an incident, an encounter, or even a single snowflake.

An hour before sunrise, he awoke his wife, and then they made breakfast for everyone, which consisted of dozens of eggs he cooked in the cooking pan over the fire, as well several loaves of bread, and last but not least, several jugs of juice.

Once done with getting everything set up conveniently for the women onto plates, glasses, and silverware, Baltor and Brishava woke the girls up one after the other, and then pointed their sleepy selves over into the direction of the food.

Once that part of their mission was accomplished, the two then began the task of unsetting all the tents.

Meanwhile, the rest of the women ate and drank by the fire—before long, they were introducing themselves and chattering happily away with each other like hens in a henhouse, most of them for the very first time.

By the time the women were done with breakfast about ten minutes before sunrise, Baltor and Brishava had neatly put everything back into the wagon, so that there was room for the two to either sit or lie down.

Chelsea was the first to arrive at the wagon, and volunteer, "Would you like me to help you get wrapped up, Baltor?"

"Please. By the way, your name is Chelsea, right?"

"Yeah."

"Nice to meet you."

Chelsea chimed back, "Nice to meet you!"

Brishava had just produced the roll of black silks, and asked, "Are we ready?"

He answered, "Let's do it."

With Chelsea's assistance, Brishava wrapped her husband back into the black silks, and once thoroughly wrapped, Brishava alone climbed into the back of the wagon. Chelsea then guided Baltor until he was comfortably lying down inside the back of the wagon, before she made her way for the wagon's driver's seat.

Only seconds before sunrise, the last thing he heard just before he fell instantly asleep was Chelsea's voice declare, "By the way, Baltor, Poila just volunteered to ride your horse today, okay?"

The sun rose just as she was finishing saying the word "okay."

When the sun had set, Baltor learned from Brishava that the caravan had only stopped for a couple of bathroom breaks, to give the horses some water, and dried rations for lunch; otherwise, they had continued non-stop all day long.

As the girls ate a quiet dinner of more dried rations, he asked, "Do you want me to set up camp for the night, or do we just want to keep traveling?"

In unison, they answered, "Keep traveling."

"By the way," Brishava asked, "what is the name of your friend and his village? We can't remember."

He answered, "As for the name of my friend, it is Yaush. As for the name of his village, it is called, Valakan."

Once he had paused after giving his answer, Poila was the first to say, "Yes, we all decided that we just want to get to Valakan as soon as possible... and relax for a week, maybe a month."

He replied, "That sounds like a good idea!"

Suddenly, his stomach made a grumbling sound that alerted Brishava's attention immediately.

"Honey," she asked, "Are you hungry?"

"Yes, I am, but I'll be all right," he answered.

"Oh."

He then explained to them all, "After all, I agree with you ladies that we should ride as long as possible, and get to Valakan as soon as possible. After all, besides the cozy town, there'll also be hot and delicious meals, cool and tasty beverages, yet most especially, warm beds for us all to sleep in. Maybe even in a day or two, if we push it to the limit!"

"Hooray!" they all agreed.

About an hour later, which was the second time that his stomach grumbled during this night, he simply took an extra shirt, and tied it tightly around his waist. Meanwhile, Brishava said nothing this time about it, though she did lightly pat her husband's belly in understanding.

Throughout this second night, not only did a single snowflake not fall from the sky yet the temperatures continued to remain unusually warm all night long.

By noon the next day, the girls could no longer take the constant riding, and after stopping the caravan, the women stretched their arms and legs around, including Brishava who had just woken up.

About an hour later or so after having eaten a small lunch and parching their thirst, as well doing some more stretching, or potty breaks, the caravan then took off. Afternoon soon turned into night, whereupon Baltor awoke.

The first thing he noticed was that the wagon he was riding in had already stopped. The second thing was that he was seriously feeling the pangs of hunger, though he kept his cravings completely under control. Meanwhile, Brishava assisted in removing the silky veils.

Once the caravan had stopped for a break about a minute later, Baltor and Brishava then went and rode back upon Grasha for most of the night.

Meanwhile, Chelsea drove the wagon, while Poila slept. By four o'clock in the morning, however, the weather had gotten quite a bit colder, which was what initially caused Brishava to wake up from a light nap while leaning back against her husband, as they rode on the warhorse.

She was also the first one to spot a very small campfire about a hundred feet up ahead to the right, because her head had been blocking Baltor's view in that direction.

"Baltor," she asked, while shifting her head over so that he could see the direction she pointed with her index finger. "Do you think that maybe that person camping up right over there next to the mountain possibly comes from your friend's town... Valakan, did you say?"

He immediately looked over in that direction. After about ten seconds or so, he simply shrugged his shoulders while answering, "Perhaps."

Just then, the camper happened to spot the travelers, and immediately he began to run on over while waving his arms around maniacally!

About thirty feet away, the camper cried out, "Help—my caravan was just attacked a few days ago, and most of our people were killed—I am pretty sure that I'm the only survivor, but I'm very lost! My horse died this morning. Can you please help me?"

He immediately realized that this camper was from the slave-trading caravan, and so he hopped off the back of his horse, while drawing his sword.

As he walked closer to the camper, Baltor soon replied, "I know exactly who you are—you are one of the worms who stole my wife away from me!"

Despite the fact that the camper could not see Baltor's face due to the darkness of night, he immediately recognized Baltor's voice—instantly he became afraid and took off into the night.

Meanwhile, Baltor had already decided that he needed to serve justice to this slave-trading criminal, and after he quickly told his wife that he'd soon be back, he then began to chase him down on foot.

Once he had entered the perimeters of the darkness, he first notched his sword back onto his belt, and then his body instantly transformed into a beastly vompareus through a willed thought. Only moments after that, Baltor's fangs took a chomp into this man's neck.

After having consumed Kartan's blood and knowledge, Baltor felt unbelievably powerful. In fact, his mind felt so powerful that with but a willed thought, he could fly to the moon, to the end of the galaxy, maybe to the very end of the universe.

Only a moment later, he began to think about his love for Brishava, and this is the sole factor that stopped him from literally flying off into space.

Instead, Baltor landed on the ground not too far away from the caravan that was still traveling eastbound, transformed back into human form, and called out so they would know that it was him returning, "Guys—I'm back!"

Brishava called out, "Good to know, my husband!"

Once Baltor had hopped back onto his horse, the caravan continued their way eastbound for the rest of the night and well through the morning—it was nearly noon the following day when the caravan reached the fork, and then took the southern route.

Two nights later, which was the third night since he had feasted—the caravan finally reached the borders of Valakan. After he had awoken, and he and Brishava had reassumed riding on Grasha, they soon arrived at Yaush's home.

Once there, and the two had dismounted, he knocked upon his friend's door, and moments later, the doorknob turned.

As soon as the door had fully opened, Yaush's mouth dropped open in astonishment at seeing his good friend standing on the other side. A smile formed, and immediately he proceeded to close his eyes, and give Baltor a good bear hug.

Another astonished look crossed Yaush's face upon opening his eyes a few seconds later, and discovering all the beautiful women who stood right behind Baltor—the girls including Brishava, all bore their own astonished faces at the size of the ten-foot, six-hundred-pound giant.

Yaush released the embrace, and with a friendly gesture of his huge hand inside, he said to all, "Vlaidim zaus!"

Even though Baltor understood the physical prompt, what surprised Baltor was the fact that his mind actually translated the words for him. Yaush had said, "Welcome all!"

Just before Baltor entered the cabin, he thankfully replied, "Gemne mao, Yaush."

Yaush, in turn, replied, "Mao sahu vlaidim, Baltor."

As Baltor remembered, his mind didn't have to translate Yaush's words, "You are welcome, Baltor."

After entering the cabin and quickly looking around, Baltor immediately began to walk over to Jimnee who sat in the couch by the fireplace.

It was only in the next moment that Jimnee turned her head to look over at Baltor, and with a very surprised look on her face, she ran over, gave Baltor a tight hug of her own, and said, "Baltor, mao've platha caloph!"

Baltor's mind quickly translated, "Baltor, you've come back!" At the same time, his peripheral vision observed that Brishava was now standing nearly right behind him.

Once Baltor and Jimnee had released the hug a moment later, he introduced the two to each other. Meanwhile, back where Yaush stood on the outside porch to his cabin, he had counted out eleven young and beautiful women bearing a warm and friendly smile, as they entered through the door.

With an amused cock to his head, Yaush closed the door behind them all after he had reentered his home. He then had to slither his massive body around the young attractive women in order to get to Baltor.

As Yaush began to draw near, he soon observed that his friend had his arm wrapped lightly around a beautiful though dirty woman's waist, and her arm wrapped around his waist.

Baltor asked in Valakanese, "How are you, my good friend?"

With a warm smile, Yaush replied back in Valakanese, "Very good, my friend!" With an inquisitive gesture while using both of his index fingers to point at all the ladies, he asked, "Now, who are they?"

Once Baltor's mind had interpreted, he explained in the same language, "To explain in a nutshell, my wife was kidnapped from me about a week and a half ago by a caravan of slave traders.

Soon after, I caught up with them and killed nearly half of them while the majority of the caravan fled like cowards into the desert. Not only did I rescue my wife from a locked cage, yet all these other women."

With a cock of his head toward the woman within his arms, he added, "By the way, this is my wife, and her name is Brishava."

Yaush shockingly realized that Baltor had said all this in Valakanese! "How is it that you have learned and mastered my language so well? You don't even have an accent!"

"A very good teacher."

Yaush shook his head in shock for a moment, but then he laughed out, "I have so many more questions for you, Baltor—however, I hardly know where to begin!"

With a gesture of his hand toward Brishava, Baltor introduced, "Well, let me once again introduce you to my wife, Brishava."

Brishava didn't understand what Baltor had just said, but she could tell that there was an introduction made, due to the gesturing prompt of his free hand. She slightly curtsied while bowing her head in greeting, as was her custom.

Baltor then spoke in Pavelian, "This is my friend, Yaush, the one I told you all about?"

Brishava threw a warm smile, and extended her hand out. Yaush took it, but he did not shake it, or even hold it.

Instead, he gently brought her hand up to his lips and gently kissed it. A moment later, he released her hand.

Baltor then asked in Valakanese, "Yaush, I need to find some rooms for us all, as we have nowhere else left to go. We should have whatever money it might cost. Is there an inn that we can stay at for awhile?"

"Well, I'm not sure what and how many rooms there might be at *Hungry Bear*, but there's only one way to find out. Jimnee, would you like to come?"

Jimnee replied with a smile, "Of course, Yaush." She immediately stood up, set her sewing materials onto the chair, and walked over to her husband's side.

They, the whole group, departed from the cabin, untied the horses from the wagon still parked outside, brought as many of their horses into the barn as possible, tied up the horses that wouldn't fit in the stalls, and then they walked their way into town.

It was during this trip that Jimnee informed Baltor, "Tell your beautiful wife that it is a pleasure to meet her!"

Baltor translated.

Brishava said, "Tell her that it is a great honor for me to have met one so highly spoken of by my husband!"

Baltor translated, to which Jimnee and Brishava clasped hands and smiled.

Jimnee turned to Baltor, and asked, "Did you find the furs to be of help for you in your quest?"

In Valakanese, Baltor replied, "Yes, they were of great help, thank you very much. But unfortunately, my camel took off into the jungles; that is, after I had gotten poisoned and captured by some sneaky cannibals. The fur suit you made was in my camel's saddle-bags. Sadly, I have no idea what happened to Valuspo."

Yaush sadly said, "Valuspo was a great animal, too. Say, can you tell me of your quest, now?"

"That," Baltor suggested, "should be told before a roasting fire with a mug of ale."

Yaush laughed at his comment, and confirmed, "You're right! Indeed, it should. I guess it is quite fortunate that we are on the way to the restaurant and inn now, isn't it?"

"Yes, it is."

Once they had reached the inn, they all entered. There were only three male patrons in the place, drinking up the suds. When they saw Yaush and Jimnee enter, they greeted, "Good evening." When all of the beautiful girls entered their haven, however, their mouths instantly dropped open, and their conversations forgotten.

Meanwhile, Baltor and Yaush approached the bar, and Yaush asked the bartender, "How many rooms do you have, Jerishan?"

Jerishan replied, "Of the fifteen rooms I have, twelve are currently available, Yaush."

"Great!" Baltor said, "We'll take them all for a week."

After figuring out the costs in his head for a second, Jerishan said, "That'll be ninety-five baushans, please."

Baltor asked, "Will you take a precious gem as payment?"

"Well," Jerishan sighed, "is it worth ninety-five baushans?"

Baltor turned to Brishava who now stood by his side, and simply asked, "Can I get a gem, please?"

Brishava pulled out an emerald the size of a chicken egg from her backpack, and as she handed it over to Baltor, she replied, "Of course, honey!"

Baltor extended it out toward the bartender while asking, "Will this cover for a week, Jerishan?"

Without having even touched the emerald to feel its quality, Jerishan's eyes bulged as he declared, "That'll easily cover a month!"

"Deal," Baltor replied. As he handed Jerishan the emerald, he asked, "Say—will that buy us all a round of ale, too?"

"Sure thing, buddy!" he replied, as he took the emerald. He then began the process of pulling out mugs, and then filling them up with for everyone in the entire bar.

Baltor picked up one of the mugs and pretended to take a small sip from it—Yaush didn't, however.

Instead, he grabbed his mug and chugged half of it down in one swallow!

"Ah." Yaush sighed, "I needed that."

A mug was set before Brishava, but she cleared her throat. When Jerishan glanced up, she shook her head negatively and pointed at the mug.

Jerishan bore a curious expression on his face.

Brishava grabbed the sleeve of Baltor's dirty shirt, and asked, "Honey, please tell the innkeeper that I don't like ale. However, do ask him if he has any wine, preferably red, please?"

Baltor translated her request.

Jerishan threw Brishava a smile and a nod with his head. He then disappeared into the backroom for a minute. When he returned, he held a corked bottle in his hand, and then told Baltor, "Tell that pretty woman that this is my best wine—reserved for only the most special of my guests!"

Once Baltor had translated, Brishava smiled at the innkeeper very appreciatively, while nodding her head, and saying, "Thank you very much!"

Baltor translated.

Yaush had just finished his second mug of ale, and then he asked Baltor, "So will you tell us about your quest—well, what you can?"

"Of course!"

Yaush stood up from his barstool, and then pointed at the three elongated tables that sat in the middle of the room that each held six chairs. The rest of the group got the idea and casually moseyed their way over there.

After the ladies had grabbed a chair or two, the two men pushed the three tables together, the ladies slid their chairs up to the table, just before everyone took a seat.

After another round of drinks had been distributed out, nearly a minute later, Baltor began to relay his tale from beginning to end, and in both languages—as before, he omitted any parts that regarded the rod, Trendon, and vampires. He also omitted the info that the wife he had rescued twice was actually the daughter of a Sultan. Meanwhile, the whole bar hovered over every word he said.

Just as Baltor's mouth had finished relaying his tale, his eyes spotted a new patron sitting in a shadowy booth at the far end of the room, alone.

This person was dressed completely in black attire, including the gloves that extended not only past the elbows, yet vanished under the shadows of the black cape and hood. As this person was currently leaning forward in their booth, Baltor assumed that this person was listening very attentively to every word that he had to say.

As soon as the hooded figure became aware that he or she had been spotted, that figure stood up and began to approach—Baltor did not make it look obvious, though his hand rested upon his sword, just in case.

Once the cloaked person reached the table, and without warning, raised his or her left hand up in order to draw back the hood. Goosebumps surged up and down Baltor's body, as he shockingly saw Humonus's face smiling down at him.

"Hey, Humonus!" Baltor exclaimed. He stepped out of his chair, turned to face his old friend, and extended his arms out for a hug—Humonus returned the embrace.

Meanwhile, the rest of the group looked over to see the commotion. Baltor finally pulled back from the hug a moment later and asked, "So how are you doing, my old friend?"

"I'm good," Humonus answered with a smile. "From the way it sounds, things are going well for you, as well!"

"Yes, they are." Baltor said. Gesturing toward Brishava, he introduced, "Have you met my wife?"

Humonus looked down toward Brishava, and replied, "No, I haven't."

Brishava extended out her hand, to which Humonus took.

He brought that hand to his lips and gently kissed it. With another bow, he added, "My... you are as beautiful and as lovely as a princess."

Baltor looked a bit surprised that he knew her identity, and asked, "How did you know?"

Humonus's face turned very serious as he answered, "Everyone in the Guild knows. That's why I came here to this town—I arrived three weeks ago. I was desperately hoping I'd run into you here, sooner or later."

"Well, I'm glad you're here," Baltor replied with a smile.

"Listen, I need to talk to you two in private, though this conversation can wait."

"You got it!"

About two in the morning, the new group of friends exchanged their warm goodnights with everyone else. Humonus, Brishava, and Baltor were the first to leave the bar area, heading to room number nine, which was Baltor and his wife's room for the night.

CHAPTER XXVI

Once the three were all comfortably seated inside with the door closed, Humonus began, "There are a few reasons why I've come looking for you, Baltor."

"I have my suspicions why."

Humonus first nodded his head twice, and then said, "Your suspicions are probably right...

"One, the Guild has a fifty thousand bounty on your head, Baltor, dead or alive. Why, you may ask?

"Because—shortly after you had made your escape with the princess, those two thieves you didn't kill, Stele and Romach, went straight to the High Council! The one named Romach clearly heard your confession to Lydia regarding the rod, and not only did he say that you admitted to finding this very powerful weapon, yet you lied about your discovery to the High Council. Not only to them did you lie if this is true, yet to me!"

"I had no choice," Baltor evenly replied.

Brishava said nothing, only listened.

After five-or-so seconds had passed, Humonus continued, "Romach also said that you killed just about everyone in a fit of murderous rage, including Lydia."

Baltor replied, "It was not because of murderous rage that I killed them but self-defense—really, you must believe me, I had no choice!"

Humonus added, "Last but not least, Romach even said," and he dropped his voice, whispering, "something else that can only be told in private."

Neither Baltor nor Brishava said a word.

Humonus said in a very hushed tone of voice, "And it is only now that I begin with reason number two. There is a seven hundred thousand reward, offered by the Sultan himself, for the one who brings his only daughter back to Pavelus, alive and well. No longer is it just the Sultan's troops scouring through the lands, but due to this extremely handsome reward, thousands of bounty hunters and adventurers have joined them in their search for the beloved princess! Now you may ask—how can reason number two possibly get any worse?"

When neither answered, nearly five seconds later, Humonus answered, "Easy—they all know exactly what Brishava looks like based off the exact-likeness sketches of her that were drawn up and posted just about everywhere across the lands—so that she could be easily identified, and brought back home to Daddy even sooner!

"Soon enough, someone will come looking for you both here and neither of you is safe."

"Is that all?" Baltor asked right away.

Humonus answered, "There is one more reason why I'm here, but I must relay this information to you in the privacy of my room, which is just down the hall in room four, just you and me."

Baltor suddenly began to look at Humonus suspiciously.

Humonus caught the "look," and said, "Listen, my ole friend, if I had come for the bounty, I would have taken her, not you—she's worth a hell of a lot more money." He then began to laugh solidly, while lightly hitting Baltor in the arm with his fist.

As soon as Humonus observed that Baltor was neither amused nor convinced, yet still suspicious, he stopped laughing. With a very serious look etched upon his face and eyes, he asked, "Why would I have said everything I did if I was going to take either of you in?"

Without waiting for an answer, he asked another question, "Baltor, is it logical for a thief to give up his greatest asset—the element of surprise?"

Just after Baltor thought about Humonus's logic, he shook his head negatively, and said, "As you have well taught me, there is no logic to a thief giving up his greatest asset—lead the way."

Immediately Baltor turned back toward Brishava, gave her a quick peck on the cheek, and then said, "Honey, I'll be right back."

"I'll be waiting for you right here, my husband," Brishava sighed with a very loving smile.

Humonus led Baltor back to his room, opened the door, politely gestured for Baltor to enter first; after both men had entered the room, Humonus shut the door behind them.

Even though he continued to face the door, he began, "There are strange rumors spreading throughout the Guild, and just about everywhere else, about a large black monster that drinks human blood."

Still facing the door, Humonus added with astonished tones, "Why—some of the zanier reports claim that this monster can even fly in the sky at incredible speeds, and can even turn invisible— wow! As for me, I've always been a skeptic of things like monsters or vampires. Both Romach and Stele, however, swore up and down that there was a beastly monster down there that night, slinking in the shadows, feasting on Lydia's blood, and roaring angrily. Did you happen to hear or see anything strange that night?"

"No," Baltor replied, and then asked, "Is that your number three reason for coming all the way out here to Valakan, to ask me about a monster?"

Baltor was certainly curious as to the reason why Humonus continued to face the door, though he did not voice his curiosity aloud.

"It leads up to reason number three, yes," Humonus replied as he turned around.

"Huh?"

"Please, sit down on the chair and get yourself comfortable."

Baltor did.

"I will tell you this reason in a moment, but let me first congratulate you for passing yet another test—which confirmed to me that my reason for coming out to see you is still doable, if you should grant it!"

"Okay, Humonus, I'm really confused now," Baltor replied honestly.

"I know that it seems like I'm being elusive, but I swear that it'll all make sense in a minute," Humonus answered. After a thoughtful look crossed his face, he then asked, "Remember when you came back from the jungles and told me of your mysterious illness which prevents you from withstanding the sunlight, and of course, your encounter with the cannibal tribe?"

Baltor nodded his head.

"Well," Humonus said, "just because I am a skeptic of mysticism and superstitious folklore does not mean that I don't recognize and consider more mundane possibilities, especially ones that seem to strangely add up.

"One possibility that I carefully considered, during the time it took me to get here, is that this might all be the clever contraption of a thief trying to gain some berth from his Guild."

After taking in a deep breath through just his nose, Humonus continued, "This particular thief that I personally know runs so fast that he does look likes he's literally flying, and fights so well that he is virtually unbeatable. Most especially, this master thief is so clever that it would be easily possible for him to make it look like the work of a 'sloppy vampiric monster trying to conceal its tracks.'"

He extended his index finger up into the air, cleared his throat several times, and then walked to the far end of the room, where rested a small table, and resting upon it, a metallic tray, pitcher, and mug. After picking up the pitcher, he poured some water into the mug, set the pitcher back down, picked up the mug, took a long draught, set the mug back down, and then turned around to face Baltor yet again.

Only then did Humonus continue, "Still another possibility that I heavily considered is the proven fact that some people do go crazy, especially after having spent long periods of time completely isolated from any other human contact. Imagine how much harder it must be for those lonely souls to retain their sanity, especially after being a prisoner for even a second. Especially upon the shocking discovery that their captors are cannibals!"

While nodding, Baltor said, "Okay, I think I see where you're going with this."

"No matter which of these possibilities exist, Baltor, they all lead to one conclusion. If you were *the monster*, yet you didn't want anyone else to find out, especially your beloved wife, wouldn't you have tried to kill me the very second my back was to you, as I started talking about the subject?"

When Humonus had said the words "the monster," he had whispered them. Still he did not pause, as he continued, "Or how about the second time my back was to you, just after I had finished talking about a particular master thief I personally know, and then I walked over to the other end of the room and then nonchalantly drank some water right after that? You had so many opportunities to make your strike on me, yet you never did...

"Therefore, my conclusion is this: You are *no monster* at all, though you made it look that way, so as to buy you and Brishava as much time as possible to safely get away! Am I right?"

Baltor nodded his head, while also bearing a very surprised look on his face.

He didn't want Humonus to know that he actually was *the monster!* A moment later, he asked, "So, what is reason number three?"

"You, your wife, and even this town are not safe, by the two of you being here," Humonus answered bluntly. "As soon as possible, you must both disappear for a very long time but before this happens, I'd like to come along with you, if you'll allow me, which is reason number three!"

Right away Baltor replied with excitement, "Of course you can come along, my friend!"

"Do you have a place already in mind where we should go?"

"As a matter of fact, I do."

"Do you have a time set as to when we'll leave, and what times do you think would be best for us to travel, during the day or night? Finally, do we have a map to get there, if we should travel during the day with you sleeping?"

"I'll have everything all planned out by tomorrow morning, which is when we'll depart!"

"Excellent," Humonus replied with a smile. "Thanks for letting me come along!"

Baltor was about to open the door that he had just walked to, but instead, he turned around, and said, "By the way, before I head back to make sure Brishava's okay, I have one more question."

"Yes?"

"Why do you want to come along?"

"Because... out of all the pupils I've had over the years, you're the only one who ever became my friend afterward!"

"Thanks, brother—for everything," Baltor replied, walking back over and giving Humonus another hug. Humonus's gruff reply was, "No problem."

A moment or two later, Baltor left the room, and headed back to his own.

After he had entered, he observed that Brishava appeared to be already asleep on the bed. He quietly set his sword onto the cushioned sofa, watched her in slumber, and relished over her delicious beauties.

Despite the fact that this room had no windows, soon after, Baltor could still sense that the sun was about to rise, and so he covered himself completely with another blanket before snuggling next to his wife and falling asleep.

The following night when he awoke, he saw that his wife was not with him though he was strangely not worried.

Nearly ten minutes later, Brishava entered through the room door, while carrying quite a few large bags, and chiming in Valakanese, "Good day!" In Pavelian, without pause, she finished, "Sweetheart."

Meanwhile, he smelled a spicy yet feminine scent protruding from her being, as he happily greeted in Valakanese, "Good day!"

A moment later, Jimnee entered the room, while also carrying a bunch of large bags in her hand. The two women began to set down the bags on the floor next to the table.

As Baltor sat up in bed against the wall, he replied, "Good evening to you, Jimnee!"

"And a good evening to you, Baltor," Jimnee said with a chipper tone. Without a pause, she excitedly added, "Tell your wife that she is so wonderful! Even though we couldn't understand each other's language, we had an absolutely wonderful day together, shopping and having fun!"

By this time, Brishava had not only carefully finished setting the last bag onto the ground, yet she had begun to take items out of the bag and set them onto the table. Meanwhile, Baltor translated the words for Brishava.

She stopped in mid-task to turn around and give Jimnee a hug. While looking into her eyes, Brishava said, "Gemne mao, Jimnee."

With a rough accent yet a gentle smile, Jimnee replied in Pavelian, "Thank you, Brishava."

"You're so welcome," Brishava said, returning that smile.

A few seconds later, Baltor revealed to Brishava, "You know that we must be leaving tonight, right?"

Brishava sighed, "I know. Humonus told me earlier today, as we ran into each other at the shops."

"Oh." he said. He then looked at Jimnee, and said in Valakanese, "It is quite unfortunate that we must be leaving tonight, but it is for all of our safeties that we do so."

Jimnee replied, "I assumed that from all the traveling gear your wife purchased today, though she was not able to explain to me why you must leave. Can you tell me why? After all, you just got here last night!"

He first sucked in a deep sigh, and as he slowly released his breath, he said, "That, I shall explain over dinner, if you and Yaush would honor us with your presence."

Without hesitation, Jimnee replied, "We'd be delighted!" She then added, "Speaking of Yaush, I must return home and wait for him to return from work, but I can assure you that we'll be back in an hour or two."

Baltor said, "Great! We'll be looking forward to see you tonight."

Once Jimnee had left and closed the door behind her, Brishava sang over her shoulder, "Guess what I got?"

He walked behind her, wrapped his arms around her, kissed her spicy neck with his lips several times, and then asked, "What?"

"Guess," she cooed.

"I don't know—new clothes."

"You're one hundred percent right, Baltor. Though it took a whole shop of tailors all day to reconstruct them from your silks, they have made you gloves and a suit with a hood to protect you from the sun! Unfortunately, they made a boo-boo and made eye-holes in the hood, so I had to purchase a hat to protect those beautiful eyes of yours, as well some new matching boots."

"Wow, that's quite a lot! You got all that for me?" he asked as he looked over her shoulder, and saw all the stuffed bags.

She released his hug, turned around, pulled the black suit out of one of the bags, and sweetly said while holding half of it out for Baltor to take, "About half of it is yours, yes—now try it all on and see how it fits."

After giving her another kiss on the cheek, he stripped down, took the outfit, and then began to dress in the one-piece black and silky suit that was sunlight impenetrable when buttoned from the ankle up to the neck—meanwhile, she watched him with ever-increasing desire.

Once he had put the black suit with the silver lining on about thirty seconds later, he found that the silk stretched throughout his muscular body exceptionally well, except for his feet and hands. He then pulled over the hood that concealed his face and neck; he could see through the holes.

"Perfect!" she exclaimed. "Now, try on the hat."

He picked the wide-brimmed black hat with a white feather sticking out of it, and then put it on.

She extended out the boots, and said, "Here are your boots."

"Thanks."

After he had put on, and laced the black leather boots with large silver buckles that also fit perfectly, she said while holding out a pair of black gloves, "Last, but not least, here are your gloves."

Once he had put these on, she chimed, "Perfect!"

He chuckled as he looked into a mirror, and said, "I kind of feel like a pirate!"

She lightly laughed at his comment for a moment, but in the next moment, she seriously ordered, "Now, I want you take it all off, my valiant swashbuckler!"

"Okay," Baltor dutifully said.

He did as ordered, and was about ready to put back on his regular attire; however, she grabbed a hold of him and slowly led him to the bed.

Meanwhile, she playfully said, "We have plenty of time to play before we go to dinner, my husband!"

Baltor growled in desire. Brishava squealed in delight....

An hour later or so, he got dressed, brought in the five buckets of hot water and a bar of soap that had been set outside the room about ten minutes earlier by a busboy, and filled the bathtub with water.

She was the first to hop into the tub, and immediately she began the process of washing herself down with soap.

Once done with her bath fifteen minutes later, he hopped into the bathtub, and scrubbed himself down; meanwhile, she began to get dressed in some new and colorful fur garments that she had purchased for herself, fixed up her hair, and then donned a bit of make-up.

By the time he hopped out of the bathtub, she was ready. He began to dry himself off, but his eyes kept falling back on his gorgeous wife—he found that he wanted her yet again! He also saw that her gaze kept falling back on his body as well, but both resisted their urges.

She looked back over to the bags and informed, "Oh, I have several more things for you in the bag, my love. Take a look-see!"

He opened the bag up. He first pulled out a long, brown and white strip of fur; he then pulled out some brown and white fur garments, and finally he pulled out a pair of brown and white fur boots—these he set down onto the floor.

Looking back into the nearly empty bag one final time, his eyes spotted a gold necklace with small gems imbedded throughout its length! He held up the necklace and asked, "Even this?"

"Yes. Why, don't you like the necklace?"

"I like it all very much, thanks—I'm just not used to be being spoiled," he said as he donned the necklace. It was a snug fit, and only enhanced the other golden necklace with the arrowhead.

She playfully replied, "Well, get used to it, mister!"

Once done with getting dressed into his fur clothes and boots, he then began the process of combing his hair with the comb that she had just given him. About a minute later, she handed him the golden hoop that Humonus had gotten him so long ago, so that he could pull his hair through it.

"Thanks," he said, as he continued his grooming procedures.

"No problem." she said, as she continued to stare at Baltor adoringly. Finally, upon observing that he was nearly complete with grooming his hair, she sighed, "No doubt you are *the finest man* I've seen by far, my bright and shining star!" When she said those three italicized words, her voice had stressed dramatically.

"Really?" he asked. "Didn't you tell something like that to me once before?"

"Yes." Brishava sighed, "I have, yet I'll certainly say it thousands of times more in thousands of other ways, I'm sure. You are h-o-t!"

He chuckled out, "Thanks, you know that I feel the same way about you. You are h-o-t! Moreover, I'd like to do something about that if you know what I mean, but I—we can't! Humonus is probably sitting in the dismal corner of the inn, alone with no one to talk to, and desperately waiting for us to come—I'm ready to go, how about you?"

"I'm ready, but have you yet inspected yourself in the mirror, my husband?"

Baltor answered with a question, "Why?"

"Because you should do this from now on before you ever go out in public—ensure for yourself that you look as good as you really do."

He looked in the mirror that was hanging from the wall to his right, and really saw his own image stare back for the first time ever! As he turned to face the mirror, he saw that his manly body had indeed become quite muscular—easily decipherable through the thin fur garments he donned.

His eyes then glanced up to his face—he saw that he had a strong jaw-line with relatively thin lips, dark-brown eyes, slightly angular eyebrows, and a slightly curvy nose—a very manly face!

He finally looked up at his hair, and then noticed the small clump of hair that stuck out at the golden hoop near the top of his head, making his hair look a bit "out of whack."

The second he had patched it up, she responded with a smile, "Let's go."

Together, hand in hand, they headed downstairs to the bar area. Upon entering the bar, Baltor was slightly amazed to see Humonus standing in the middle of the bar, talking happily away to all of the former slave girls with mug in hand—that and a slight slur! In between taking long sips, it was obvious that he was telling some sort of tale through his showy arm gestures.

Meanwhile, the girls all appeared to be completely enrapt.

When Humonus saw his friend, however, he stopped his tale in mid-sentence. With a prompting gesture of his hand, he said with a slightly drunken slur, "Baltor! Come here, my friend."

Baltor replied with a smile, "I'm already on the way."

Humonus added with a laugh, "On the double!"

Baltor began to suspect that Humonus might have been talking about his old training days. With a laugh, he replied, "Sir, yes, sir!" This triggered an outburst from the girls, which confirmed his suspicions.

Once he had speedily reached Humonus, only eight seconds later, he could totally smell the alcohol reeking off his friend's breath—whew!

Humonus wrapped his arm around Baltor and asked the girls, "Did you know that when I first saw him, he was nothing more than a raggedy, thin, and mud-caked boy! Now look at what I've made him into. A simply magnificent beast, he is!"

He then threw a hard slap into Baltor's gut. He didn't even flinch.

The women looked over with admiring glances. Poila was the one to sigh, "Really? I thought you were a prince from the get-go. Nevertheless, what a handsome hero you still are!"

A couple of the other girls began to giggle. Meanwhile, Brishava noticed the looks but said nothing. She didn't feel the pangs of jealousy—well, maybe a little.

Meanwhile, Baltor said in humility, "I just did what I had to do, that's all! Anybody else would have done the same thing."

"Oh come on, Baltor!" said Humonus. "How many people would have dared to fight an entire caravan of slave traders just to become a hero to a bunch of beautiful women, besides me?"

All of the girls giggled for a few moments. Once the giggling had almost subsided, Baltor shrugged his shoulders and laughed, "I don't know. Perhaps everyone, perhaps only us two, I don't know."

He could see from his peripherals that Yaush and Jimnee had just entered the bar. In the Valakanese language, Baltor called out with a smile, "Yaush and Jimnee, we're over here."

Immediately, they began to walk over. Meanwhile, Humonus leaned in close toward Baltor, and whispered, "I must confess, my friend... I'm pretty drunk... and pretty hungry. How about we get something to eat?"

"Good idea, Humonus."

In both languages, Baltor asked, "Are we all ready to sit down and then order some dinner?"

From the nodding of heads, Baltor escorted Humonus over to a table and gently sat him down into a chair. He then took the seat next to his friend, and Brishava took the seat next to Baltor on the other side.

After Yaush had asked the innkeeper for permission, he then linked together several other tables so that they could all sit together. Yaush and Jimnee then took seats on the other side of the table, while the girls filled in the remaining seats.

Humonus must have already arranged dinner with the innkeeper somehow, or someone did—for the moment that they had all gotten comfortable, several of the serving girls began to pass out the steaming plates of steak and potatoes, while the rest began to bring out the mugs of ale.

Amongst those serving girls, Baltor noticed Yeea—she had long known that Baltor was amongst the customers, but had also seen the extremely beautiful woman sitting and clinging next to him, which is why Yeea said nothing but only kept her gaze focused on her task.

Once everything had been set down onto the table, which included mugs, glasses, silverware, etc., almost everyone had begun to eat, except for the serving girls, including Yeea, who left.

Even though Baltor found he was strangely hungry, he had learned how to ignore his hunger pains. However, as the smells of the spicy food wafted up his nose, he could hear his stomach begin to growl.

He wondered for the first time whether he could tolerate eating the food, and so he gave it a shot.

Baltor did find that everything tasted quite delicious, and that he was able to stomach the food and the ale, even though dinner didn't curb his hunger one iota. He was starting to crave fresh blood, once again.

Meanwhile, as Brishava ate, she also watched in amazement as her husband ate the offered food, as she had never forgotten or been allowed to forget that Baltor had his own special diet. Despite her curiosities, she said nothing about her thoughts.

Once dinner had been finished, the conversations began. Baltor found that he was the sole interpreter between the two different languages, which he could still fortunately speak on the fourth night since having feasted last.

Everyone had to ask him the questions. The first important question came from Yaush, as he asked, "Where are the three of you guys going, and why do you have to leave so soon after having just arrived?"

After Baltor had interpreted the question to Humonus and the girls, he then answered in both languages, "Let me say that it's best for everyone that we disappear as soon as possible and for awhile.

As to the why and the where, I really can't answer those questions for all our safeties..."

Even though there were many more important questions asked that night, a very important one that regarded the plans of the girls and their futures.

Baltor interpreted the girls' answers that they had voted to stay in town, acquire a large cabin to accommodate them all, learn the Valakanese language, and get jobs.

Brishava, who happened to have her backpack on her, took it off, opened it, poured out the remaining jewels onto the table, and offered, "This should help you get started!"

At that, the girls all squealed in delight over this unexpected generosity and exclaimed, "Thanks!"

Brishava smiled humbly, nodded her head, and replied, "You are most welcome."

Several more hours of friendly conversation and drinking alcohol passed, as everyone attempted to learn the very basics of the Valakanese language through Baltor—even though Baltor continued to drink wine, he did not even so much as get a slight buzz.

Finally, around two in the morning, Baltor made the sobering announcement that the time had come for he and his wife to go to bed, especially since they were going to have to leave before sunrise. Except for the girls who didn't have to get up early in the morning, everyone else agreed that the time had come to call it a night.

After all the goodnights had been made a few minutes later, Baltor held on to an intoxicated Brishava with Humonus staggering in the lead; meanwhile, Yaush carried a very drunk Jimnee home; finally, the girls continued to drink at the table.

Chelsea, who had not been drinking at all the whole night, hurried over to the staircase, and purposefully blocked Humonus's path at the base of the stairwell.

As Humonus stopped in his tracks and threw an inquisitively drunk look, Chelsea answered the look with a question of her own, "Humonus, guys, would it be all right if... if I—if I came along with y'all?"

Humonus turned his drunken head to look at Baltor and Brishava, who had also stopped in their tracks; Humonus noted that both were nodding their smiling faces in the affirmative.

After a slight pause, Humonus laughed out in a slur, "Surrre... Soo, what room you in... Chelsssha?"

"Close enough. I'm in room six!"

With another laugh, Humonus said, "I'll be at room shix firsht thing in the morning."

"Thanks!" Chelsea said before giving each of them a quick hug, and then getting out of the way, so they could head to their respective bedrooms. She then headed back over to the girls, told everyone the news, said her fond farewells, and then headed to bed.

Brishava, now in her bedroom, had immediately fallen into bed and passed out. Baltor stayed awake all night long preparing for the ensuing journey, which would commence first thing after sunrise.

Not only did he get everything neatly packed up, but he also spent several hours drawing up a map based off memory. The specific route he had taken to safely get through the Bospa Mountains and into the Jungles of Galgaa.

As Baltor already learned the first time—take the wrong turn and there would be some very serious, perhaps deadly repercussions.

By the time he had nearly completed all of his tasks, there remained about an hour or so until sunrise, or so Baltor approximated upon looking through the glass windows that revealed the lightening skies.

He decided that the time had come to change into his new daily/sleeping attire, though he would wait until the last minute to wear the hat with the optional facial visor that had eyeholes. Therefore, he opened the black, leather waterproof bag, and after pulling the hat out by the top of the crown, he dropped it nonchalantly onto the bed, where it came to rest after a slight thudding noise.

The next thing to catch his eye within the bag was the one-piece black suit. Just after having pulled the suit out of the bag, putting it on, and then buttoning it up, he threw a quick glance over into the mirror.

He quietly chuckled, as he muttered aloud, "Looks like kiddy pajamas."

After he had donned the socks that had been lying right under the suit, he pulled the final item out of the bag—the black boots. After securing the boots to his feet, he then donned the necklace Brishava had gotten for him.

He took one last look over to the bed, in order to pick up the hat and put it back into the bag, but then he noticed a string that was now poking out from underneath the visor.

He picked up the hat and then flipped it, while noting in surprise that Brishava had added two extra features to the hat, since last he saw it. Not only did the hat now have a front pocket that held the now pocketed facial visor, yet it also had a thick, black string sewn into the opposite ends at the base of the crown.

He realized that whenever he didn't want to wear the hat on his head, he could simply hang the cord around his neck, thus allowing the hat to hang loosely upon his back.

After choosing the second route, he finally strapped on the black sheath that still held his beloved sword, and looked again into the mirror. Instead of laughing this time, there was only a very pleased smile imbedded upon his face, while his head nodded in approval at the man who nodded right back in the mirror.

Several seconds later, he wondered at how much time he had until sunrise, so he opened his bedroom door, peeked out the window on the other side of the hallway, which revealed the colors of dawn that fast approaching. There was still about a half an hour or so left until sunrise, so he closed the door, walked back over to Brishava, who was still sleeping in bed, and ever so gently shook her while calling her name.

"Hmmm?" she finally responded very sleepily.

"It's almost time to wake up. Everything's packed, and hot water will be on its way shortly, so you can take a bath. Right now, I need to talk to Humonus about something important, which he will later explain to you when you're conscious, so I'll be right back—love you!"

After planting a light kiss on her cheek, Baltor grabbed the map, exited the bedroom, and closed the door behind him. He then walked over to Humonus's room, and knocked on the door.

A few moments later, Humonus said from the other side of the door, "Come in."

Baltor opened the door, entered, and then closed the door behind him. As he turned back around, he noticed that Humonus was still packing his belongings away, and that Chelsea soundly slept on the bed.

A few moments later, Baltor half whispered, "Humonus, I made a map that will get us to the Galgaa Jungles safely. It is important that I explain this map to you right now. Later, you can explain it to Brishava and Chelsea.

"Most likely, I'll be sleep by the time we leave, so you'll have to carry me to the wagon parked behind Yaush's barn. You know where that's at, right?"

Humonus answered, "Yeah, I know where Yaush's barn is. Hold one more second... okay." He then stopped packing, and met Baltor halfway in the bedroom. It only took Baltor several minutes to explain the route based off his map, while Humonus continuously nodded his head in understanding.

Once completed with the directions, Baltor concluded, "...and that's it!"

"Gotcha, buddy," Humonus replied, "I'll explain the map to Brishava and Chelsea later, as you requested. Once I'm done packing, we'll meet you over at your room, okay?"

"Okay."

Baltor exited the room, and he headed back to his room. Immediately upon entering, he became quite a bit surprised to see Yaush and Jimnee standing inside.

Brishava was now awake yet still only wearing her pajamas. Once Baltor had closed the door behind him, he turned around, and noted that Yaush was looking very sad.

In confirmation, Yaush said in a sad tone of voice, "My friend, I am going to miss you so much!"

Baltor responded, "And I you, my friend!"

Yaush appeared to fight back some tears, as he said with his arms extended out, "Come here."

Baltor approached and accepted the tight hug from Yaush. A minute passed until Yaush finally released his embrace, and Baltor could see tears sprout down the giant's face.

Through his unabated tears, Yaush said, "You must promise me that you'll come back again. You and your beautiful wife can stay in our home anytime!"

While trying to fight back tears, Baltor replied, "I swear that I will come back, but only once our situation has fully been resolved."

Yaush replied seriously, "I know that you are the man to resolve any situation that comes your way. And I know that Brishava is the woman to help and support you along the way! Did you know that the two of you are soulmates, just like me and Jimnee?"

Without waiting for a response, Yaush immediately walked over to where Brishava stood—though she listened, she did not understand a word they said.

Upon drawing near, Yaush extended his massive arms out and gave her a tight hug for a few moments. He then relaxed the hug until he looked down into her eyes, and said, "Baltor, please tell Brishava, 'It truly was a pleasure, and an honor, to meet you!'"

Baltor interpreted.

Brishava responded, "Tell Yaush that rarely have I met someone who is as noble as he! And I've met many nobles."

Baltor interpreted.

Jimnee then walked over to Baltor, gave him a tight hug, and with tears flowing out of her eyes, she said, "Baltor, as my husband says, you two are more than welcome to stay at our home at any time. If you should ever need any more clothes made, you'll always know where to come!"

She released her hold on Baltor, but then immediately clasped onto his hands as she laughed, "Oh—did you know some of the townsfolk of Valakan conjured a little nickname for you after you left the first time? They began to call you, 'Volfenpakslaer'!"

Baltor's mind had already instantly translated the words as "the slayer of a whole pack of wolves!" As he laughed, he gave Jimnee another tight embrace; from all the high emotions in the room, he could no longer fight back the bloody tears that began to pour from his eye sockets.

As soon as Jimnee pulled back from the hug, and she saw all the blood on Baltor's face, she stammered out in shock, "My God? What, what is this—blood pouring from your eyes?"

Baltor wiped the tears, which only smeared the blood further upon his face as he tried to explain, "I've obtained a mysterious illness from the jungles."

"How strange," Yaush added with astonishment—Jimnee replied at the same time, "Oh my goodness!"

Even though Brishava couldn't understand the language, she understood the strange and shocked expressions, and said to Baltor, "They're wondering about your illness, aren't they? Tell them that your illness may be strange—but that you are the most noble man I've ever met!"

While still trying to wipe off the remaining blood with his hands, Baltor translated the words.

Jimnee spoke first, "Tell Brishava that I know this to be true, but I've never seen anything quite like it before, and I, well, we were just in shock, that's all. I am sorry if our comments hurt you, or your husband's feelings."

As Baltor translated, Brishava soon relaxed. Once completed, she then replied with a curtsy, "Gemne mao, Jimnee."

Just then, a knock on the door interrupted their conversation. Brishava walked over to the door and opened it, and there stood Humonus and Chelsea with bags in hand.

There was still a tad bit of dried blood on Baltor's face that he had missed—Jimnee noticed it, licked the sleeve of her shirt, and then quickly wiped the blood off until gone.

Humonus didn't step in the room, yet instead asked, "Well guys—are we ready to go?"

Baltor said, "Yeah, just about. Are you ready, honey?"

"I haven't taken my bath or gotten dressed yet in my traveling attire."

Humonus asked, "You haven't? Why not?"

"Long story, Humonus," Brishava answered. "Give us ten more minutes and we'll be ready to go."

Baltor's gaze fell to the window, and the skies that were seriously lighting up—he figured it'd be about two to three minutes until the sun rose.

"Baltor, please tell your friends, Yaush and Jimnee," Humonus said, "that it was a pleasure to meet them."

Baltor translated.

"And tell Humonus and Chelsea the same thing," was Jimnee's response.

Baltor translated. He then added in Valakanese, "Oh, we'll all be dropping by to pick up the wagon and five horses, including Grasha—someone will have to ride her separately as we will use her for scouting purposes. As I will be sound asleep very soon, I must make my final farewell now. My friends, Yaush and Jimnee— farewell!"

At the same time, Yaush and Jimnee came over and gave Baltor a group hug, while saying, "Farewell!" Brishava joined in a moment later. A few moments later Humonus and Chelsea joined in on the group hug.

About twenty seconds later, once the hug had been released, Yaush and Jimnee gave their farewells to Humonus and Chelsea, and then exited the room; hand in hand, Yaush and Jimnee returned home.

Once gone, Humonus informed, "We'll be back in the room, whenever you guys are ready."

Brishava replied, "Okay."

After Chelsea and Humonus had left, Brishava took off her nightclothes and hopped in the still-hot bathtub—meanwhile, Baltor pulled out the visor, laid the hat and visor right over his face and neck, and fell asleep upon the bed.

Once Brishava was ready to go, she retrieved Humonus and Chelsea. Together they walked to Yaush's place, retrieved four of their horses from the barn, attaching them to tow the wagon— Grasha was, only minutes later, ready to go with her own saddle and reins.

After saying their final farewells to Yaush and Jimnee, they traveled to the inn. Brishava rode on Grasha.

Upon arrival at the inn, they packed everything up into the back of the wagon, which included Baltor's sleeping body, and once everyone had taken a quick potty break, the group began to make their way east. By the time they left the borders of Valakan, it was an hour and a half after sunrise.

CHAPTER XXVII

For the entire day, filled mostly with cloudy skies and periodical light rains, Humonus followed the directions of the map, all the while scouting the areas out for danger and the best routes for the wagon—he rode upon Grasha. All the while, either Brishava or Chelsea steered the wagon, and Baltor slept in the back.

Never did they take any breaks, other than breakfast, lunch, and one other fifteen-minute break in the late afternoon.

That evening, around seven or so, the rain had once again stopped for the dozenth time. It was then that Humonus found a perfect spot for them to camp, which area was a small clearing between three tree-covered mountains. Immediately the girls began the process of setting up a four-man tent, while he began building a campfire using timber they had stored in the back of the wagon.

Just after the sun had set about forty minutes later, Baltor awoke feeling famished! Without haste, he set his hat onto the bag, and booked out of camp at top speed.

As Baltor was starving, his single mission was to scour the area out for fresh animal blood. Very fortunate for him, it only took four and a half minutes to track down and capture a fox, seven more minutes to consume its blood, fifteen minutes to track a sheep down and consume that, and fifteen minutes to get back to camp.

By the time he had returned, feeling a little better but still a little hungry, he saw that the camp was now fully set up with a tent and a campfire. Furthermore, a metallic tripod grill stood over the fire itself, which grill held a small, black cauldron that had steam pouring out. He didn't see either girl, but Humonus was continuously stirring something in the cauldron with a large spoon.

"Where'd you go, Baltor?" Humonus asked, while looking over.

"I checked the area out for about a mile every direction. Area's clear."

"Great," was Humonus's even reply. "Dinner will be ready in an hour... my secret-recipe chicken stew tonight! Oh, and in case you're wondering, the girls are reorganizing the wagon."

"Perfect," Baltor said contentedly, before plopping down near the fire and relaxing.

Nearly an hour later, they all silently ate the stew, because it turned out to be that delicious—food, unfortunately, that did nothing to quench Baltor's hunger pains! Thus, when no one was looking, he tied a strip of cloth tightly around his waist, under his shirt.

After everyone but Baltor had drunk a few rounds of ale, coupled with some light and pleasant conversations, Humonus, Brishava and Chelsea went to sleep in the tent.

All night long, Baltor stayed awake and guarded their camp, which night passed on by without incident.

About an hour before sunrise, after having cooked breakfast of eggs and bacon in a frying pan, Baltor woke everyone up by announcing, "Breakfast!"

Following breakfast, in which Baltor was the only one still very, very hungry even though he ate, they began to break camp. Once complete, he climbed into the back of the wagon, put on his sleeping clothes and hat, and fell asleep the very second the sun rose.

As soon as the rest of the group was ready to go, only a minute after the sun had risen on this beautiful day without any clouds, they continued their journey east. Early that evening, they stopped at another place that Humonus thought looked good to camp at.

Sometime after they had set up camp, between then and the time that Baltor awoke right at sunset, he had a strange dream, though he could not recall any of the details except for one—there was a huge white bear involved.

When he awoke right after sunset and climbed out the wagon, he saw that Humonus lay on the ground nearby with his eyes closed, and then he noticed that there were several additional layers of clothing wrapped around his chest and back. The girls were kneeling on either side of him.

Upon seeing the pained expression upon Humonus's face, Baltor asked with great concern, "What the hell happened? You all right?" It was only then when he inhaled that he smelled iron in the air.

Humonus first slowly opened his eyes, and then slowly turned his head until he faced Baltor. With pain etched into his half-whispering voice, he began to explain, "While you were asleep about thirty minutes ago, Brishava and Chelsea had left to take a bath in the lagoon located nearby..."

After painfully wincing aloud, he said, "Meanwhile, I was happily roasting a couple of rabbits for our dinner tonight, and stupidly wasn't paying attention to my surroundings."

At this point in Humonus's story, he was forced to take a lengthy pause, due to yet another painful spasm in his chest.

Therefore, Chelsea who had already heard the story, continued, "A giant white bear also smelled the meat Humonus was cooking. Not even ten minutes ago, it quietly entered the camp directly right behind Humonus, at which point he was turning the skew right next to the fire, and then he said that—"

Humonus, who had just put his hand on Chelsea's arm to silence her, then weakly interrupted, "That by the time I turned around, the bear was on all fours about three feet away from where I stood, while the fire pit was only about two feet behind me."

He took another lengthy pause, and just as Chelsea was about to continue in the story, he pointed his index finger up into the air for her to remain silent.

About twenty seconds later, he finally continued, "In the next moment, I attempted to nicely shoo him away as he was on all fours, but he wouldn't go away—no matter what!

"Not three seconds later, he decides to get mad at me, probably because I was standing in the way of the food, and he rears back onto his hind paws, growing to fifteen feet tall while growling angrily at me."

When Humonus took still another lengthy pause, Chelsea didn't say anything this time, nor did anyone else.

Perhaps ten seconds later, he finally continued, "By this time, I realized that I was in serious danger, and I thought had already planned out a good solution to this problem—I was oh so very wrong!"

Upon hearing all of this, Baltor looked quite shocked, especially since he was hearing it from his friend, teacher, and truly a master thief, though not technically. When Humonus didn't continue a minute later, he had to ask, "What was your plan?"

"It was my plan to wait for him to drop down onto all fours, figuring that he would charge at me, and that just before reaching me, I would have rolled to the right or left, and he would plunge into the fire—he didn't do that!"

"What did he do?"

"I kid you not—this bear had arms that were five feet long! I t threw one unexpected swipe of his paw into my direction, and my chest was already shredded open!"

Chelsea gently lifted up the clothing on Humonus's chest; Baltor saw three bleeding slashes that spanned from one side of his chest to the other. The smell of the blood was *deliciously intoxicating*!

Barely was Baltor able to resist the vampire urges by forcibly looking away, not breathe in, and ask, "Where's the bear now?"

"On the far side of the fire pit—dead," Chelsea answered.

Humonus added with weak excitement, "Yeah—I got so mad that I pulled my daggers out of my belt, and then I leapt up at him, while swinging both of my daggers up and at him! Only a split second later, each dagger went through each eyeball and both plunged into his brain, instantly killing him—they did!"

Still fighting the urges, Baltor asked, "Should we go back to Valakan, and get you some medical treatment?"

"No, my friend," Humonus answered, "we can do that here. Thankfully, I brought my first-aid kit, located in the back of the wagon, which kit has disinfectant, bandages, and even better, a week's worth of that numbing elixir. Can you get that for me Chelsea, please?"

"Got ya, babe," she replied before hurrying for the wagon.

Meanwhile, Humonus said, "After I'm all bandaged up, I'll need some help into the back of the wagon, and so long as whoever's driving the wagon tomorrow goes real slow because it is a very bumpy ride, especially around these mountains... then we can be on our merry way."

After wincing very loud in pain, he added with a small smile, "Trust me, my friend of friends—I'll be all right."

"Are you sure?" Baltor asked, still not convinced.

"Yeah, I'm sure," Humonus answered confidently.

Cocking his head to the side, Baltor said, "Okay..."

It was then that Chelsea returned with the kit. Baltor excused himself by saying, "I'll be back, guys. Gonna check the area out. I know you two girls can help him with the medical procedure... right?" What he didn't say was that he needed blood, oh so bad!

"Right," Brishava was the first to answer.

Right away, he left camp, so he could hunt.

Perhaps an hour later, he finally ran across a pack of coyotes ... six of them he hunted, one after the other, and consumed. Barely did any of this animal blood help, as his stomach ever so painfully clenched and unclenched—*still*!

On his way back to camp, he began to visually contemplate the possibility of taking his warhorse tonight and galloping her at top speed to the cannibal tribe, perhaps four hundred miles and many weeks away, and feast. After all, it had long ago been his top-secret plan to use the cannibals as dinner for many years to come.

Specifically, his thoughtful conclusions were: *Because neither girl knows how to fight, and Humonus can't fight, I have no choice but to stay and protect. While, of course, continuously resisting the bloodthirsty vampire inside me, which is getting harder and harder to control... Why, I almost took a bite into his neck tonight!*

Right away upon his return, he saw that Brishava and Chelsea had fallen asleep on the ground, perhaps thirteen feet away from the campfire—in turn, he picked each girl up and lay her down in the tent, before pulling guard duty all night long.

The next morning after breakfast Brishava had cooked and served, Chelsea changed all of Humonus's bandages in the back of the wagon, noting happily to everyone that the wounds had finally stopped bleeding—now in a soft-scab form.

Only after she had exited, nearly five minutes later, did Baltor enter with suit on. He forthwith leaned against the railing, put the hat and visor on, and fell asleep as the sun rose only seconds later.

A minute-or-so later, Chelsea began steering the wagon at half the speed, while Brishava rode on Grasha, and the two men rode in the back and slept: The group continued riding east.

As the days and nights passed, Humonus slowly got better and stronger; still, due to their slow movement, it took a week and a half before they reached the jungles. By the time they entered, he was almost back to full health, and they could ride at a normal speed. Needful to say, nearly every waking moment was torturous for poor Baltor; only his even stronger love for his wife kept him going....

Three days later, Humonus finally regained full mobility without any pain. That night, Baltor took his nightly disappearance for food.

However, unlike the previous times where he hunted in the vicinity on foot, this time he steered his horse through the wide variety of jungle terrains (frequently at a gallop). S o m e h o w he knew that the cannibals' village lay somewhere nearby to the southeast. *Perhaps fifty or sixty miles away?*

Shortly before midnight, he luckily chanced upon an unsuspecting cannibal guard patrolling the external borders of their territory, perhaps an eighth of a mile away from Baltor's location.

Therefore, he climbed off his horse, ran about a hundred feet, transformed into the vompareus, flew on over and feasted on the man's blood. At the end of this delicious feast, Baltor felt not only satisfied and powerful, yet for the first time in a very, very long time—*full!*!

Although he knew he could have flown anywhere he wanted to in the world, he had never forgotten that he had his warhorse to contend with, and so he transformed back into a human, and rode Grasha back to camp ... they arrived a little before four in the morning.

Not surprisingly, Humonus was up and guarding with sword drawn. Upon seeing that it was Baltor, he sheathed his sword and sleepily asked, "So.... anything to report?"

"Nothing bad," Baltor said, while climbing down to his feet and tethering his horse to a tree. "Why don't you get yourself some sleep? It's my turn for guard duty anyway."

"Ok, buddy...."

The next morning before sunrise, Baltor whistled a very chipper tune as he cooked breakfast of pancakes and sausage for everyone. After all, for the first time in weeks, he wasn't hungry one iota. Once ready, he woke each person up in turn, by handing that person a plate of food that had a fork stuffed into it.

It took another two solid days and nights of traveling, without stopping to camp or take hardly any breaks at all, before the group finally reached the borders of Chao-chu-sha-maen.

Nearly an hour after sunset, the group finally arrived at the village's outskirts. Baltor was in the lead, riding on his warhorse. Humonus steered the wagon, while the girls sat beside him.

It was then that Baltor signaled for Humonus to park the wagon—he did. As soon as they climbed off, stood on their feet and began to stretch out, Brishava, Chelsea and Humonus looked around in amazement—for never before had the latter two seen black people. Brishava, on the other hand, had seen them quite a few times in her life, either visiting royalty or their slaves: She was amazed because these people were primitive, and short.

Despite their amazements, they followed behind Baltor after he had tethered his horse to a tree, waved for them to follow and walked into the village. The villagers remembered Baltor from his first visit, for there was no alarm—just curiosity at these newcomers, so they stopped whatever they were doing and also began to follow.

Soon enough, the very large group of people reached the tribal palace—with Baltor still in the lead. As he approached the entryway, neither of the two guards crossed their spears just before he could enter. Surprisingly, they let him pass.

Only a split-second after Baltor had entered the palace, however, he heard the guards click their spears together, barring everyone else entry. Including his friends and wife.

331

Right away, Baltor cocked just his head around and said nonchalantly, "Just wait a little bit, guys. Trust me, you're completely safe—I'll be back as soon as I can."

After the group nodded, Baltor looked forward, before briskly making his way up to the throne room.

As before, at the throne room's entryway, there were the two guards with spears. Baltor definitely expected these guards to cross their spears before him, forbidding him entry; that is, until the king, queen, or prince had granted permission.

Even more surprise came to Baltor when those two guards didn't cross their spears this time, thus allowing him to enter the throne room, which he did.

As his feet walked toward the three thrones, his eyes saw that the king, queen and prince all bore excited smiles upon their faces!

Once he had neared, Baltor bowed in the same way he had done just before he left the last time.

When he looked back up, a few moments later, he saw that the prince was now standing up, and had begun to use the sign language; he drew the symbol of the tower into the air.

Baltor next cocked his head from side to side, which indicated the affirmative. He then pointed his own index finger into the air, pointed at his own mouth, pointed at Prince Cheo's mouth, and then said in Pavelian, "How are you doing, Prince Cheo?"

Right away, the prince looked very confused, looked to his parents, and then said something in less than five seconds.

Baltor's mind heard Prince Cheo's words interpret into, "I believe he wants me to speak to him. As we've clearly proven, however, there is no way for him to speak our language or for us to learn his, other than names, drawings, and a very crude form of sign language—of course!"

The king asked something in his native tongue, which Baltor's mind interpreted a bit faster, "Why don't you try saying something to him?"

As Baltor stood back onto his feet, Prince Cheo asked in his own language, "So... you found the tower?"

Baltor threw a smile, and replied slowly in their tongue, "Yes... I... did."

Everyone in the room threw gasps of shock at the same time!

Once silence filled the room, a few moments later, Baltor added, "Your highnesses, the language barriers that we once had no longer apply. From now on, we can now communicate by speech."

More gasps of shock coursed throughout the room!

With a stammer, Prince Cheo was finally able to ask, "How—how did you master our language while you were away, and with no one to teach you?"

Baltor evenly answered, "To answer your question requires understanding a bit of my history, which I will now commence to explain. I am from a city called Pavelus, which city consists of a population of around one hundred and twenty thousand—a massive and powerful city that is far, far, far away from here."

Before Baltor had a chance to continue with his briefing, he became interrupted as every last one of the villagers excitedly yelped out the word "coo" or the word "caw!"

His mind instantly interpreted that "this custom" was similar to his own of saying "ooh" or "aah" whenever being utterly amazed.

Continuing his briefing only five seconds after he had stopped, he said, "Now the reason I have traveled such a great distance is because of my mission to locate the tower that I had found drawn upon an ancient map and retrieve a magical item that is a rod. Though I no longer have this rod in my possession, it magically taught me how to overcome any language barriers, as you guys have just learned."

Again came the "coo" or the "caw," this time with a mega amount of excitement and happiness, which Baltor's mind easily interpreted as cheering!

"Unfortunately," he added, "before I had left the jungles, I also contracted a mysterious illness which prevents me from bearing the sun's rays at all, which makes me nocturnal. Also, I have my own very special diet that if I don't live by religiously, I will die within days."

This time, the cooing or the cawing from the villagers either sounded sympathetic, sad, shocked, and/or horror-stricken—Baltor's mind didn't have to interpret a thing.

The king replied with a thoughtful look, "I am sorry to hear about your illness, but is it wrong of me to rejoice in the fact that we can now fully communicate?"

"No, your majesty, the king—it is not wrong of you at all to rejoice. As for my illness, I deal with it as best I can."

The prince said excitedly, "Welcome back to Chao-chu-sha-maen, my brother! So tell me, and please do not take offense, but is there a particular reason that you have traveled all the way back here so soon, Prince Baltor?"

Baltor's mind seriously didn't acknowledge the added title, as his mouth explained, "Yes, there is—I have several friends of mine waiting outside. We are on the run from others who wish to take away our happiness, and our lives. For a time, we will need a place to stay, perhaps for quite awhile."

After a sigh, Baltor hesitantly suggested in the form of a question, "I was hoping that maybe we could stay here, if your highnesses would be so gracious?"

The queen answered, "Prince Baltor, you and your friends are most welcome here. Since your departure, we all have missed you very greatly!"

Baltor smiled. Suddenly, the added title registered in his brain, and then he asked with doubt to his voice, "My Queen, did I hear you just call me a prince, or am I simply misinterpreting what you're saying?"

Instead of her or anyone else answering, the king looked over to a servant and informed, "Allow his friends, and ours, to enter."

The servant bowed, just before running out of the throne room, up to the window, and cawing twice to the guards downstairs to allow Baltor's friends to enter.

The prince walked in front of Baltor, touched his own face just below the eye, and then put that pinky upon Baltor's forehead. He asked, "You know that you are also royalty here, right?"

Baltor looked confused at that, as he asked, "What do you mean?"

"We have been soul brothers since the day you left, which officially makes you a prince by our customs," Prince Cheo informed.

"I did not know that," Baltor said. A smile crossed his lips as he added, "My brother."

The two princes gave each other a brotherly hug, just as the rest of the group slowly entered the throne room, looking about in wonder and amazement.

"Tell your friends to approach," the king said.

Baltor looked back, and called out in Pavelian, "Guys. The royalty of this land wish to meet you."

They approached closer. Once they had neared the area, they all bowed almost in unison.

"Tell them," the queen said, "that they are most welcome to stay within our lands for as long as they wish."

Baltor interpreted.

The group verbally expressed their sincerest gratitude, to which Baltor translated.

A moment later, the king, queen, and prince all began cocking their heads from side to side.

Baltor informed, "By the way, guys, when they do that head gesture, it means yes. When they roll their heads around in a circle, that means no. Okay?"

"Okay." the group stated.

As Baltor's eyes scanned Brishava for a moment, a proud smile crossed his face. A few moments later, he said in the villagers' language, "There is one more part of my history that I need to inform you all."

"What is that?" Cheo asked with curiosity.

"I have since become married, and this." Baltor said. He gestured his right hand toward Brishava, and introduced, "This... is my beloved wife, Brishava!"

Even though Brishava couldn't even begin to understand what her husband had just said in under a second, she assumed that he was introducing her, and so she curtsied toward the thrones.

Cheo looked very surprised to hear this information, yet he said a few moments later, "Tell *Princess* Brishava, as she is your wife, that it is an honor to meet her!"

Baltor interpreted.

He then fully explained to the group that he had been designated a prince in this land, and that Brishava was now a princess here, as well!

For a moment, Brishava's face betrayed bewilderment and awe at this additional entitlement, but then she smiled, nodded, and then curtsied before the thrones.

Out of respect, Humonus and Chelsea both bowed before Prince Baltor and the princess of two countries, Brishava.

Baltor responded, "My friends, that's not necessary."

Humonus then replied, "Oh, but it is necessary, your highness!"

The king declared emphatically, "Tomorrow night, there shall be both a coronation, and then a celebration for the return of Prince Baltor and his bride, Princess Brishava!"

Many cheers rang out in the room, but Baltor's friends looked around in confusion.

Once the din had quieted a minute later, he translated what the king had just said—in turn, Humonus and Chelsea began to cheer, and then the villagers joined in yet again. Baltor and Brishava both remained humble. That night they all partied quite hearty!

The following morning, while Baltor still slept in his special clothes within a hut designated for him and Brishava, the villagers began packing a tar-like substance into the sides of the hut, which would make the room sunlight impenetrable during the day.

Brishava couldn't take the smell of the substance, so she exited the hut and passed out in Humonus and Chelsea's hut.

Only moments after sunset the following evening, after Baltor had removed his hat, he saw an old woman who had already entered the hut.

With the torch this villager held in her left hand, she was just about to light a torch posted about four feet away from the front door.

After she had lit the torch, Baltor sat up in bed. He then said in the villagers' language, "Good evening."

The villager bowed and replied, "Good evening to you, Prince Baltor. My name is Pa-cheu. Just so you know, it has been assigned to me to light the torch in your hut just after sunset every night by King-Cha-Abduja-Chem-Masgaran-Chai. This way you will know that the sun has indeed set."

"Oh." he replied with a smile, "well, thank you, Pa-cheu."

"It is my pleasure to serve you, my prince," she said with a toothless smile, bowed, and exited the hut.

That night, Baltor and Brishava were tribally crowned a prince and princess of the Chao-chu-sha-maen village.

Following the coronations, the partying commenced that lasted the entire night!

The next evening, unusually shaped clouds filled the skies. Just as the sun was about to set, the skies were infuriated with nearly a half dozen colors—Baltor was still sleeping of course.

Suddenly, the villagers began to get very excited as they dropped to the ground on their backs, extended their arms and hands into the air, and appeared to be clutching for the very skies.

Meanwhile, Brishava was eating dinner with Humonus and Chelsea outside, and the group of friends stared confusedly at the spastic villagers.

Even more confusing to the three was the moment the colors in the dusky sky had started to fade, the villagers got back to their feet, and acted as if nothing at all had happened.

A few minutes later, as soon as Baltor had arrived at their hut, he saw Brishava, Humonus, and Chelsea still sitting at a table and chatting quietly amongst one another.

Once Baltor had drawn near, Humonus was the first to look up and greet, "Good evening, Your Highness!"

A moment later, the group similarly greeted Baltor.

He responded with a smile, "Good evening to you all, my friends, but please, just call me Baltor."

Humonus asked, "Say Baltor, can you tell me why the villagers get so worked up whenever the sun is about to set and the skies are infuriated with colors?"

Baltor laughed as he replied, "I've seen them do this before, during my last visit here. However, to be honest with you, I have no idea what it means. Let's go ask Prince Cheo, okay?"

"Good idea."

Once they had found Cheo, who was currently sitting in the throne room, Baltor asked him, "We've got a question. What's with the ritual that you guys do at every colorful sunset?"

"Oh that?" Cheo asked. "This is our way of communicating with our God who shines his beautiful lights upon us! Did you not know that Chao-chu-sha-maen means 'the nation of heavenly lights'?"

"No, I didn't—thanks." Baltor next translated this information to the group.

Because Brishava, Humonus, and Chelsea could not learn even the basics of the verbal language, other than shortened versions of peoples' names, Baltor began to teach them the sign language that he and Cheo had already begun to expand, along with the rest of the tribe.

For the next couple of months, as the group stayed in the village, there were no incidents to report regarding the cannibals' village, which was only twenty-eight miles to the south of this village.

That was—except for the weekly trips that Baltor would make in order to quench the beast. He soon gained a new and powerful psychic ability to read minds, amongst his other ones—all but one of his powers lasted three days before they faded away, which power he classified: "interpreting unknown languages."

Two months and five nights after their arrival, however, the cannibal tribe launched a surprise attack, perhaps in retaliation to the mysterious attacks launched upon their own members!

Unfortunately, fifteen villagers had been killed before they were able to drive back the bloodthirsty cannibals, with Baltor and Humonus's help!

Fortune only smiled on the villagers that it had been a night attack and not a day, or Baltor would not have been able to help, and they might have all lost the battle and their lives.

Only a half an hour after the last of the cannibals had retreated back home, King Cha immediately called a meeting in the throne room for the whole tribe, and he even invited the group to join.

Once fully assembled, two minutes later, he declared, "Chao-chu-sha-maen can no longer tolerate these merciless attacks from

Conga-chasa-casua-craen. Enough is enough! The time has come for war to be declared!"

Throughout the room, many whooping noises erupted from the villagers—Baltor's mind translated that the name of the cannibals' village actually meant, "The warring gods that dominate over the blood-thirsty gorilla and vulture!"

Once the whooping noises had ceased, Baltor verbally translated the king's message to his Pavelian-speaking friends.

The king waited for Baltor to finish, and then he spoke to Baltor, "Tell your friends that our wars are not your wars. You and your friends may stay here if you wish."

As Baltor translated the message to the group, Humonus began stroking his bearded face while he squinted.

Once translated, Humonus pointed his index finger into the sky, and suggested, "Tell King Cha that I have a better plan! What if we were to train the villagers in our fighting style? Give it a year, that's all we'll need, and then we can decimate the cannibals for good. In the meantime, we can also help the villagers to build some defensive fortifications around the village, in order to give us better protection. Ask him."

The plan sounded good in Baltor's opinion, so he translated the words to the king and queen and prince.

King Cha said, "Tell Humonus that my warriors already know how to fight!"

Instead of translating the words to Humonus, Baltor replied, "Not like this." In Pavelian, he barked, "Humonus, face me!"

Humonus did.

"Humonus, attack me!"

Humonus threw a punch at Baltor, aimed for his face—easily, Baltor caught the fist, grabbed his wrist, and simply twisted—Humonus's body flew over Baltor's, just before slamming hard into the ground.

Baltor continued to twist on his wrist until Humonus yelped out in pain, and slapped the floor hard with his hand.

Baltor let go, faced the king, queen, and prince, and then bowed—throughout and after the split-second demonstration, they all bore amazed and shocked expressions upon their faces.

After taking two steps back, Baltor added, "This is but a taste of what we can teach your troops."

Several more moments of silence had passed. The queen was the next to ask, "Can we see more, please?"

"Of course, Queen Che-Baesucse," Baltor said with a smile.

For the next hour, Baltor and Humonus demonstrated nearly two dozen more techniques of their fighting skills with blinding speeds. The second that the demonstrations were over, the king, queen, and prince immediately agreed to Humonus's idea.

It only took two days of hard work to set up a good defensive perimeter—also thanks to Humonus's ideas. What they did was to collect an enormous amount of bamboo sticks, create spears out of them, and bury one-quarter of the spears' lengths into the ground while angling the sharp points in an outwards direction around the entire village, except for two different positions where constant guards were set.

Once the defenses were completed, Humonus and Baltor then began to teach the villagers how to fight.

In total, there were one hundred and twenty-seven villagers that attended class, ranging from ten to sixty years old. Brishava and Chelsea even took classes.

During these night classes, Humonus would instruct the lessons and the movements; meanwhile, Baltor translated, and typically was the dummy—no pun intended.

When not learning martial arts, eating, partying, or sleeping—everyone (friends, villagers, and royalty) would all come together to learn, enhance, and master the sign language.

After about three months' time had passed, Humonus got good enough where he could teach solely through the art of motion or sign language. No more yelling for him, not that it did any good anyway, as far as the villagers were concerned. They actually thought it very funny whenever Humonus would yell and his face turned beet red.

By the end of the year, there were one hundred and thirty-one highly skilled warriors of the Chao-chu-sha-maen tribe. Of course, Baltor, Humonus, Brishava, and Chelsea were among the numbers. In return, the Chao-chu-sha-maen taught the entire group how to do ventriloquism, the art of casting their voices into other locations.

Thanks to Humonus's strategic planning, a "battle-plan" formed that all immediately agreed was sound. The army quickly prepared for the trip and the upcoming battle, and then they left just after sunset.

Just before sunrise, the army camped about halfway to the cannibals' village. That day, there were no incidents or encounters at all while Baltor slept in the back of the wagon—night came, he woke up, hopped onto Grasha, and the troops moved on.

About an hour before the battle was to commence, at two in the morning, Baltor had gone ahead of his troops and killed an unsuspecting cannibal guard.

With his powers once again in full force, he headed back—he had learned that the original vulture-woman had been killed in the same battle when he and the prince had escaped, but the same gorilla-man was still alive.

Nearly three in the morning, the three squadrons of forty troops split up, and silently surrounded the cannibals' village—Cheo led the first squadron of troops, Baltor led the second, and Humonus led the final.

At four in the morning, once the simulated bird-cries erupted throughout the jungle—the army silently stormed into the village, eliminating anyone that was armed!

Not even two minutes had passed before the war was over, as most of the cannibals surrendered without a fight. There were only twelve casualties total—all of them were the enemy. Those cannibals that survived were gathered into the center of the village, right in front of the fire pit.

Without a word spoken, Baltor sliced the ringleader's head off before he could even think to react, and then he cocked his head from side to side at Cheo.

Cheo then proclaimed, "Cannibalism shall no longer be allowed here! Attacks upon the village of Chao-chu-sha-maen will not be tolerated either! We shall be leaving troops to ensure that our rules remain in place. If so much as one of our soldiers gets hurt, we shall decimate you all completely! Do you understand?"

The villagers responded by cocking their heads from side to side. All but fifty of the glorious warriors returned home; those fifty remained behind to guard.

It was quite ironic that at the beginning of the second night of their journey back, Baltor happened to observe these rather large gray-colored bats with huge wings circling and landing at a green bush filled with red berries not too far away.

He asked a nearby tribesman, named Hoo, "Are those bats?"

Hoo replied, "Those are vampire bats, my prince."

"Vampire bats," Baltor asked, "What are they doing at the bush?"

"They are eating the berries from the cah-su-mahn bush. That is why we never cut them down, so that they will not feast on us, my prince."

"Really," Baltor replied, just before climbing off his horse. He began to walk closer, but Hoo stuck out his arm to block his path.

With a lot of worry in his voice, Hoo warned, "My prince, I wouldn't get any closer to them if I was you—they will bite!"

Baltor laughed, "You—you guys go on ahead without me. I'll catch up in a minute. That's an order from your prince."

He waited until everyone was out of sight, before tethering his horse to a nearby true. He next walked over to the bush, observing that the giant bats did not pay him the slightest bit of heed. He picked up a berry and chewed on it—it was *wonderfully delicious*!

After he ate a dozen more berries, he could already tell that the juices were actually *quenching his vampiric thirsts*—suddenly Baltor realized with *ever-growing excitement* that he would no longer have to be a killer to survive!!

Several more months passed, as the group stayed safely hidden away in the massive jungle province of Chao-chu-sha-maen, now consisting of the two villages, as well approximately a thousand square miles of land.

During one of those nights, at a bonfire party, Baltor had finally learned the mystery from Prince Cheo of how he had acquired Baltor's possessions, right before he had left for the tower long ago. The day after Baltor's arrival to their village, several kids had been playing in a large pile of dead leaves in their playground, and there they were just lying inside—his map, saber and sheath. Nearly right away the kids delivered the objects to their parents, who delivered to the prince. For some unknown reason, Prince Cheo suspected they belonged to Baltor. However, there had never been any sighting of his camel, nor any of his other gear, by anyone of either tribe ... whatsoever. Valuspo's fate remained an unsolved mystery.

Another mystery that Baltor solved on his own, which he had figured out through experimentation only a few nights prior to this party, is that if he dried the cah-su-mahn berries and ground them into dust, and then dusting the powder into his food or drinks, he quenched his thirsts and hungers. Only one of his powers remained, language comprehension, and that was okay by him.

After all, the more that Baltor and Brishava got to know one another, the more their love flourished, and reigned—the power of "True Love." Finally came the day, nearly a year after their arrival, when they got officially married—the Chao-chu-sha-maen way.

And only one day later, Humonus and Chelsea got married in the same tribal fashion. The group, now a part of the Chao-chu-sha-maen tribe and family, had grown very strong and inseparable throughout all of these most wonderful of times....

CHAPTER XXVIII

Only a minute or so before the sun had set, a little over a year later, upon a particular evening that had partly-cloudy skies— those dull-gray clouds unexpectedly lit themselves up into a dazzling array of beautiful colors and patterns—pinks, peaches, oranges, purples, yellows, blues (light to dark), and yes, even greens!

As always, this spectacle of nature instantly drew the attention of the villagers of Chao-chu-sha-maen, and excited them so greatly that they stopped whatever they were doing, dropped to the ground, and began chanting, whooping and rolling all around on their backs.

While their arms and hands remained extended above them reaching for the skies, their fingers continuously opened and shut, as if trying to clutch the skies.

As for Baltor during this timeframe, he remained "obliviously asleep" on his back, in his bed in his hut, as it was still during his slumber time. Sleeping next to him in bed but facing the other direction was his wife Brishava.

Only seconds after the loud noises had begun, however, she got awoken from her slumber. But as she understood all-too-well their unique religious customs, she simply shifted her body close to her husband in bed, placed her head on his stomach, and drifted right back to sleep.

It was one second later that Baltor's sleeping mind began to have a lucid dream.

At first, he could only see that he was standing within a black area of unknown proportions, floating in the middle of the air. Though there were no sources of light, he, upon glancing down, could see his own body as if he were standing in broad daylight.

Just after he had physically pinched himself to be sure that he wasn't dreaming while surprisingly feeling substance, he began to suspect that maybe he wasn't dreaming at all, but more likely, fully conscious in another dimension.

As he looked around one more time, he confirmed yet again that there were absolutely no sources of light—or anything else anywhere else.

Until, about a minute after his arrival, just off to his right about fifteen feet away, this emperor-sized bed unexpectedly popped out of nowhere!

As he turned his head to look over, the first thing about this bed that caught his eye were the mahogany posts at each of the four corners, which he estimated to be ten feet tall and circular in shape.

In addition, wrapped around each post were two see-through veils of silk, red and blue, which began at the base, and then gently wrapped their way around until they reached the very top, where there was a golden hoop that the veils went through and streamed to the opposite post on the bed, forming a loose x pattern.

Upon closer examination of the bed's mahogany base, he also saw various predator-styled animals etched throughout and that there was a neatly made purple velvet blanket upon the bed, embroidered with dozens of rows of golden diamonds.

Last not but least, though there was no headboard, there was still a wide assortment of colorful pillows neatly arranged at the head, each embroidered with one large golden diamond.

Now, even though the bed was very elegant in his opinion, he didn't much see the relevance in it, so he began to look elsewhere to see if anything else would pop out. It does, but not where he was looking at the time when it happens.

For, only a short time later, as he glanced again to the bed, he surprisingly saw a very thin and old man lying under the blanket near the edge of the bed, who looked as if he had been there all along.

As Baltor looked closer, he saw that this man appeared to be venerable, bearing a few scattered strands of silvery hair upon his head, dark and sunken eyes, a very pale complexion, and skeletal hands that extend from underneath his purple pajamas.

Still, despite this man's venerability, Baltor observed that this old man's staring rather sternly at him.

A moment later, the old man tried to sit up by propping his hands into the bed and pushing up, but failed miserably. Instead of trying a second time, he looked over to Baltor angrily, pointed his bony index finger at him, and growled out the word, "You."

Immediately Baltor began to feel these slight electrifying chills running up and down his spine, and he also noticed that with each passing moment, those chills intensified in degree until they started to get more and more painful like he was being electrocuted to death—and that's when he woke up.

Or did I? Baltor began to wonder upon hearing two final whooping noises coming from outside, followed by complete silence. And at the same time, he felt his wife still sleeping on his belly.

Ironically enough, it was then that the door to the hut quietly opened up as Pa-cheu entered, allowing a tiny bit of the dusky light to enter.

That light allowed Baltor not only to see that Brishava's eyes remained closed, yet she looked really comfortable.

He then thought with a bit of amusement, *I must've been dreaming, or she would have felt the electrical surges, too.*

In the next moment, perhaps because of the tiny amount of light that now cast onto her face, she released a deep sigh.

Pa-cheu threw a sweet smile at Baltor, who returned it. She then exited the hut, closing the door behind her.

Once alone, Baltor asked lightly, "Honey?"

"Yes?" she sighed, half in sleep.

"I just had the strangest dream."

"Tell me your dream?"

"Okay," Baltor said. After telling her the dream in precise detail, he added, "I know now that it must have been a dream because you obviously didn't feel a thing. So, what do you suppose this dream means?"

Brishava shifted her head so that she could look directly into Baltor's eyes and then she said, "I think that this is the sign, my husband, that we need to head back to Pavelus, so that we can claim our thrones before my father dies."

After taking a deep breath through her nose, she said, "If my father should die without me there, the next person to become the Sultan would be my older half-brother, Imperious-Lord Rasta...

"After all, my father has permanently forbidden my Uncle Vaspan from inheriting the kingdom. Unfortunately, although my brother pretends to look all just and noble, he is really just as ruthless and sinister as both my father and uncle."

"But we have a kingdom here, as well," Baltor countered.

"Then let us unite the two kingdoms, my love!" Brishava said as she sat up in bed. "But do not fight our destiny, for Pavelus needs us as well—we are Pavelus!"

"But so is Chao-chu-sha-maen," Baltor argued though he continued to lie down.

She replied calmly, "We must make our own kingdom—not take theirs away from them. Besides, who says that we can't honor them as royal kin whenever they come to our cities…?

"Know this, my husband—I was born as the heiress to the throne of Pavelus, for a reason. We cannot let that reason be for naught. Besides, perhaps I can change even my father's stern mind, especially when he sees on just how much love I have for you, my husband!"

"You are right, my love," Baltor sighed. "When do you wish to leave?"

After Brishava had playfully snuggled the side of her face back into his chest, she then suggested, "How about two weeks? That'll give us plenty of time to say our farewells to our wonderful friends!"

"Ok," he said. After a few seconds, he chuckled, "I love you, my Princess!"

"And I love you, my Sultan!"

That was the first time she had ever called him sultan before.

Several hours later, as soon as they had informed Humonus and Chelsea of the decision to return to Pavelus in two weeks hence— they also agreed to come along and help.

That night at the campfire, after Baltor had officially announced the group's decision to the villagers, the prince appeared to expect it, as he immediately signed, "Can you guys go on a journey with me before you head home to Pavelus?"

"Sure, my brother. You got it, but as you know, we need to be heading back in two weeks," Baltor signed back.

"I know… my brother…" Cheo replied in the language of Pavelian, which indicated that he had been listening and learning when the group spoke to each other in their native language, and which surprised the heck out of them all, too. He then added, "To-morrow night we go. We back… seven nights… from tomorrow night… okay?" A sheepish smile crossed his face.

"Okay," they all answered back in unison—though several different languages, including sign language, were used to answer Cheo back. This caused everyone to burst out laughing a moment later from the hilarity of the situation.

The next night, the party of five began to travel straight north. Over the course of the next three and a half nights, they saw several breathtaking sights along the way, including the abrupt addition of jagged mountain peaks that went hundreds of feet up in the air amongst the thick and lush jungle vegetation.

Continuously, the temperatures remained in the high 80's coupled with thick humidity. The only person who never sweat was Baltor.

About two hours before sunrise, Cheo stopped next to a gigantic bush that bore thick leaves, resting right in front of a cliff face, and said in his native language, "We're going to need some light to see in here."

"In where?" Baltor asked back.

Cheo orally answered, "In the cave behind this bush."

Baltor translated Cheo's request to Humonus.

Humonus pulled a torch and some flint out of his backpack, and began the process of lighting it. Once lit, a few seconds later, he then handed the torch to Cheo.

Carefully keeping the torch flames away from the bush, Cheo walked around it into a small cave with a tunnel at the end of it angling downwards—the rest of the group followed behind.

About fifteen minutes later, and still in the same tunnel that continuously angled downward, the group began to see something glowing a strange gold color far ahead of them.

About two minutes later, the tunnel transformed itself into a huge cavern that literally consisted of pure molten gold, covering the floors, the walls, the stalactites and stalagmites, and even the ceiling.

"*Wooooow!*" Chelsea was the first to say in disbelief.

Baltor sighed aloud, "My God. This is unbelievable!"

Cheo asked in Pavelian, "What is God?"

"God is that which made us all, I guess," Baltor said in the Chao-chu-sha-maen language. "I just used that phrase as a figure of speech, for I was amazed by the heavenly qualities of this place!"

"Oh. As you already know, we call God, Shava-Tula-Suah-Lakasa-Casusea. We never use God as figure of speech."

"I see. I'm sorry if I offended you."

"Ah, do not apologize to me, my brother. Apologize to God. Come, if you think you were amazed by the heavenly qualities of this place, wait till you see what lies ahead!"

Cheo then led the group to the far end of the cavern, where there was yet another tunnel leading downwards.

After having passed two other junctions, yet still going straight for another half an hour, they entered another immense cavern.

This breathtaking chamber even had an underground waterfall that cascaded into an underground lagoon. Now, the reasons that everyone could see everything so crystal clear here wasn't because of gold—but from the small, medium, large, and even enormous colored lights reflecting back from a wide assortment of precious crystalline emeralds, sapphires, rubies, and even diamonds.

"Whoa," was the group's response.

Humonus signed, "Do you know how much money this all is worth?"

Cheo signed, "What is money?"

Humonus answered, "Money is used to buy and sell things like food, clothes, homes, whatever."

"I see, as you know, we have no such thing, as we are a utopian society. Do you think that these are worth a lot of money?"

"You have no idea... perhaps billions of parsecs!"

A smile formed on Cheo's face, as he signed, "Really. We did not know that they were valuable—we just liked them because they are pretty to look at!"

"Aren't they though?" Humonus signed back.

"Perhaps we could establish a trade sometime; after all, we have lots of pretty and useful things in Pavelus," Brishava suggested in sign language.

Cheo verbally answered in Pavelian, "Yes, maybe we can."

The group decided to set camp in the cave just near the surface, until the following night.

Just after sunset, everyone in the group but Humonus left. Meanwhile, he stayed back to conceal all of the tracks, and once done several minutes later, he then ran to catch back up to the group.

After the group had returned to the village three and a half nights later, they partied almost non-stop for the next six days and nights. On the final night, hundreds of fond farewells were exchanged between everyone, including King Cha, Queen Che and Prince Cheo.

The night before they left, they launched a party and during this party, more ideas were shared about establishing trade between Pavelus and Chao-chu-sha-maen, sometime soon. After the discussions were over, the celebrating continued until the wee hours of the morning.

They—Baltor, Brishava, Humonus, and Chelsea—all began their journey west the following night. Right before they had left, Baltor had hung on the outside of the wagon two very large sacks, each containing a cah-su-mahn berry bush with roots and dirt. He figured that he could plant them once they reached Pavelus. During the course of their trip, which included a month-long stay in

Valakan, they even discussed and perfected a plan on how to get to the Sultan, himself.

The plan's conclusion was to simply walk in through the front gates, inform the guards that they had rescued the Sultan's daughter, and that they were coming to collect the reward. The guards would have no choice but to bring them before the Sultan. It was in all their greatest hopes that the Sultan would then accept Baltor as her husband! A little over four months of time passed until they reached the borders of Pavelus.

After arriving at the city gates, fortune smiled upon them as the plan worked out exactly that way, up to a point. When the guards informed the Sultan that a group of three people had found his daughter, he was overjoyed, though he truly was lying on his deathbed.

Because he heard the news that there were others with his Brishava, he commanded that two squads of guards fill his bedroom, just in case things should turn underhanded. The Sultan knew that his Ruling-General Glacius couldn't attend, as he was very busy training the troops for war in the coliseum.

Once the guards had escorted the group into the bedchambers of the Sultan, Baltor realized that this was the same old man and the same exact bed he had seen in his dreams! However, he was not too surprised at the revelation, nor that guards filled the entire room, either.

Without hindrance, Brishava immediately passed the guards surrounding the Sultan, and sat next to her father as he still lay down in his bed. Once she had passed, the guards immediately blocked the way leading up to their Sultan.

Sultan Brishavus said gently to his daughter, "Oh how I have missed you these last few years, my Brishava."

"I've missed you too, Father!" She laid her head upon his chest and looked up into his face.

After giving his daughter a tender smile, he revealed, "Soon I will die, and the kingdom will become yours, and Duke Marlborough of Vispano. I have just dispatched word for your marriage to be prepared for tomorrow. For the last year, he has been eagerly waiting here in Pavelus for your return, my daughter. He has also brought along with him seventy thousand of his best knights and troops. They are all camped to the north of the city, in order to help protect us from—" A sudden seizure of coughing erupted!

Once the coughing had abated, several minutes later, Brishava countered, "But Father... I cannot marry the duke, for I am already married! Actually, I have been married these last couple of years, since my disappearance. Baltor, my husband, is standing over there." She pointed toward Baltor.

"Impossible," the Sultan retaliated without even having looked where she pointed. "You must marry the duke or this empire will fall. My brother is already on his way to attack Pavelus—he has even hired several divisions of mercenaries to assist. So tell me then, who in the hell authenticated your marriage?"

"God did," Brishava answered. "And I will not marry any other man, ever."

The Sultan said, "Let me see this man."

The guards made space so that Baltor could pass, and as he neared the bed, he saw the Sultan tried to sit up in bed but fail, point at him, and then heard him growl out the word, "You."

Just like in Baltor's dream! Also just like the dream, chills now ran up and down his spine, but this time, he was wide awake. Despite the chills, Baltor took a deep breath through his nose before replying boldly to his father-in-law, "I am Prince Baltor Elysian."

"Prince? Prince of what? I have never heard that name of Elysian before," the Sultan scoffed. "Where is your kingdom?"

"I am the Prince of Chao-chu-sha-maen."

A myriad of chuckles erupted around the room from the guards. Brishava snapped, "That's not funny!"

The guards stopped laughing.

"How many soldiers did you bring with you from Chaoshu, or whatever the hell was the name of that place you just called it?" the Sultan asked most of his question seriously, but found himself bursting out laughing at the end.

Only a moment later, more voracious laughter erupted from everyone, except from the small group of friends.

Brishava snapped, "Father!"

Perhaps ten seconds later, the Sultan was finally able to ask through his own dissipating laughter, "Well?"

Very seriously, Baltor answered through the dissipating laughter, "I brought none back with me. All we will need to do is to unite and train all the able-bodied citizens of Pavelus in martial arts, and then we can handle any foes that come our way, my Sultan—no matter the numbers!"

Upon hearing Baltor's ridiculous solution, the Sultan immediately became enraged as he cried out, "Guards, kill him... In fact kill them all!"

As the guards drew their swords and began to encircle the bunch, the Sultan quietly said to Brishava, "You will marry the duke—do you understand me, young lady?"

What the Sultan didn't expect was that his only beloved daughter would pluck a small boot knife out, plunge it straight into his heart, and then twist!

His eyes bulged out in surprise and pain, yet without so much as a peeped sound from his lips he instantaneously died with that look of surprise upon his face!

Brishava quickly closed her father's lifeless eyes, and tucked the knife under the mattress with one hand; with the other hand, she pulled up both the silky blue sheet and the royal purple blanket until tucked neatly under her father's neck.

She immediately stood up, turned around, and commanded, "Stop—I order you! The Sultan has just died. As you all well know, I am Brishava, his daughter—the next in line to the throne of Pavelus. In other words, I am now your Sultaness! I command you to stop your attack on my husband and friends!"

For a moment, the guards stopped their original order, in order to look back over to the bed. Despite the fact that all of the guards knew, or found to be true, all of Brishava's words, they also observed that their Sultan's blanket was now forming a small circular pool of blood, right over his heart area!

For another few moments, silence reigned in the room, as the guards confusedly looked around for their officer-in-charge, General Hawkins. They came to discover that their general was staring at their obviously murdered Sultan, bearing his own look of shock.

Even though it was obvious to all that the one who had been nearest to the Sultan had done the assassinating—there were two reasons for all the confusion, surprise, and shock.

One—even though the palace guards didn't much like the Sultan and his extremely obnoxious and mean behaviors, he was actually dead. And two, the main reason, most of these guards, including their general, had very much come to know and love Princess Brishava since infancy, as they had watched over and protected her—it had never before been like her to hurt even a fly, much less kill her own father.

Once Brishava saw the looks of confusion, surprise, and of course shock, she confidently said, "Yes, it is true that my father has died by my hand, but all present know that his tyrannical ways had to be stopped. Most also know that I have been both kind and just for all of my life! Finally yet most importantly, my husband's plan is strategically sound that we can save Pavelus without the duke or his men! On our own, the Sharia Empire can become glorious."

Hawkins ordered, "Sheath your swords, men."

The guards did.

Brishava then pointed to Baltor, and added, "By my marriage to him, this is your soon-to-be Sultan, Prince Baltor Elysian. Kneel before your ruler!"

Again, the guards looked to Hawkins. Once they observed that he had already gone down onto his knees, they immediately followed suit.

A few moments later, as Brishava looked over to Baltor and saw that he looked unsure of what to say, Brishava commanded, "You may all rise."

Once they had risen, she added, "None will ever speak of what transpired in this room to anyone—ever. Understand?"

"Yes, Sultaness!"

"Good," she replied. "Commanding-General Hawkins, before I personally assign you to secretly dispose of my father's body in the furnace, though we will have a public funeral, I would like to introduce to you all to the new Ruling-General.

"You will listen and obey every word that this man has to say, as he has already successfully demonstrated his skills at training and governing troops to maximum proficiency! General Hawkins, this is Ruling-General Humonus."

Humonus's eyes looked a bit in shock for a moment, but then the newly promoted Ruling General regained his poker face as he said, "Pleasure to meet you, Commanding-General Hawkins."

Hawkins snapped a salute and said, "Ruling-General Humonus—I, and my ranks, are under your command, sir!"

Humonus replied, "Excellent. Once you have completed the Sultaness' command, I want you to call forth all my other generals, and inform them that we shall conduct a meeting in one hour. I shall need as many statistics as possible...

"How long do we have until Sedious Vaspan arrives? How many troops is he bringing along with him? What types of machines of war does he have? How many troops do we have? What types of defenses and offenses do we possess? Etc., etc. Statistics, General Hawkins."

"Yes, sir!" Hawkins said. He snapped a salute, and began to walk toward the door. Just before he had exited the room, Humonus added, "Oh, one more thing, General."

Hawkins stopped, turned around and asked, "Yes, sir?"

Humonus turned his head toward Brishava. "My Sultaness, what are you going to do about the former ruling general Glacius? We can't have him wandering about freely, and possibly starting up any revolts, especially now."

Brishava snapped her fingers as she replied, "Excellent point! General Hawkins, I want Glacius arrested for his crimes against humanity, which I know quite a few that he is guilty of, but I do not want you to arrest him in front of his men...

"Instead, simply tell him that the Sultan has commanded his presence—escort him directly to my husband and me with two squads of your most loyal soldiers!

"When he arrives here, I will personally deliver the order as the Sultaness that he is to be arrested and locked in the dungeon with maximum security."

Hawkins said, "Yes, my Sultaness! Because of the commands to secretly dispose of the Sultan's body in the furnace, and to locate and bring Glacius here before the Sultaness, however, it'll take me at least a couple hours to have all the other generals tabulate statistics into reports for you, Ruling-General Humonus."

Humonus asked, "How much time will you need, General?"

"I believe two hours, sir."

Humonus said, "Done."

Hawkins snapped another salute, delivered a bow, and then left the room; the two troops that had just finished wrapping up the Sultan's body in the blanket followed.

Once the double doors had closed, Chelsea looked over to Brishava and asked, "My Sultaness, I was wondering—which room will Humonus and I stay in?"

Brishava answered, "Ask the guards posted outside to direct you to the nearest spare bedroom on this floor. Make sure they let me know which room you'll be staying in, so it'll be easy for me to find you, okay?"

Chelsea answered, "No problem and thanks."

Humonus added, "I will most likely be very busy with the generals soon enough, so I wish to spend a little quality time with my wife first, if that's okay with you, my Sultaness?"

Brishava lightly laughed and said, "Go right ahead."

Humonus looked over to Baltor, and added with a look of remembrance, "Oh, Prince Baltor, I have a present for you when the time is right."

Baltor asked with a very curious expression on his face, "What is it?"

"You'll soon see," Humonus said with a small smile, which became reflected by Chelsea's own smile—a second later, the two left the room.

"Guards," Baltor said, "I want you to wait outside for a minute as I need to speak to your Sultaness alone. I will let you know when you can come back in."

"Yes, Prince Baltor!"

Once the two were alone, his smile disappeared, and he stated incredulously, "I can't believe you murdered your own father!"

As she stared back into his eyes, evenly and softly, she replied in the same tone of voice as her eyes showed, "Yes, I did. I did murder him."

Her eyes then cast to the ground as she added, "Remember when you first came here to this palace to assassinate my father, and we bumped into each other? Remember the following conversations we had?"

"Of course I do, but—"

She looked back up and interrupted, "Well, everything you said about him was and has been true. You told me that he is a tyrant that needed to be stopped—but that is not the sole reason I killed him now. There are several others. For one, he has never respected my thoughts and opinions, ever! For two, you are my husband, and I will never have another! But the third and main reason is that we can save Pavelus without the Duke's men, and make the Sharia Empire truly glorious!"

He said nothing, though his eyes squinted in contemplation.

She added softly, after a short pause, "I hope that you don't think of me differently now, do you?"

He shook his head a bit to clear out the shock, and then he answered, "I'm just incredibly surprised. What's to stop you from plunging a dagger into me?"

She breathed out a light laugh as she drew near her husband, wrapped her arms around his waist, looked deep into his eyes, and almost innocently said, "Just don't be a tyrant, is all."

As he looked back into her eyes, he first inhaled deeply. Upon release, he said, "No problem there." He then wrapped his arms around his wife, pulling her tightly into his body.

A few moments later, as another thought popped into his head, he asked, "So, where are we going to sleep? I don't think it wise to sleep in here with the balcony and windows."

"Hmmm?" she hummed as if she had awoken from slumber.

He leaned back from the embrace. "Where should we sleep?"

"Oh. I think it wise if we get a bedroom without windows; that is, until we can have curtains made to block out the light in here during the day. In fact, why don't we just get this whole room remodeled, my husband?"

He cocked his head to the side, smiled, and then replied, "Good idea, my wife."

Several moments later, still another question formed in his mind, so he asked it, "Oh—where should we have my bushes planted?"

"I'll make sure they're well taken care of first thing in the morning, under guard of course. I'll also ensure that our cooks put the dried powder into a seasoning shaker."

"You really do have everything covered, don't you?"

"Of course!" she replied with a giggle.

He affirmed, "I love you!"

"I love you too, my Sultan!"

After delivering a gentle kiss on his wife's lips, he called aloud, "Guards, you can come back in."

The guards posted outside opened the double doors, and allowed the two squads of guards to enter.

About twenty minutes later, Hawkins and Glacius arrived. To make a long and dramatic story short, after Brishava had ordered Glacius's arrest, he pleaded for his freedom stating he didn't have any choice, but to follow the commands of the Sultan! Brishava, in turn, promised that he would be allowed trial at a later time, but that for now, he would be incarcerated in the dungeon with maximum security. The guards, in turn, bound him in handcuffs, and escorted the still-pleading Glacius to the dungeon with Hawkins in the lead.

Soon after Baltor and Brishava had moved into a guest bedroom without windows, she fell asleep upon his chest. Though he stayed awake all night long until morning, he neither minded, nor moved.

Come morning, just after Baltor had fallen asleep, Brishava woke up, and six handmaidens dressed her up into an elegant yellow dress that had small silky red embroidered flowers hemmed chaotically abroad, from top to bottom. The girls had finally pulled her hair into a tight weave that wrapped itself back into the diamond-encrusted crown, which rested upon her head.

Once done, she then entered the throne room and took her place upon the throne. The Sultaness' first decree began with the order to plant the berry bushes into the botanical gardens. She then ordered that these bushes be guarded on a twenty-four-hour basis, and that only the cooks be allowed to enter the area and pluck the berries, so that they could dry it into powder, and then place that powder into their soon-to-be Sultan's seasoning shaker.

Her second decree regarded the harem room on the top floor of the palace, and the dozens of girls who resided there. Her order was that the harem girls be given real jobs within the palace, and new quarters with the other servants. As for the harem room itself, Brishava stated that they would probably turn this into a recreation room one day, but not for a while.

Her third decree regarded the coronation ceremony that would be conducted for them both at 8:30 p.m. that night. She spent a little more than an hour giving all the specifics she wanted for this "extremely important event" to the Chief Foreman, whose name's Jamar, a handsome-looking and well-dressed man in his late 20s.

Just as Jamar was about to exit the throne room to execute her orders, Brishava called out, "Jamar? Can you please ensure that the invitations get sent out to all the nobles of Pavelus, A.S.A.P.? Can you also please ensure that you do not forget that the coronation ceremony is to be held at 8:30 p.m., for which only the nobles are invited to attend the ritual? In addition, don't forget that the official welcoming of the new Sultan and Sultaness commences at 9:30 p.m., for which all the citizens of Pavelus will need to be notified so that they can attend? Got it all?"

With a very confident smile upon his face, Jamar replied evenly, "I will not let you down, your highness. Let me assure you that I have every last specification you said already pictured in my mind's eye—you and the Sultan will not be disappointed."

Brishava smiled in genuine appreciation, and replied, "Thanks, Jamar."

Jamar bowed, and then left to turn his picture into reality.

Not even ten seconds later, she spotted Humonus, who had just entered the throne room; without hesitation, she declared, "Ruling-General—what perfect timing for you to arrive! I can assure you that I will only need a minute of your time, as I know that you are a very busy man."

Humonus first bowed, and then asked, "Yes, my Sultaness?"

Brishava answered, "Please ensure that only those nobles' names written upon the list, which will shortly be delivered to you by our Chief Foreman Jamar, be allowed to enter the palace itself at 7:00 p.m. In addition, at 9:00 p.m., I want all of the city's inner gates, including the gates of the palace grounds, opened. From what I understand, this will be the first time the palace gates have been open to the public since her construction five and a half centuries ago!"

"Finally yet importantly," she concluded, "as I know you are brand new to your job, please doubly ensure that the safety of both myself and my husband are properly placed in and around the palace grounds. Understand?"

"Yes, my Sultaness," Humonus replied with a low bow. "Your wish is my command." He then left to carry out her orders.

Her forth decree of the day was that a messenger be dispatched to politely invite the Duke of Vispano to the throne room.

About an hour later, Jamar was the next to arrive with a report that the total cost would approximate around nine million parsecs. Finally, he mentioned that the treasury held over sixty-nine million parsecs, which did not include her family's personal treasures.

Without hesitation, Brishava nodded and with a pleased smile. Jamar bowed again, and left to get things rolling.

Not even two minutes after Jamar had left, Duke Marlborough of Vispano arrived.

After waving his hand flamboyantly outwards, the duke began with a very pleased smile upon his face, "Princess Brishava—how nice it is of you to return."

"Thank you. It is good to be back, Duke Marlborough."

After looking around the throne room just to be sure, Marlborough's face straightened out as he asked, "So, where is your father?"

Without emotion or explanation, Brishava replied, "He died last night."

He asked with a bit of shock to his voice, "Really?" Now with sympathy to his voice, he added, "I'm so sorry to hear that."

"Me too."

The duke's bushy eyebrows rose sharply, just before his thin-lipped mouth asked, "So... I totally understand that you must be in a state of mourning with your father gone... but are we to still be married tonight, as was the word dispatched to me by his messenger last night?"

"Well... actually. Here's the situation: My father never knew until just moments before he died last night, that I have been married these last few years to a man named Prince Baltor Elysian."

With a look of agitation now upon his face, he replied slowly, "Prince... Baltor... Elysian... I have never heard of this man."

"Even though you've never heard of my husband, this does not change the fact that he is a ruler of a kingdom far to the east...."

After curiously looking all around the throne room for this prince, but seeing no men wearing the crown of a prince, the duke finally asked, "Where is this prince now, and what kingdom does he rule, if you don't mind me asking?"

"Of course I don't mind, Duke. My husband is sleeping now, as he is quite weary from our long, long, long journey back home. He is the prince of a kingdom that is about a thousand miles to the east, called Chao-chu-sha-maen."

After a minute's pause, yet now bearing a clear look of anger upon his face, the duke growled, "I see.... Well, it would have been nice to know this information before I transported seventy thousand of my best troops nearly six hundred miles around the continent to get here nearly a year ago, pointlessly!"

"Even worse," the duke whined, "I waited for many years to marry the girl of my dreams, you, only to painfully find out just now that my betrothed is already married!"

Brishava replied with sympathy, "I understand that you're upset, so let me ask you this question. What will it cost so that we can continue our trade and peace between our two noble nations?"

"Hmmm. That's a tough one. How about ten million parsecs?"

"Ten million?" she asked incredulously.

"Yes. Would you like me to go over every last item of what I'm going to be missing out on, especially you?"

"Fine. You can have your ten million."

"Excellent—I'm now confident that the Sharia Empire and Vispano Province will continue with our trade and peace," the duke said with a pleased smile.

"See my treasurer on the way out, and have a good day, Duke," Brishava replied, bearing a forced political smile upon her face.

The duke nodded and then made his way out of the throne room. Once he had collected his money, he immediately left Pavelus via horseback, and made his way up to his seventy thousand troops camped to the north of the city. By that afternoon, they were all making their way back north to the borders of Vispano.

For just about the entire day, Brishava kept busy by managing the transformation of the throne room into the coronation room.

Just after sunset and without having experienced any dreams, Baltor returned to consciousness. Yet before he had opened his eyes, he not only felt a soft bed under his back, yet an even softer woman's face lying on his stomach, coupled with her equally silky hair that splashed almost everywhere like a waterfall—based off experience, he presumed this head belonged to his wife.

After opening his eyes a second later, his suspicions were indeed confirmed—Brishava had been deeply studying his face while he slept, as she so very often liked to do.

Right away she gave him a quick peck on his stomach, before looking back up and cooing, "Good evening to you, my husband."

After releasing a deep sigh, he replied, "Good evening, my wife!"

She said, "I have some wonderful news to share with you."

"Yes, my love, what is it?"

After sitting up in bed, she answered with excitement growing in her voice, "Tonight, we are to be officially crowned the new Sultan and Sultaness of the Sharia Empire! Following that there will be two back-to-back ceremonies—the first to be formally introduced to our subjects, and the second for the nobles—the whole city of Pavelus will be celebrating here at the palace tonight!"

He asked, "Just like that?"

"Just like that," she cooed. "I will teach you how to make things work for you on much broader scales, my love."

He said emphatically, "That's great!"

As a curious expression grew on his face, he asked, "So did you talk to Humonus at all today?"

She nodded her head a single time before answering, "Yes I did. Ruling-General Humonus reported to me about a half an hour ago that he had just received 'an urgent report' from the advanced naval scouts, which report stated that my uncle now has six divisions of troops under his command, more than one hundred and twenty thousand men! Per the report, they left Mauritia three weeks ago—on foot, on horse, or on ship—and in three to four weeks, they are expected to arrive here at Pavelus.

"This gives us very little time to prepare, and certainly not enough time to hire any mercenary divisions ourselves. I have already hired out the services of dozens of merchant ships to dispatch to other cities and request for mercenaries and volunteers."

"I see," he said.

She nodded her head one time, before continuing her briefing, "Basically, as our troop count stands now versus theirs, we are outnumbered three to one—we have a little over forty thousand soldiers—both army and navy. Even though the strong fortifications to our outer walls will stop them for quite awhile—perhaps a month—it will not stop them forever because they have hundreds of powerful siege and catapulting machines."

After taking in a deep breath through just her nose, she added, "While half of our naval fleet is continuing to protect the harbor, the other half has been dispatched to retrieve ten thousand soldiers from Lasparus—half of the troops originally stationed in our other city. Unfortunately they won't be arriving here until but a few days before Uncle Vaspan and his army."

"So therefore," she concluded, "it is in my hopes and prayers that we shall be able to recruit citizens with promise of payment and training. After I have formally introduced you to the citizens of Pavelus at nine-thirty tonight, I want you to be straight with them and tell them of the upcoming attack, and to call upon their assistance in defending the city. Speak from the heart—got it?"

"Yes, ma'am."

She lightly kissed her husband's chest, before she smiled and sighed, "Good. Before we get ready for our coronations, let's have fun first!"

She began to giggle. He began to growl with desire.

An hour later, after the two had even shared a nice bubble bath together, they finally went their separate ways. Baltor now blankly allowed himself to become dressed, tailored, and groomed by six assistants in the master bedroom, while Brishava was similarly taken care of in her own dressing room by six handmaidens.

Once his assistants were done with their multitude of tasks, which tasks took thirty minutes, they finally bowed; the supervisor asked, "Are you pleased, Your Majesty, with the way you look?"

Only then did Baltor begin to gaze closely at his reflection in the mirror. The first thing to catch his attention was the *very* princely crown now secured on his head; the second was his *very* grandfather's sword, which weapon was now nicely secured on his back inside a sheath that possessed all these magnificent qualities: brand-new, made with black and gold vertical stripes, and polished to a gleam. Baltor assumed the black material was marble and the gold was real. The third and fourth things were his two *very* precious necklaces, especially the gold necklace with a polished gold arrowhead pendant, despite the multiple complaints of all his assistants to take them off. Baltor had won the argument in the end.

As for the rest of his *royal attire,* they had perfectly tailored his purple, gold, and blue-striped shirt made of silk, as well his silky black pants that had a golden-stripe going down the outside hem. At knee-level those pants were crisply folded and held in place inside his shiny black boots, bearing its own vertical-stripe made of actual gold.

Next, he gazed at his hair, shockingly noting that it was no longer long and straight, but short and very wavy, as it had been cut shoulder's length. His gaze finally looked at just his face, observing that his braided goat-tee was thankfully still there, yet one of the assistants had drawn a smooth-and-crisp line using black eyeliner right around his eyelids, which made his eyes and face look all that much more "hawkish!"

"Well, Your Majesty?" the supervisor asked.

"Umm," Baltor said with a small smile, "Yeah, I am. Thanks."

"Thank you, Your Majesty," he happily said with a smile, just before he delivered a final bow and left with his other assistants.

Only seconds after the assistants had left, Humonus entered the bedroom. Though he donned the formal uniform of a ruling-general, he said rather casually, "My friend—you look good!"

"Thank you... as do you!"

After nodding appreciatively one time, Humonus got right down to business as he said, "The time has just about arrived for me to escort you to the ritual room, where you will be officially crowned the Sultan of the Sharia Empire! But before we do all of this, I, Humonus, have a gift for you Baltor—friend to friend—come with me, please?"

Looking surprised, Baltor nodded his head, delivered a smile, and began to follow Humonus out the doors—though a dozen guards followed the pair to Humonus's unguarded bedroom down the hall and to the right, they stayed outside as the two entered the room.

Once two of the guards had shut the doors, Humonus turned around and said, "Now, close your eyes."

Baltor closed them. Thus he couldn't see as Humonus walked over to the bed, slid *something* out from underneath the mattress, and then walked back with that *something*.

Nearly a minute later, Humonus finally said, "Open them, and surprise."

Baltor opened his eyes and his mouth dropped open in shock—for within Humonus's extended hands, he held a duplicate sword!

In shock, Baltor exclaimed, "No way!" His hand unconsciously strayed to the handle of his own sword on his back just to make sure it was still there—it was.

Nearly a minute later, Baltor finally stammered, "How—how on earth did you have that made?"

"I'll tell you the whole story later—for now, let me just say that I have a very-well-trained eye! Take it. It's yours, my friend."

Baltor took the sword from Humonus's extended hands, and closely examined it—it even felt the same weight! Just to be sure, he pulled the original sword out, and confirmed not only the weight, yet every single detail on both swords was "perfectly identical." He could only ask, "How in the heavens?"

Humonus smiled, and asked, "Do you like it?"

"I—I love it, my friend! Thank you!"

Baltor set both swords down on the bed, and then gave his friend a strong hug of gratitude.

"Oh, I also have an identical sheath that I will help strap on your back—my friend, and my prince!" Humonus added.

After he had picked up a duplicate sheath from on top of his table, he next assisted Baltor in clamping it on, while adding, "It appears that the leader has become the follower!"

Even though Baltor laughed, Humonus didn't laugh whatsoever as he delicately picked up both swords by the handles off the bed, and flipped them around in one quick movement so that he was now gripping the paper-thin blades—the handles were extended toward Baltor.

Once he gripped both swords by their handles, Humonus released his grip and placed his hands to his sides.

Still bearing an "ear to ear smile," Baltor sheathed both swords upon his back in one quick movement! His right hand next clasped firmly onto Humonus's left shoulder, just before he said with a whole lot of appreciation, "Thank you very much, my best friend."

Instantly Humonus snapped to the position of attention, threw his crispest salute, and declared, "The time for your crowning has come—my best friend, my prince of two nations, and my soon-to-be Sultan of the Sharia Empire!"

Baltor glanced over to the mirror for another moment, and upon seeing that everything was as it should be, he looked back at Humonus and half-whispered, "Yes, it has, Ruling-General Humonus, yes, it has!"

After an affirming nod, Humonus released his salute, performed a right face, and walked for the bedroom doors—Baltor followed.

Ten seconds later, Humonus called out, "Open the doors!"

Simultaneously, two of the guards standing out in the hallway opened the two doors.

Together—with Baltor and Humonus in the middle of the procession—they made their way down several hallways, and one staircase that led down, until they reached the final hallway that led to the double doors of the throne room. Doors made of pure gold with large diamond doorknobs; in the middle of each door was the carving of a curvy saber.

Furthermore, Brishava stood in the middle of this hallway, as well a platoon of her own guards who surrounded her.

Upon arrival, the guards automatically shuffled around, so their leaders could unite at the entryway—they did.

Brishava next reminded, "Just remember that you'll each be called in turn to enter the room by the Justice of the Peace—you first Ruling-General, then me, then you, my Sultan. Before we are crowned in front of the nobles and officers, my love, we have certain oaths that we will have to swear to, and after we are crowned, we can take our thrones. Trust me that this coronation ceremony will be long and tedious, not unlike a wedding. And at the end, about an hour from now, only you and I, my love, will be standing out here in this hallway. Oh, and of course our personal guards."

Without pause, Brishava concluded, "Right after that, I have some really important errands to take care of, so just head on down to our bedroom and wait for me, okay?"

"Okay."

Just then, the trumpets blew, as the ceremony began—this turned out to be a very ornate ritual that lasted exactly an hour—it appeared that Jamar the coordinator had every reason to be as confident as he claimed, as all the "t's" were crossed, and all the "i's" were dotted.

Following the ceremony, Brishava gave her husband a quick kiss on the cheek, before she said, "Love ya. Gotta go."

With that, she left for another part of the palace with half a platoon of guards. Meanwhile Baltor and the other half of the platoon made their way back to the bedroom with the balcony.

Once inside the room by himself, as the guards had returned to their other duty posts, he heard the sounds of tens of thousands of people talking outside.

When he peeked outside the balcony, he first noticed the night sky above, and then it was the palace grounds that were packed with tons of people! A little nervous, he snuck into the back parts of his bedroom, sat on a comfortable couch, and waited for his friends.

Only a minute later, Humonus entered the room—after the doors were closed behind him, he snapped a sharp salute, and said just as sharply, "Good evening, my Sultan!"

"Humonus, when we are alone, please just call me Baltor."

"As you command, Baltor," Humonus replied at a normal volume.

Baltor cocked his head toward the balcony, and said, "I must confess that I'm a bit nervous, my friend."

Humonus declared, "We all get nervous, Baltor. Use those nerves and make them steel—that is what shall make you truly powerful! Show Pavelus you are her Emperor, and Pavelus will be yours! Show the world you are her Sultan, and the world will become your Empire!"

Baltor was surprised for but a moment as Brishava seemingly came out from nowhere and said, "Ruling-General Humonus is correct and wise. So, my Husband and Sultan, are you ready to meet your subjects?"

It was then that Baltor happily noticed that Brishava had not changed her appearance one iota.

She still wore that beautiful green silky dress, filled of course with actual diamonds and emeralds that ran along dozens of vertical seams on her bodice and arms. Her hair was tightly pulled up into a bun, which then gently splashed and curled its way halfway down her back—can't forget to mention the tiny platinum crown, stuffed with diamonds and emeralds.

The one thing that really grabbed his attention was her absolutely adorable face—light-green eye-shadow around her doe-brown eyes, and glossy red lipstick on her thick, luscious lips. In Baltor's opinion, she looked like a beautiful porcelain doll.

After giving him the sweetest smile, Brishava asked her earlier question, "Are you ready to meet your subjects, my gorgeous Sultan?"

Baltor stood to his feet, cleared his throat, returned the smile, and then said, "Yes, I am, my Wife and Sultaness."

She turned to the guards stationed at the doors, commanding, "Allow Ruksha to enter, so that he can make the royal announcement."

Without word, the guards opened his respective door.

A man, who appeared to be in his late fifties and regally dressed, entered the room. He bowed upon hands and knees.

Brishava commanded, "Ruksha, you may rise and call me out."

Ruksha rose to his feet, and declared with enthusiasm to his voice, "Yes, my Sultaness!"

As soon as he had stepped out onto the balcony, dozens of trumpeters began to play the royal anthem, which quieted the crowds.

Once the tune was over, Ruksha proclaimed with pride, "Citizens of Pavelus.... It is my privilege and honor to introduce to you the firstborn daughter and princess of the sultan, who sadly passed away last night. Please welcome our new Sultaness of the Sharia Empire—her married name is Sultaness Brishava Elysian!"

The crowds immediately took to their "Sultaness" as she stepped out onto the balcony, for a myriad of cheering and applause erupted; she waved her hands out joyously to the people.

Once the crowd had settled down, several minutes later, she then proclaimed, "First of all my beloved citizens, you should know that the time of my father's cruel and unjust reign is over!"

Yet again, the crowds broke out into cheering and applause.

Once settled, many minutes later, the Sultaness proudly introduced, "And now, it is my honor to introduce my husband, the new Sultan of the Sharia Empire—his name is Baltor Elysian!"

This time, silence immediately reigned in the city, for the citizens became afraid that their "new sultan" might ultimately turn out to be a tyrant like all the other rulers for the last five centuries.

Baltor cocked his head over to look into the mirror one last time. Not only did he see his present and his past, yet he also saw his future—a future cast in the present! He now knew what he needed to be—his nerves became as steely as the swords on his back—his eyes darted forward—his feet walked onto the balcony.

As soon as he stood to Brishava's right, he stopped in his tracks—in that very moment, Baltor's mind mysteriously tabulated to him that all of his citizens, nearly eighty-two thousand, as well forty thousand, two hundred and fifty-six soldiers of Pavelus had attended, even though only thirty thousand people could fit inside the palace walls. Most were outside the palace gates and in the surrounding streets for about two miles every direction.

With a lightning-quick flick of Baltor's wrists, his swords crossed each other above his head and toward the heavens, as he proudly proclaimed: "I have been officially crowned your Sultan, though not too long ago, I was once a peasant...

"Please listen to my words of warning, or of wisdom, your choice. As I speak, there are more than 120,000 enemy soldiers making their way toward Pavelus—by land and by sea—led none other than by Sedious Vaspan. They will try to rape and plunder us of all our riches until bone dry, and they will try to make all our women and children their slaves—the men will all be executed...

"Unfortunately with my forces alone, we are outnumbered three to one—so the time's come for me to ask for volunteers. You will be paid just the same as my regular foot soldiers—you will be trained by the best of the best, I swear to that on my honor!

"Those who can't fight or will refuse to fight—we shall provide you with safe haven within Pavelus's strong defenses, or you may attempt an escape on your own, by land or by sea, if you so wish...."

Nearly ten seconds later, he sheathed his swords in one quick motion, thrust his open-palmed hands out to the crowds, and suggested with fervency, "But consider this option for a minute... Declare me your Sultan and fight for me, and I will lead you all toward successes that are beyond imagination. Believe me, it is my intention to pave the entire streets of Pavelus from gold, even if it means that the walls of this palace be used to build them....

"So who amongst you shall hail me... *your Sultan*?!"

The End

COMING SOON: BOOK II OF III:

THE REIGN OF THE SULTAN!

VALAKANESE TRANSLATIONS

1) "Kid—are you okay?"
2) "I think he's still out cold—boy was that kid really lucky I saw him when I did, or he'd be cat chow!"
3) "Kid—are you okay?"
4) "I'm glad to see that the kid's going to survive!"
5) "Lie down."
6) "Are you hungry?"
7) "Are you feeling better this morning, kid?"
8) "If he can talk, then that is definitely a sign of improvement!"
9) "Follow me!"
10) "Oopsy-daisy."
11) "Baltor, please follow me, friend. Follow me—follow!"
12) "I see Baltor."
13) "I see saber tooth tiger."
14) "I shot saber tooth tiger."
15) "I killed saber tooth tiger."
16) "Thank you."
17) "You are welcome, Baltor."
18) "Good morning to you, Valuspo! My, you are such a beautiful creature, and so strong and powerful!"
19) "Follow me, Baltor."
20) "Yes, Baltor."
21) "No."
22) "Hungry?"
23) "Honey, do we have anything to eat for Baltor? He's hungry, Jimnee."
24) "Sorry no, I've been very busy making these fur coats for him and his animal.
25) "Yaush, why don't you take him to *Starving Bear*?"
26) "You are welcome, Baltor."
27) "Follow me, Baltor."
28) "Good morning to you."
29) "Everyone, this is my new friend, Baltor! Baltor, these are all my good friends!"
30) "Good morning to you, Baltor!"
31) "Baltor, sit."
32) "Good morning to you, Yaush!"
33) "And good morning to you, Yeea."
34) "How is Jimnee?"
35) "She is great—thanks for asking!"

36) "Good morning to you, Baltor."

37) "So Yaush, what can I get you and your friend for break-fast?"

38) "Can we please have two orders of omelets, eggs and sau-sage, along with some alasvo juice, please?"

39) "Sure thing!"

40) "Salami my old friend, will you please join us for breakfast?"

41) "Salami, this is my new friend, Baltor. It appears that my friend can speak quite a few other languages, though he cannot speak Valakanese. I, being a simple local hunter, can only speak our native tongue. Will you please try and see if you can speak any of his languages, my friend?"

42) "Yeea. One second, please?"

43) "Yes?"

44) "Salami, what would you like for breakfast?"

45) "I'll have what they're having."

46) "Sure thing."

47) "Thank you, Yaush."

48) "Good morning, my friends. I have a quick though serious question—were you guys by chance laughing at Yeea?"

49) "Absolutely not, Paelsho. My friend, the only thing we were laughing about was our own silliness—that's all, I swear! Where is Yeea now, so I can explain to her about the misunderstanding, and apologize?"

50) "I let her go for the morning. Yeea seemed so convinced, and shaken up, that you guys were laughing at her—that she was liter-ally in tears when she gave me Salami's order! Just so you know, I didn't believe a word of it to be true, as I've known you two gen-tlemen for many-many years, and we all know how women can be at times—emotional wrecks!"

51) "We must also apologize for the inconvenience it has cost you as well, Paelsho—apology accepted?"

52) "Ahhh, don't worry about it—breakfast's crowds almost gone anyway. Oh, don't worry about Yeea either—I'll explain the misunderstanding and extend the apology when she comes back this afternoon. She'll be just fine! Come back soon, friends."

53) "Thank you, Paelsho."

54) "God speed!"

CHAO-CHU-SHA-MAEN TRANSLATIONS

55) "Follow me!"

56) "Let him pass."

57) "Father and mother, our attack on the cannibals of Cheu-sha failed miserably—they were somehow ready for us and launched their own surprise attack, while we were camped the night before! Those not instantly killed or able to escape were taken prisoner, including myself. Even though I was next on the list to become sacrificed that very night, this brown-skinned man who now stands behind me fought valiantly for his escape, but there were too many of them on him—he took my spot as the next to be sacrificed. At that moment that he was about to have the ivory tusk implanted into his chest, and his heart removed, eaten, and tossed into the fire, our rescuers arrived and saved the day."

58) "Had it not been for this man who now stands before me, I would have been sacrificed, and not be alive now. I shall forever be grateful to this man who is now my brother..."

59) "Come, come."

60) "Allow this young man to pass."

61) "Come, come."

62) "Stop."

63) "This man has the heart and strength of a tiger!"

64) "That tiger desperately needs a bath, as you do. By the way, I love you, my son."

65) "Servant girls, we need your assistance."

66) "The black tower—that is taboo! No—no!"

67) "No, no, please don't draw this picture again—very bad luck!"

68) "Escort this prince by royal procession to the black tower."

ABOUT THE AUTHOR

When the author, J. Eric Booker, is not creating his literary or musical masterpieces upon "cloud 9," which is seldom, he and his business partner run their own mobile recording studio, called BluColla Inc. Despite the fact that J. Eric Booker hasn't attended a single day of college, it is in his belief that though an education is important, it is not the crux to writing or music—it is the imagination and the determination.

To learn more about the author, check out his websites:

www.soundcloud.com/e-main-1

www.facebook.com/j.eric.booker

www.goodreads.com/j.eric.booker

www.amazon.com/author/j.eric.booker

ACKNOWLEDGMENTS

First, I'd like to thank my wonderful family! I'd also like to thank.
Brian Kuhn
Dave Barr
Dave Jones
Dr. Joel Bolton
Dr. Masaaki Hatsumi (Soke)
Dr. T
Em Petrova – Editor of this book & Spicy Romance Author
Eric Ondoy
Eric Smolich
General (retired) Patrick E. Rea
George Craig
Glen Woodsides
Griffin Kisner
Henry Miller
James Clausen
Jamie Caldwell
Janice Korzik
Jason Williams
JT, Geo and Jeanty Etienne
Margaret Weis (NYT Best Selling Author)
Marlene Hamilton
Marshane, Mandy, "Monkey" and Malachi Kitt
Mason, Liz, Alyssa, Connor and Trinity Meyer
Matt Jones
Mike, Deanna and Larry Behning
M n T Glenn
Mike Janzcak
Randy Roberts
R.A. Salvatore (NYT Best Selling Author)
Raul Cuevas
Ray, Tracy, Hailey, Joey, Jaden and Rusty Fjeldheim
Raymayne Gray
Ryan and Kacey Stevenson
Shanna Caldwell
Tracy and Laura Hickman (NYT Best Selling Authors)

LITERARY WORKS WRITTEN BY J. ERIC BOOKER

THE Making © 2004—MYSTERY

"The Elysian Dynasty Trilogy" © 2008—FANTASY
BOOK I: *THE SWORDS OF THE SULTAN*
BOOK II: *THE REIGN OF THE SULTAN* (coming soon)
BOOK III: *THE WAR OF ALL WARS* (coming soon)